POKÉMON™

ADVENTURES

RUBY & SAPPHIRE

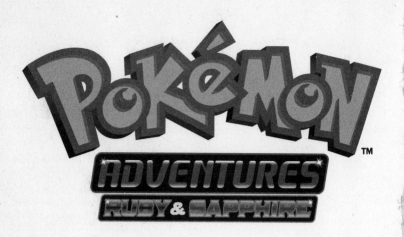

Pokémon® ADVENTURES

Volume 16
VIZ Kids Edition

Story by **HIDENORI KUSAKA**
Art by **SATOSHI YAMAMOTO**

© 2013 Pokémon.
© 1995-2013 Nintendo/Creatures Inc./GAME FREAK inc.
TM and ® and character names are trademarks of Nintendo.
POCKET MONSTER SPECIAL Vol. 16
by Hidenori KUSAKA, Satoshi YAMAMOTO
© 1997 Hidenori KUSAKA, Satoshi YAMAMOTO
All rights reserved.
Original Japanese edition published by SHOGAKUKAN.
English translation rights in the United States of America, Canada, the
United Kingdom and Ireland arranged with SHOGAKUKAN.

English Adaptation/Bryant Turnage
Translation/Tetsuichiro Miyaki
Touch-up & Lettering/Annaliese Christman
Design/Shawn Carrico
Editor/Annette Roman

Printed in the U.S.A.

Published by VIZ Media, LLC
P.O. Box 77010
San Francisco, CA 94107

10 9 8 7 6 5 4 3 2 1
First printing, May 2013

www.vizkids.com

www.viz.com

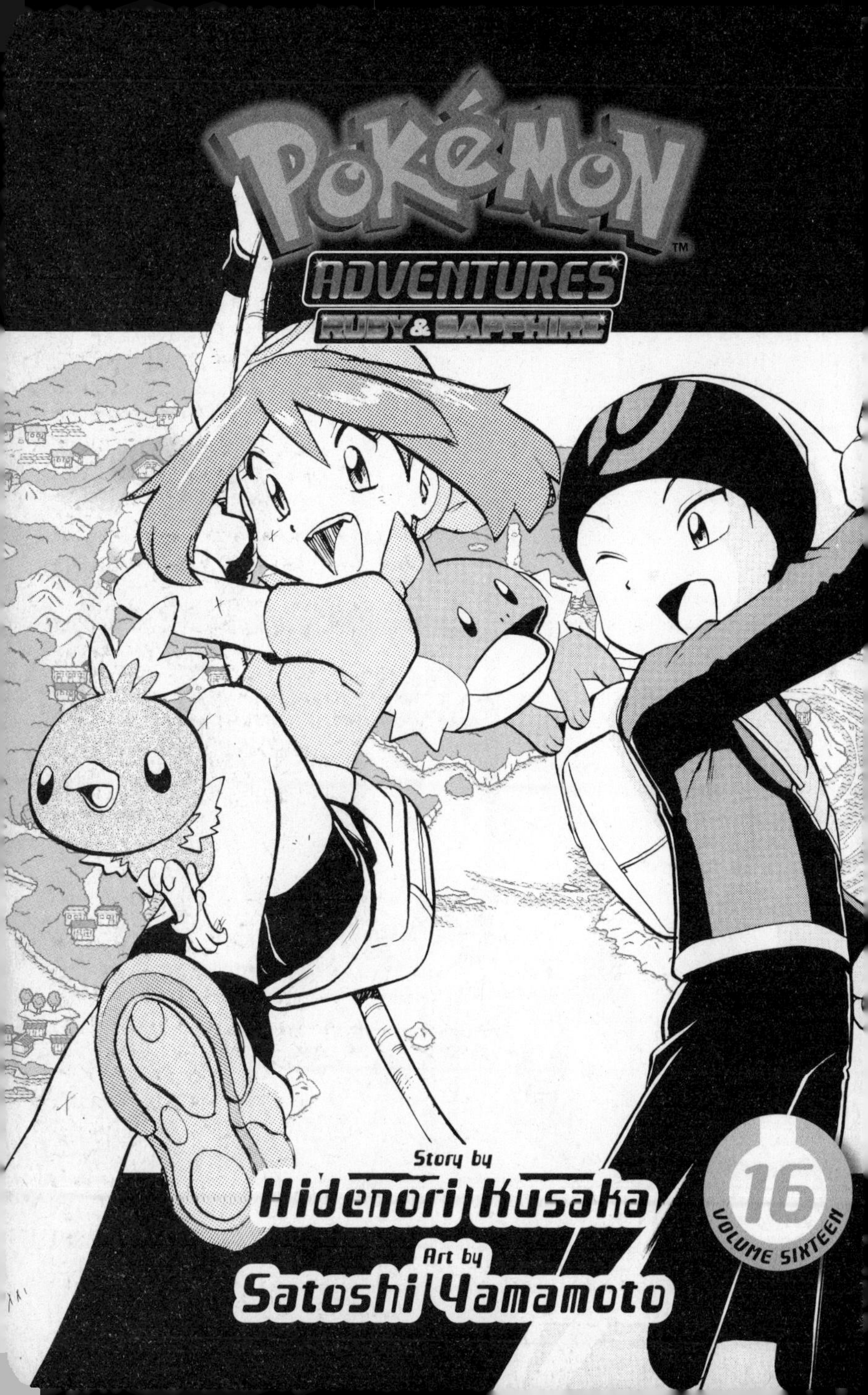

POKÉMON™
ADVENTURES
RUBY & SAPPHIRE
Story by
Hidenori Kusaka
Art by
Satoshi Yamamoto
16
VOLUME SIXTEEN

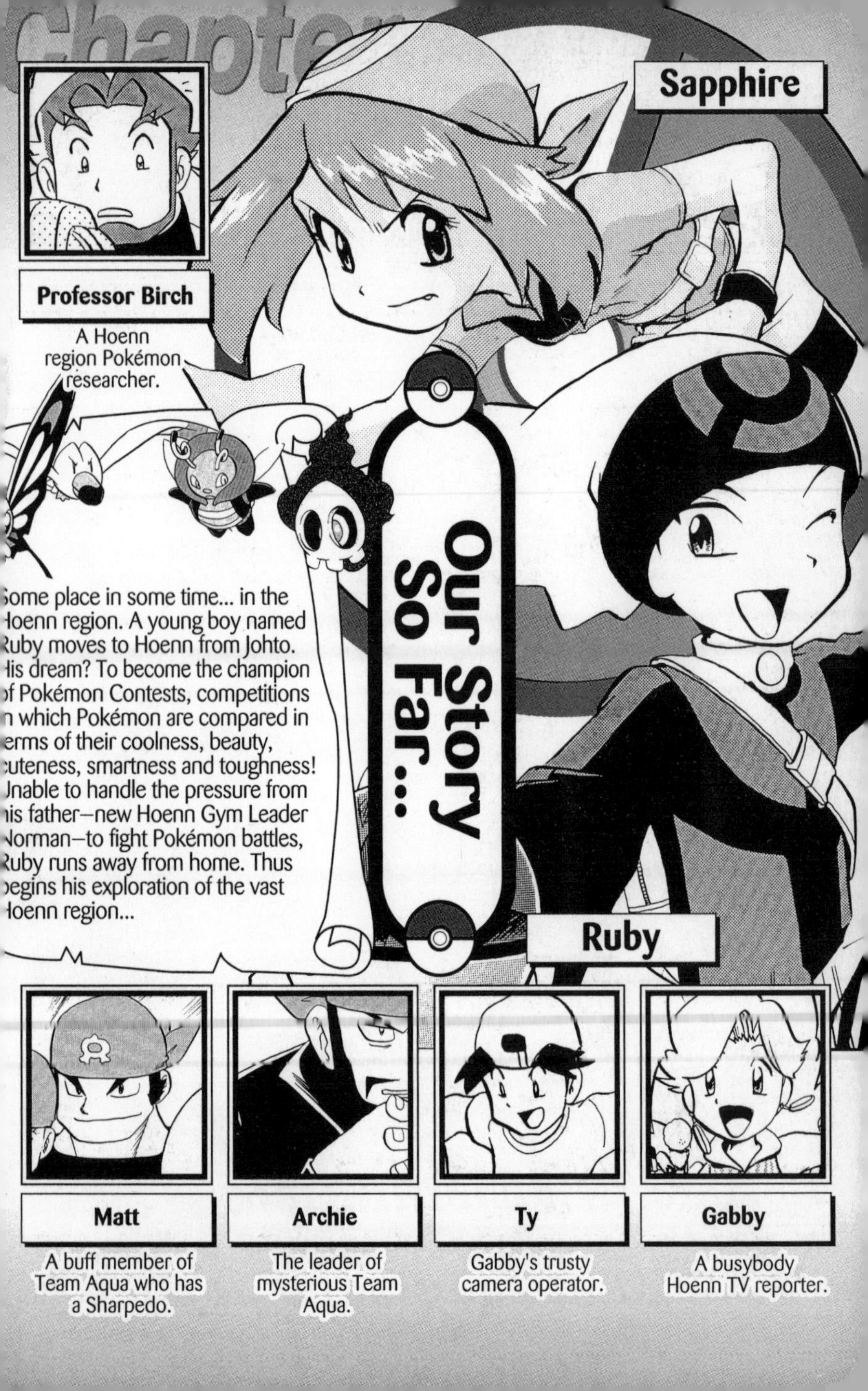

Sapphire
Professor Birch
A Hoenn region Pokémon researcher.
Our Story So Far...
ome place in some time... in the
oenn region. A young boy named
uby moves to Hoenn from Johto.
is dream? To become the champion
f Pokémon Contests, competitions
n which Pokémon are compared in
erms of their coolness, beauty,
uteness, smartness and toughness!
nable to handle the pressure from
is father—new Hoenn Gym Leader
orman—to fight Pokémon battles,
uby runs away from home. Thus
egins his exploration of the vast
oenn region...
Ruby
Gabby
A busybody Hoenn TV reporter.
Ty
Gabby's trusty camera operator.
Archie
The leader of mysterious Team Aqua.
Matt
A buff member of Team Aqua who has a Sharpedo.

Story of The Fou

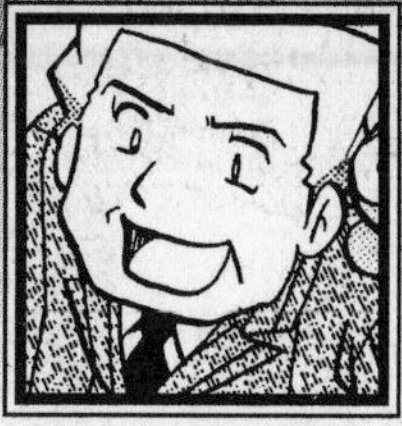

President Stone

C.E.O. of the giant Devon Corporation. Currently unconscious.

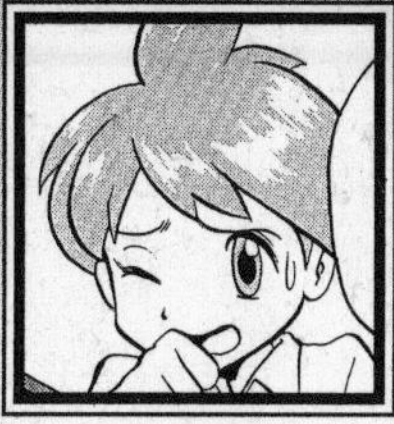

Wally

A frail boy who longs for a Pokémon of his own.

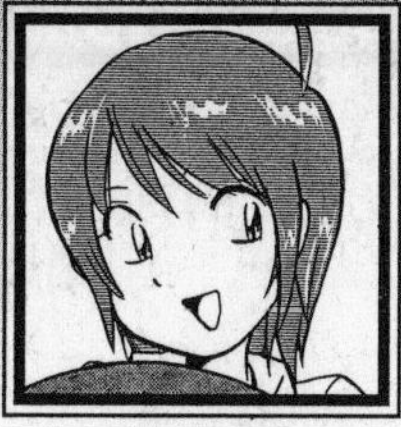

Mother

Ruby's mother, a sweet and gentle homemaker.

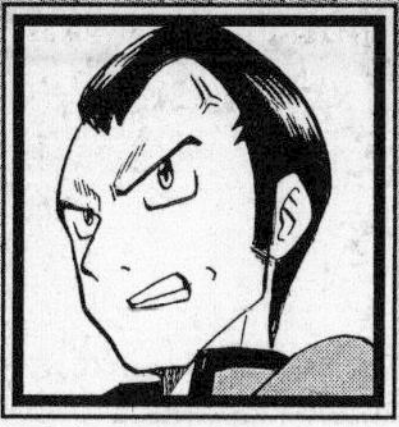

Norman

Ruby's father, the Gym Leader of Petalburg City.

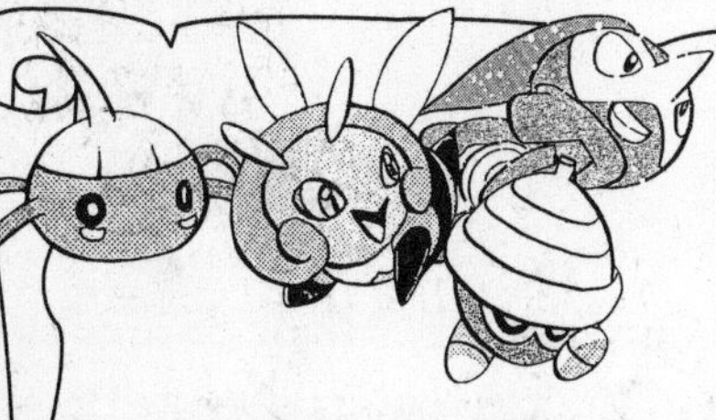

Ruby meets a girl named Sapphire who lives in a cave. Like Ruby, she has a dream. Hers is to defeat all the Gym Leaders in the Hoenn region. The two agree to pursue their dreams for 80 days, then reunite at the spot where they first met. And thus, Ruby and Sapphire's 80-day journey through Hoenn begins.

First, Ruby helps a frail boy named Wally capture his first Pokémon near Petalburg City. But then Ruby is washed away by a tsunami caused by a mysterious earthquake! Meanwhile, Sapphire faces her first Gym Leader near Rustboro City...

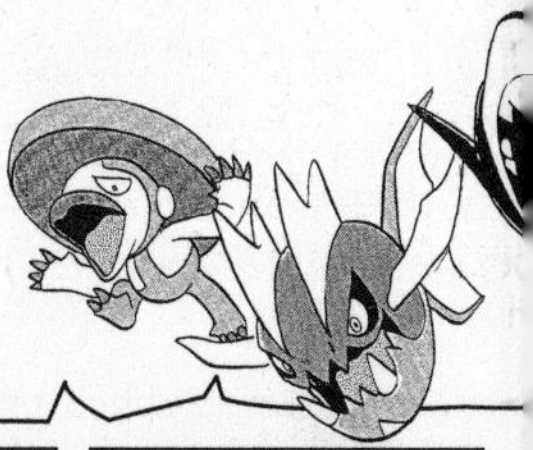

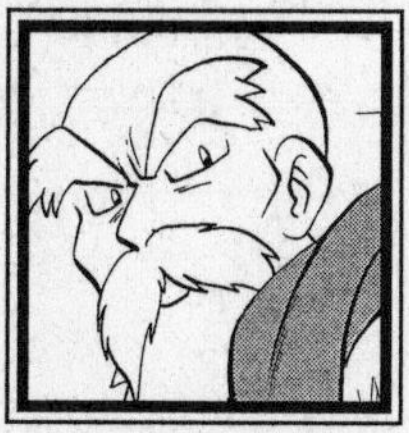

Mr. Briney

A former sailor, skilled in the ways of the maritime.

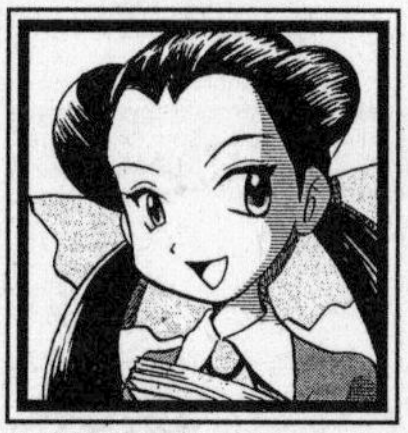

Roxanne

The Gym Leader of Rustboro City. She loves to study and learn.

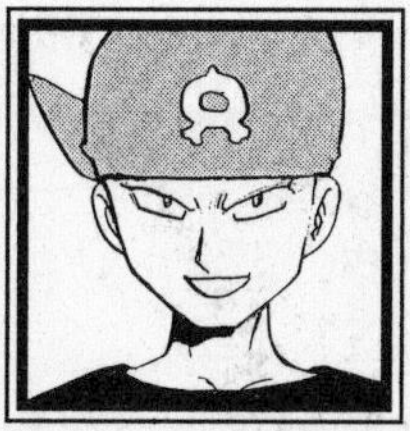

Amber

Archie's most trusted follower. He has a Carvanha.

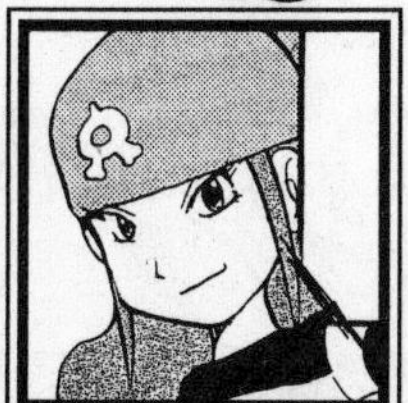

Shelly

A member of Team Aqua who has a Ludicolo.

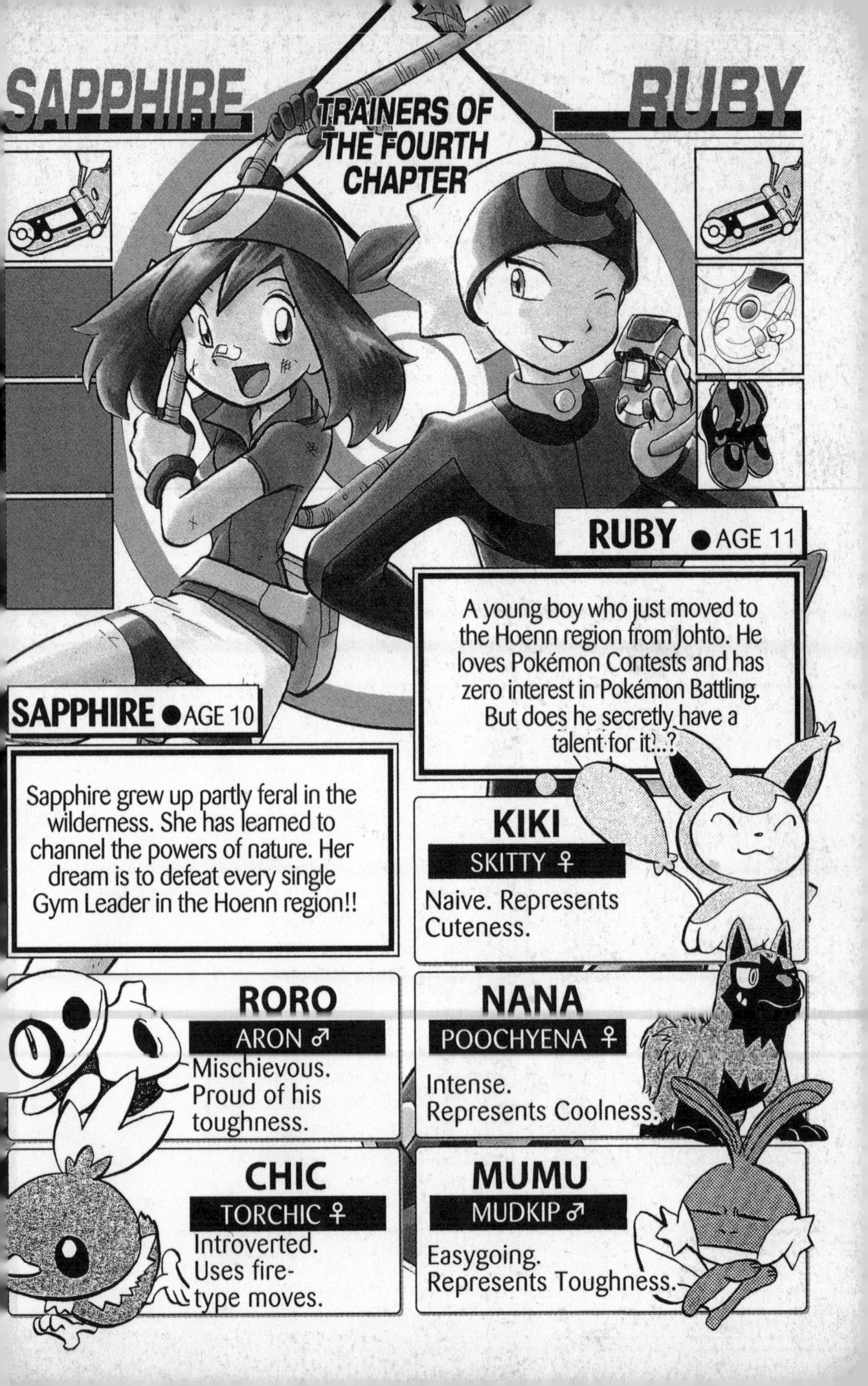
TRAINERS OF THE FOURTH CHAPTER
RUBY
SAPPHIRE
RUBY ●AGE 11
A young boy who just moved to the Hoenn region from Johto. He loves Pokémon Contests and has zero interest in Pokémon Battling. But does he secretly have a talent for it...?
SAPPHIRE ●AGE 10
Sapphire grew up partly feral in the wilderness. She has learned to channel the powers of nature. Her dream is to defeat every single Gym Leader in the Hoenn region!!
KIKI
SKITTY ♀
Naive. Represents Cuteness.
NANA
POOCHYENA ♀
Intense. Represents Coolness.
RORO
ARON ♂
Mischievous. Proud of his toughness.
MUMU
MUDKIP ♂
Easygoing. Represents Toughness.
CHIC
TORCHIC ♀
Introverted. Uses fire-type moves.

POKÉMON
ADVENTURES
RUBY & SAPPHIRE

CONTENTS

16
VOLUME SIXTEEN

ADVENTURE 191
Blowing Past Nosepass II 8

ADVENTURE 192
Stick This in Your Craw, Crawdaunt! I 22

ADVENTURE 193
Stick This in Your Craw, Crawdaunt! II 42

ADVENTURE 194
Guile from Mawile 62

ADVENTURE 195
Mashing Makuhita 77

ADVENTURE 196
Ring Ring Goes Beldum 94

ADVENTURE 197
Heavy Hitting Hariyama 108

ADVENTURE 198
Adding It Up with Plusle & Minun I 122

ADVENTURE 199
Adding It Up with Plusle & Minun II 136

ADVENTURE 200
Tripped Up by Torkoal 161

ADVENTURE 201
Slugging It Out with Slugma 177

● Chapter 191 ●
Blowing Past Nosepass II

Pokémon Adventures Ruby & Sapphire The Fourth Chapter

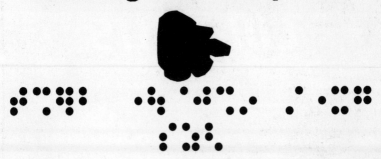

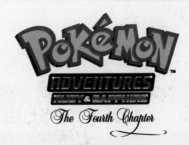

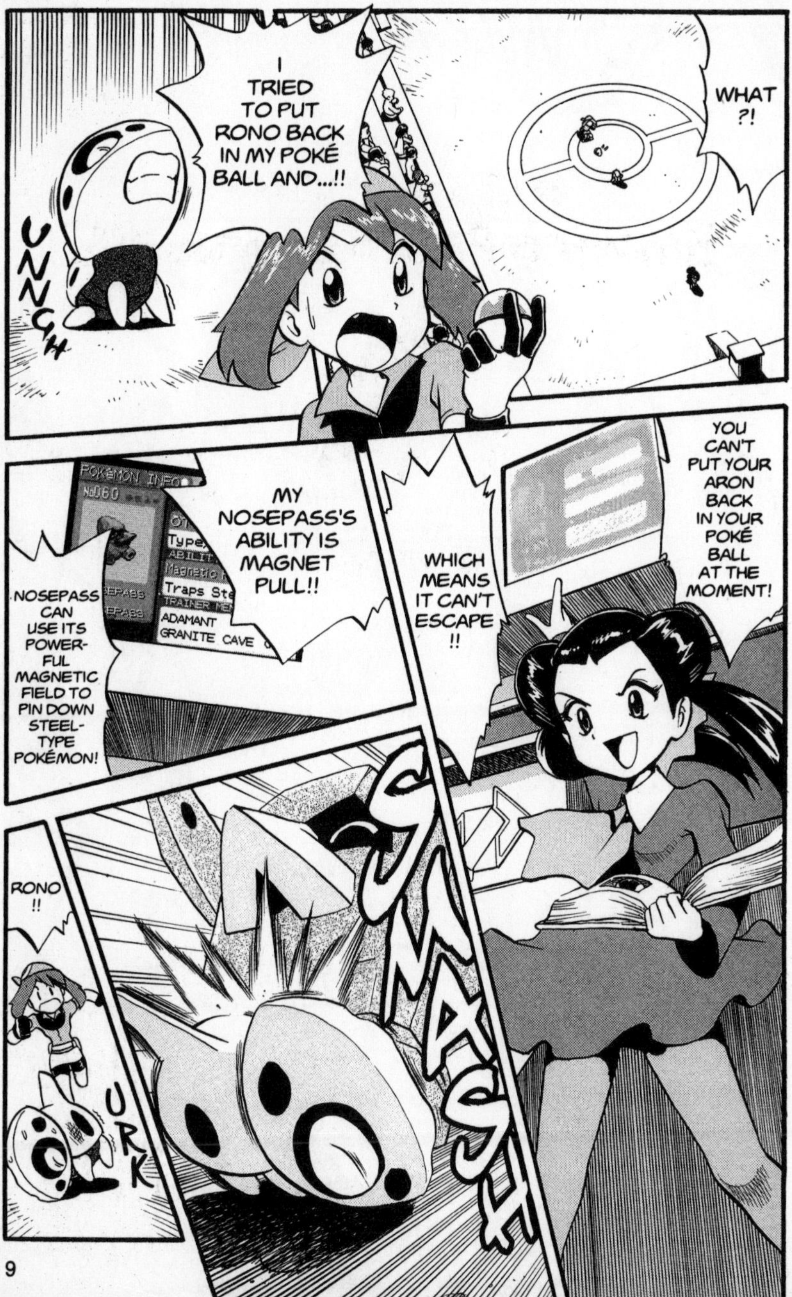

WHAT?!
I TRIED TO PUT RONO BACK IN MY POKÉ BALL AND...!!
UNNNGH
YOU CAN'T PUT YOUR ARON BACK IN YOUR POKÉ BALL AT THE MOMENT!
WHICH MEANS IT CAN'T ESCAPE!!
MY NOSEPASS'S ABILITY IS MAGNET PULL!!
POKéMON INFO
ADAMANT
GRANITE CAVE
NOSEPASS CAN USE ITS POWERFUL MAGNETIC FIELD TO PIN DOWN STEEL-TYPE POKÉMON!
SMASH
RONO!!
URK

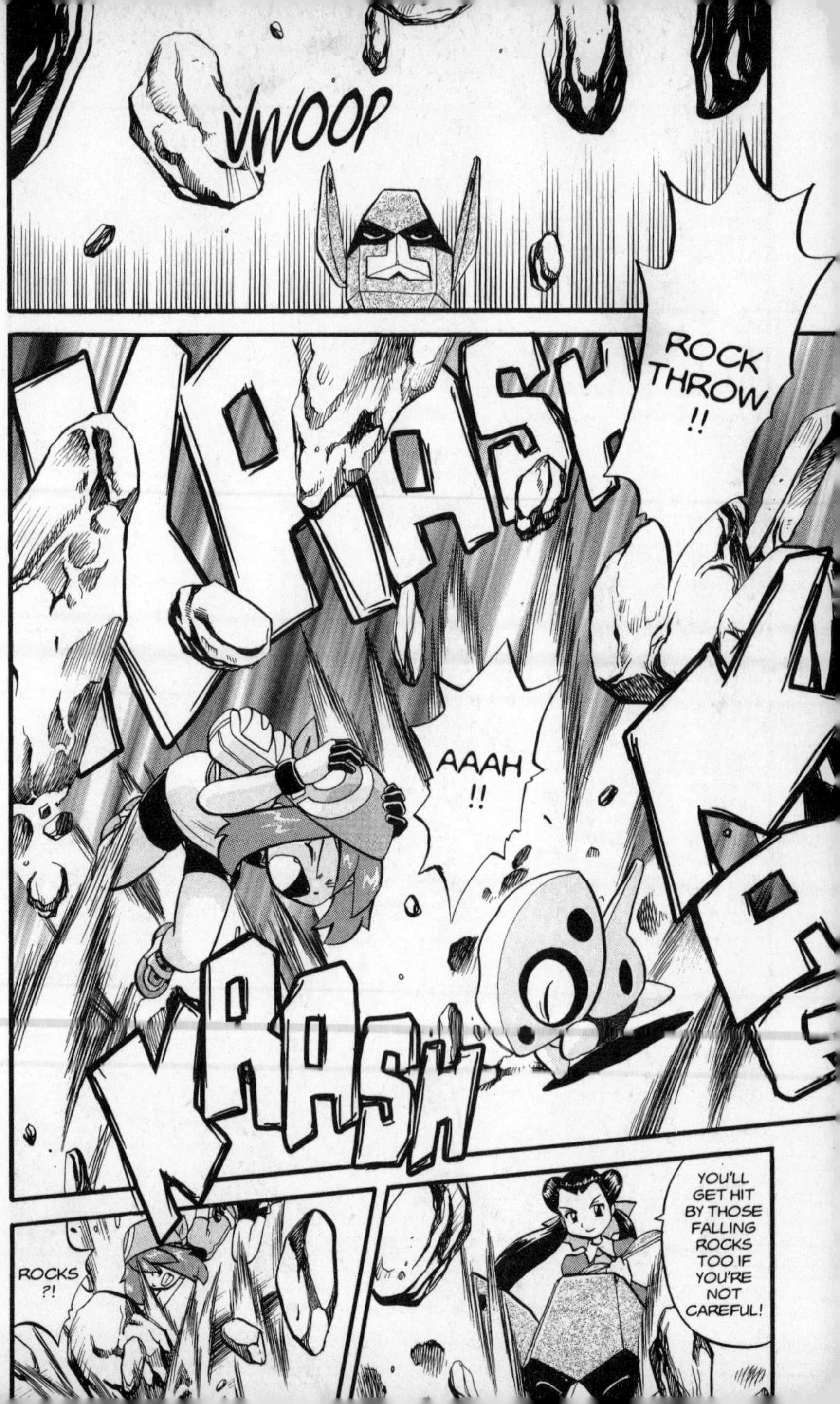
VWOOP
ROCK THROW!!
AAAH!!
YOU'LL GET HIT BY THOSE FALLING ROCKS TOO IF YOU'RE NOT CAREFUL!
ROCKS?!

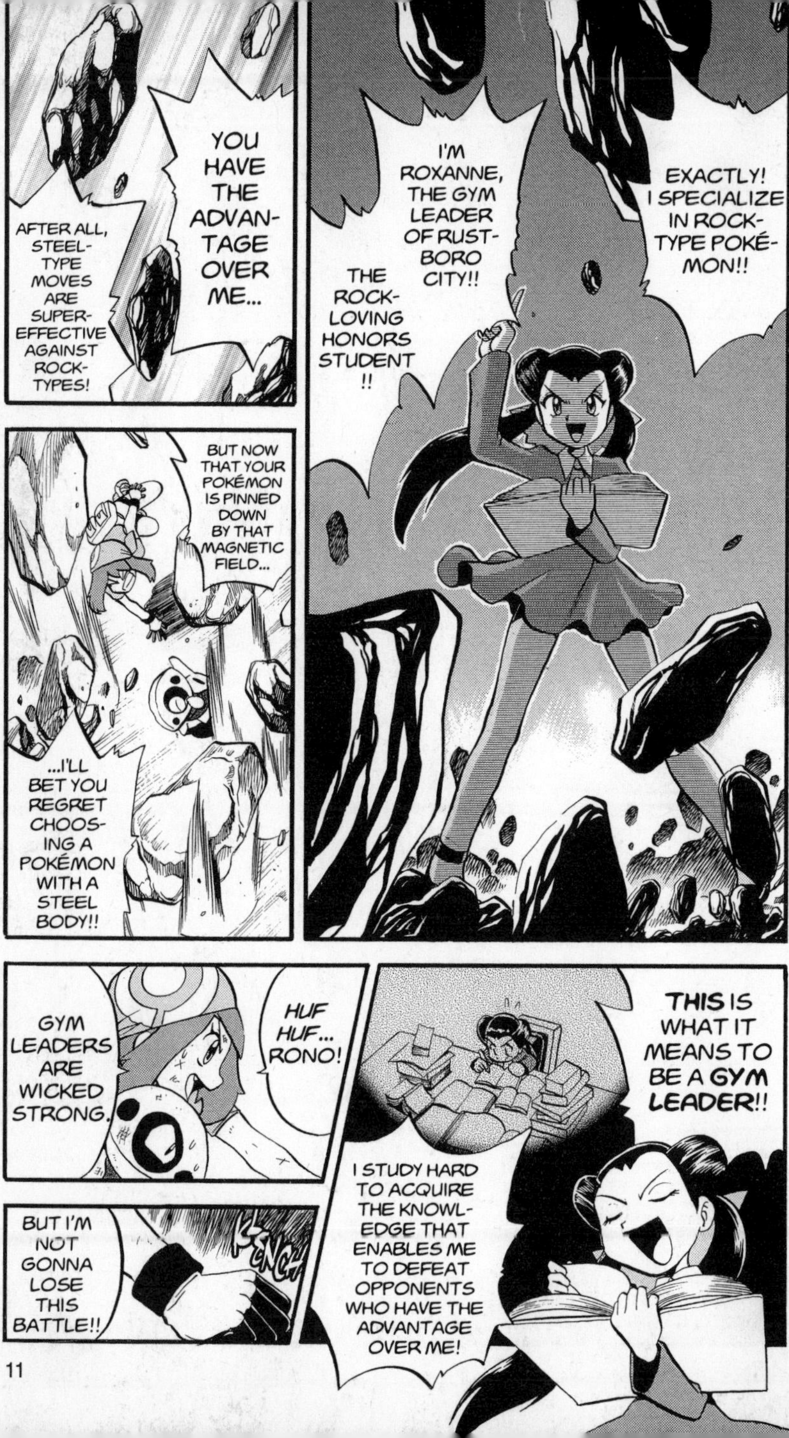

EXACTLY! I SPECIALIZE IN ROCK-TYPE POKÉMON!!
I'M ROXANNE, THE GYM LEADER OF RUSTBORO CITY!!
THE ROCK-LOVING HONORS STUDENT!!
YOU HAVE THE ADVANTAGE OVER ME...
AFTER ALL, STEEL-TYPE MOVES ARE SUPER-EFFECTIVE AGAINST ROCK-TYPES!
BUT NOW THAT YOUR POKÉMON IS PINNED DOWN BY THAT MAGNETIC FIELD...
...I'LL BET YOU REGRET CHOOSING A POKÉMON WITH A STEEL BODY!!
THIS IS WHAT IT MEANS TO BE A **GYM LEADER**!!
I STUDY HARD TO ACQUIRE THE KNOWLEDGE THAT ENABLES ME TO DEFEAT OPPONENTS WHO HAVE THE ADVANTAGE OVER ME!
HUF HUF... RONO!
GYM LEADERS ARE WICKED STRONG.
KLENCH
BUT I'M NOT GONNA LOSE THIS BATTLE!!

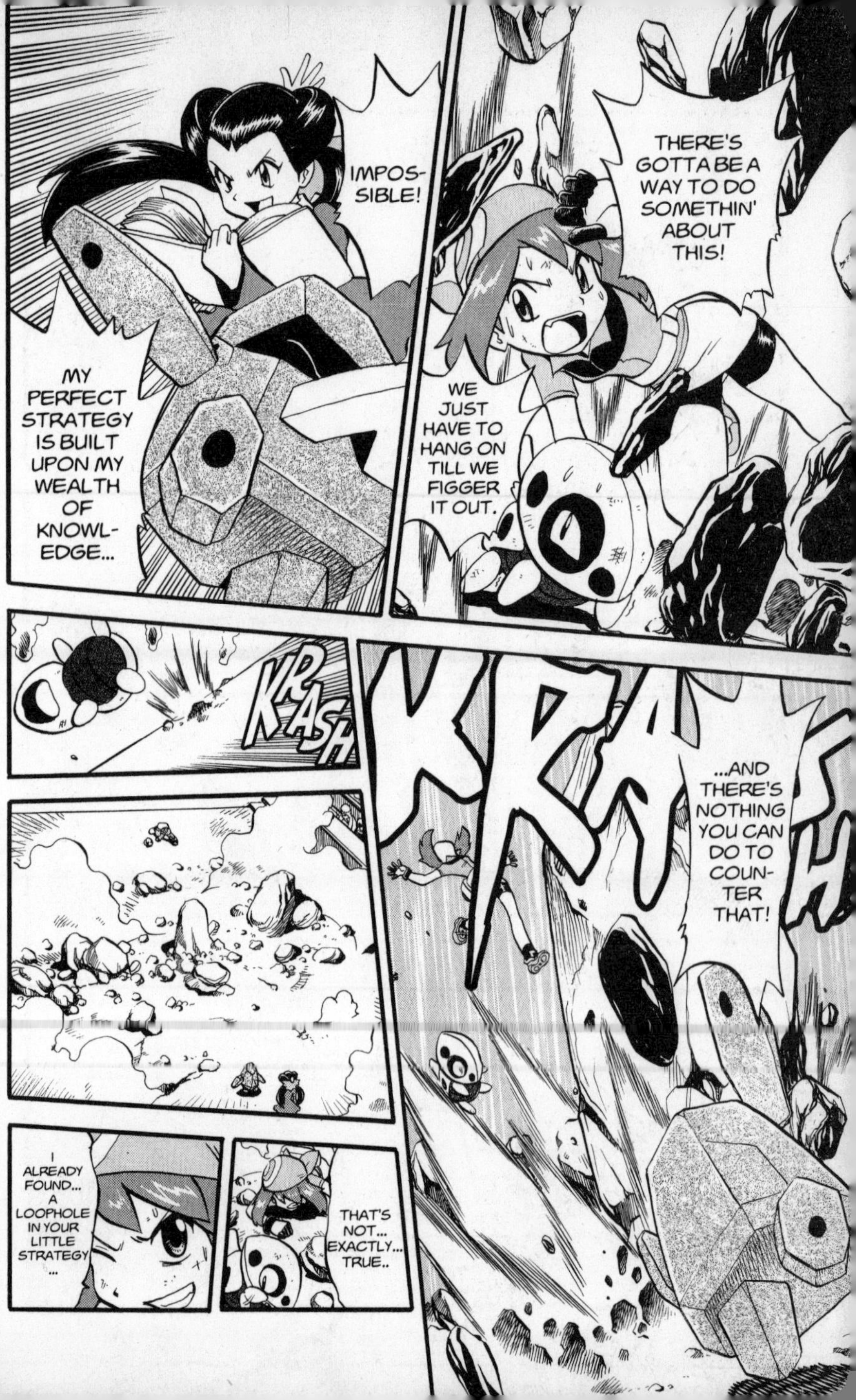
THERE'S GOTTA BE A WAY TO DO SOMETHIN' ABOUT THIS!
WE JUST HAVE TO HANG ON TILL WE FIGGER IT OUT.
IMPOSSIBLE!
MY PERFECT STRATEGY IS BUILT UPON MY WEALTH OF KNOWLEDGE...
KRASH
...AND THERE'S NOTHING YOU CAN DO TO COUNTER THAT!
KRASH
THAT'S NOT... EXACTLY... TRUE..
I ALREADY FOUND... A LOOPHOLE IN YOUR LITTLE STRATEGY...

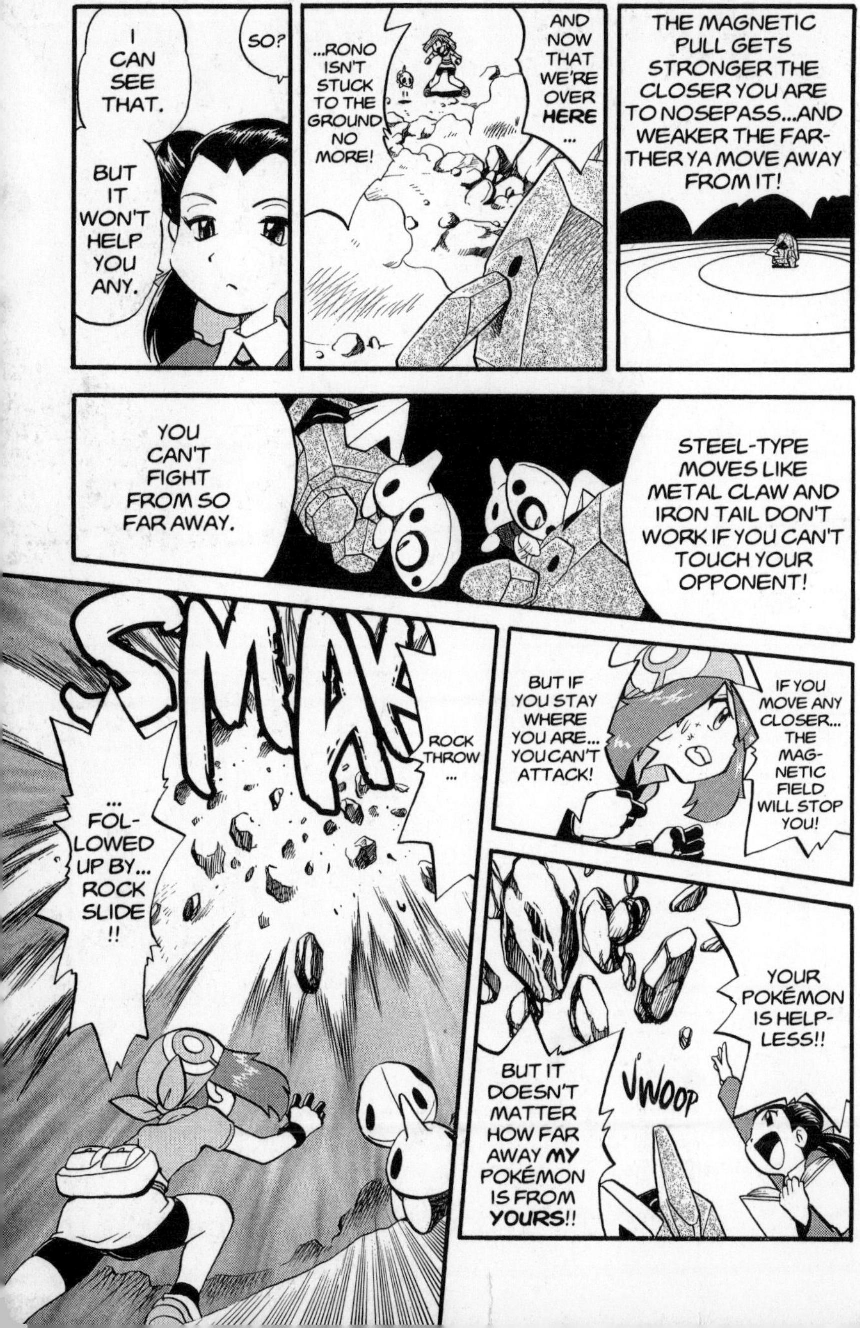
THE MAGNETIC PULL GETS STRONGER THE CLOSER YOU ARE TO NOSEPASS...AND WEAKER THE FARTHER YA MOVE AWAY FROM IT!
AND NOW THAT WE'RE OVER **HERE**...
...RONO ISN'T STUCK TO THE GROUND NO MORE!
SO?
I CAN SEE THAT.
BUT IT WON'T HELP YOU ANY.
STEEL-TYPE MOVES LIKE METAL CLAW AND IRON TAIL DON'T WORK IF YOU CAN'T TOUCH YOUR OPPONENT!
YOU CAN'T FIGHT FROM SO FAR AWAY.
IF YOU MOVE ANY CLOSER... THE MAGNETIC FIELD WILL STOP YOU!
BUT IF YOU STAY WHERE YOU ARE... YOU CAN'T ATTACK!
YOUR POKÉMON IS HELPLESS!!
VWOOP
BUT IT DOESN'T MATTER HOW FAR AWAY **MY** POKÉMON IS FROM **YOURS**!!
SMAK
ROCK THROW...
...FOLLOWED UP BY... ROCK SLIDE!!

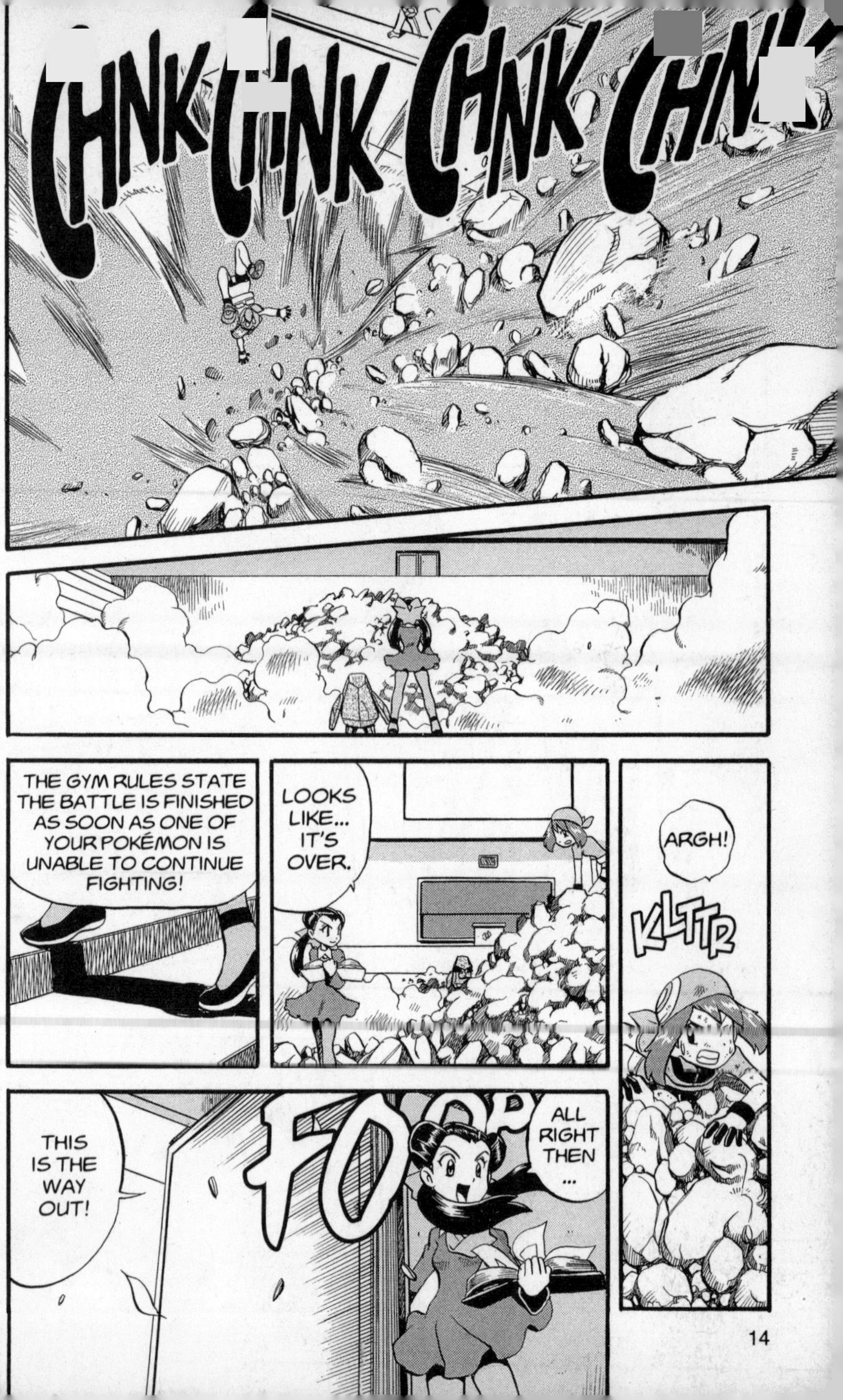
CHNK CHNK CHNK CHN
ARGH!
KLTTR
LOOKS LIKE... IT'S OVER.
THE GYM RULES STATE THE BATTLE IS FINISHED AS SOON AS ONE OF YOUR POKÉMON IS UNABLE TO CONTINUE FIGHTING!
ALL RIGHT THEN ...
THIS IS THE WAY OUT!

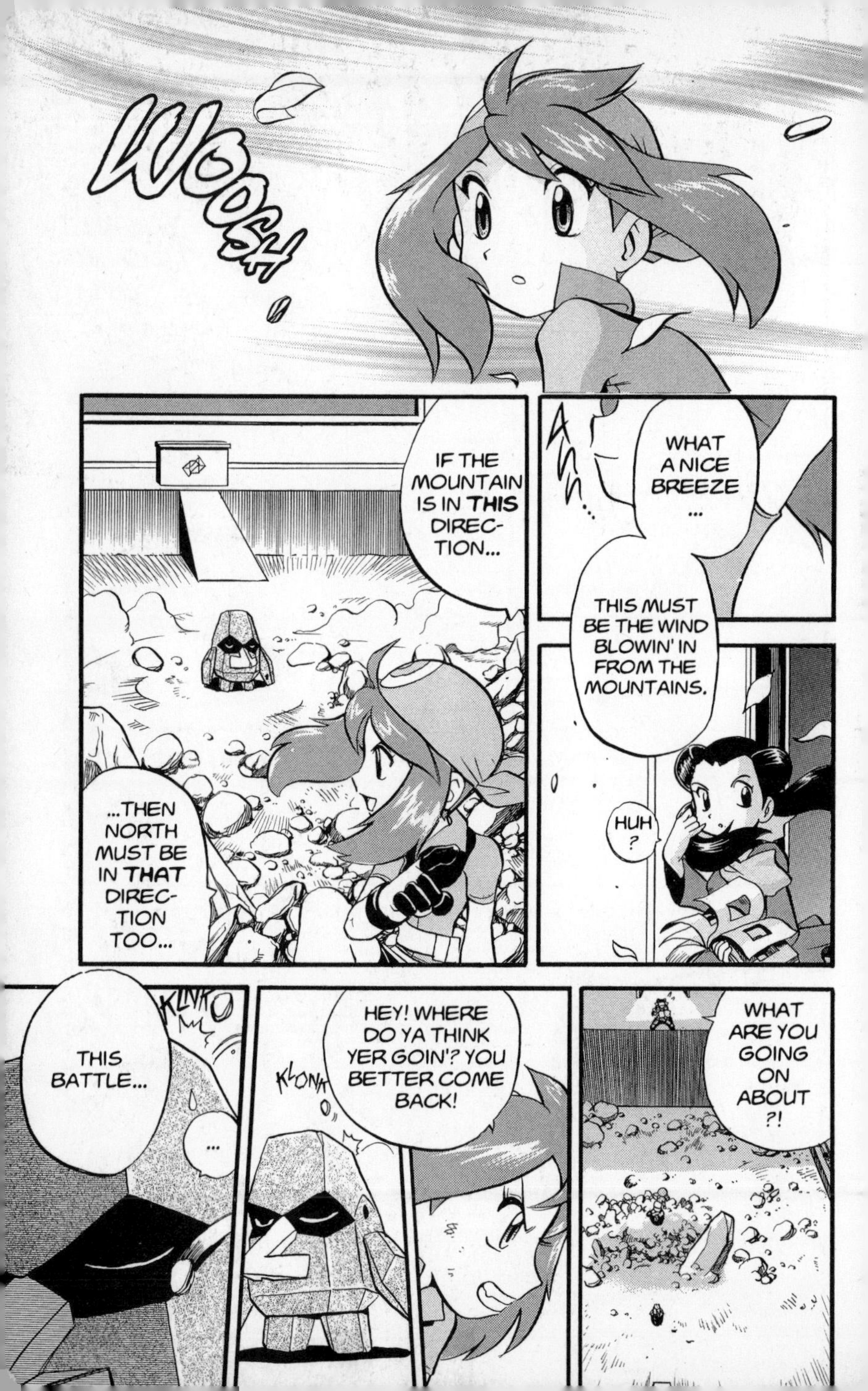
WOOSH
WHAT A NICE BREEZE ...
THIS MUST BE THE WIND BLOWIN' IN FROM THE MOUNTAINS.
HUH ?
IF THE MOUNTAIN IS IN **THIS** DIRECTION...
...THEN NORTH MUST BE IN **THAT** DIRECTION TOO...
WHAT ARE YOU GOING ON ABOUT ?!
HEY! WHERE DO YA THINK YER GOIN'? YOU BETTER COME BACK!
KLONK
KLINK
THIS BATTLE...
...

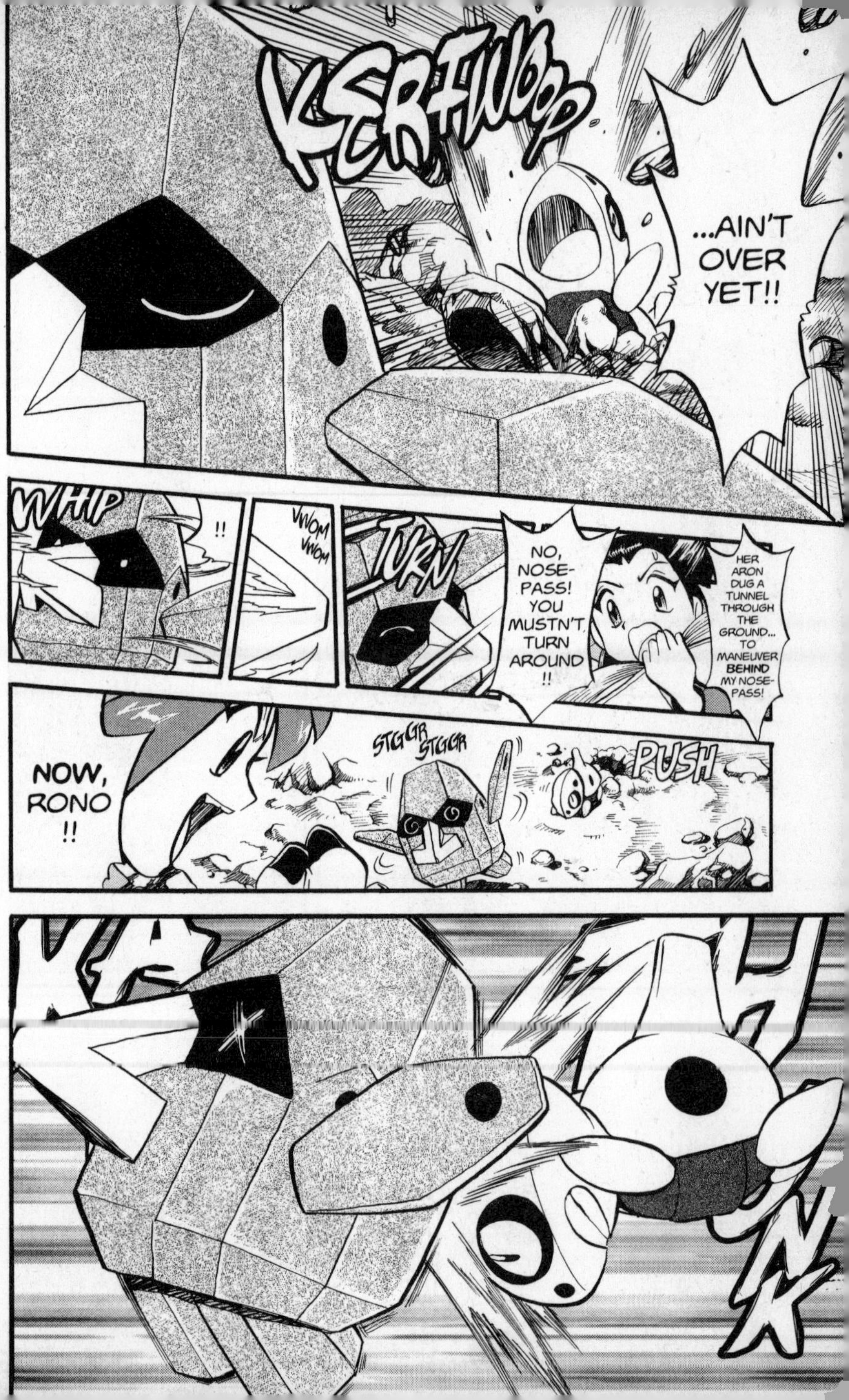
KERFWOOP
...AIN'T OVER YET!!
HER ARON DUG A TUNNEL THROUGH THE GROUND... TO MANEUVER **BEHIND** MY NOSE-PASS!
NO, NOSE-PASS! YOU MUSTN'T TURN AROUND !!
TURN
VWOM VWOM
WHIP
!!
PUSH
STGGR STGGR
NOW, RONO !!

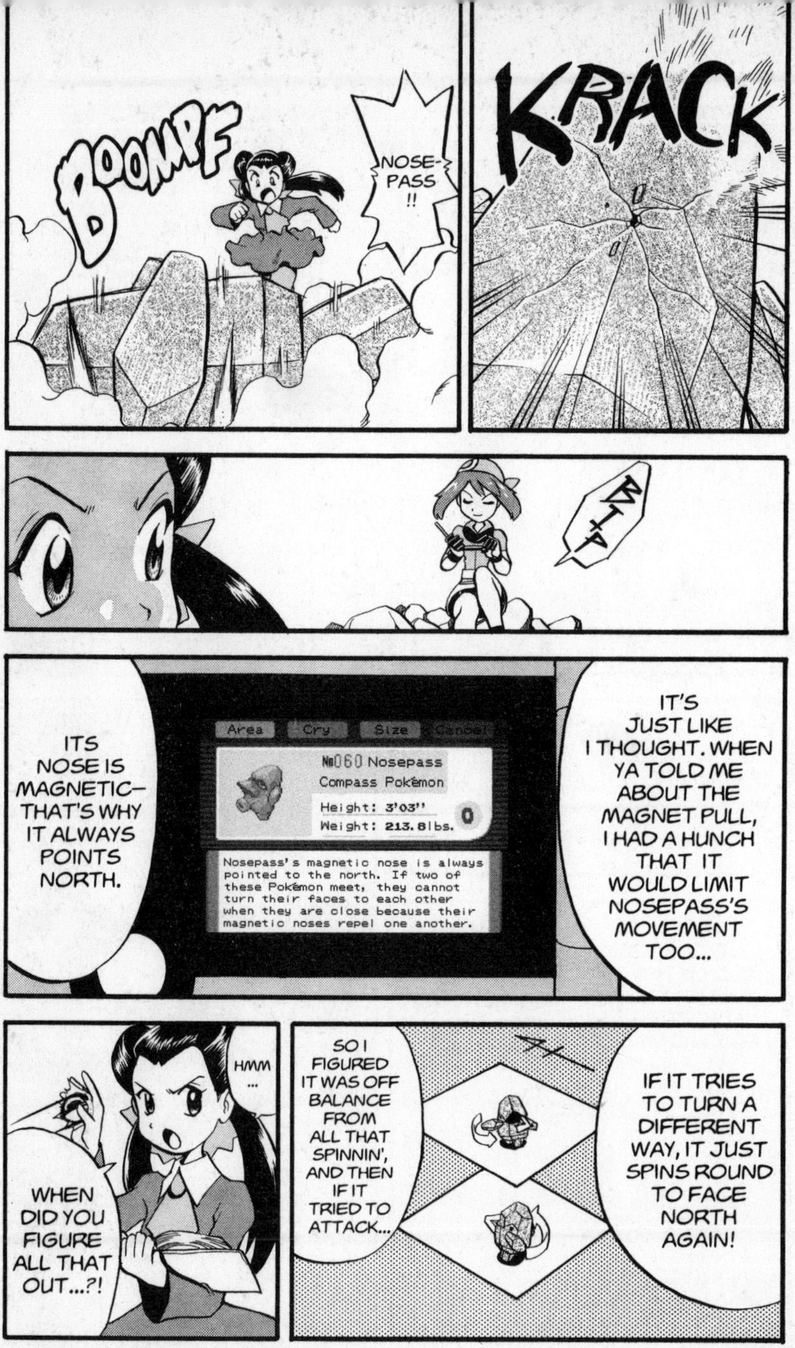
KRACK
NOSE-PASS !!
BOOMPF
IT'S JUST LIKE I THOUGHT. WHEN YA TOLD ME ABOUT THE MAGNET PULL, I HAD A HUNCH THAT IT WOULD LIMIT NOSEPASS'S MOVEMENT TOO...
Area Cry Size Cancel
№060 Nosepass
Compass Pokémon
Height: 3'03''
Weight: 213.8lbs.
Nosepass's magnetic nose is always pointed to the north. If two of these Pokémon meet, they cannot turn their faces to each other when they are close because their magnetic noses repel one another.
ITS NOSE IS MAGNETIC—THAT'S WHY IT ALWAYS POINTS NORTH.
IF IT TRIES TO TURN A DIFFERENT WAY, IT JUST SPINS ROUND TO FACE NORTH AGAIN!
SO I FIGURED IT WAS OFF BALANCE FROM ALL THAT SPINNIN', AND THEN IF IT TRIED TO ATTACK...
HMM ...
WHEN DID YOU FIGURE ALL THAT OUT...?!

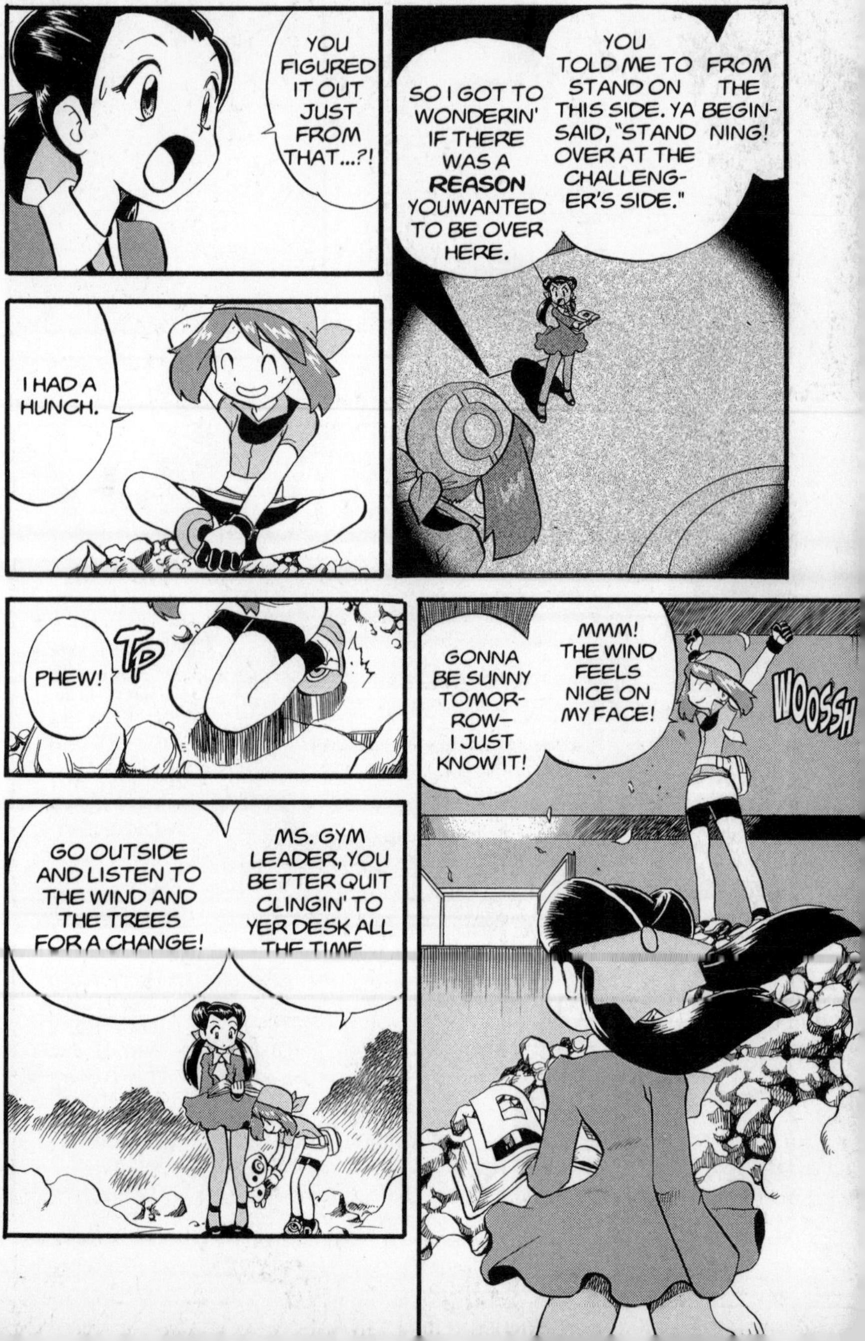
YOU TOLD ME TO STAND ON THIS SIDE. YA SAID, "STAND OVER AT THE CHALLENGER'S SIDE." FROM THE BEGINNING!
SO I GOT TO WONDERIN' IF THERE WAS A **REASON** YOU WANTED TO BE OVER HERE.
YOU FIGURED IT OUT JUST FROM THAT...?!
I HAD A HUNCH.
MMM! THE WIND FEELS NICE ON MY FACE!
GONNA BE SUNNY TOMORROW— I JUST KNOW IT!
WOOSSH
TP
PHEW!
MS. GYM LEADER, YOU BETTER QUIT CLINGIN' TO YER DESK ALL THE TIME
GO OUTSIDE AND LISTEN TO THE WIND AND THE TREES FOR A CHANGE!

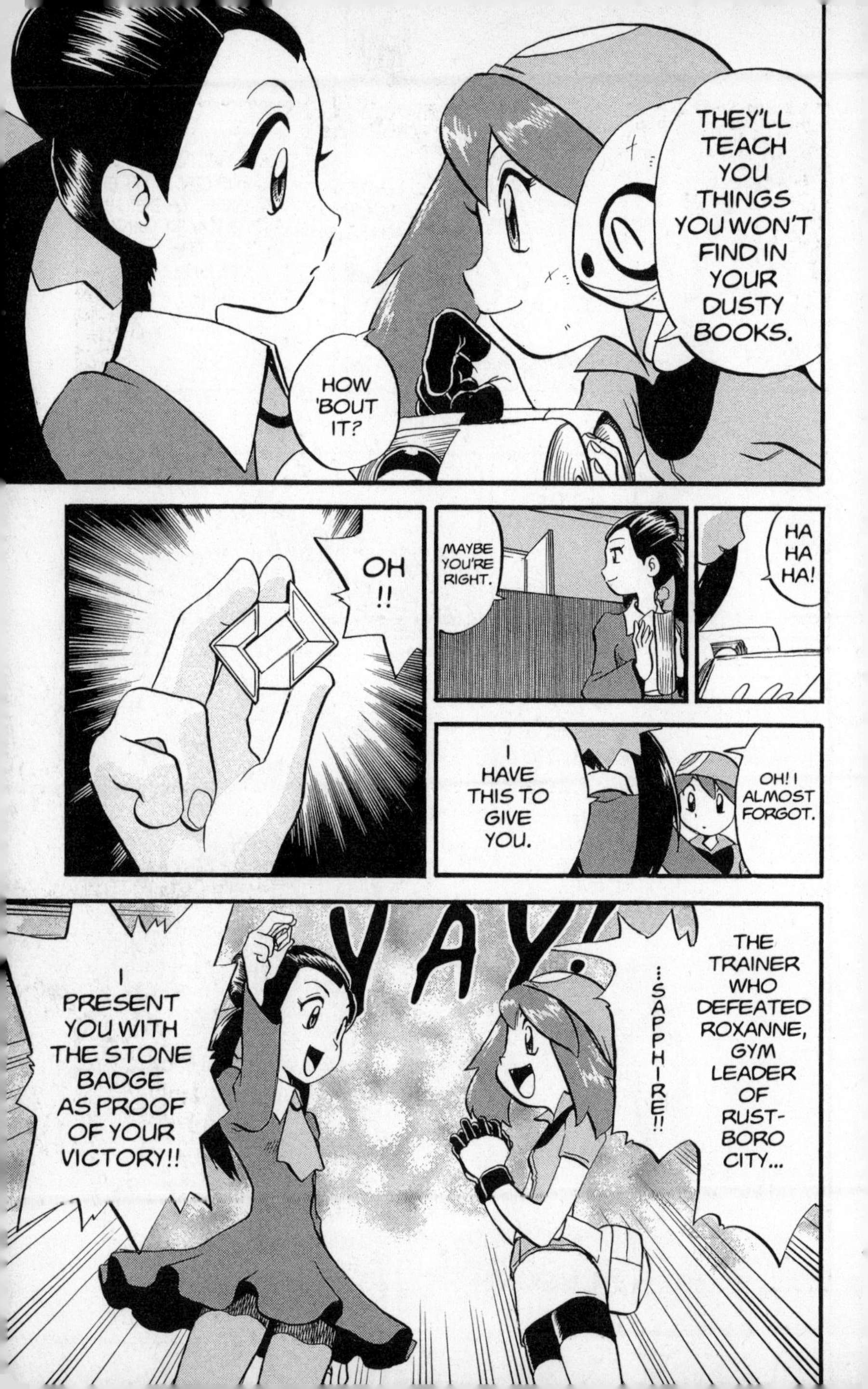
THEY'LL TEACH YOU THINGS YOU WON'T FIND IN YOUR DUSTY BOOKS.
HOW 'BOUT IT?
HA HA HA!
MAYBE YOU'RE RIGHT.
OH! I ALMOST FORGOT.
I HAVE THIS TO GIVE YOU.
OH !!
THE TRAINER WHO DEFEATED ROXANNE, GYM LEADER OF RUST-BORO CITY...
...SAPPHIRE!!
YAY!
I PRESENT YOU WITH THE STONE BADGE AS PROOF OF YOUR VICTORY!!

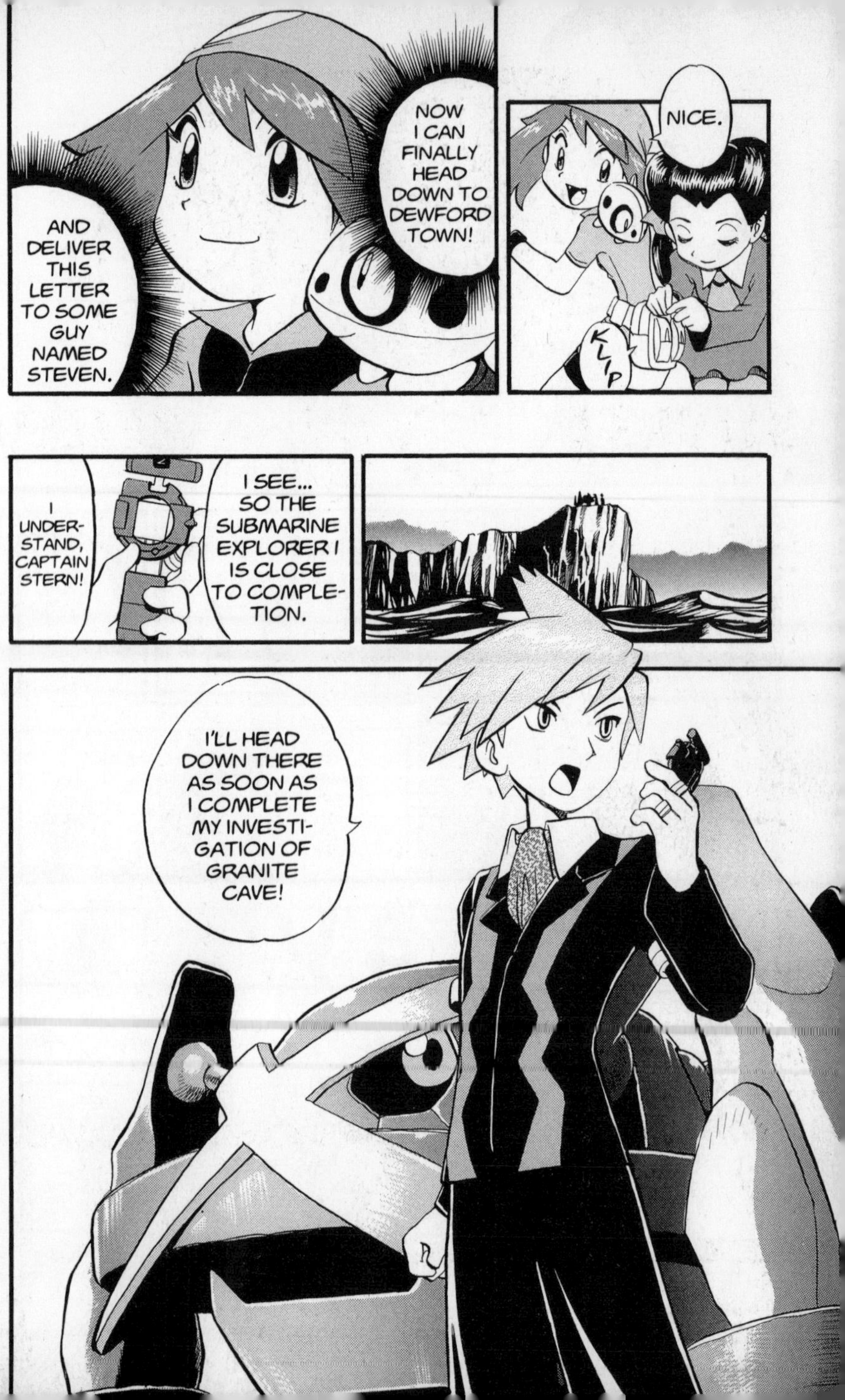
NICE.
KLIP
NOW I CAN FINALLY HEAD DOWN TO DEWFORD TOWN!
AND DELIVER THIS LETTER TO SOME GUY NAMED STEVEN.
I SEE... SO THE SUBMARINE EXPLORER I IS CLOSE TO COMPLETION.
I UNDER-STAND, CAPTAIN STERN!
I'LL HEAD DOWN THERE AS SOON AS I COMPLETE MY INVESTI-GATION OF GRANITE CAVE!

ADVENTURE MAP

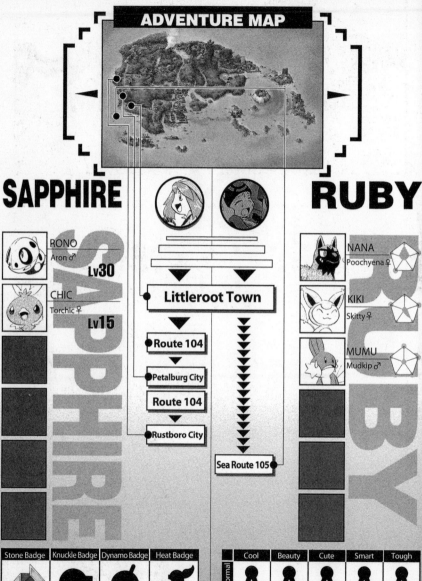

SAPPHIRE

RONO
Aron ♂
Lv30

CHIC
Torchic ♀
Lv15

RUBY

NANA
Poochyena ♀

KIKI
Skitty ♀

MUMU
Mudkip ♂

Littleroot Town

Route 104

Petalburg City

Route 104

Rustboro City

Sea Route 105

Stone Badge	Knuckle Badge	Dynamo Badge	Heat Badge
Balance Badge	Feather Badge	Mind Badge	Rain Badge

		Cool	Beauty	Cute	Smart	Tough
Normal						
Super						
Hyper						
Master						

● Chapter 192 ●
Stick This in Your Craw, Crawdaunt! I

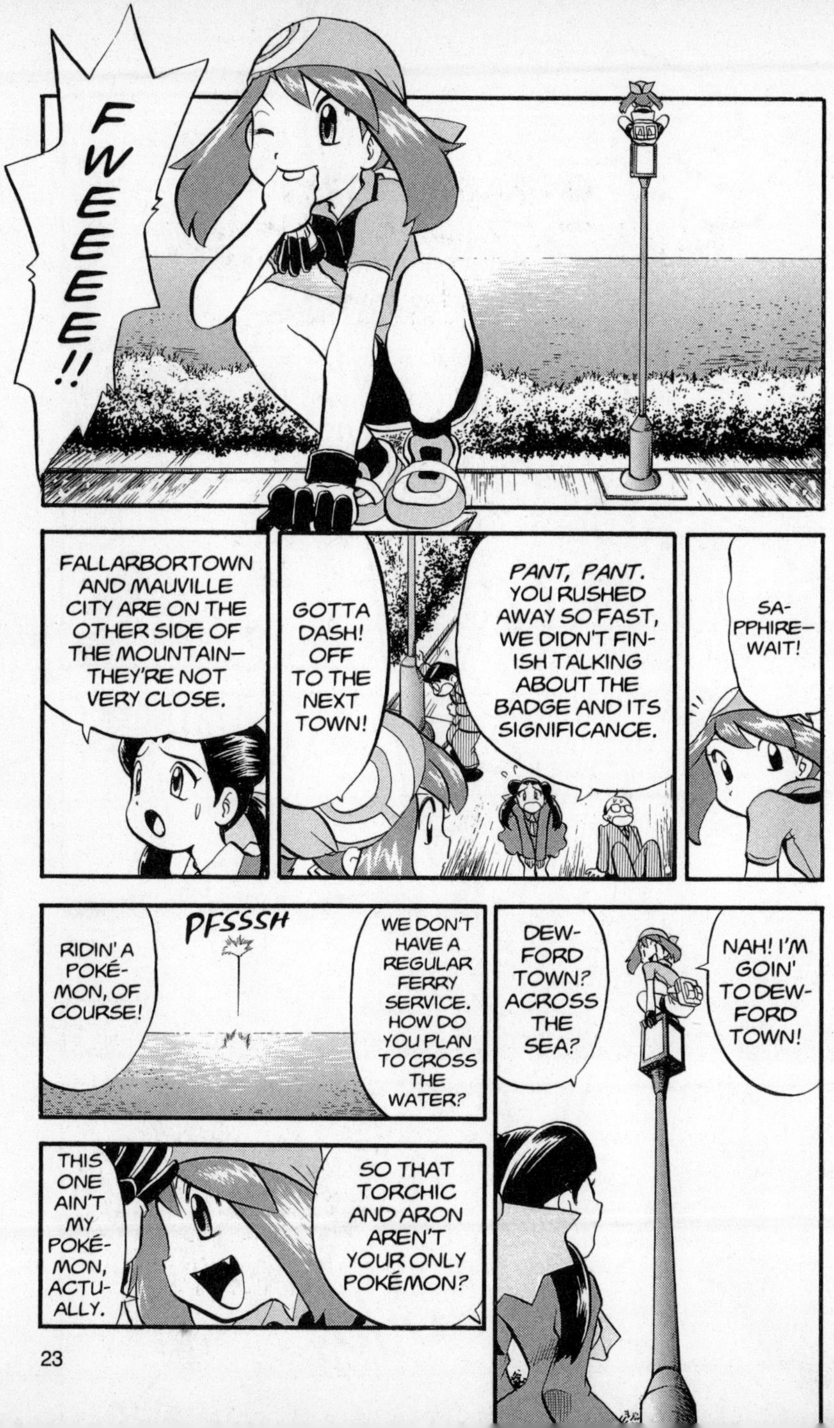
FWEEEEE!!
SAPPHIRE—WAIT!
PANT, PANT. YOU RUSHED AWAY SO FAST, WE DIDN'T FINISH TALKING ABOUT THE BADGE AND ITS SIGNIFICANCE.
GOTTA DASH! OFF TO THE NEXT TOWN!
FALLARBORTOWN AND MAUVILLE CITY ARE ON THE OTHER SIDE OF THE MOUNTAIN—THEY'RE NOT VERY CLOSE.
NAH! I'M GOIN' TO DEWFORD TOWN!
DEWFORD TOWN? ACROSS THE SEA?
WE DON'T HAVE A REGULAR FERRY SERVICE. HOW DO YOU PLAN TO CROSS THE WATER?
PFSSSH
RIDIN' A POKÉMON, OF COURSE!
SO THAT TORCHIC AND ARON AREN'T YOUR ONLY POKÉMON?
THIS ONE AIN'T MY POKÉMON, ACTUALLY.

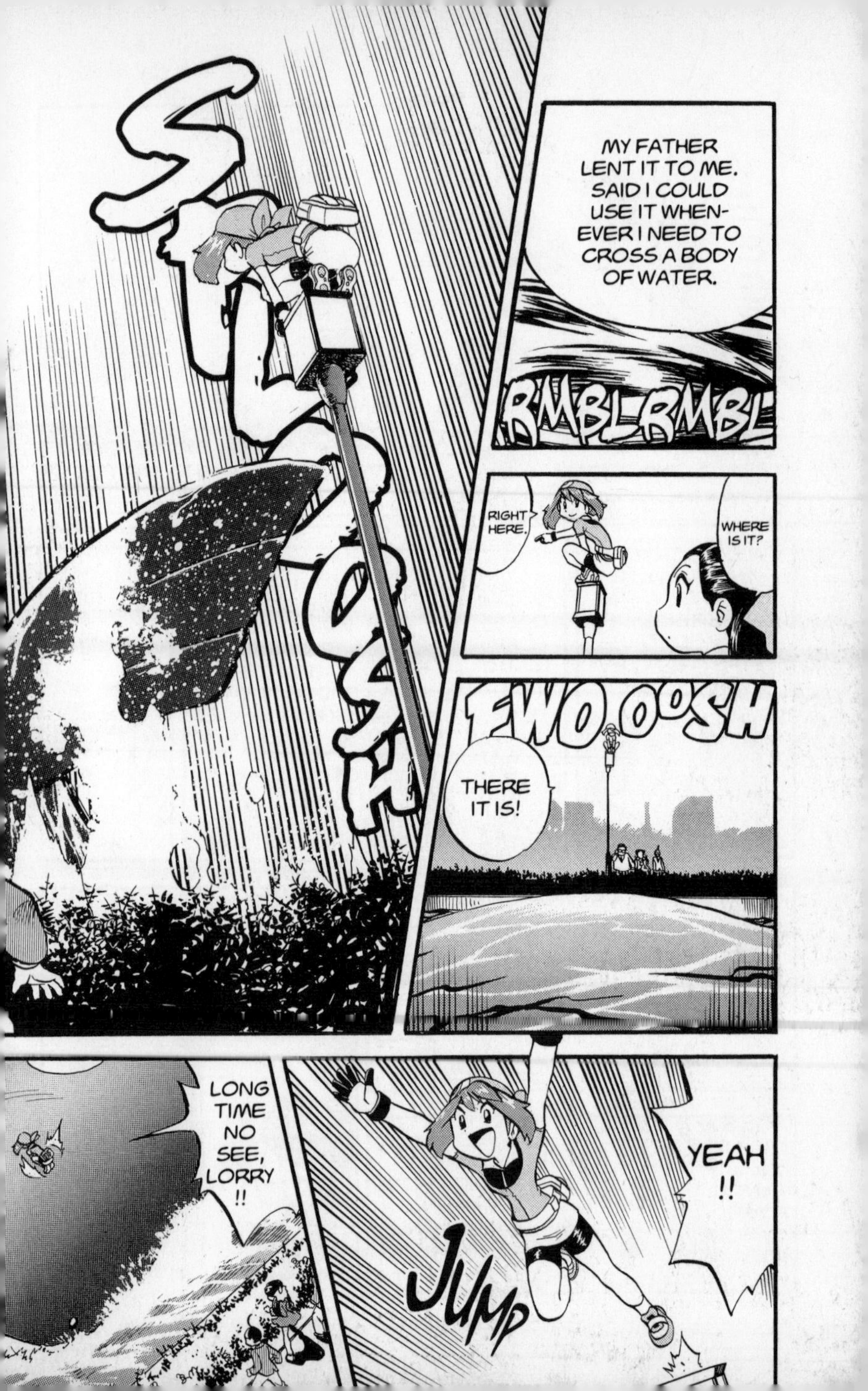
MY FATHER LENT IT TO ME. SAID I COULD USE IT WHENEVER I NEED TO CROSS A BODY OF WATER.
RMBLRMBL
WHERE IS IT?
RIGHT HERE.
FWOOOSH
THERE IT IS!
S
OOSH
YEAH !!
JUMP
LONG TIME NO SEE, LORRY !!

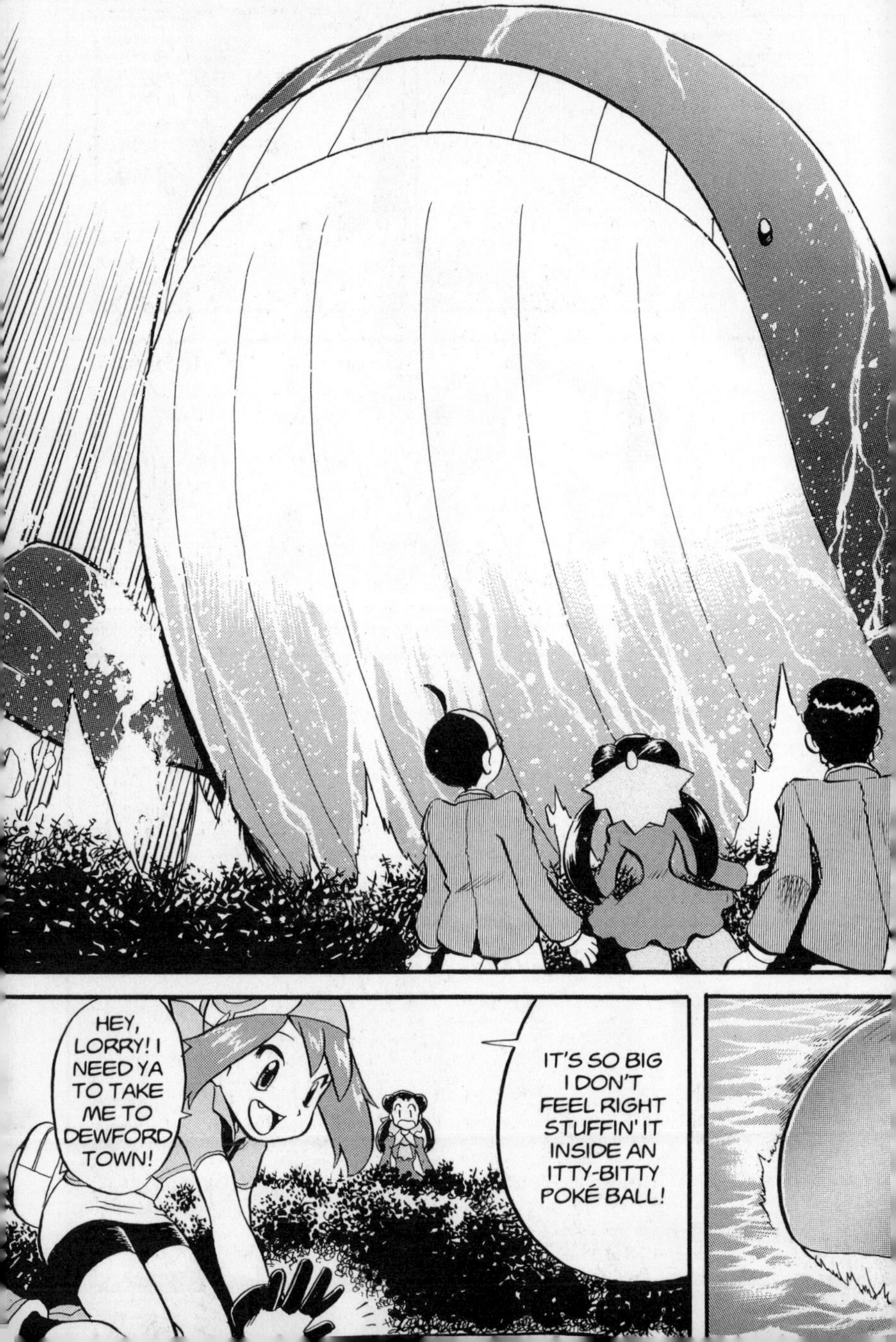
IT'S SO BIG I DON'T FEEL RIGHT STUFFIN' IT INSIDE AN ITTY-BITTY POKÉ BALL!
HEY, LORRY! I NEED YA TO TAKE ME TO DEWFORD TOWN!

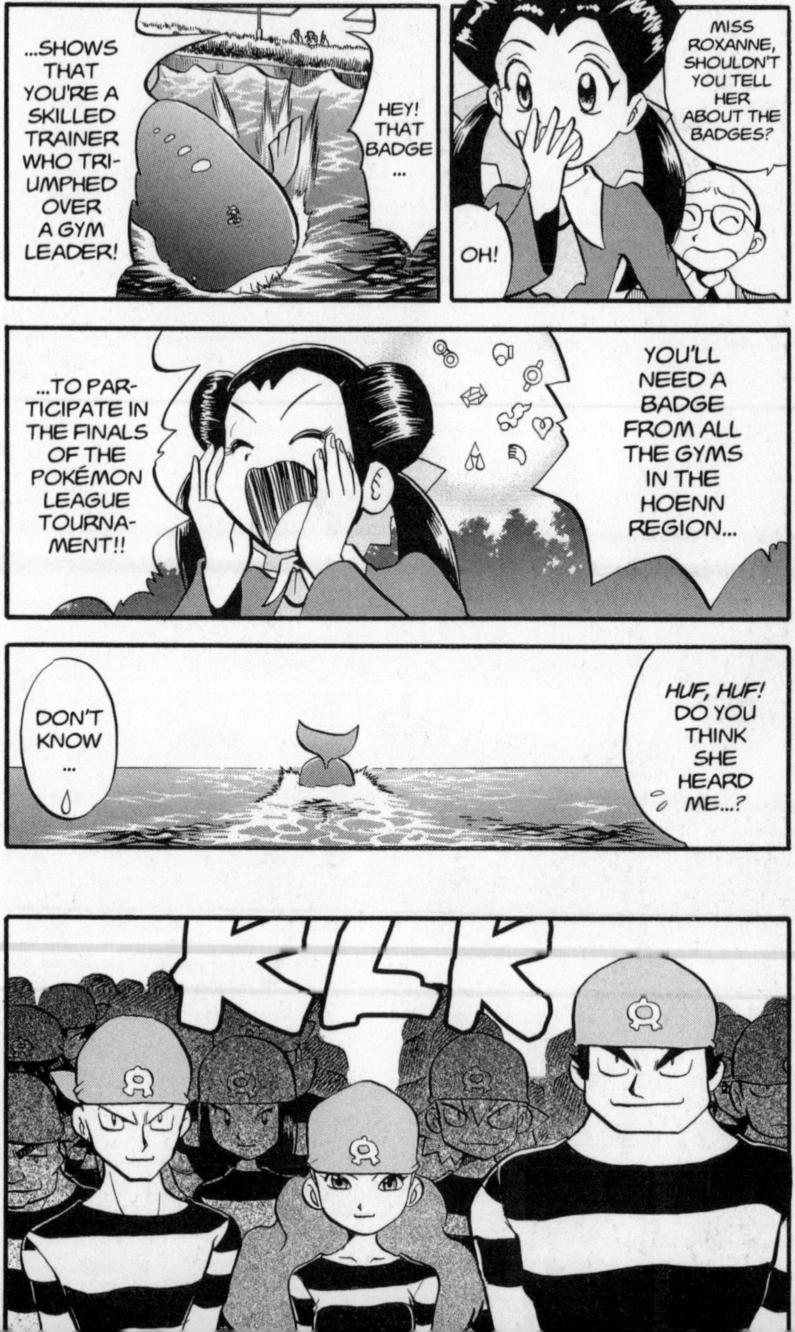
MISS ROXANNE, SHOULDN'T YOU TELL HER ABOUT THE BADGES?
OH!
HEY! THAT BADGE ...
...SHOWS THAT YOU'RE A SKILLED TRAINER WHO TRIUMPHED OVER A GYM LEADER!
YOU'LL NEED A BADGE FROM ALL THE GYMS IN THE HOENN REGION...
...TO PARTICIPATE IN THE FINALS OF THE POKÉMON LEAGUE TOURNAMENT!!
HUF, HUF! DO YOU THINK SHE HEARD ME...?
DON'T KNOW ...

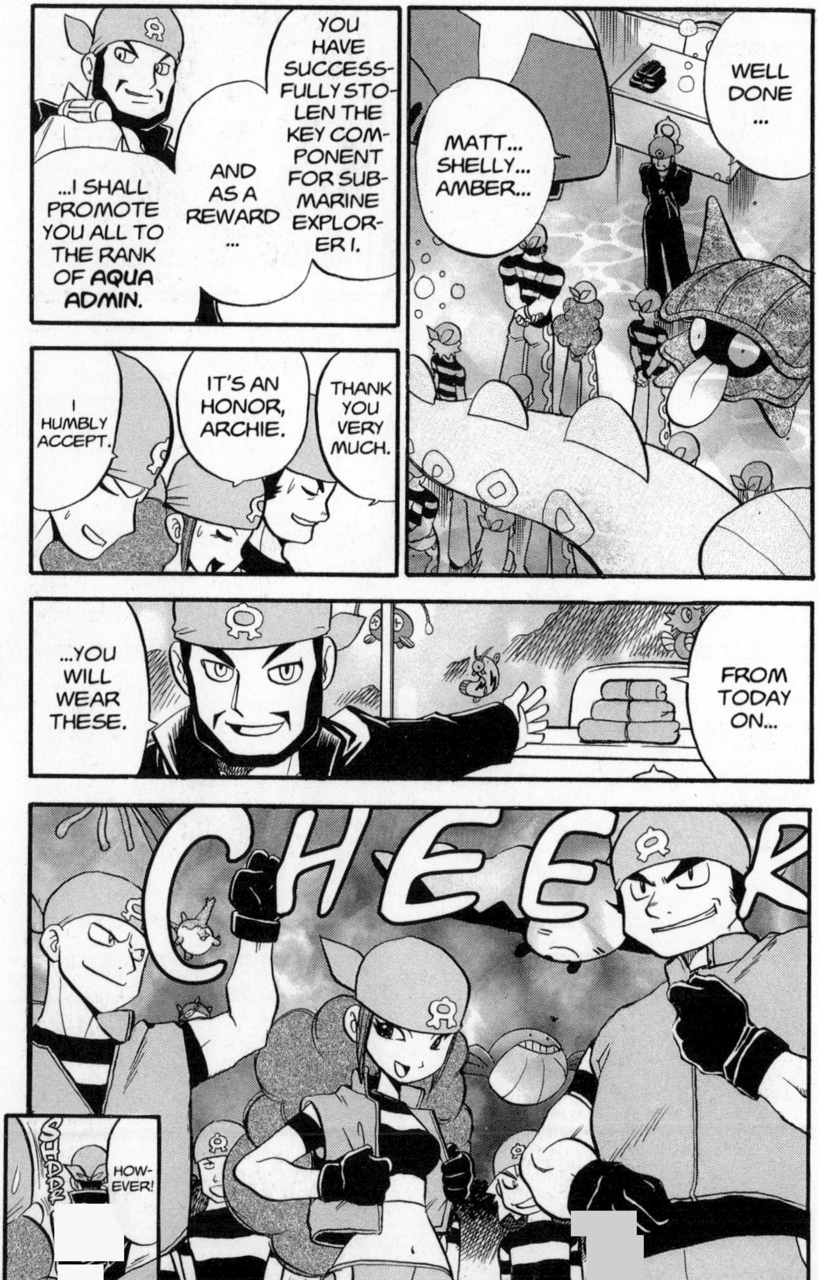
WELL DONE ...
MATT... SHELLY... AMBER...
YOU HAVE SUCCESSFULLY STOLEN THE KEY COMPONENT FOR SUBMARINE EXPLORER I.
AND AS A REWARD ...
...I SHALL PROMOTE YOU ALL TO THE RANK OF **AQUA ADMIN.**
THANK YOU VERY MUCH.
IT'S AN HONOR, ARCHIE.
I HUMBLY ACCEPT.
FROM TODAY ON...
...YOU WILL WEAR THESE.
CHEER
HOW-EVER!

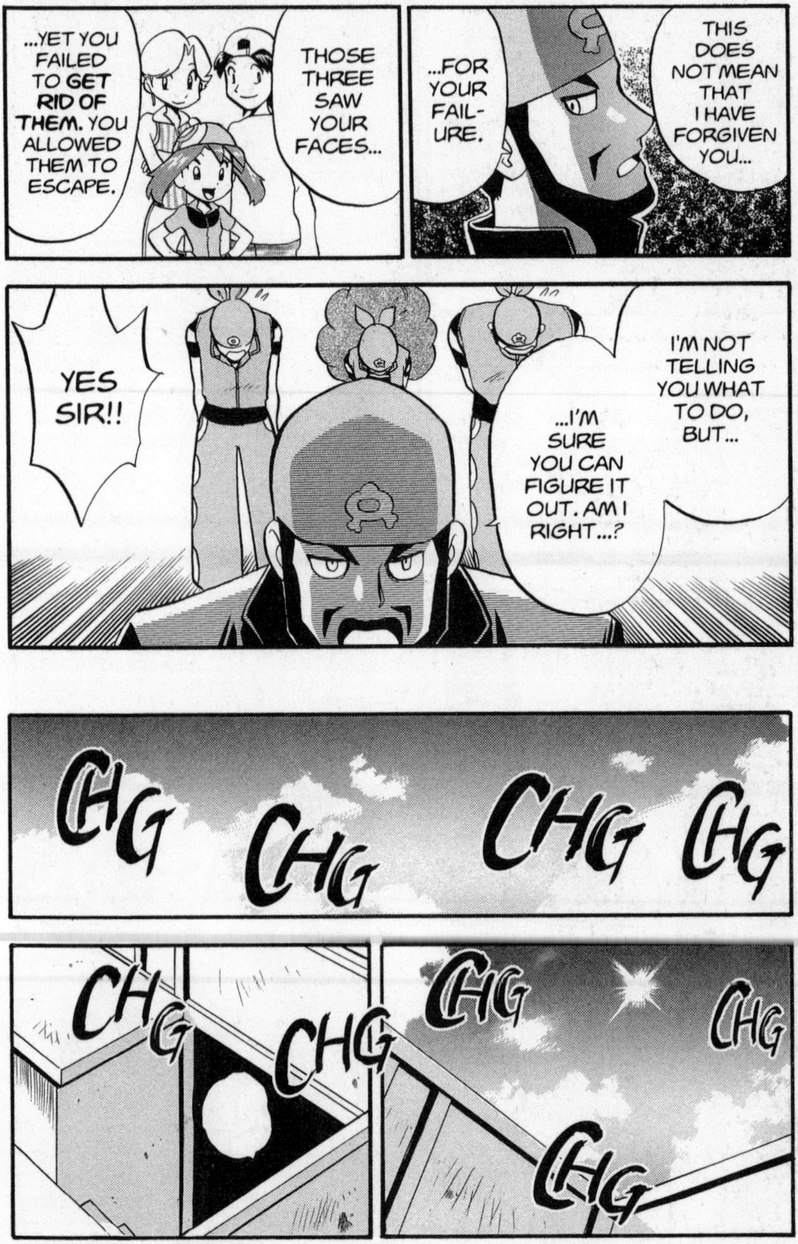
THIS DOES NOT MEAN THAT I HAVE FORGIVEN YOU...
...FOR YOUR FAIL- URE.
THOSE THREE SAW YOUR FACES...
...YET YOU FAILED TO GET RID OF THEM. YOU ALLOWED THEM TO ESCAPE.
I'M NOT TELLING YOU WHAT TO DO, BUT...
...I'M SURE YOU CAN FIGURE IT OUT. AM I RIGHT...?
YES SIR!!
CHG
CHG
CHG
CHG
CHG
CHG
CHG
CHG
CHG

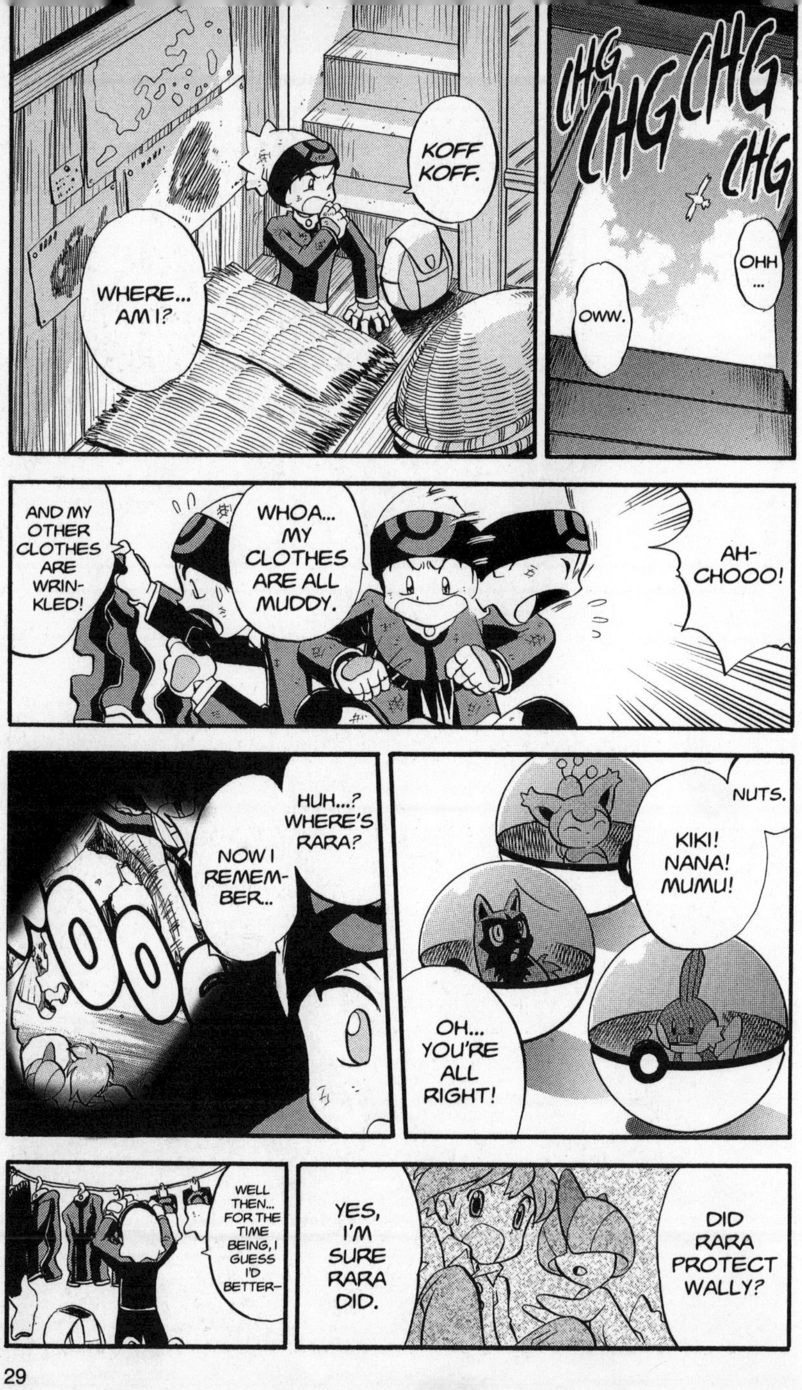
CHG CHG CHG CHG
OHH...
OWW.
KOFF KOFF.
WHERE... AM I?
AH-CHOOO!
WHOA... MY CLOTHES ARE ALL MUDDY.
AND MY OTHER CLOTHES ARE WRIN-KLED!
NUTS.
KIKI! NANA! MUMU!
OH... YOU'RE ALL RIGHT!
HUH...? WHERE'S RARA?
NOW I REMEM-BER...
DID RARA PROTECT WALLY?
YES, I'M SURE RARA DID.
WELL THEN... FOR THE TIME BEING, I GUESS I'D BETTER—

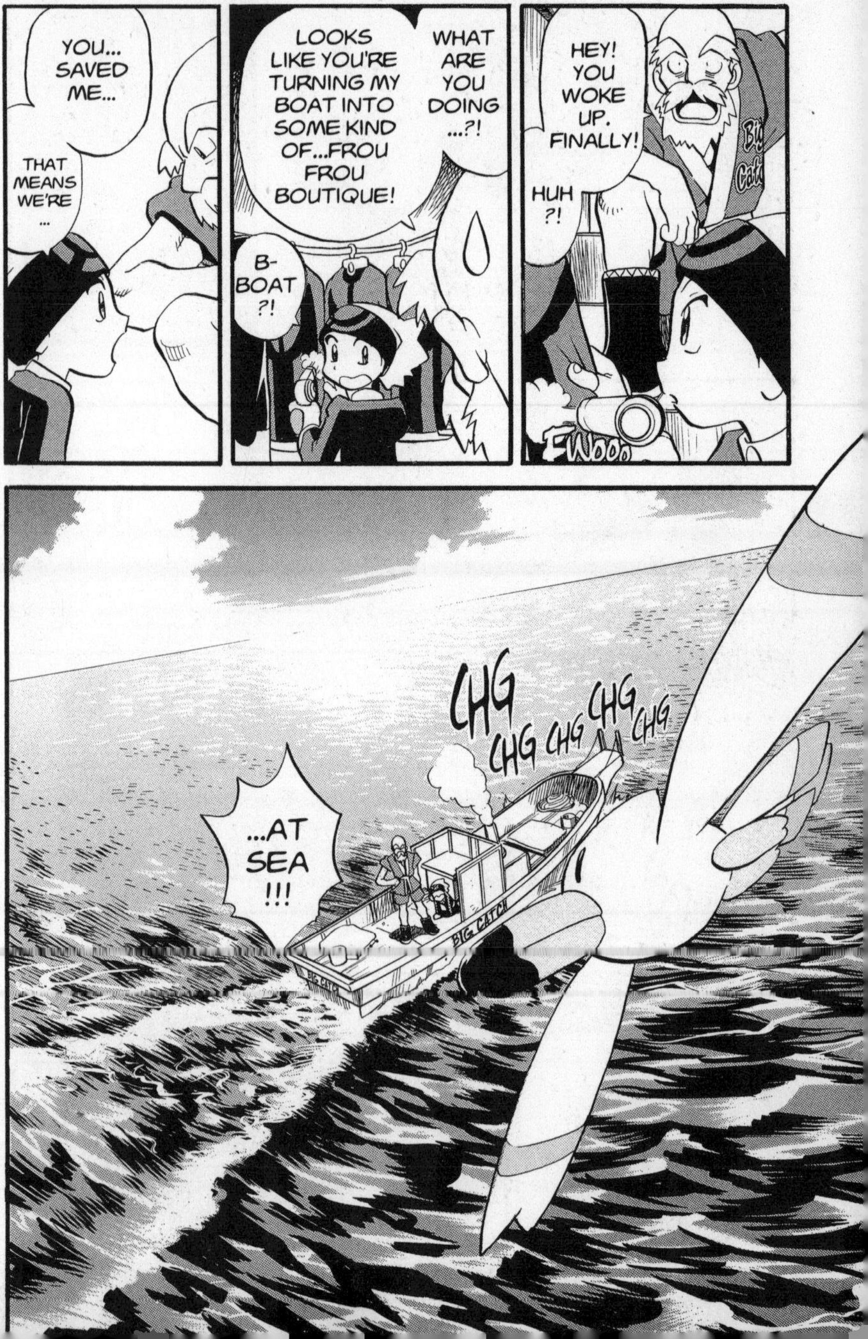
HEY! YOU WOKE UP. FINALLY!
HUH ?!
FWOOO
WHAT ARE YOU DOING ...?!
LOOKS LIKE YOU'RE TURNING MY BOAT INTO SOME KIND OF...FROU FROU BOUTIQUE!
B-BOAT ?!
YOU... SAVED ME...
THAT MEANS WE'RE ...
CHG CHG CHG CHG CHG CHG
...AT SEA !!!

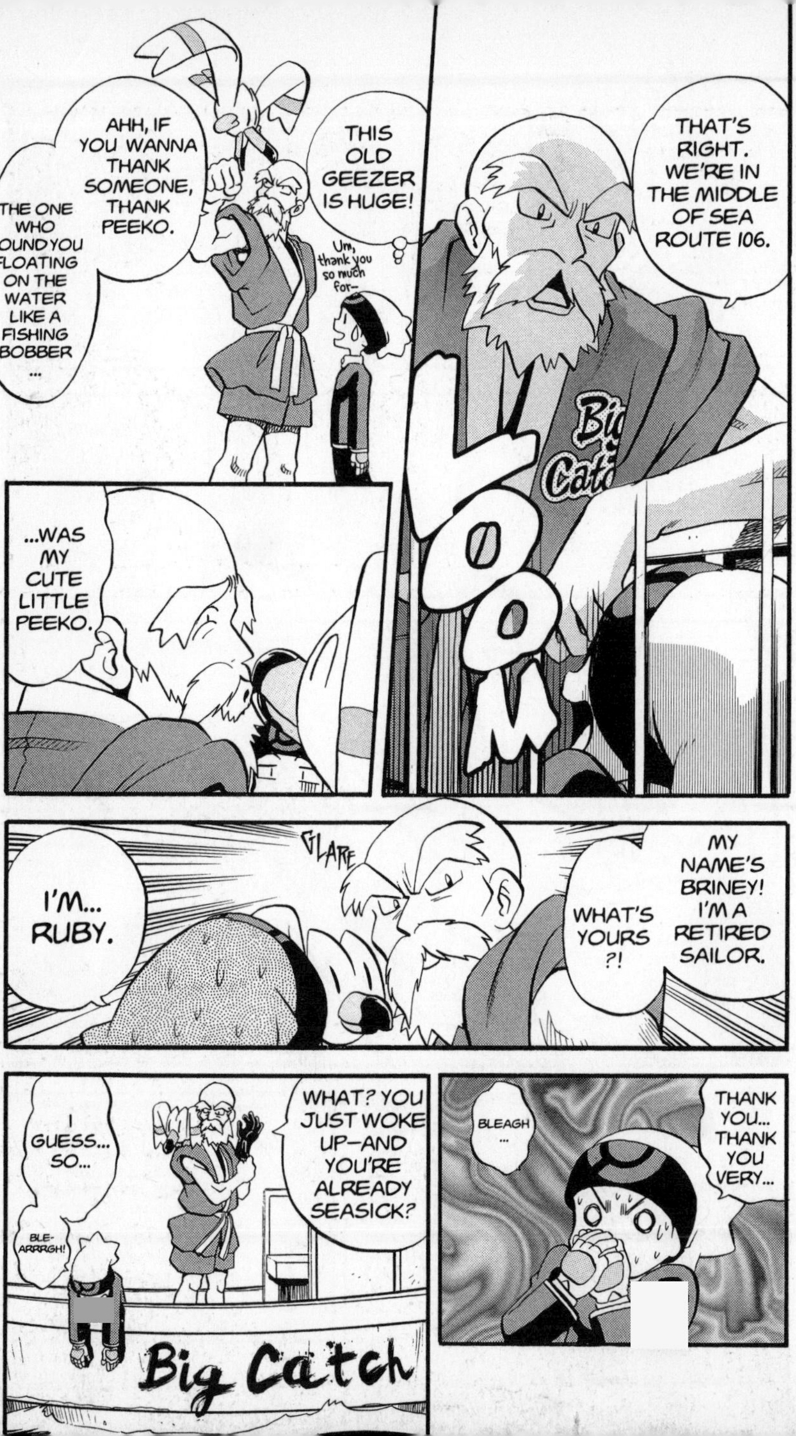
THAT'S RIGHT. WE'RE IN THE MIDDLE OF SEA ROUTE 106.
Big Catch
VOOM
THIS OLD GEEZER IS HUGE!
Um, thank you so much for–
AHH, IF YOU WANNA THANK SOMEONE, THANK PEEKO.
THE ONE WHO FOUND YOU FLOATING ON THE WATER LIKE A FISHING BOBBER ...
...WAS MY CUTE LITTLE PEEKO.
MY NAME'S BRINEY! I'M A RETIRED SAILOR.
WHAT'S YOURS ?!
GLARE
I'M... RUBY.
THANK YOU... THANK YOU VERY...
BLEAGH ...
WHAT? YOU JUST WOKE UP–AND YOU'RE ALREADY SEASICK?
I GUESS... SO...
BLE-ARRRGH!
Big Catch

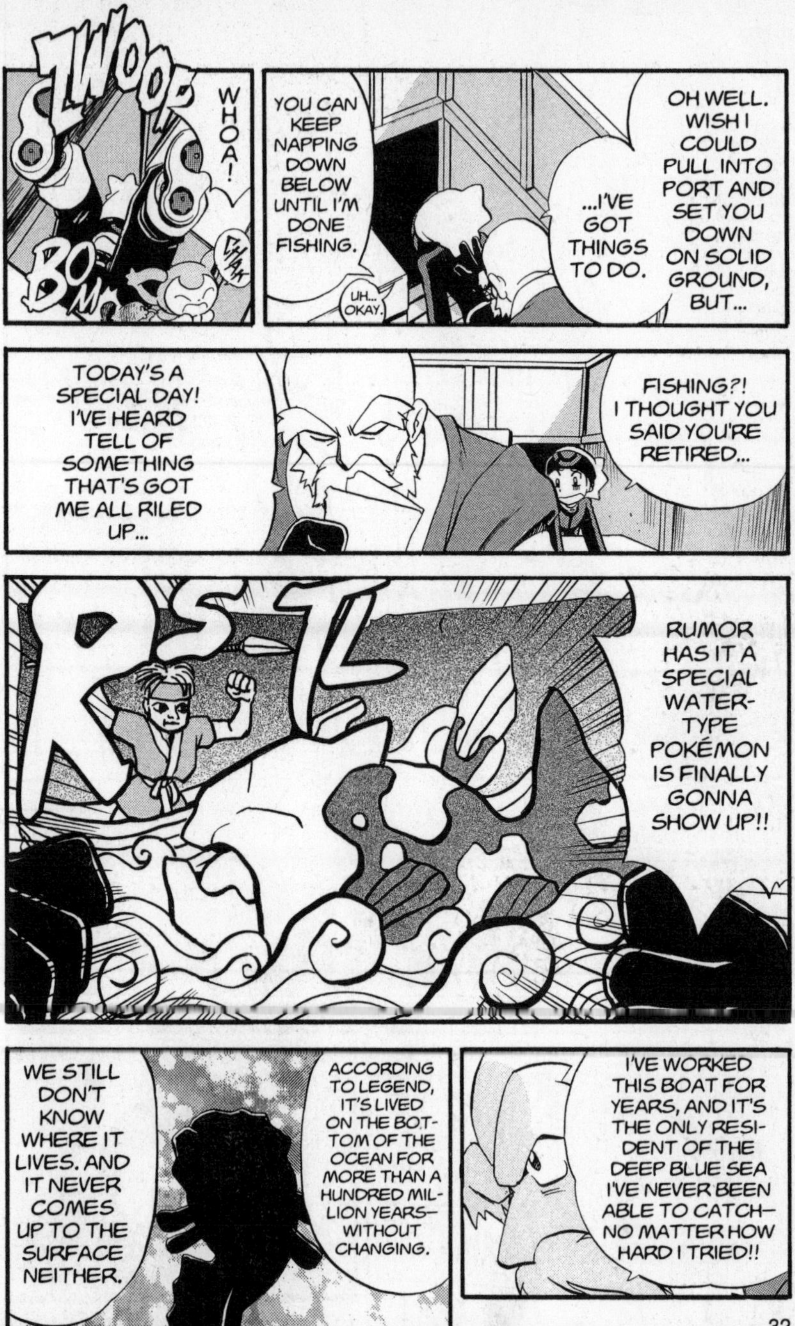
OH WELL. WISH I COULD PULL INTO PORT AND SET YOU DOWN ON SOLID GROUND, BUT...
...I'VE GOT THINGS TO DO.
YOU CAN KEEP NAPPING DOWN BELOW UNTIL I'M DONE FISHING.
UH... OKAY.
ZWOOP
WHOA!
CHAK
BOM
FISHING?! I THOUGHT YOU SAID YOU'RE RETIRED...
TODAY'S A SPECIAL DAY! I'VE HEARD TELL OF SOMETHING THAT'S GOT ME ALL RILED UP...
RUMOR HAS IT A SPECIAL WATER-TYPE POKÉMON IS FINALLY GONNA SHOW UP!!
I'VE WORKED THIS BOAT FOR YEARS, AND IT'S THE ONLY RESIDENT OF THE DEEP BLUE SEA I'VE NEVER BEEN ABLE TO CATCH—NO MATTER HOW HARD I TRIED!!
ACCORDING TO LEGEND, IT'S LIVED ON THE BOTTOM OF THE OCEAN FOR MORE THAN A HUNDRED MILLION YEARS—WITHOUT CHANGING.
WE STILL DON'T KNOW WHERE IT LIVES. AND IT NEVER COMES UP TO THE SURFACE NEITHER.

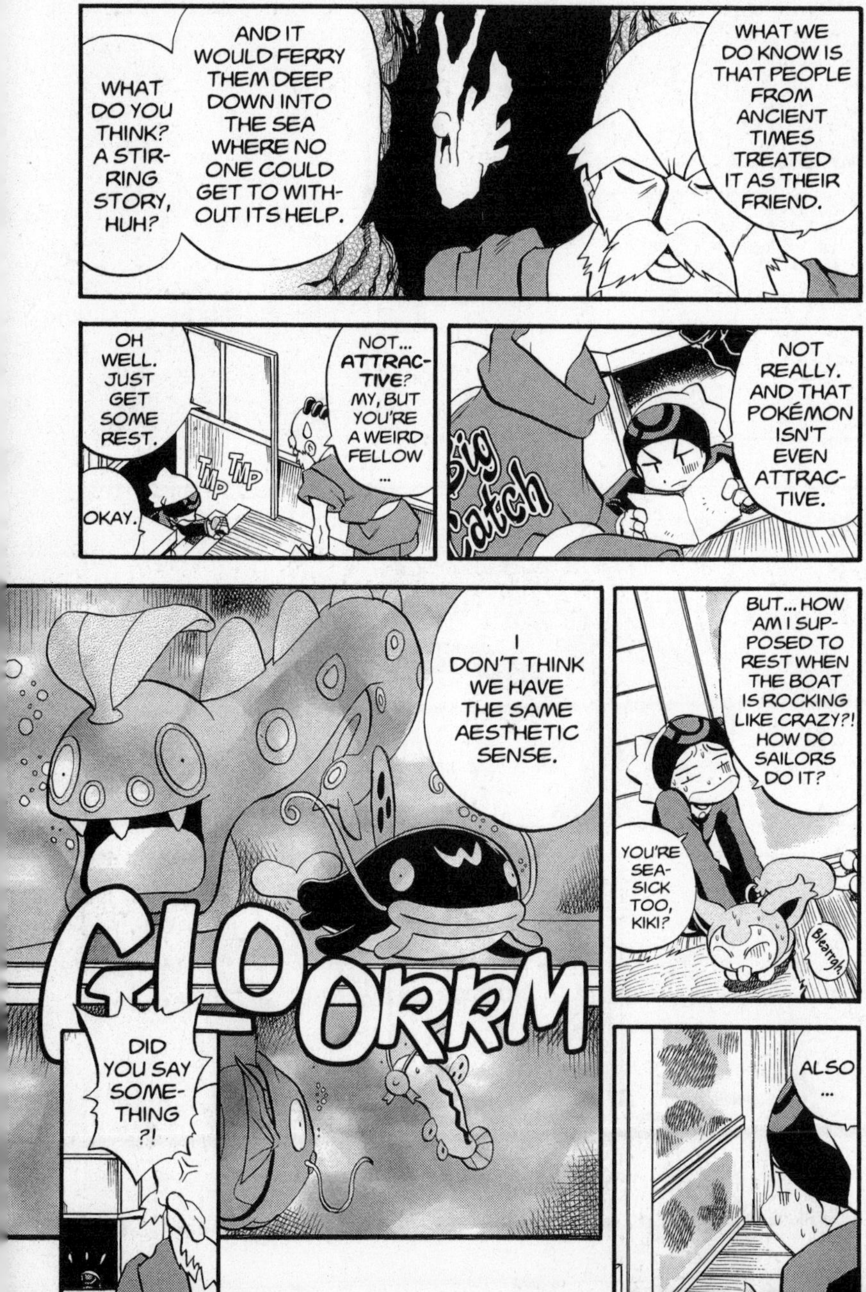
WHAT WE DO KNOW IS THAT PEOPLE FROM ANCIENT TIMES TREATED IT AS THEIR FRIEND.
AND IT WOULD FERRY THEM DEEP DOWN INTO THE SEA WHERE NO ONE COULD GET TO WITHOUT ITS HELP.
WHAT DO YOU THINK? A STIRRING STORY, HUH?
NOT REALLY. AND THAT POKÉMON ISN'T EVEN ATTRACTIVE.
Big Catch
NOT... **ATTRACTIVE**? MY, BUT YOU'RE A WEIRD FELLOW...
OH WELL. JUST GET SOME REST.
TMP TMP
OKAY.
BUT... HOW AM I SUPPOSED TO REST WHEN THE BOAT IS ROCKING LIKE CRAZY?! HOW DO SAILORS DO IT?
YOU'RE SEASICK TOO, KIKI?
Blearrgh
ALSO...
I DON'T THINK WE HAVE THE SAME AESTHETIC SENSE.
GLOORRKM
DID YOU SAY SOMETHING?!

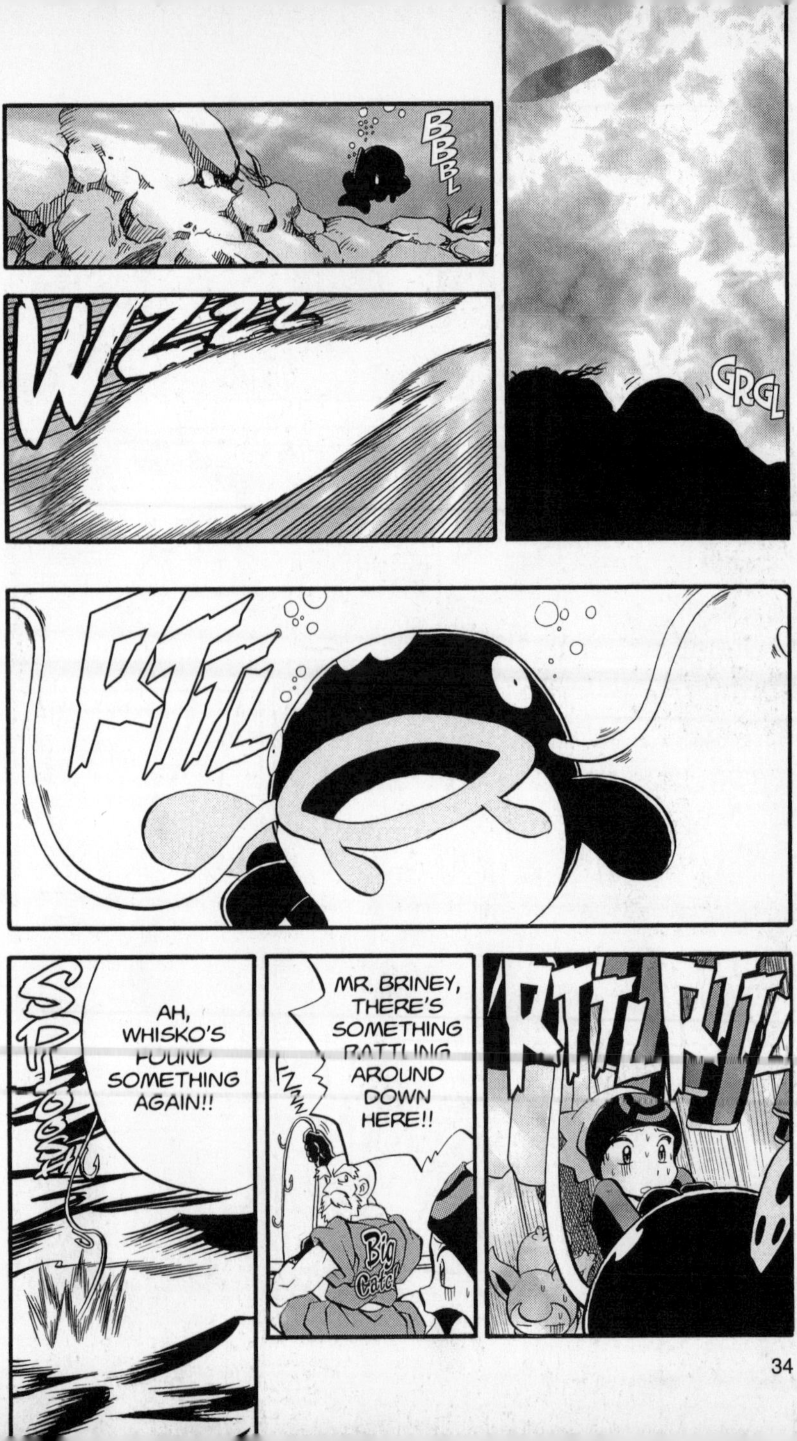
GRGL
BBBL
WZZZ
PTTL
RTTL RTTL
MR. BRINEY, THERE'S SOMETHING RATTLING AROUND DOWN HERE!!
FZZZ
AH, WHISKO'S FOUND SOMETHING AGAIN!!
SPLOOSH
Big Catch

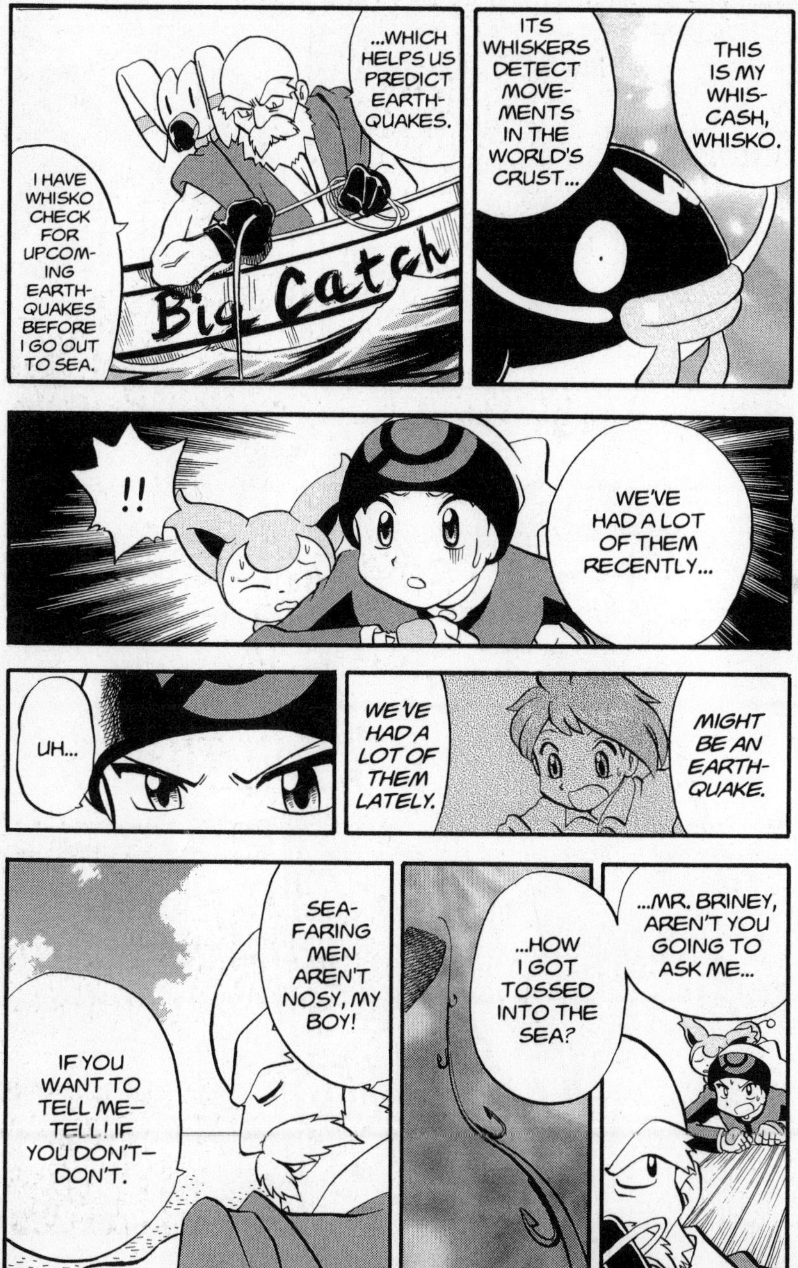
THIS IS MY WHIS-CASH, WHISKO.
ITS WHISKERS DETECT MOVE-MENTS IN THE WORLD'S CRUST...
...WHICH HELPS US PREDICT EARTH-QUAKES.
Big Catch
I HAVE WHISKO CHECK FOR UPCOM-ING EARTH-QUAKES BEFORE I GO OUT TO SEA.
WE'VE HAD A LOT OF THEM RECENTLY...
!!
MIGHT BE AN EARTH-QUAKE.
WE'VE HAD A LOT OF THEM LATELY.
UH...
...MR. BRINEY, AREN'T YOU GOING TO ASK ME...
...HOW I GOT TOSSED INTO THE SEA?
SEA-FARING MEN AREN'T NOSY, MY BOY!
IF YOU WANT TO TELL ME— TELL! IF YOU DON'T— DON'T.

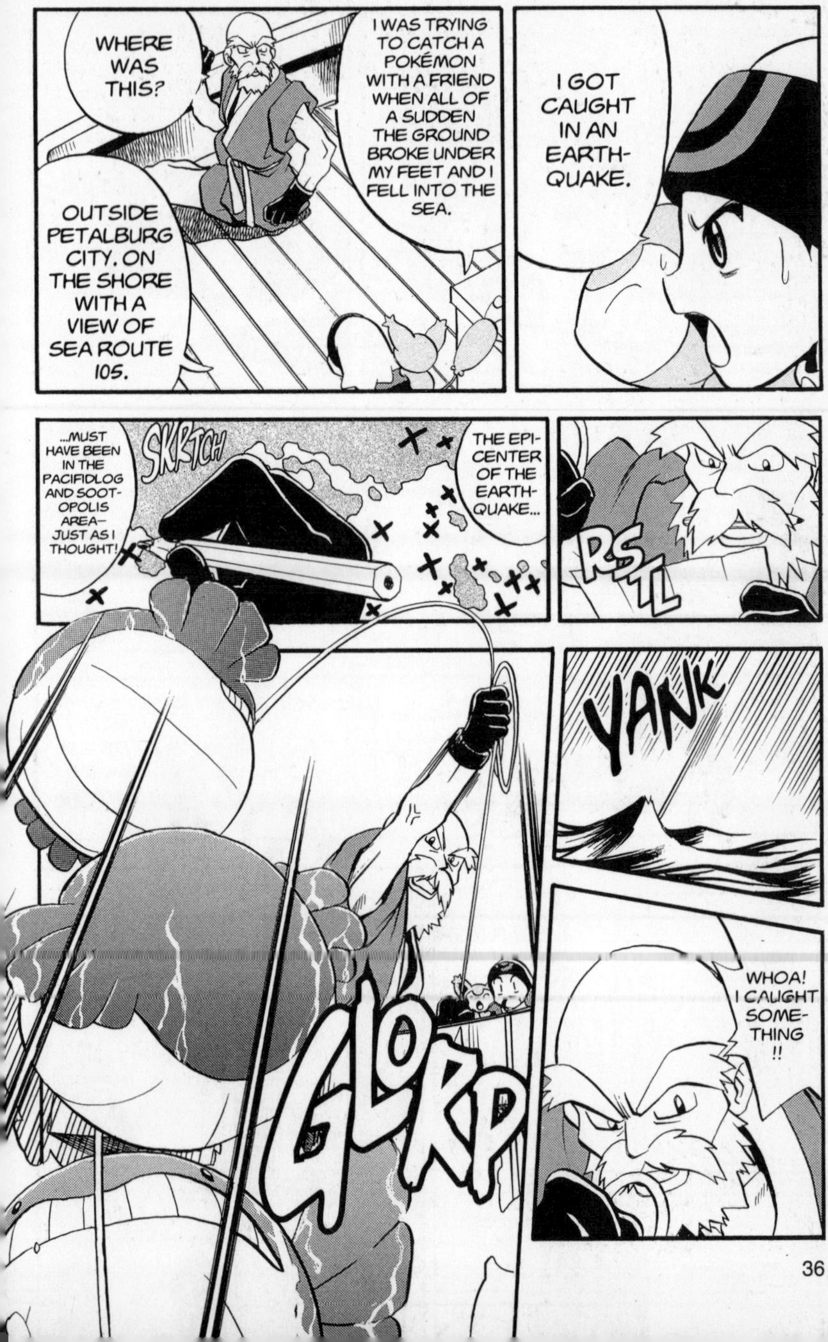
I GOT CAUGHT IN AN EARTH-QUAKE.
I WAS TRYING TO CATCH A POKÉMON WITH A FRIEND WHEN ALL OF A SUDDEN THE GROUND BROKE UNDER MY FEET AND I FELL INTO THE SEA.
WHERE WAS THIS?
OUTSIDE PETALBURG CITY. ON THE SHORE WITH A VIEW OF SEA ROUTE 105.
RSTL
THE EPI-CENTER OF THE EARTH-QUAKE...
SKRTCH
...MUST HAVE BEEN IN THE PACIFIDLOG AND SOOT-OPOLIS AREA— JUST AS I THOUGHT!
YANK
WHOA! I CAUGHT SOME-THING !!
GLORP

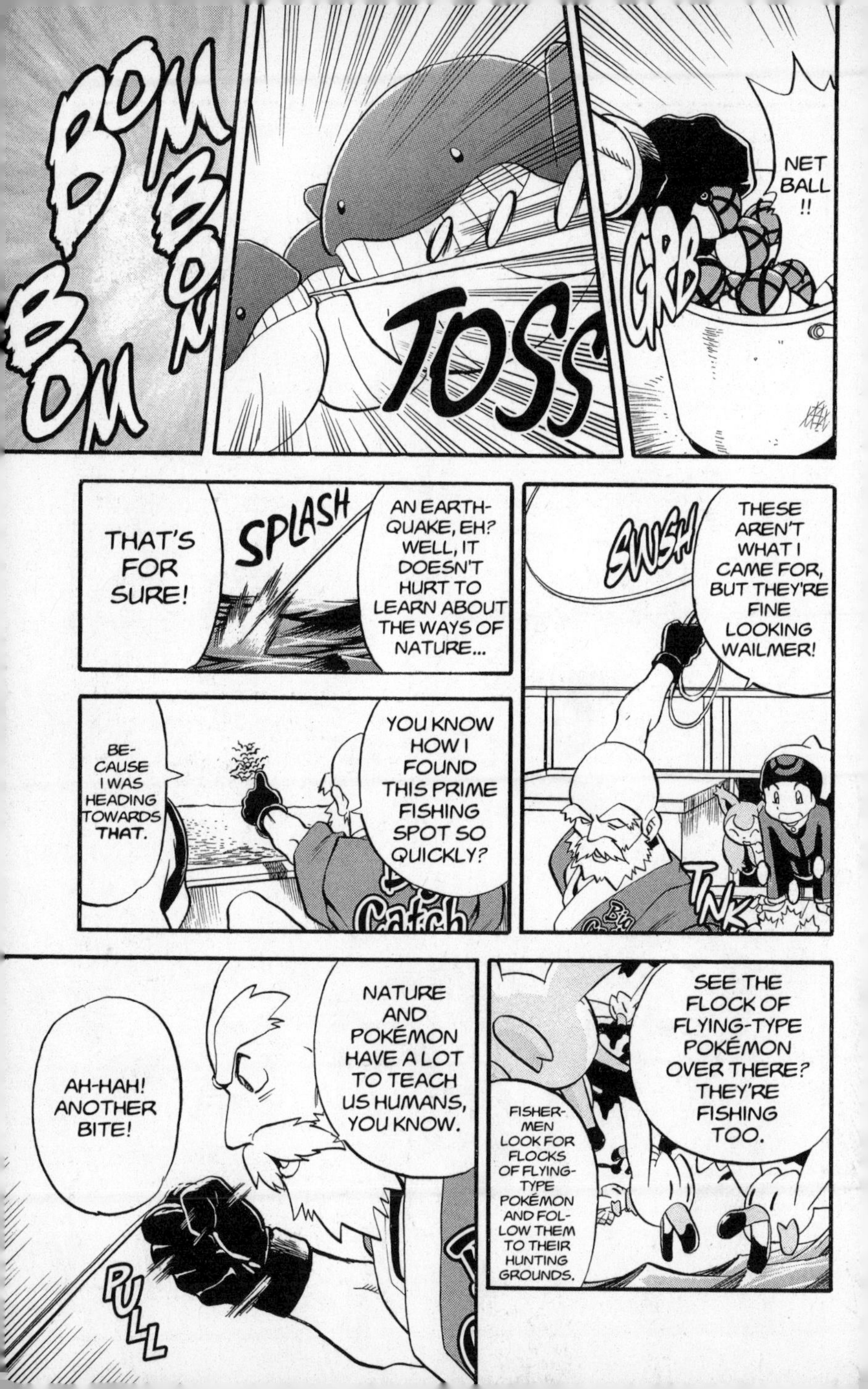
NET BALL!!
GRB
TOSS
BOM BOM
BOM BOM
SWISH
THESE AREN'T WHAT I CAME FOR, BUT THEY'RE FINE LOOKING WAILMER!
TNK
AN EARTH-QUAKE, EH? WELL, IT DOESN'T HURT TO LEARN ABOUT THE WAYS OF NATURE...
SPLASH
THAT'S FOR SURE!
YOU KNOW HOW I FOUND THIS PRIME FISHING SPOT SO QUICKLY?
BE-CAUSE I WAS HEADING TOWARDS THAT.
SEE THE FLOCK OF FLYING-TYPE POKÉMON OVER THERE? THEY'RE FISHING TOO.
FISHER-MEN LOOK FOR FLOCKS OF FLYING-TYPE POKÉMON AND FOL-LOW THEM TO THEIR HUNTING GROUNDS.
NATURE AND POKÉMON HAVE A LOT TO TEACH US HUMANS, YOU KNOW.
AH-HAH! ANOTHER BITE!
PULL

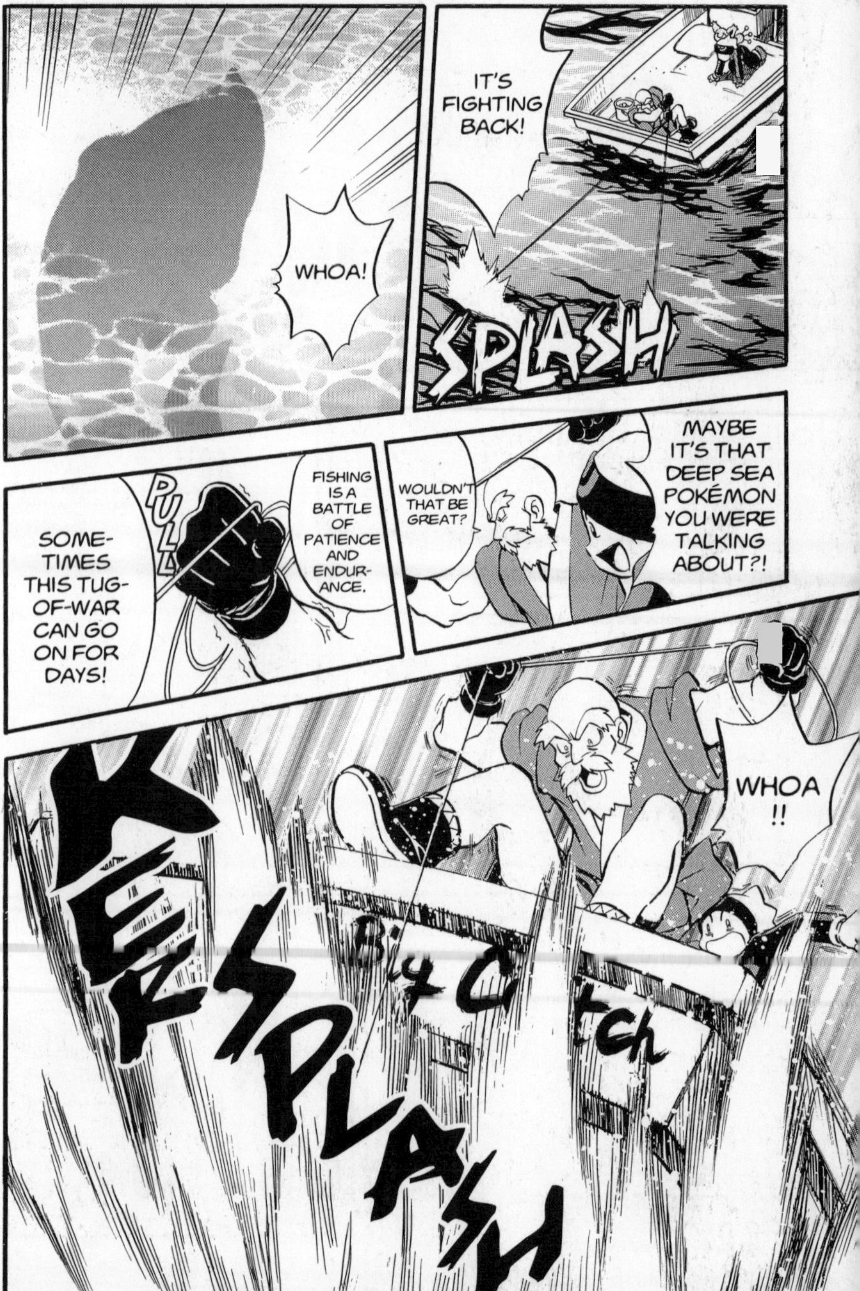
IT'S FIGHTING BACK!
SPLASH
WHOA!
MAYBE IT'S THAT DEEP SEA POKÉMON YOU WERE TALKING ABOUT?!
WOULDN'T THAT BE GREAT?
FISHING IS A BATTLE OF PATIENCE AND ENDURANCE.
PULL
SOMETIMES THIS TUG-OF-WAR CAN GO ON FOR DAYS!
WHOA !!
KERSPLASH

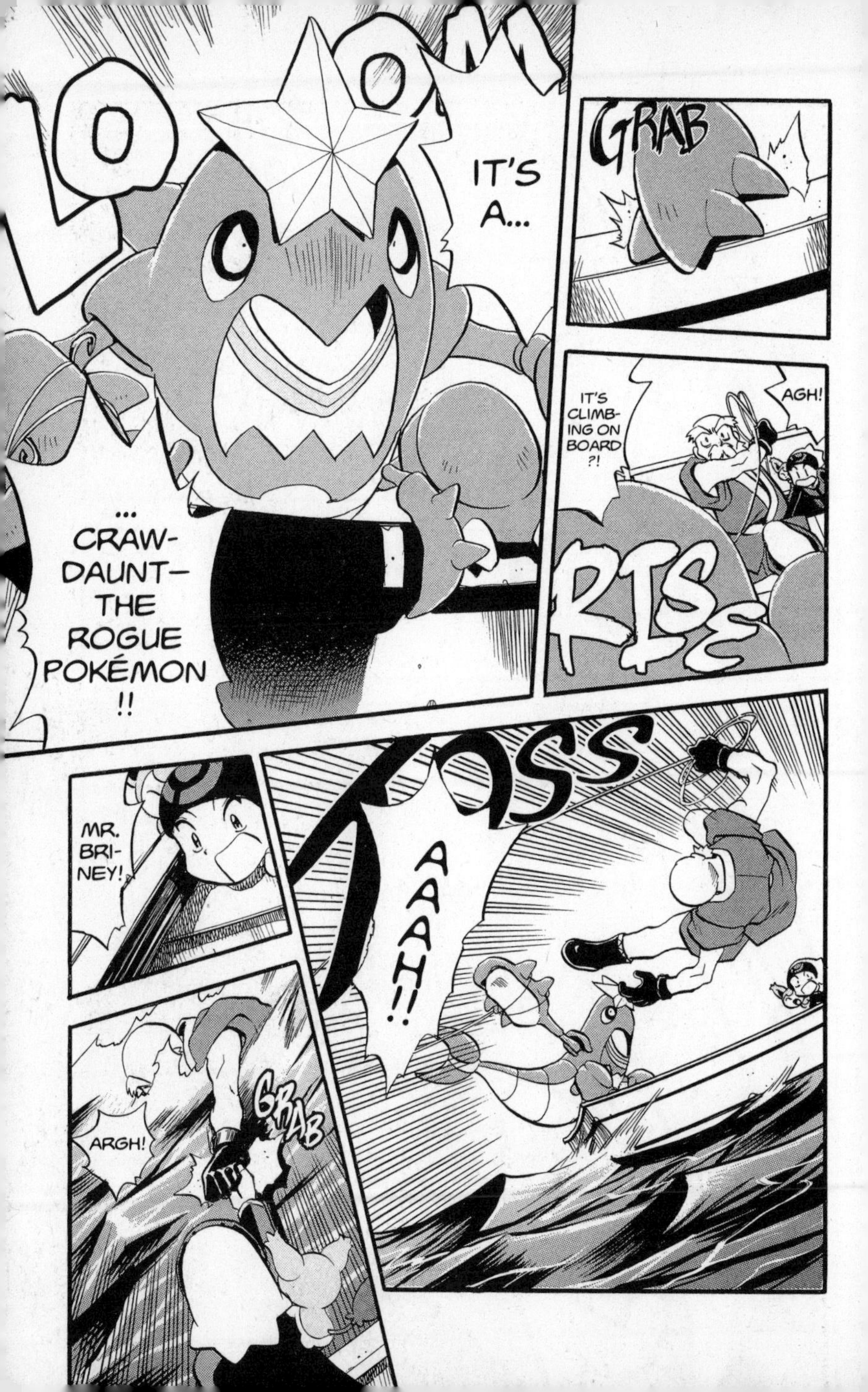
GRAB
AGH!
IT'S CLIMBING ON BOARD?!
RISE
LOOOM
IT'S A...
...CRAWDAUNT—THE ROGUE POKÉMON!!
TOSS
AAAAH!!
MR. BRINEY!
GRAB
ARGH!

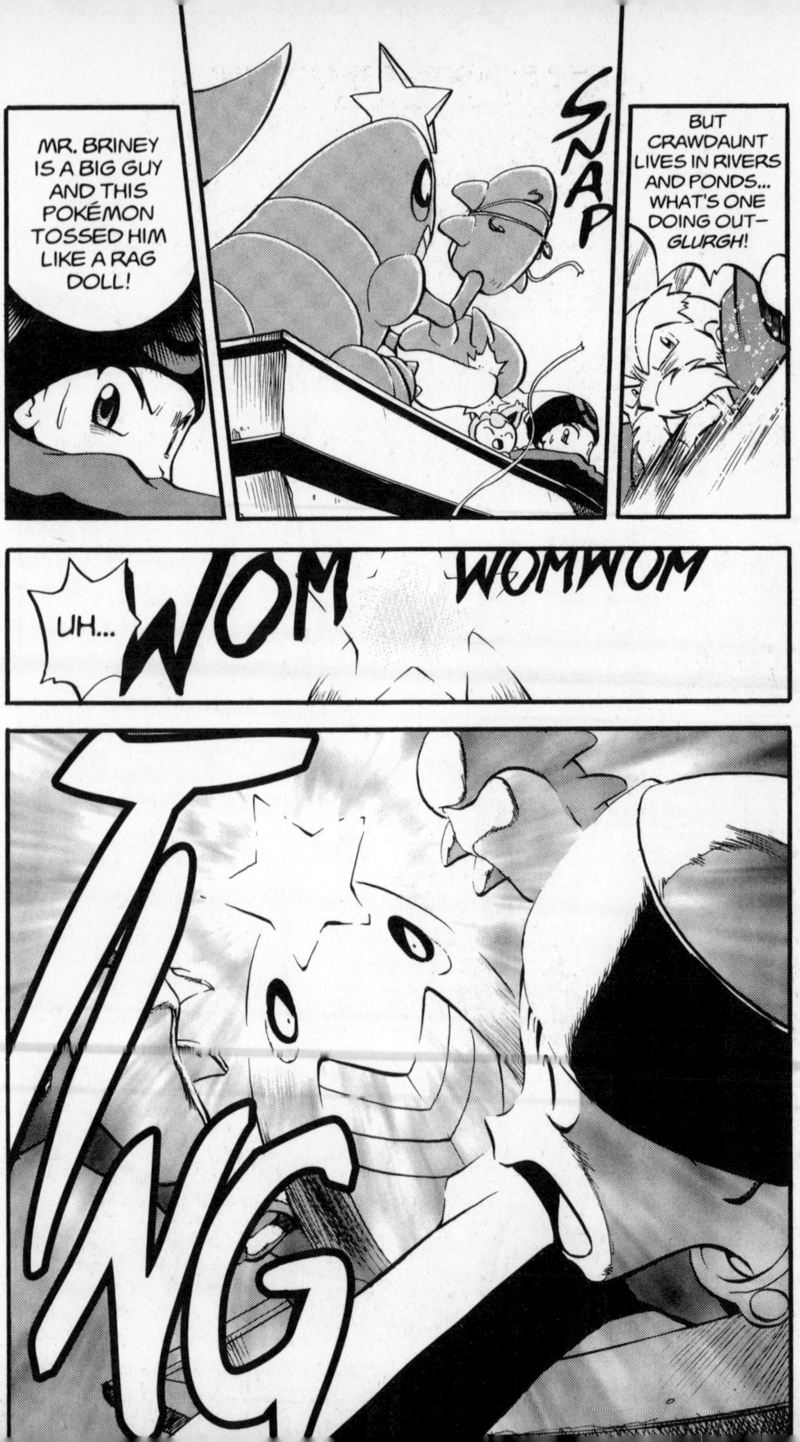
BUT CRAWDAUNT LIVES IN RIVERS AND PONDS... WHAT'S ONE DOING OUT— GLURGH!
SNAP
MR. BRINEY IS A BIG GUY AND THIS POKÉMON TOSSED HIM LIKE A RAG DOLL!
WOMWOM
WOM
UH...

ADVENTURE MAP

SAPPHIRE

CHIC
Torchic ♀
Lv15

RONO
Aron ♂
Lv30

LORRY
Wailord ♂
Lv41

RUBY

KIKI
Skitty ♀

NANA
Poochyena ♀

MUMU
Mudkip ♂

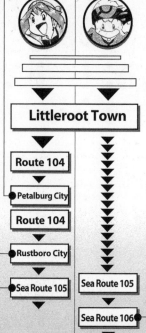

Littleroot Town

Route 104

Petalburg City

Route 104

Rustboro City

Sea Route 105

Sea Route 105

Sea Route 106

	Stone Badge	Knuckle Badge	Dynamo Badge	Heat Badge
	Balance Badge	Feather Badge	Mind Badge	Rain Badge

		Cool	Beauty	Cute	Smart	Tough
Normal		♛	♛	♛	♛	♛
Super		♛	♛	♛	♛	♛
Hyper	Master					

● Chapter 193 ●
Stick This in Your Craw, Crawdaunt! II

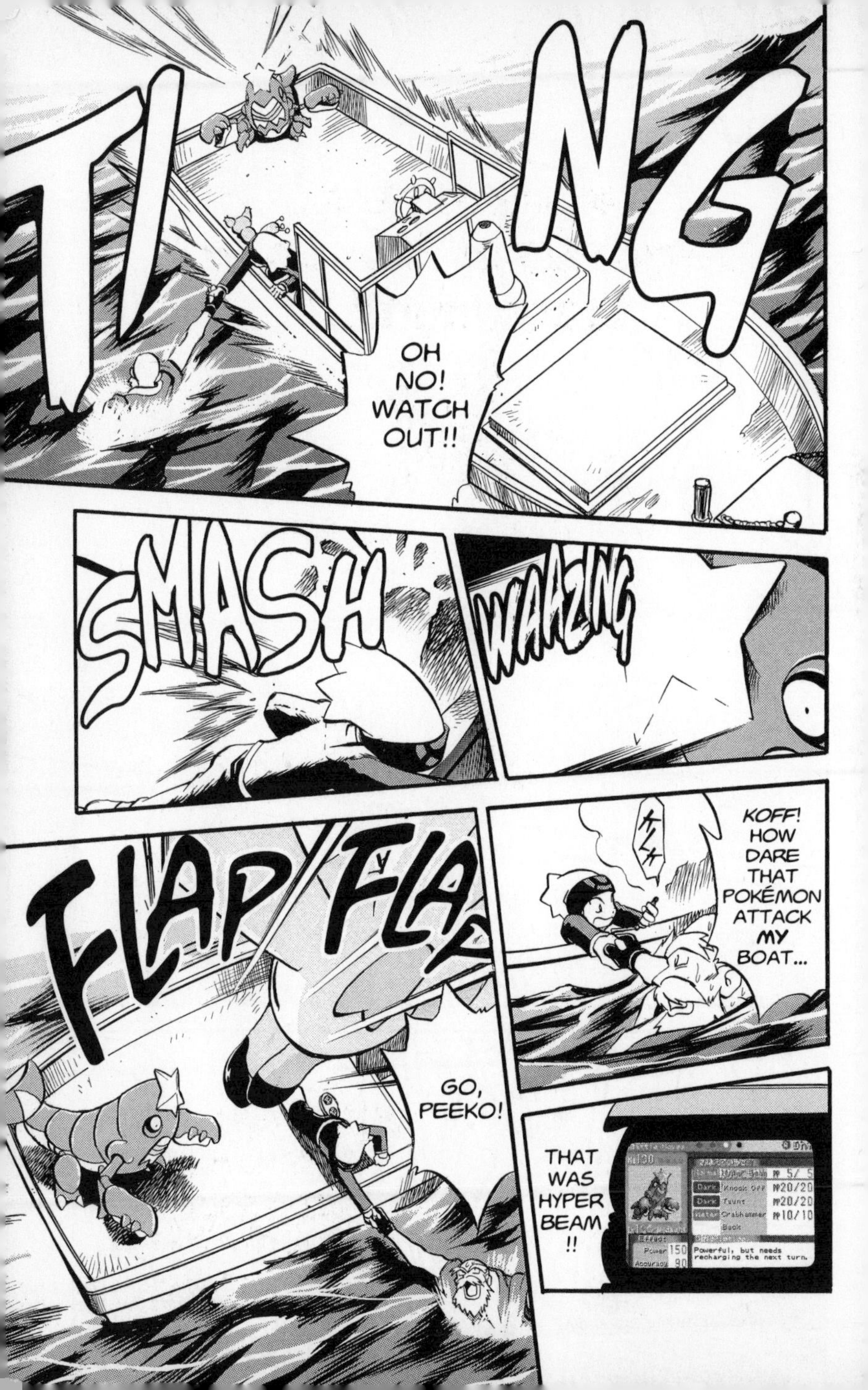
TING
OH NO! WATCH OUT!!
WHAZING
SMASH
KLK
KOFF! HOW DARE THAT POKÉMON ATTACK MY BOAT...
THAT WAS HYPER BEAM!!
Dark Knock Off PP20/20
Dark Taunt PP20/20
Water Crabhammer PP10/10
Back
Effect
Power 150
Accuracy 90
Powerful, but needs recharging the next turn.
FLAP FLAP
GO, PEEKO!

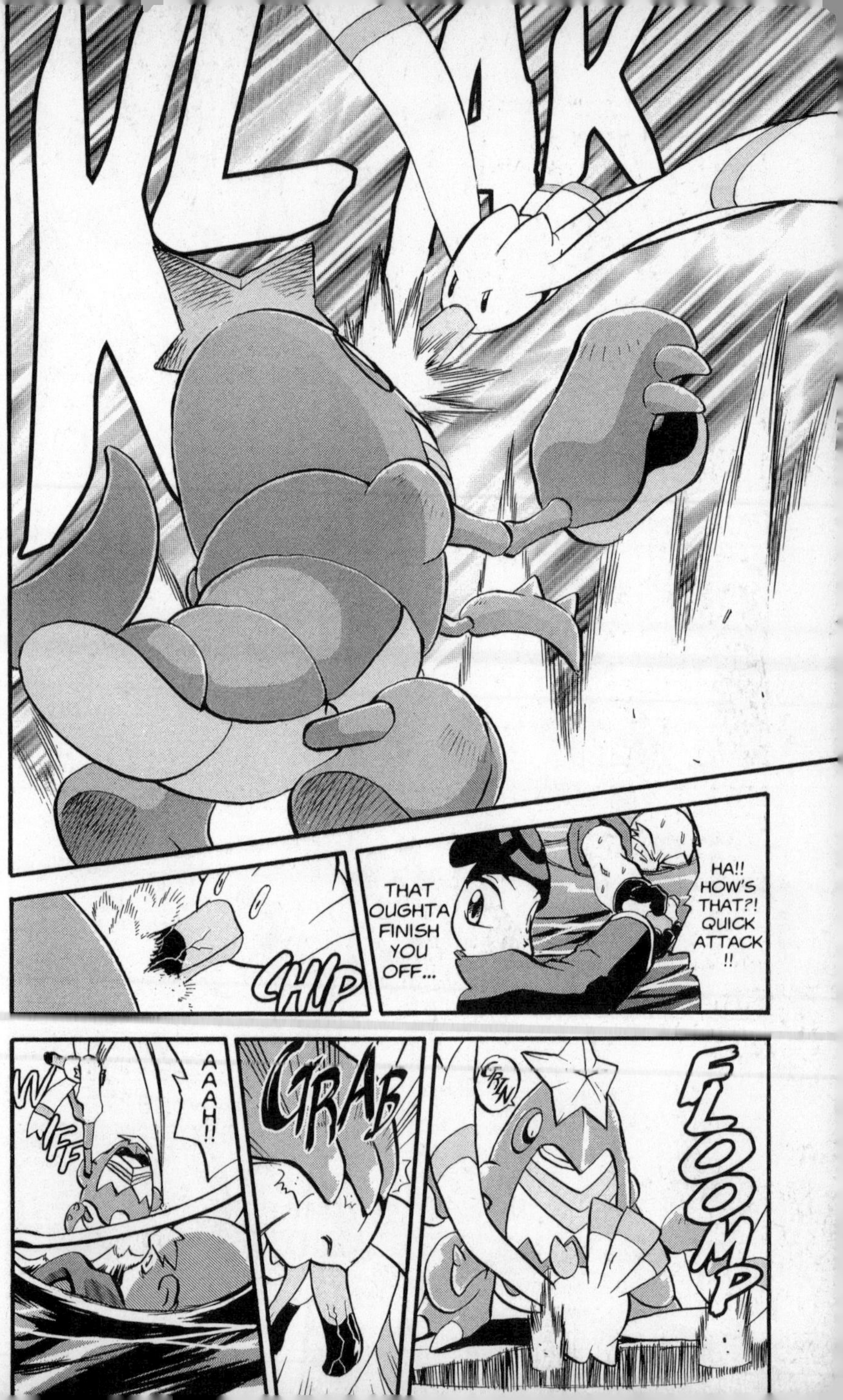
HA!! HOW'S THAT?! QUICK ATTACK !!
THAT OUGHTA FINISH YOU OFF...
CHIP
GRIN
FLOOMP
GRAB
AAAH!!
WIFF

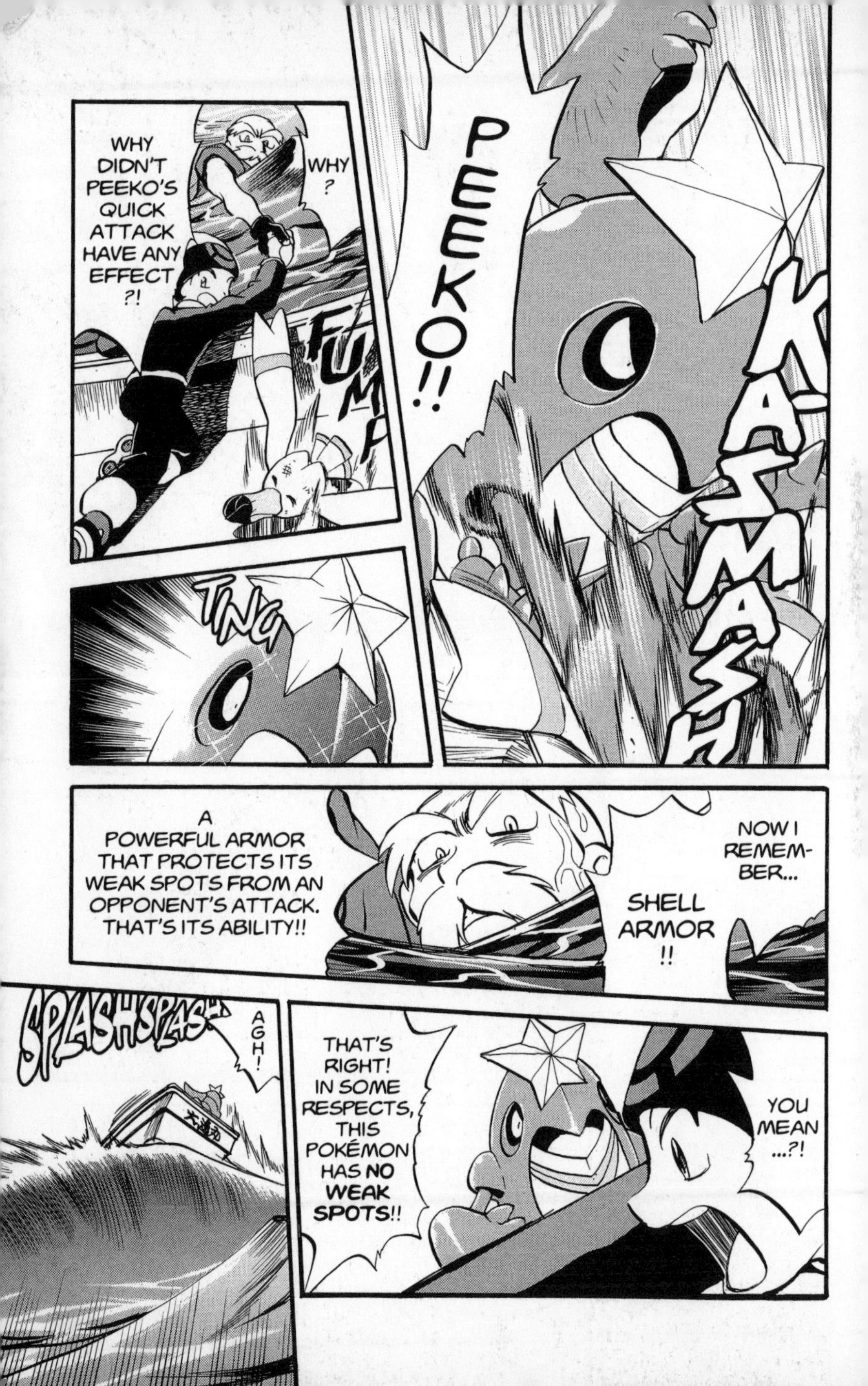
PEEKO!!
KASMASH
WHY?
WHY DIDN'T PEEKO'S QUICK ATTACK HAVE ANY EFFECT?!
FUMP
TING
NOW I REMEMBER...
SHELL ARMOR!!
A POWERFUL ARMOR THAT PROTECTS ITS WEAK SPOTS FROM AN OPPONENT'S ATTACK. THAT'S ITS ABILITY!!
YOU MEAN...?!
THAT'S RIGHT! IN SOME RESPECTS, THIS POKÉMON HAS **NO WEAK SPOTS**!!
AGH!
SPLASHSPLASH

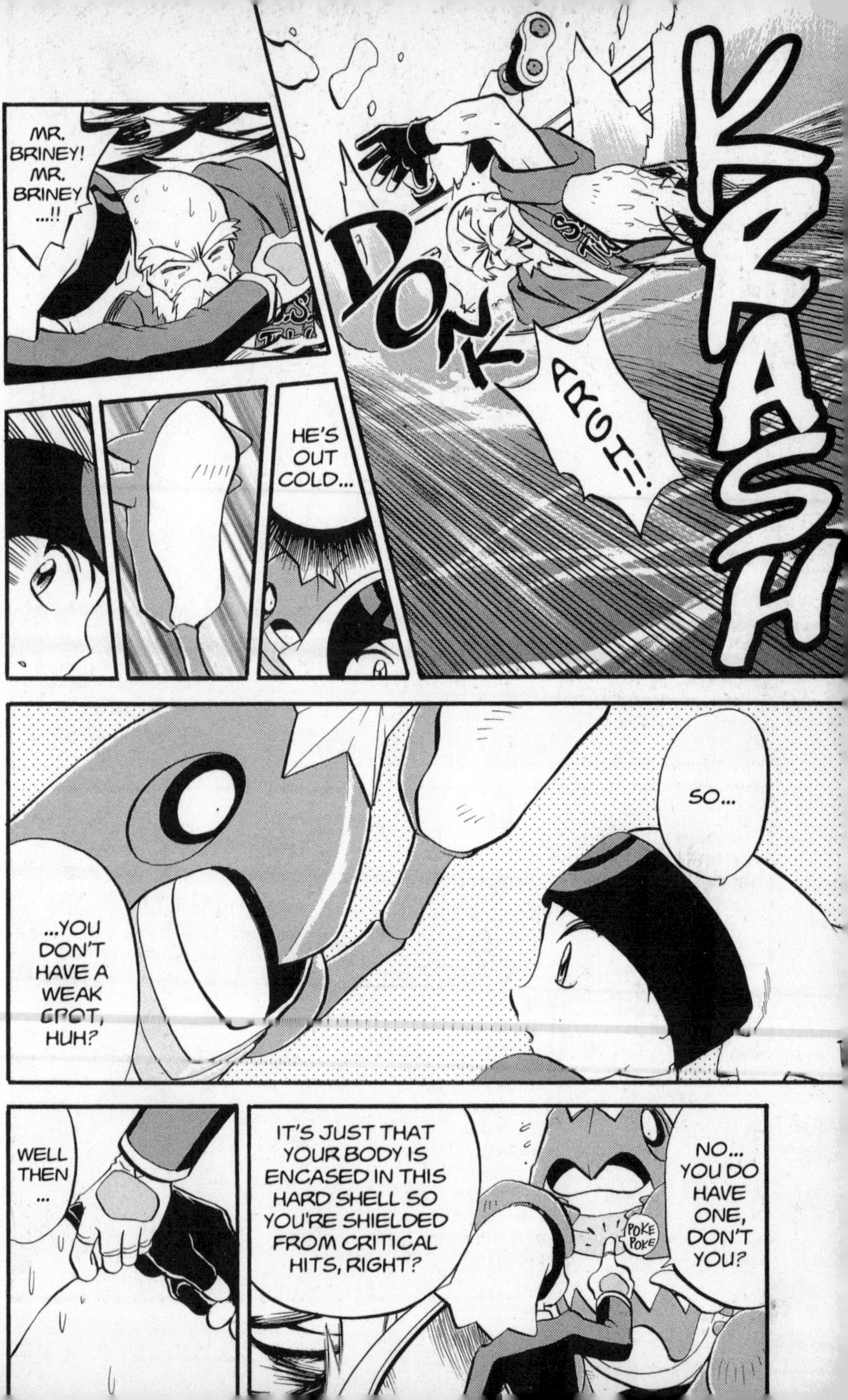
KRASH
DONK
ARGH!!
MR. BRINEY! MR. BRINEY ...!!
HE'S OUT COLD...
SO...
...YOU DON'T HAVE A WEAK SPOT, HUH?
NO... YOU DO HAVE ONE, DON'T YOU?
POKE POKE
IT'S JUST THAT YOUR BODY IS ENCASED IN THIS HARD SHELL SO YOU'RE SHIELDED FROM CRITICAL HITS, RIGHT?
WELL THEN ...

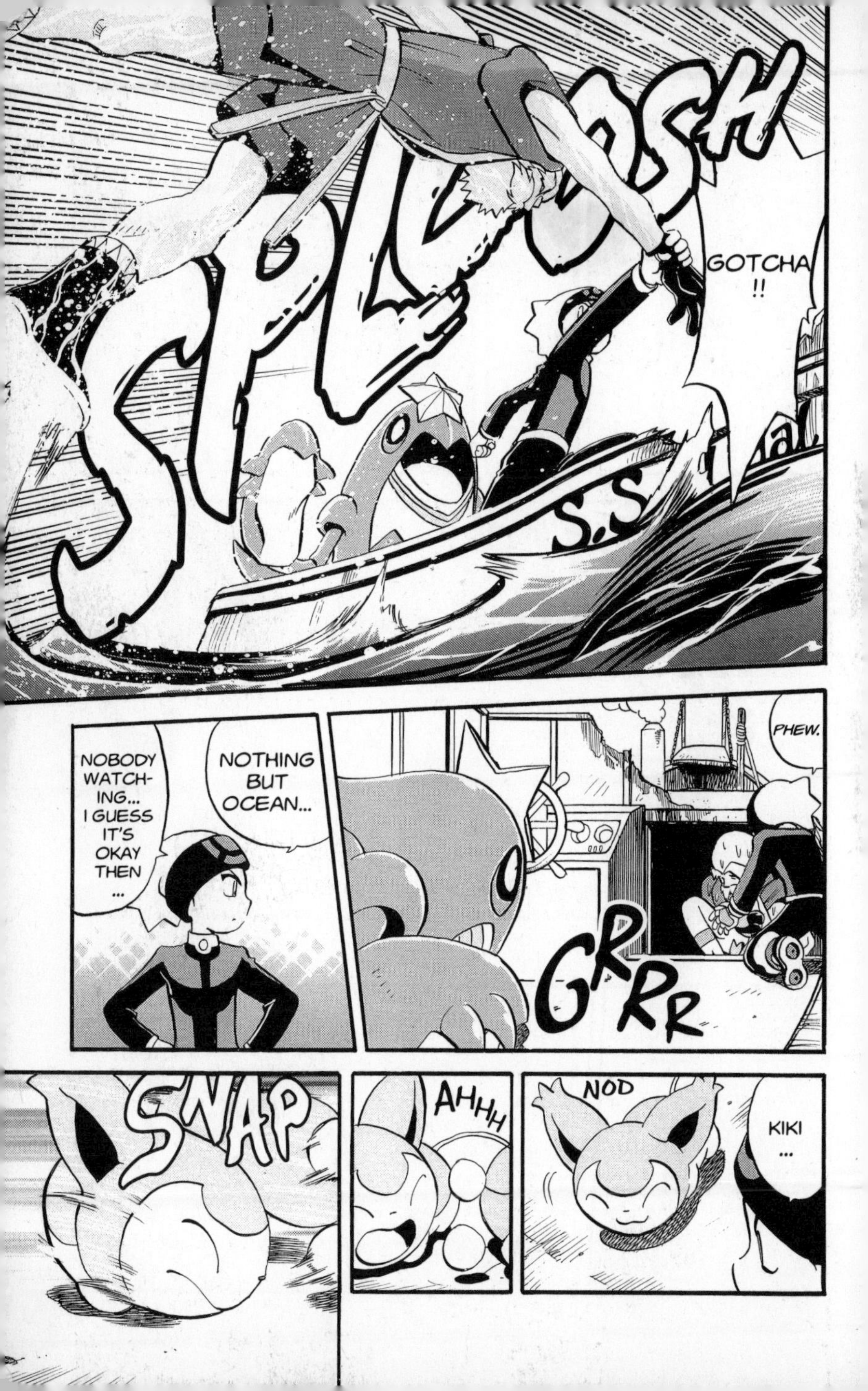

SPLOOSH
GOTCHA!!
S.S.
PHEW.
GRRR
NOTHING BUT OCEAN...
NOBODY WATCH-ING... I GUESS IT'S OKAY THEN ...
KIKI ...
NOD
AHHH
SNAP

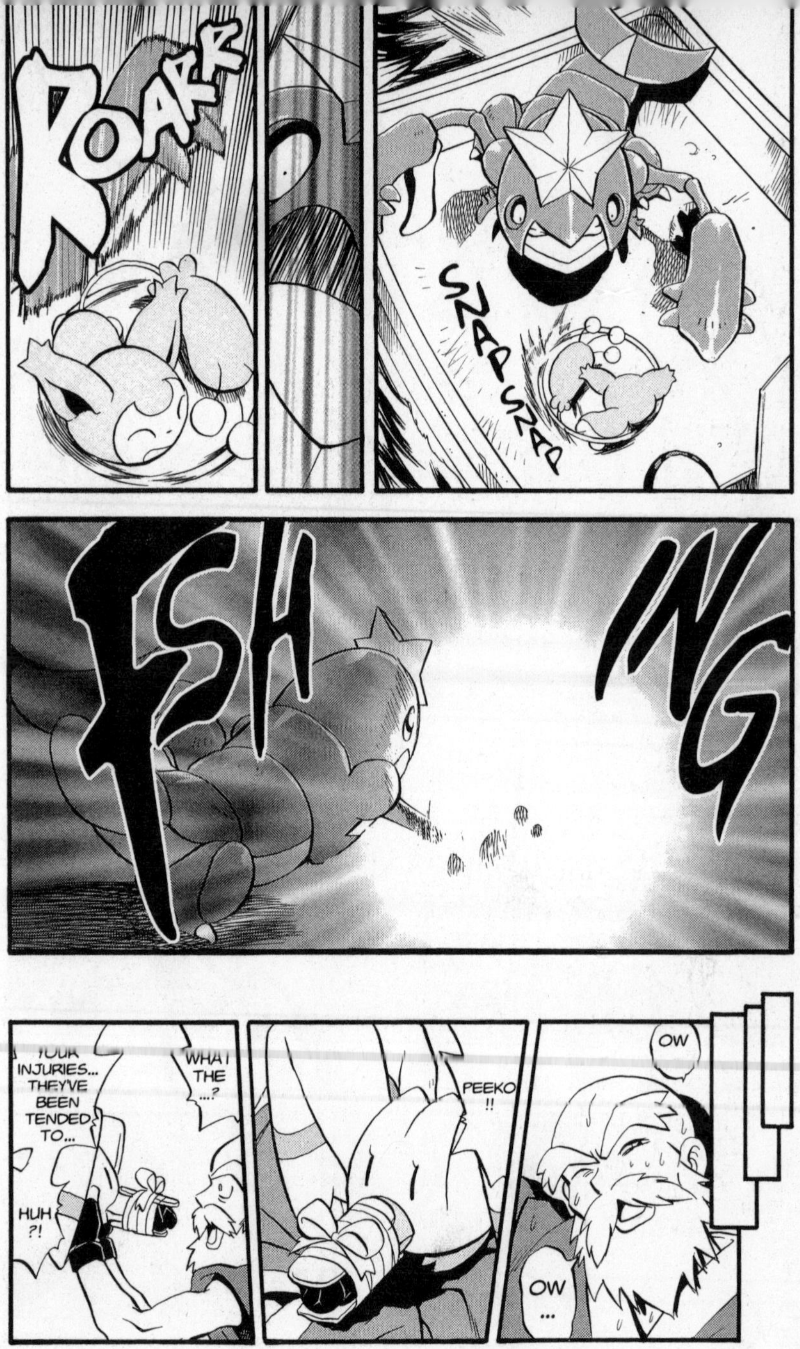
SNAP SNAP SNAP
ROAR
FSH ING
OW
OW ...
PEEKO !!
WHAT THE ...?
YOUR INJURIES... THEY'VE BEEN TENDED TO...
HUH ?!

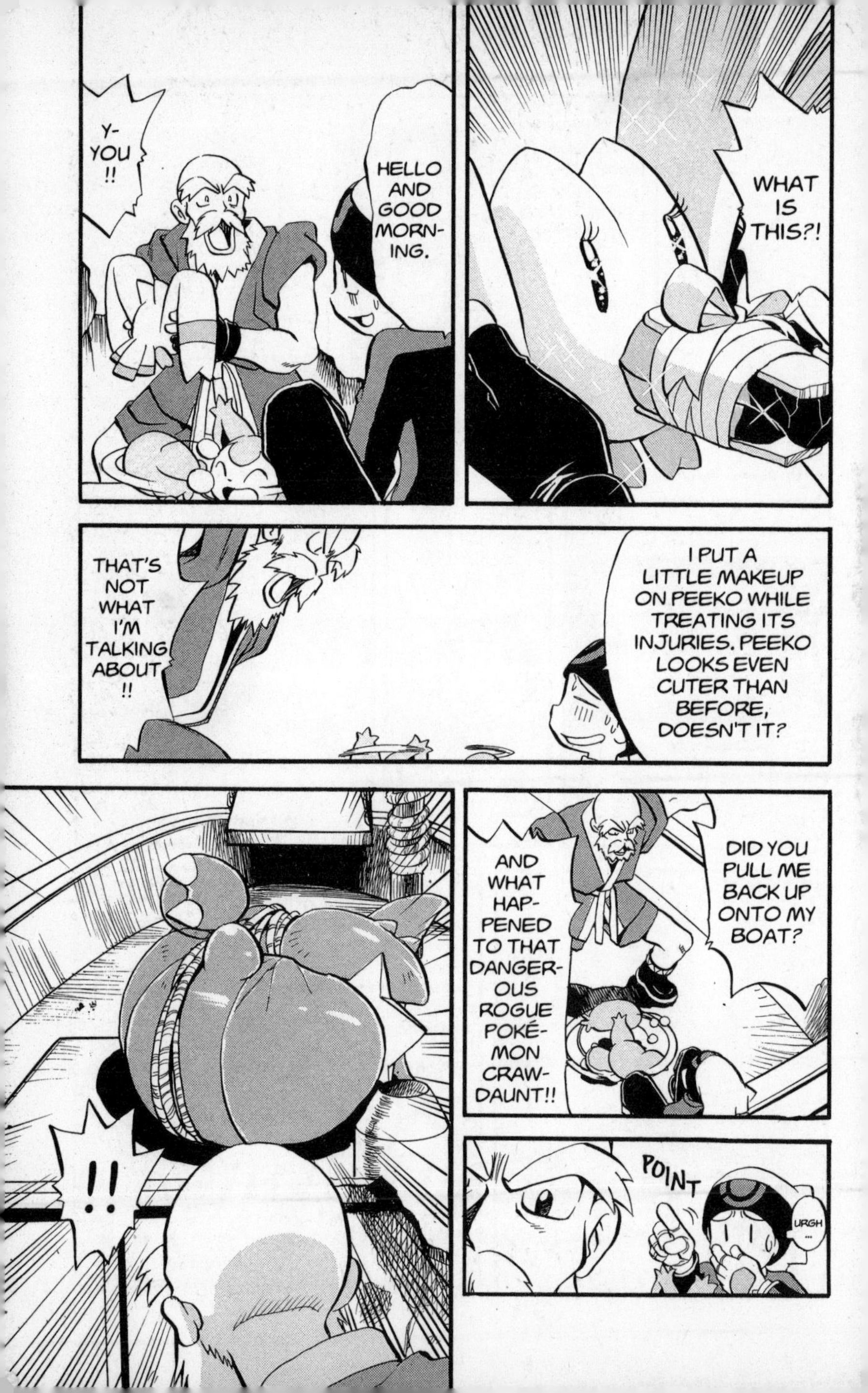
WHAT IS THIS?!
HELLO AND GOOD MORNING.
Y-YOU!!
I PUT A LITTLE MAKEUP ON PEEKO WHILE TREATING ITS INJURIES. PEEKO LOOKS EVEN CUTER THAN BEFORE, DOESN'T IT?
THAT'S NOT WHAT I'M TALKING ABOUT!!
DID YOU PULL ME BACK UP ONTO MY BOAT?
AND WHAT HAPPENED TO THAT DANGEROUS ROGUE POKÉMON CRAWDAUNT!!
POINT
URGH...
!!

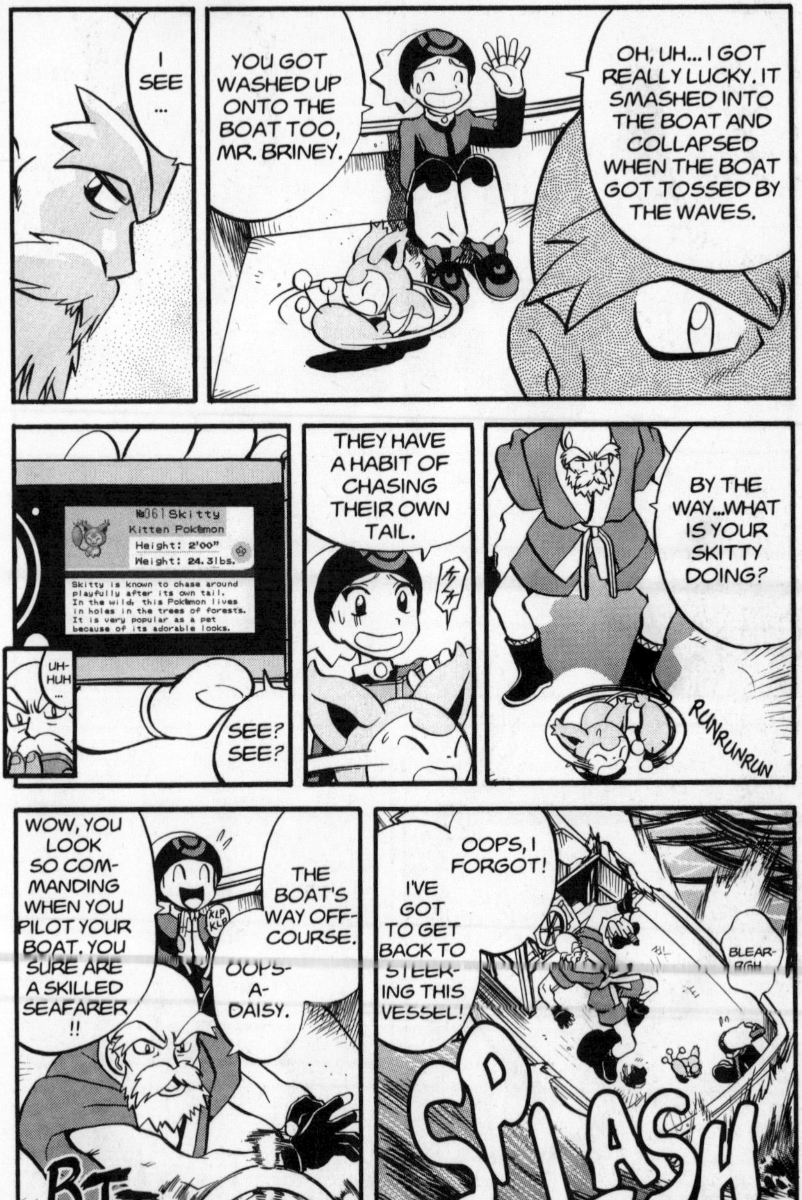
OH, UH... I GOT REALLY LUCKY. IT SMASHED INTO THE BOAT AND COLLAPSED WHEN THE BOAT GOT TOSSED BY THE WAVES.
YOU GOT WASHED UP ONTO THE BOAT TOO, MR. BRINEY.
I SEE ...
BY THE WAY...WHAT IS YOUR SKITTY DOING?
RUNRUNRUN
THEY HAVE A HABIT OF CHASING THEIR OWN TAIL.
SEE? SEE?
No061 Skitty
Kitten Pokémon
Height: 2'00"
Weight: 24.3lbs.
Skitty is known to chase around playfully after its own tail. In the wild, this Pokémon lives in holes in the trees of forests. It is very popular as a pet because of its adorable looks.
UH-HUH ...
OOPS, I FORGOT!
I'VE GOT TO GET BACK TO STEERING THIS VESSEL!
BLEAR-RGH
SPLASH
WOW, YOU LOOK SO COMMANDING WHEN YOU PILOT YOUR BOAT. YOU SURE ARE A SKILLED SEAFARER !!
KLP KLP
THE BOAT'S WAY OFF-COURSE.
OOPS-A-DAISY.
RTTL

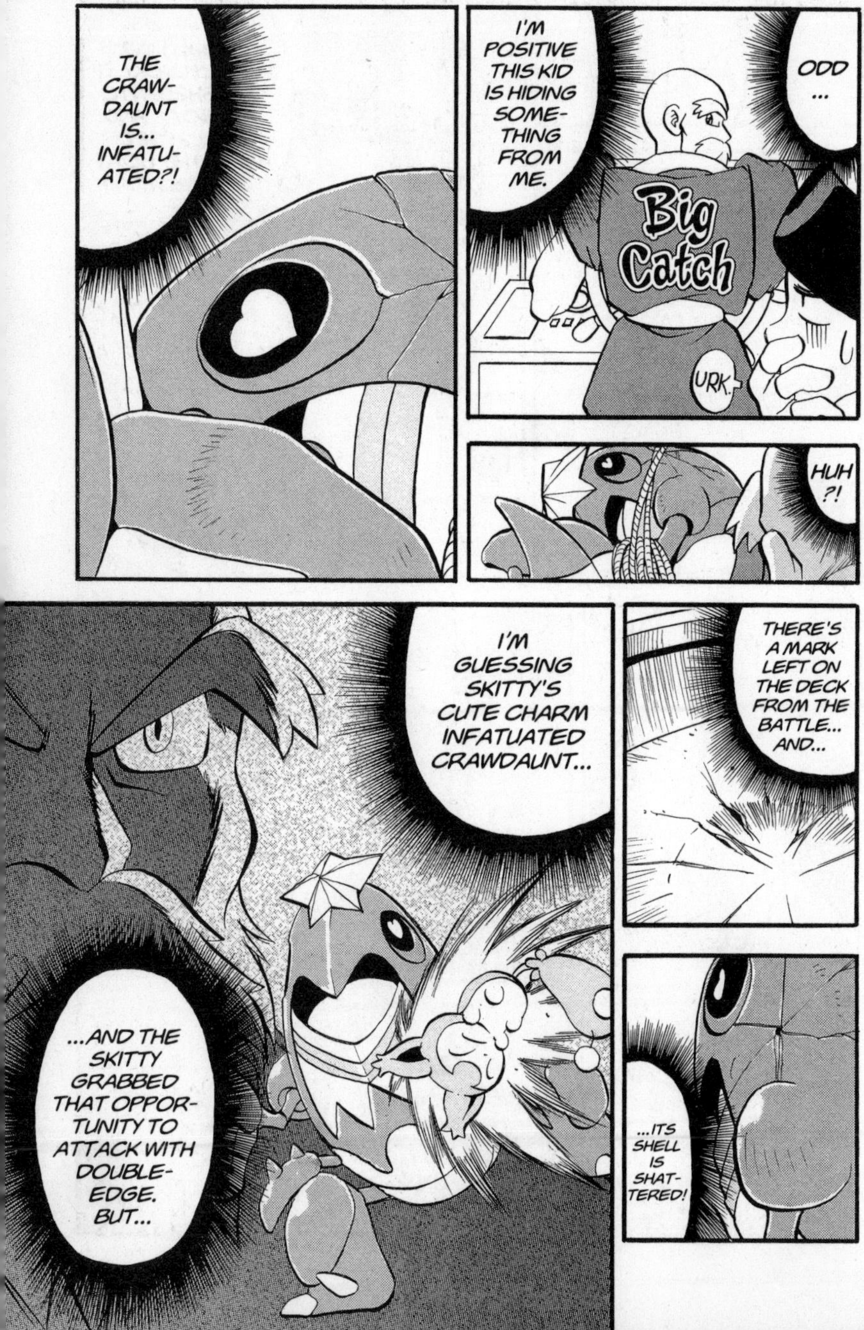
ODD ...
I'M POSITIVE THIS KID IS HIDING SOMETHING FROM ME.
URK.
HUH ?!
THE CRAWDAUNT IS... INFATUATED?!
THERE'S A MARK LEFT ON THE DECK FROM THE BATTLE... AND...
...ITS SHELL IS SHATTERED!
I'M GUESSING SKITTY'S CUTE CHARM INFATUATED CRAWDAUNT...
...AND THE SKITTY GRABBED THAT OPPORTUNITY TO ATTACK WITH DOUBLE-EDGE. BUT...

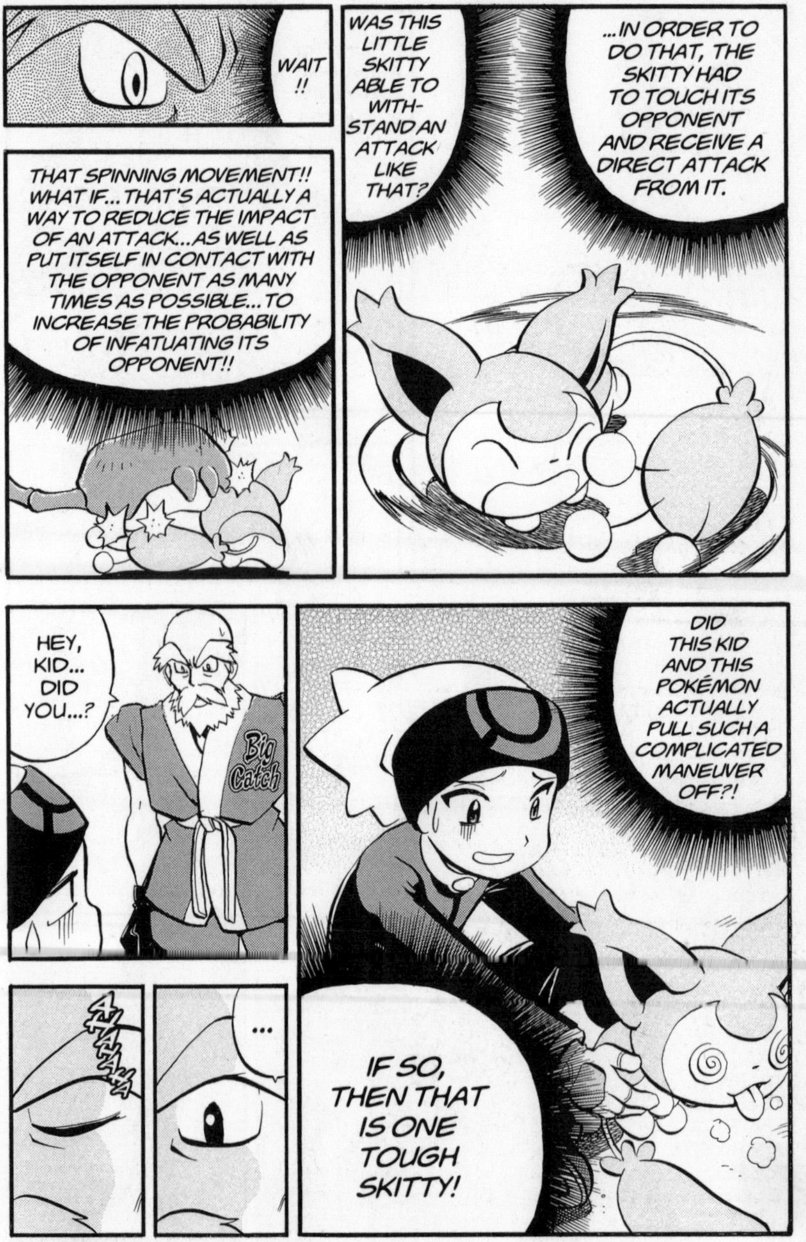
...IN ORDER TO DO THAT, THE SKITTY HAD TO TOUCH ITS OPPONENT AND RECEIVE A DIRECT ATTACK FROM IT.
WAS THIS LITTLE SKITTY ABLE TO WITH-STAND AN ATTACK LIKE THAT?
WAIT!!
THAT SPINNING MOVEMENT!! WHAT IF... THAT'S ACTUALLY A WAY TO REDUCE THE IMPACT OF AN ATTACK...AS WELL AS PUT ITSELF IN CONTACT WITH THE OPPONENT AS MANY TIMES AS POSSIBLE... TO INCREASE THE PROBABILITY OF INFATUATING ITS OPPONENT!!
DID THIS KID AND THIS POKÉMON ACTUALLY PULL SUCH A COMPLICATED MANEUVER OFF?!
IF SO, THEN THAT IS ONE TOUGH SKITTY!
HEY, KID... DID YOU...?
Big Catch
...

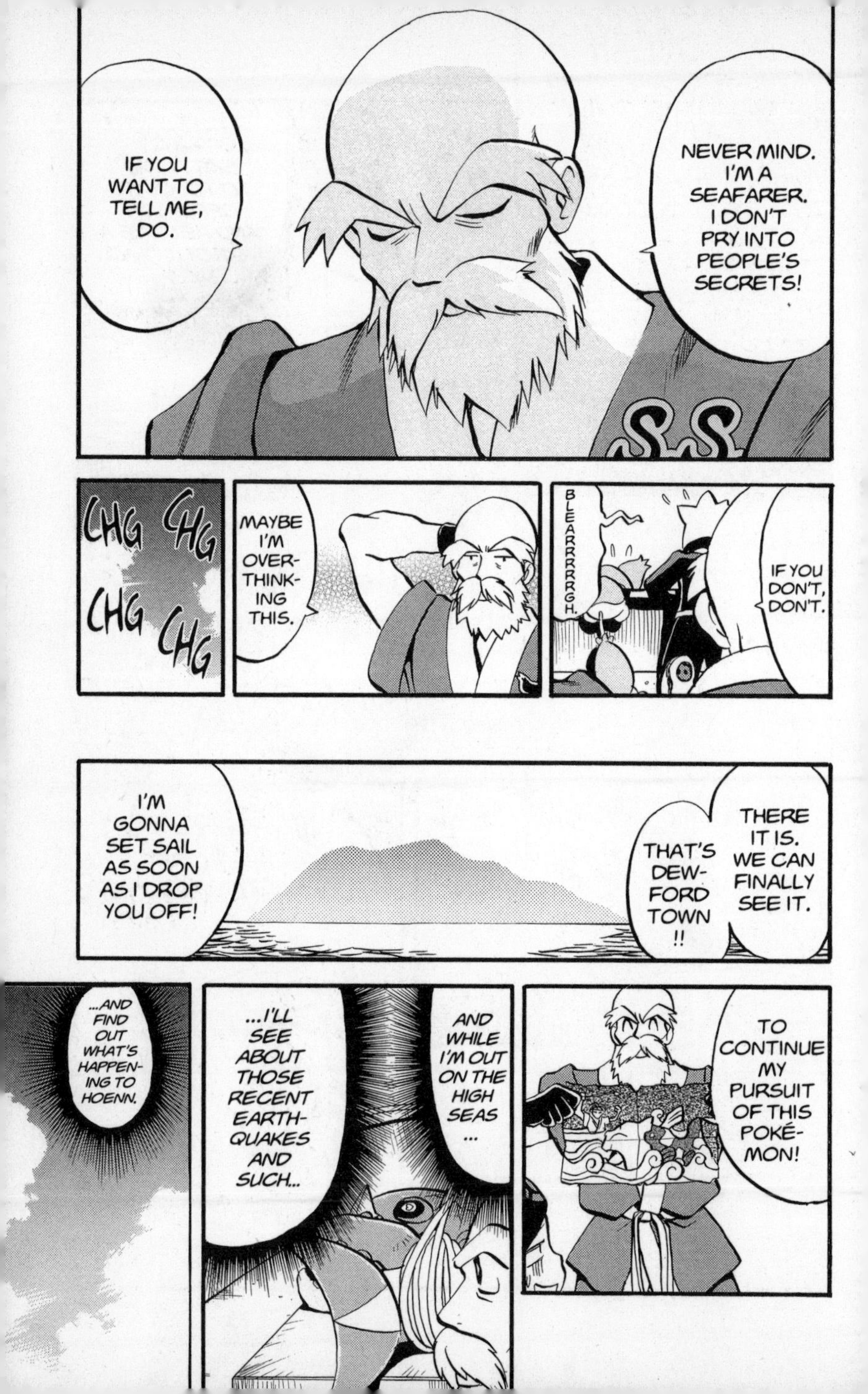
NEVER MIND. I'M A SEAFARER. I DON'T PRY INTO PEOPLE'S SECRETS!
IF YOU WANT TO TELL ME, DO.
IF YOU DON'T, DON'T.
BLEARRRRRGH.
MAYBE I'M OVER-THINKING THIS.
CHG CHG CHG CHG
THERE IT IS. WE CAN FINALLY SEE IT.
THAT'S DEW-FORD TOWN!!
I'M GONNA SET SAIL AS SOON AS I DROP YOU OFF!
TO CONTINUE MY PURSUIT OF THIS POKÉ-MON!
AND WHILE I'M OUT ON THE HIGH SEAS...
...I'LL SEE ABOUT THOSE RECENT EARTH-QUAKES AND SUCH...
...AND FIND OUT WHAT'S HAPPEN-ING TO HOENN.

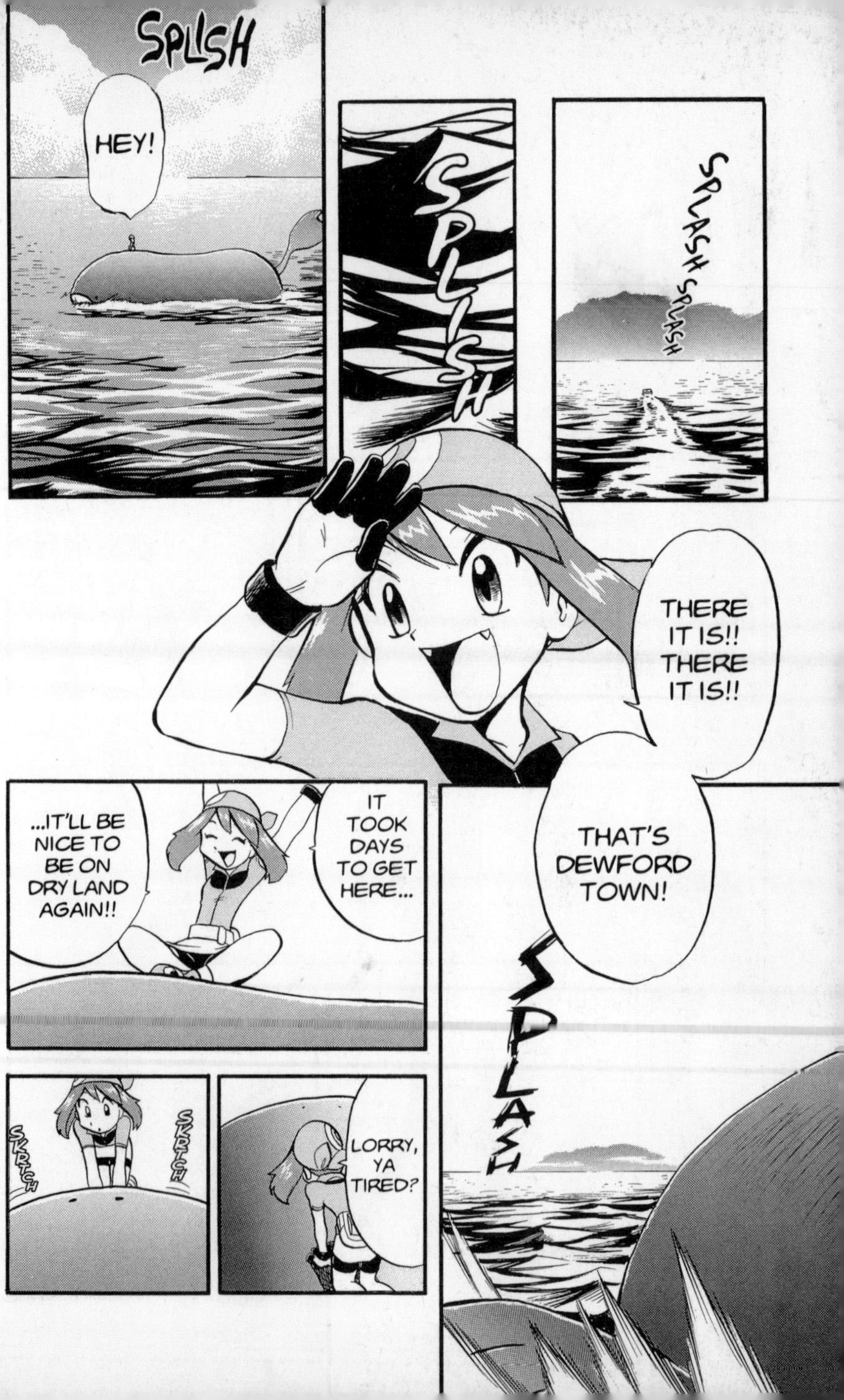

SPLASH SPLASH SPLASH
SPLISH
SPLISH
HEY!
THERE IT IS!! THERE IT IS!!
THAT'S DEWFORD TOWN!
SPLASH
IT TOOK DAYS TO GET HERE...
...IT'LL BE NICE TO BE ON DRY LAND AGAIN!!
LORRY, YA TIRED?
SKRTCH
SKRTCH

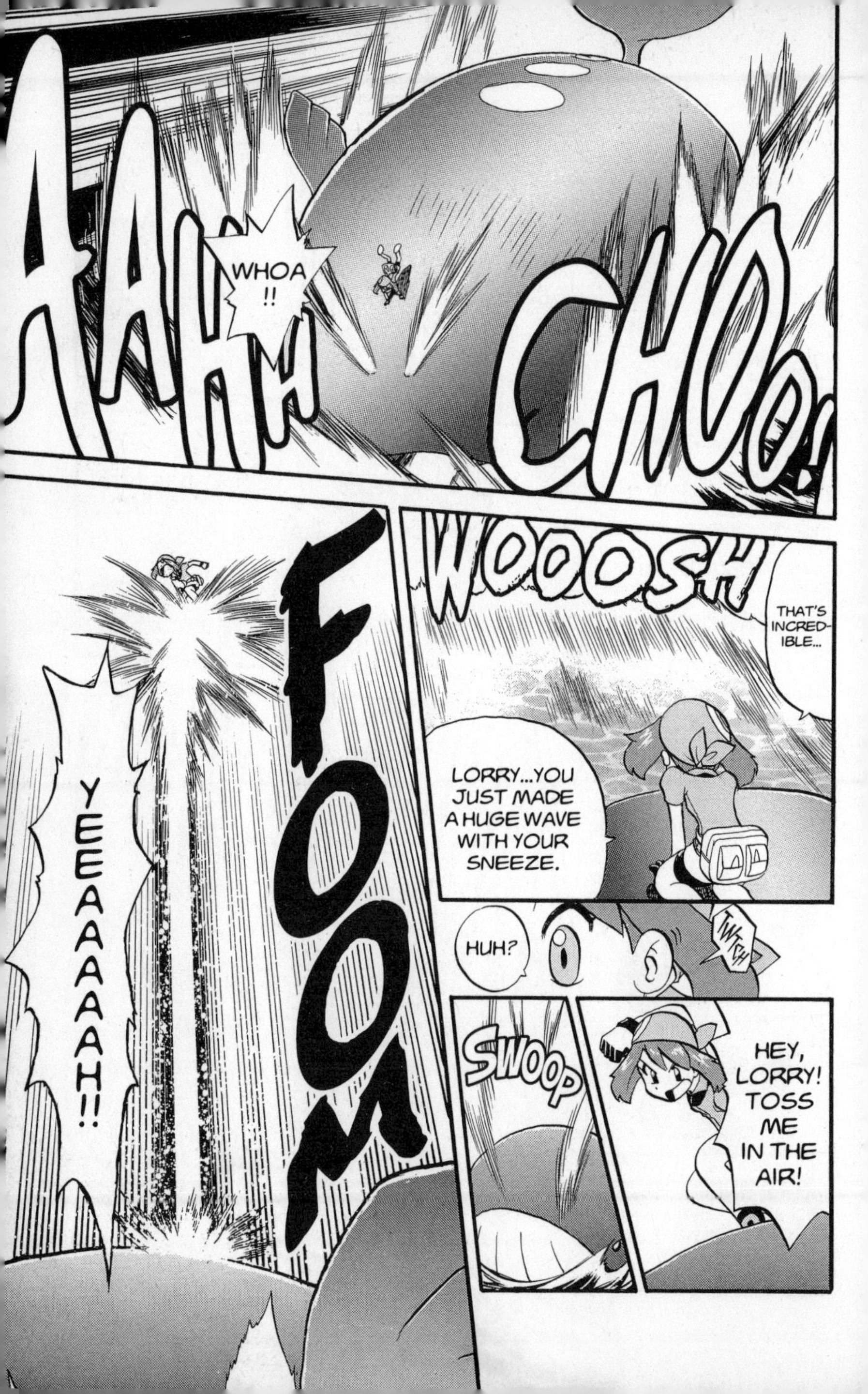
AAHH
CHOO
WHOA!!
WOOOSH
THAT'S INCREDIBLE...
LORRY...YOU JUST MADE A HUGE WAVE WITH YOUR SNEEZE.
TWITCH
HUH?
HEY, LORRY! TOSS ME IN THE AIR!
SWOOP
FOOM
YEEAAAAAAH!!

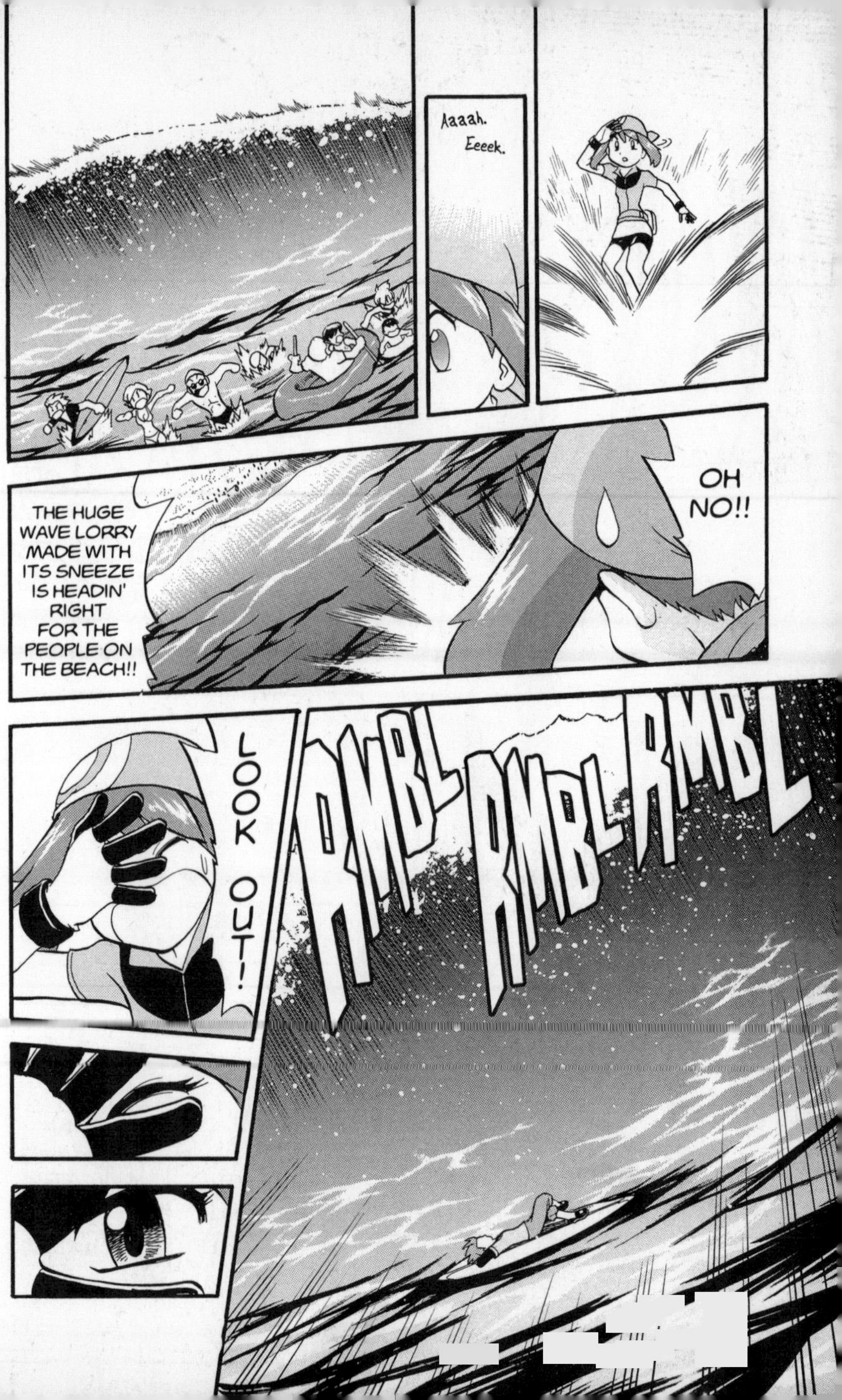
Aaaah.
Eeeek.
OH NO!!
THE HUGE WAVE LORRY MADE WITH ITS SNEEZE IS HEADIN' RIGHT FOR THE PEOPLE ON THE BEACH!!
RMBL RMBL RMBL
LOOK OUT!

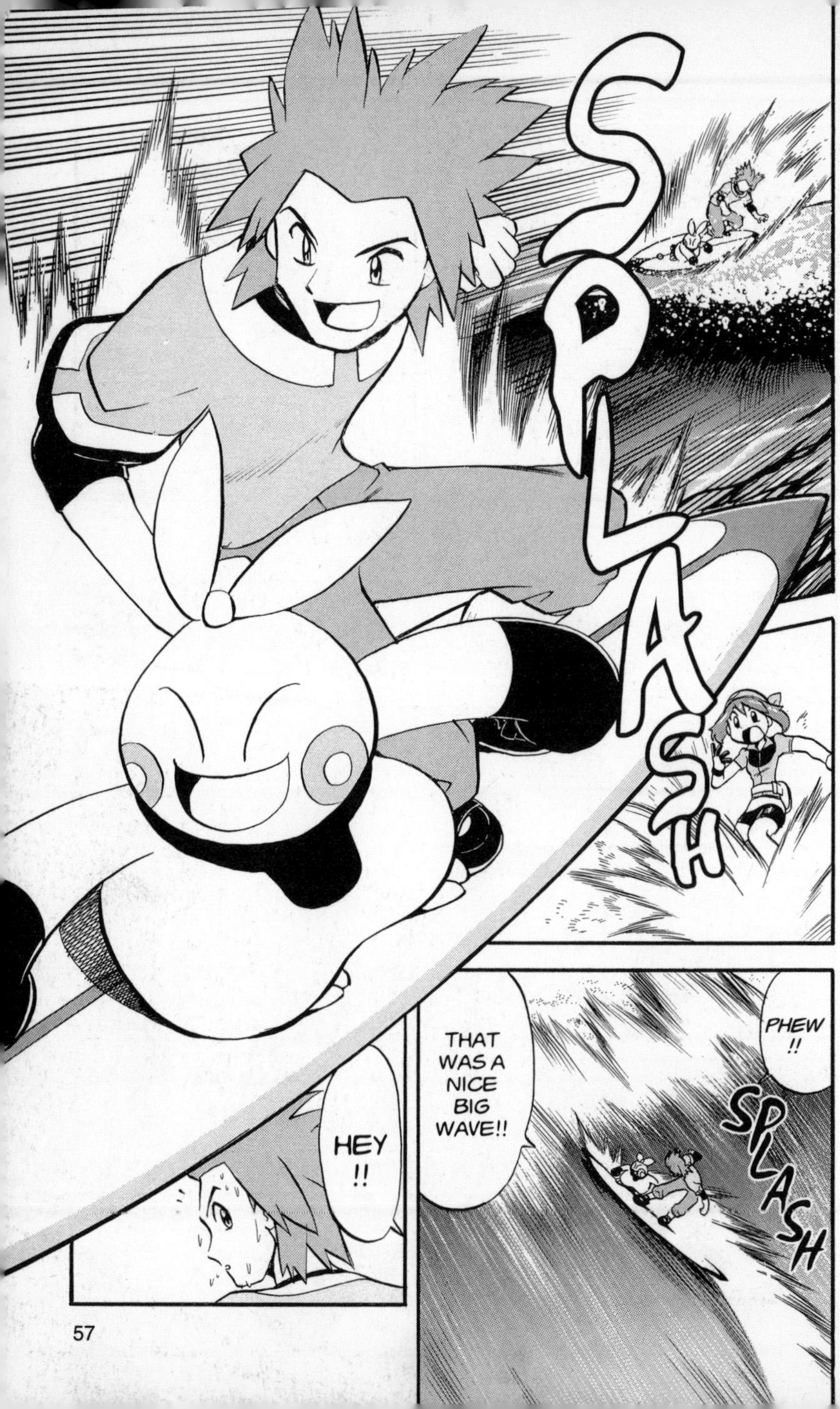

SPLASH
PHEW!!
THAT WAS A NICE BIG WAVE!!
SPLASH
HEY!!

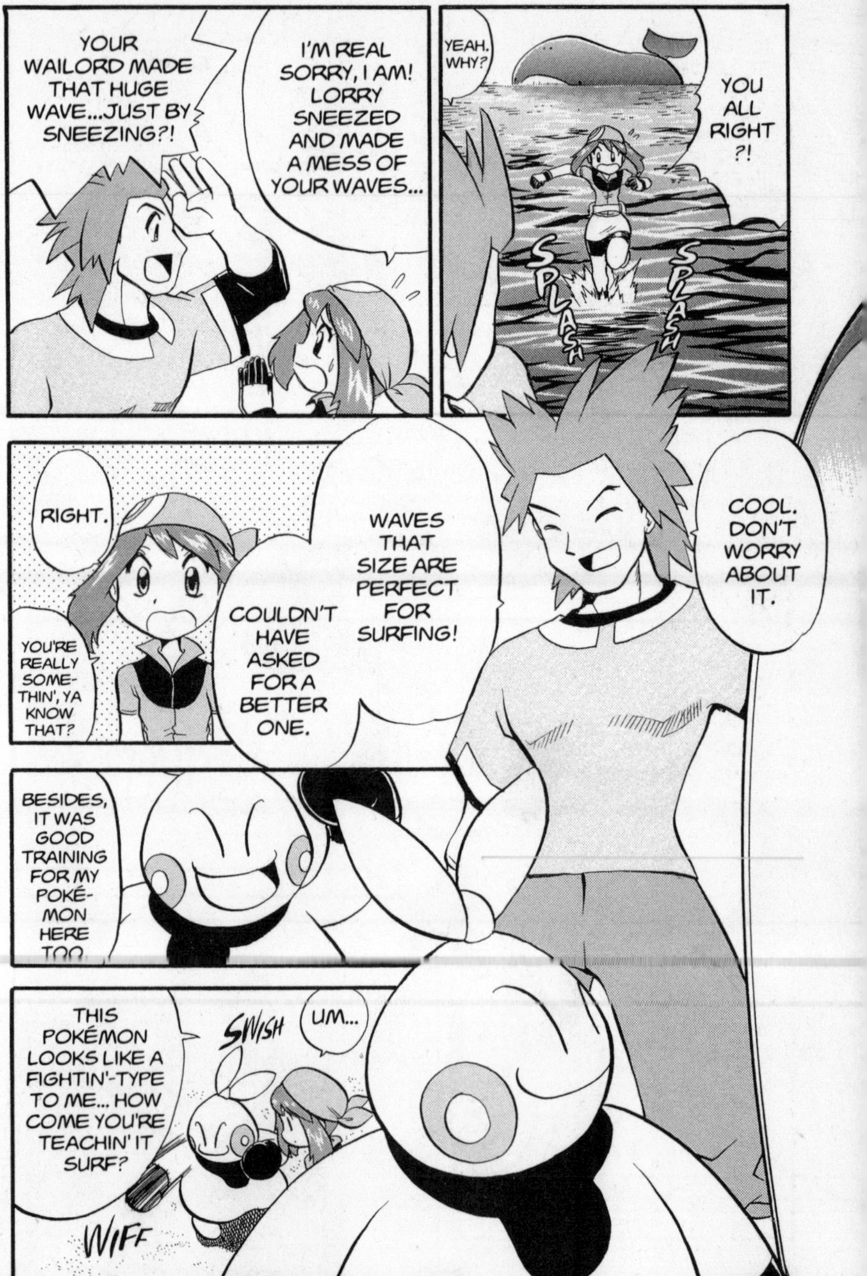
YOU ALL RIGHT ?!
YEAH. WHY?
SPLASH
SPLASH
I'M REAL SORRY, I AM! LORRY SNEEZED AND MADE A MESS OF YOUR WAVES...
YOUR WAILORD MADE THAT HUGE WAVE...JUST BY SNEEZING?!
COOL. DON'T WORRY ABOUT IT.
WAVES THAT SIZE ARE PERFECT FOR SURFING!
COULDN'T HAVE ASKED FOR A BETTER ONE.
RIGHT.
YOU'RE REALLY SOME-THIN', YA KNOW THAT?
BESIDES, IT WAS GOOD TRAINING FOR MY POKÉ-MON HERE TOO.
UM...
SWISH
THIS POKÉMON LOOKS LIKE A FIGHTIN'-TYPE TO ME... HOW COME YOU'RE TEACHIN' IT SURF?
WIFF

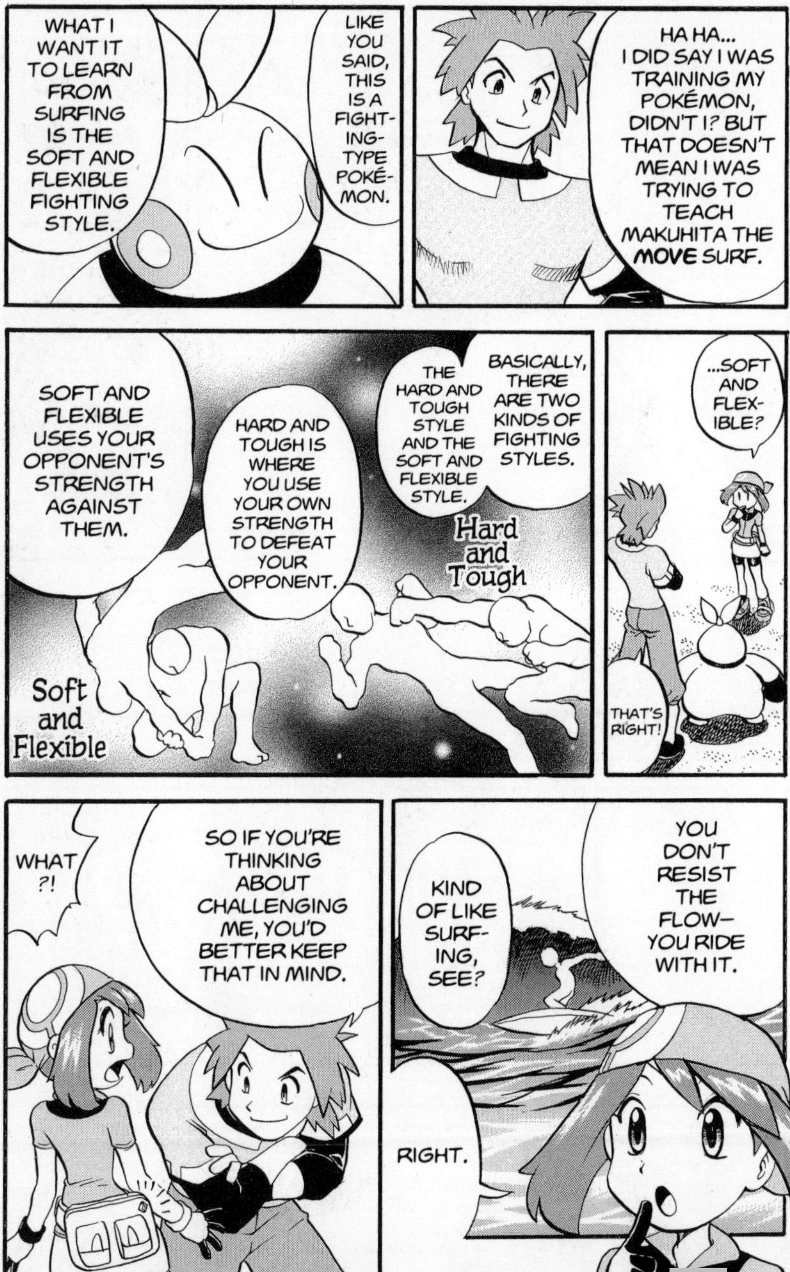
HA HA... I DID SAY I WAS TRAINING MY POKÉMON, DIDN'T I? BUT THAT DOESN'T MEAN I WAS TRYING TO TEACH MAKUHITA THE MOVE SURF.
LIKE YOU SAID, THIS IS A FIGHTING-TYPE POKÉMON.
WHAT I WANT IT TO LEARN FROM SURFING IS THE SOFT AND FLEXIBLE FIGHTING STYLE.
...SOFT AND FLEXIBLE?
THAT'S RIGHT!
BASICALLY, THERE ARE TWO KINDS OF FIGHTING STYLES.
THE HARD AND TOUGH STYLE AND THE SOFT AND FLEXIBLE STYLE.
HARD AND TOUGH IS WHERE YOU USE YOUR OWN STRENGTH TO DEFEAT YOUR OPPONENT.
SOFT AND FLEXIBLE USES YOUR OPPONENT'S STRENGTH AGAINST THEM.
Hard and Tough
Soft and Flexible
YOU DON'T RESIST THE FLOW—YOU RIDE WITH IT.
KIND OF LIKE SURFING, SEE?
RIGHT.
SO IF YOU'RE THINKING ABOUT CHALLENGING ME, YOU'D BETTER KEEP THAT IN MIND.
WHAT?!

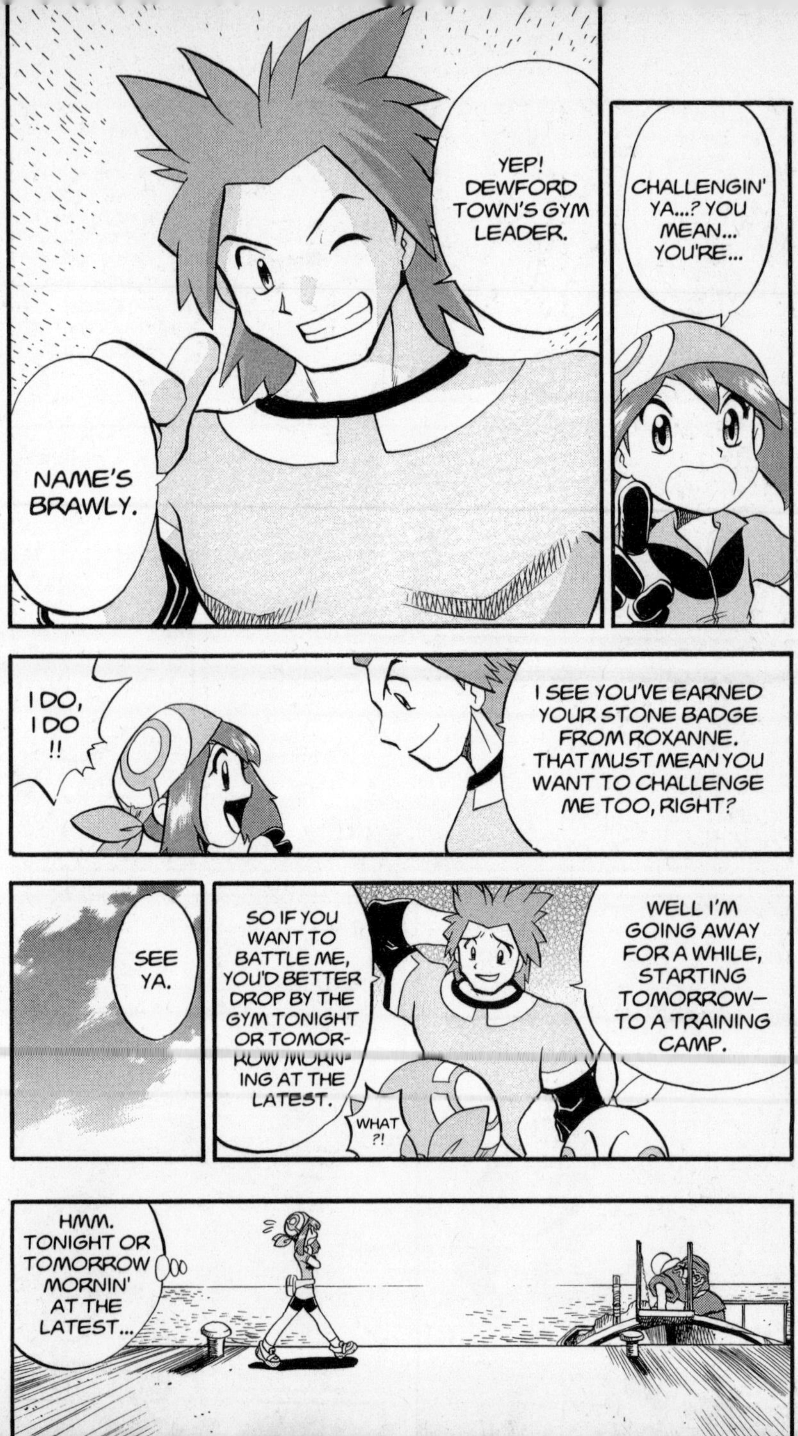
CHALLENGIN' YA...? YOU MEAN... YOU'RE...
YEP! DEWFORD TOWN'S GYM LEADER.
NAME'S BRAWLY.
I SEE YOU'VE EARNED YOUR STONE BADGE FROM ROXANNE. THAT MUST MEAN YOU WANT TO CHALLENGE ME TOO, RIGHT?
I DO, I DO !!
WELL I'M GOING AWAY FOR A WHILE, STARTING TOMORROW— TO A TRAINING CAMP.
SO IF YOU WANT TO BATTLE ME, YOU'D BETTER DROP BY THE GYM TONIGHT OR TOMORROW MORNING AT THE LATEST.
WHAT ?!
SEE YA.
HMM. TONIGHT OR TOMORROW MORNIN' AT THE LATEST...

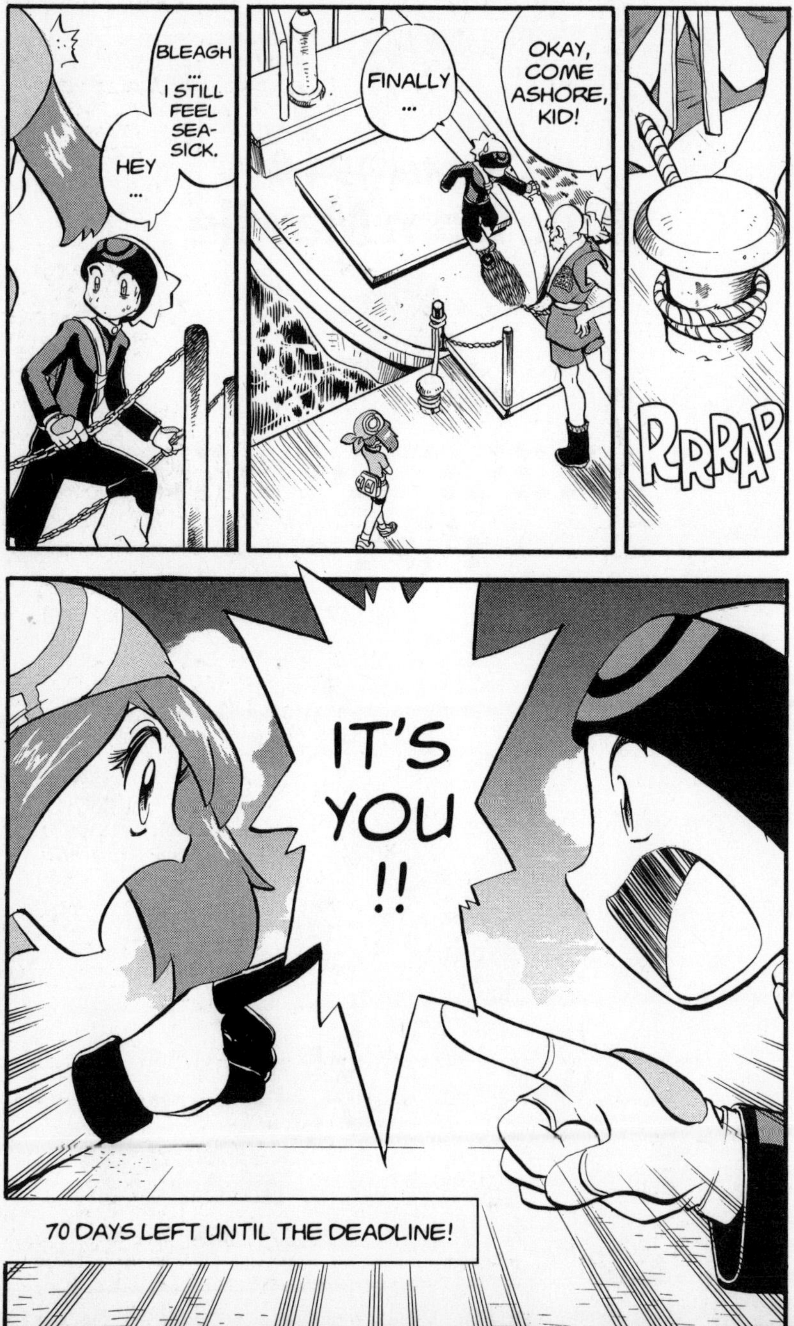
RRRAP
OKAY, COME ASHORE, KID!
FINALLY ...
BLEAGH ... I STILL FEEL SEA-SICK.
HEY ...
IT'S YOU !!
70 DAYS LEFT UNTIL THE DEADLINE!

● Chapter 194 ●
Guile from Mawile

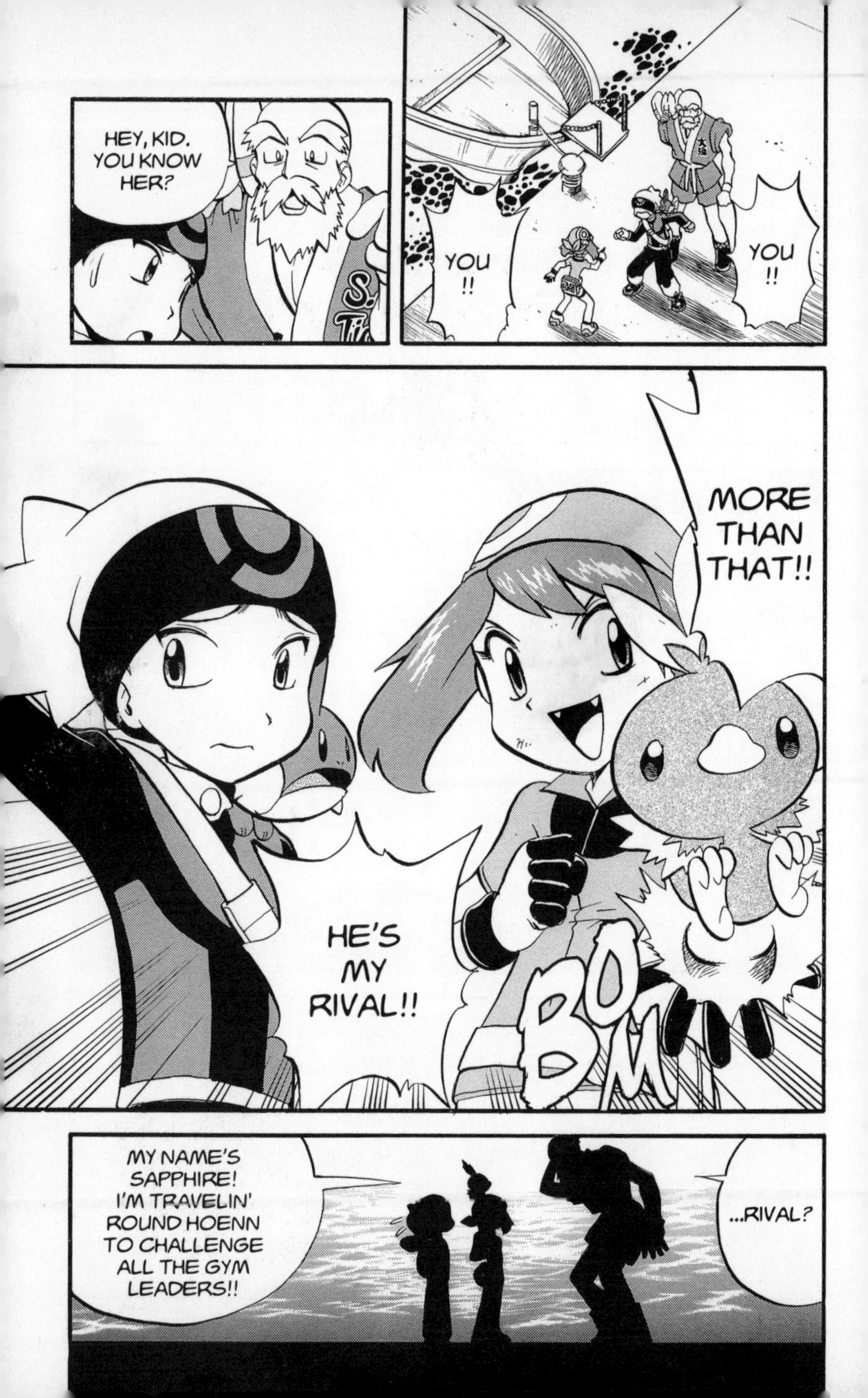
YOU !!
YOU !!
HEY, KID. YOU KNOW HER?
MORE THAN THAT!!
HE'S MY RIVAL!!
...RIVAL?
MY NAME'S SAPPHIRE! I'M TRAVELIN' ROUND HOENN TO CHALLENGE ALL THE GYM LEADERS!!

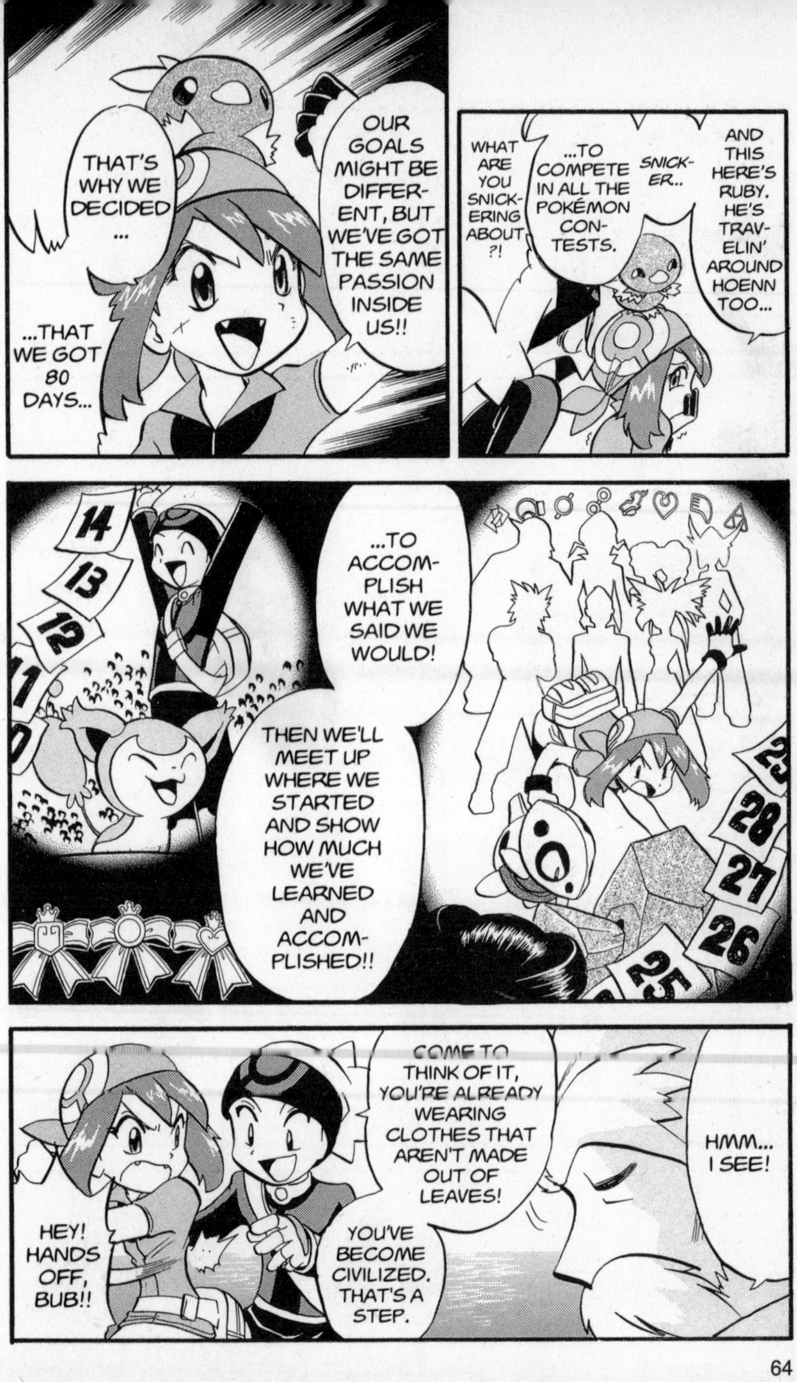
AND THIS HERE'S RUBY. HE'S TRAVELIN' AROUND HOENN TOO...
SNICKER..
...TO COMPETE IN ALL THE POKÉMON CONTESTS.
WHAT ARE YOU SNICKERING ABOUT?!
OUR GOALS MIGHT BE DIFFERENT, BUT WE'VE GOT THE SAME PASSION INSIDE US!!
THAT'S WHY WE DECIDED...
...THAT WE GOT 80 DAYS...
...TO ACCOMPLISH WHAT WE SAID WE WOULD!
THEN WE'LL MEET UP WHERE WE STARTED AND SHOW HOW MUCH WE'VE LEARNED AND ACCOMPLISHED!!
HMM... I SEE!
COME TO THINK OF IT, YOU'RE ALREADY WEARING CLOTHES THAT AREN'T MADE OUT OF LEAVES!
YOU'VE BECOME CIVILIZED. THAT'S A STEP.
HEY! HANDS OFF, BUB!!

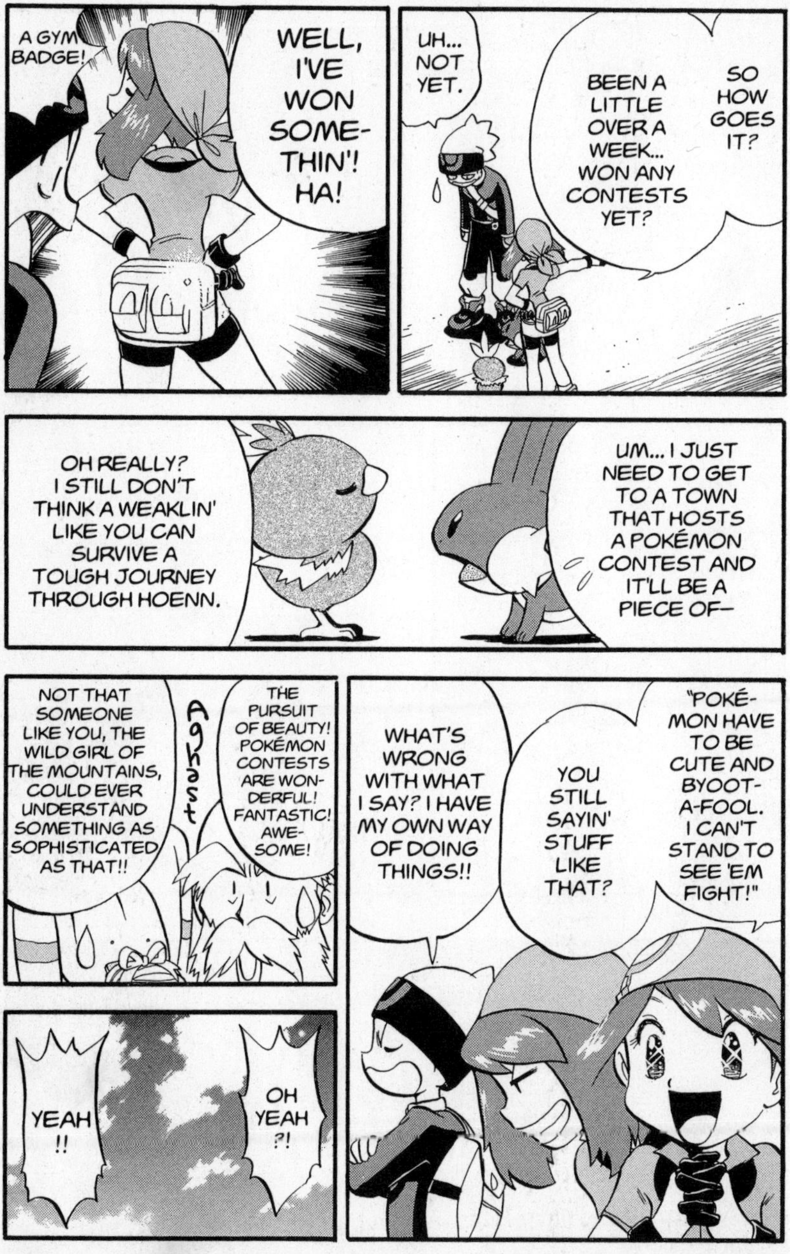
SO HOW GOES IT?
BEEN A LITTLE OVER A WEEK... WON ANY CONTESTS YET?
UH... NOT YET.
WELL, I'VE WON SOME-THIN'! HA!
A GYM BADGE!
UM... I JUST NEED TO GET TO A TOWN THAT HOSTS A POKÉMON CONTEST AND IT'LL BE A PIECE OF—
OH REALLY? I STILL DON'T THINK A WEAKLIN' LIKE YOU CAN SURVIVE A TOUGH JOURNEY THROUGH HOENN.
"POKÉ-MON HAVE TO BE CUTE AND BYOOT-A-FOOL. I CAN'T STAND TO SEE 'EM FIGHT!"
YOU STILL SAYIN' STUFF LIKE THAT?
WHAT'S WRONG WITH WHAT I SAY? I HAVE MY OWN WAY OF DOING THINGS!!
THE PURSUIT OF BEAUTY! POKÉMON CONTESTS ARE WON-DERFUL! FANTASTIC! AWE-SOME!
Aghast
NOT THAT SOMEONE LIKE YOU, THE WILD GIRL OF THE MOUNTAINS, COULD EVER UNDERSTAND SOMETHING AS SOPHISTICATED AS THAT!!
OH YEAH?!
YEAH!!

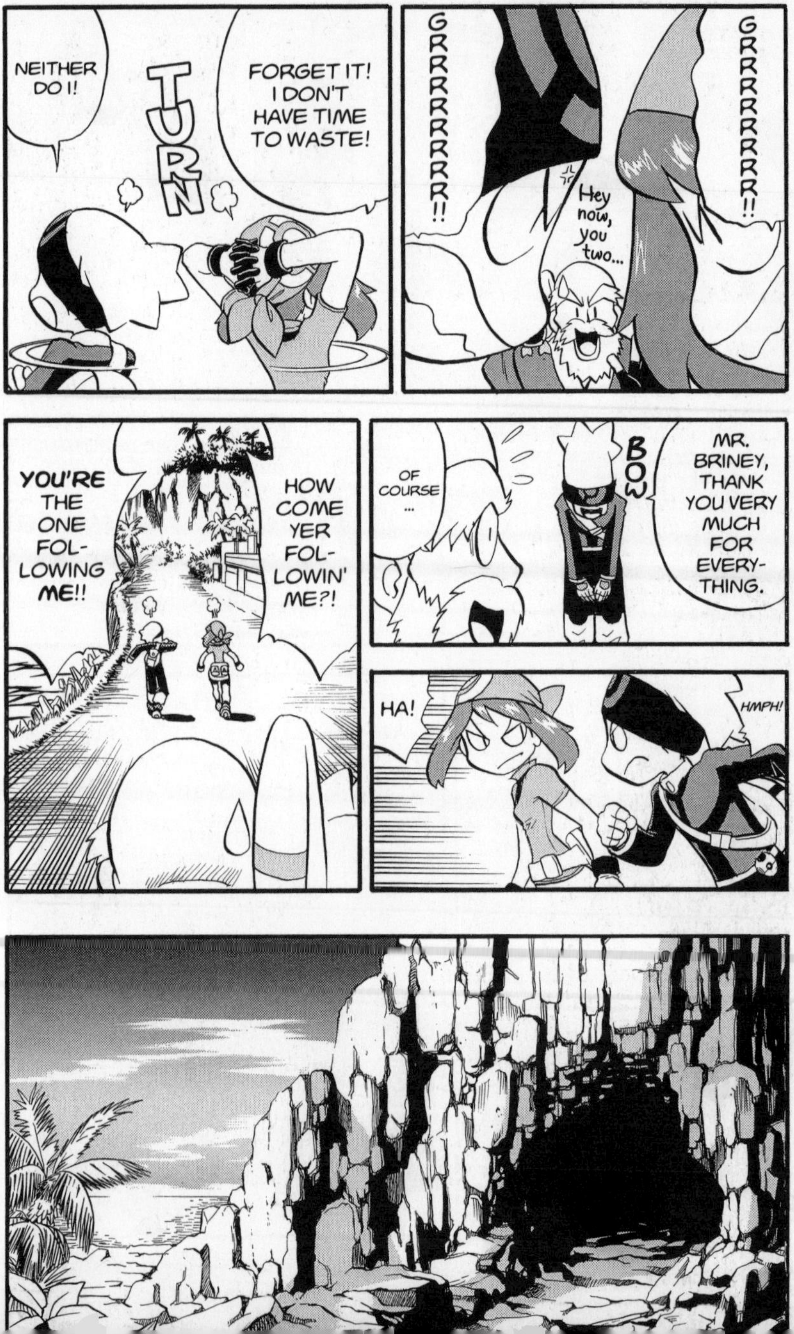
GRRRRRRRR!!
Hey now, you two...
GRRRRRRRR!!
FORGET IT! I DON'T HAVE TIME TO WASTE!
TURN
NEITHER DO I!
MR. BRINEY, THANK YOU VERY MUCH FOR EVERYTHING.
BOW
OF COURSE ...
HMPH!
HA!
HOW COME YER FOLLOWIN' ME?!
YOU'RE THE ONE FOL-LOWING ME!!

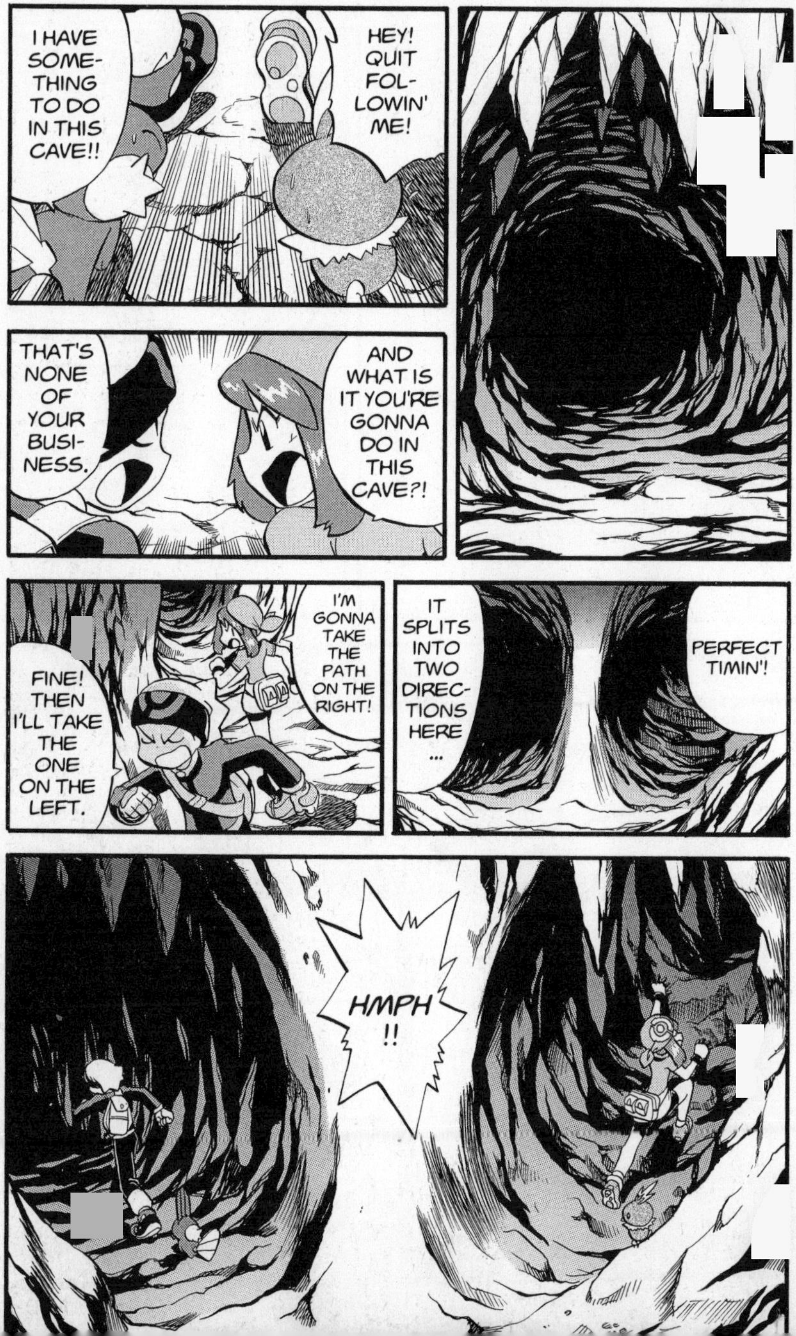
HEY! QUIT FOL-LOWIN' ME!
I HAVE SOME-THING TO DO IN THIS CAVE!!
AND WHAT IS IT YOU'RE GONNA DO IN THIS CAVE?!
THAT'S NONE OF YOUR BUSI-NESS.
PERFECT TIMIN'!
IT SPLITS INTO TWO DIREC-TIONS HERE ...
I'M GONNA TAKE THE PATH ON THE RIGHT!
FINE! THEN I'LL TAKE THE ONE ON THE LEFT.
HMPH!!

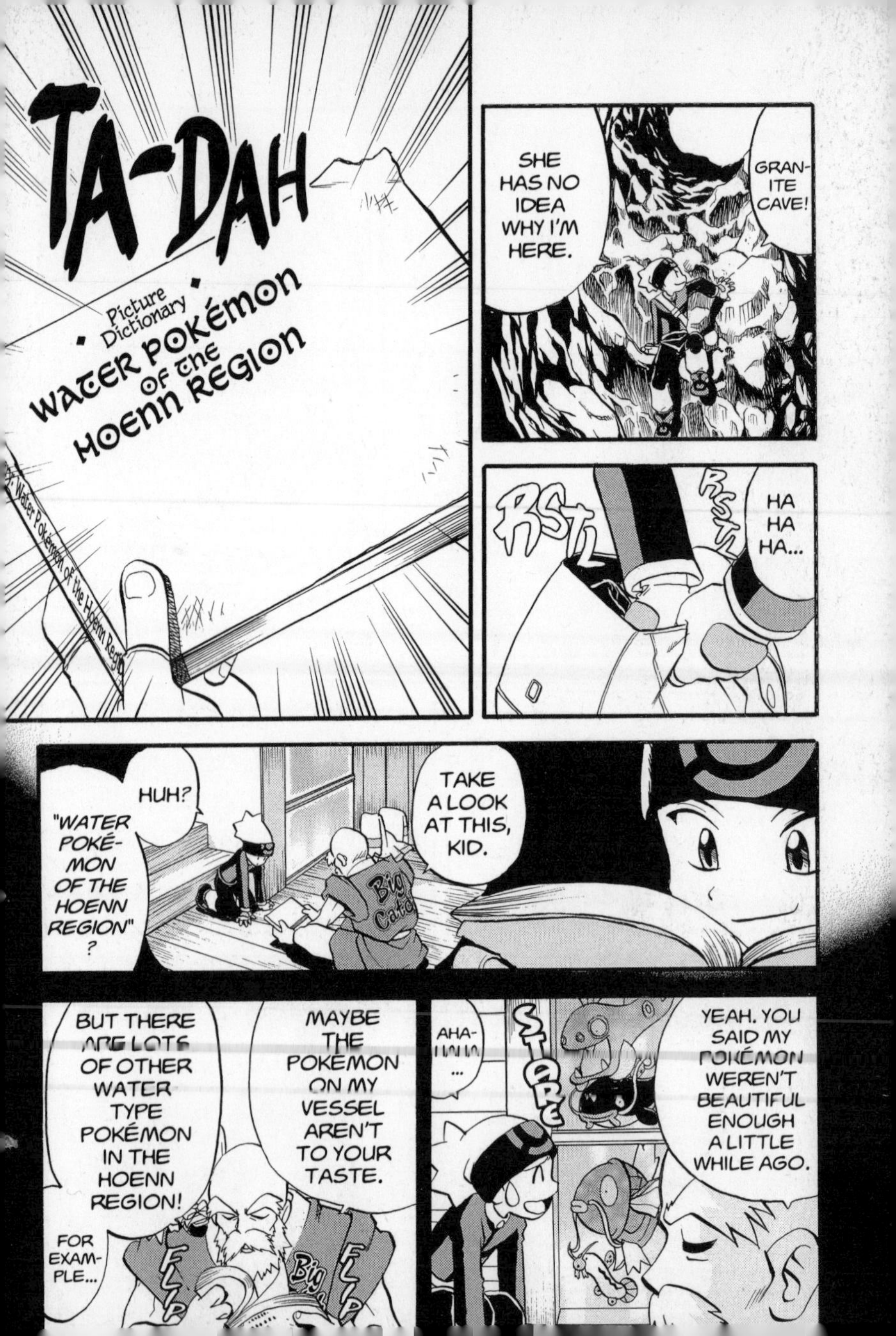
GRAN-ITE CAVE!
SHE HAS NO IDEA WHY I'M HERE.
RSTL
RSTL
HA HA HA...
TA-DAH
Picture Dictionary
WATER POKÉMON OF THE HOENN REGION
TAKE A LOOK AT THIS, KID.
HUH? "WATER POKÉMON OF THE HOENN REGION"?
YEAH. YOU SAID MY POKÉMON WEREN'T BEAUTIFUL ENOUGH A LITTLE WHILE AGO.
STARE
AHA-
...
MAYBE THE POKÉMON ON MY VESSEL AREN'T TO YOUR TASTE.
BUT THERE ARE LOTS OF OTHER WATER-TYPE POKÉMON IN THE HOENN REGION!
FOR EXAMPLE...
FLIP
FLIP

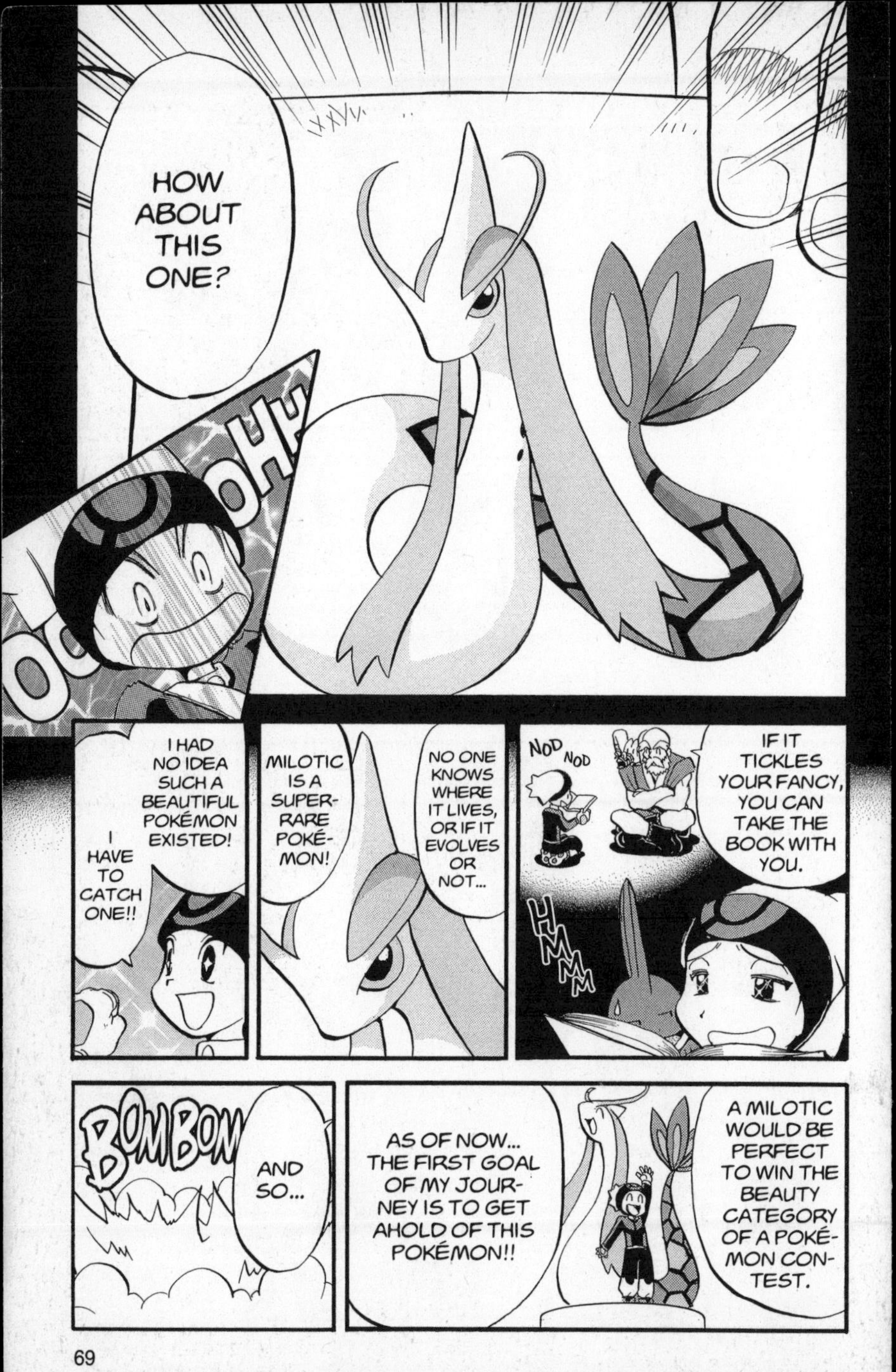
HOW ABOUT THIS ONE?
OOOOH
IF IT TICKLES YOUR FANCY, YOU CAN TAKE THE BOOK WITH YOU.
NOD NOD
HMMMM
NO ONE KNOWS WHERE IT LIVES, OR IF IT EVOLVES OR NOT...
MILOTIC IS A SUPER-RARE POKÉMON!
I HAD NO IDEA SUCH A BEAUTIFUL POKÉMON EXISTED!
I HAVE TO CATCH ONE!!
A MILOTIC WOULD BE PERFECT TO WIN THE BEAUTY CATEGORY OF A POKÉMON CONTEST.
AS OF NOW... THE FIRST GOAL OF MY JOURNEY IS TO GET AHOLD OF THIS POKÉMON!!
AND SO...
BOM BOM

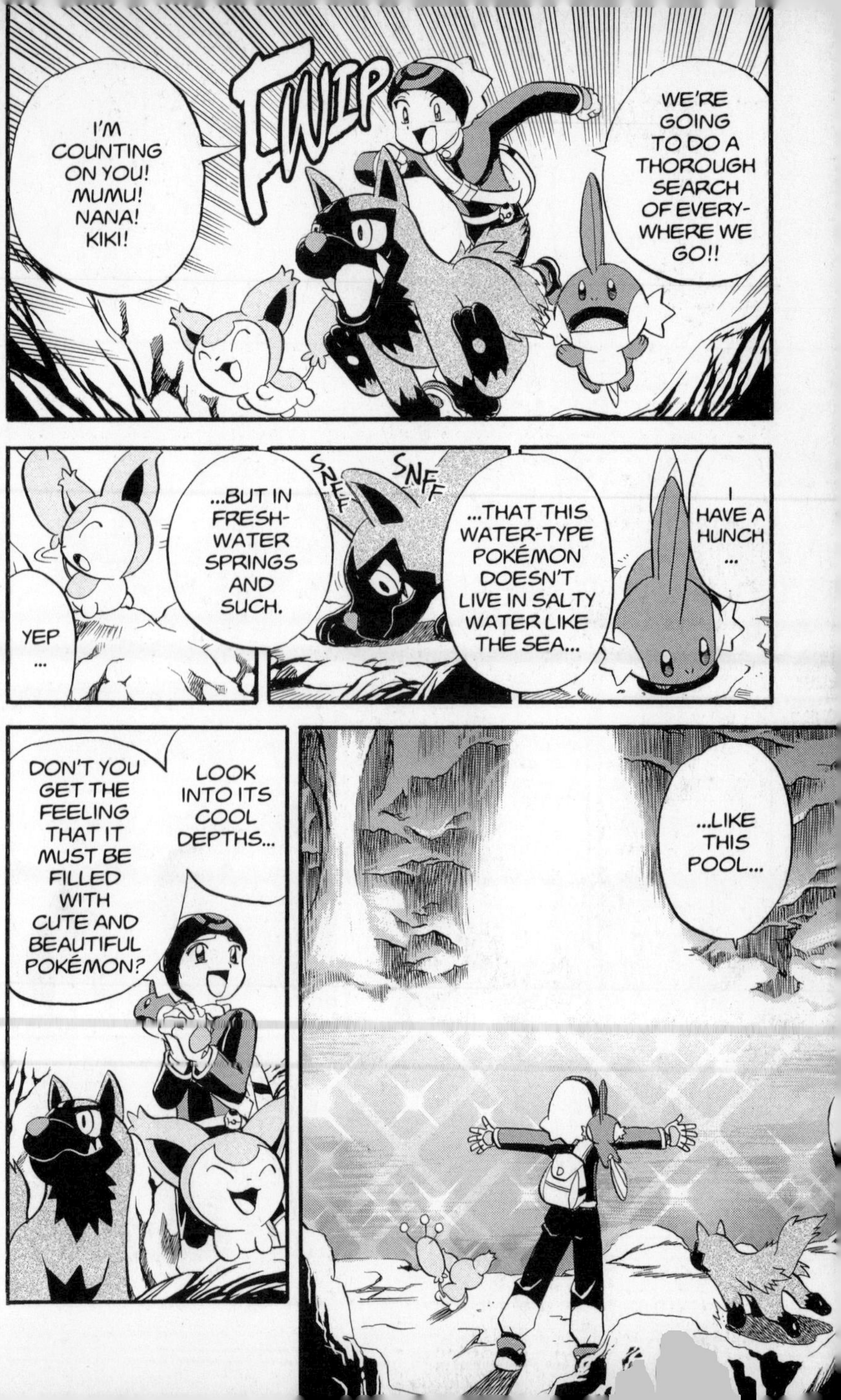
WE'RE GOING TO DO A THOROUGH SEARCH OF EVERY-WHERE WE GO!!
FWIP
I'M COUNTING ON YOU! MUMU! NANA! KIKI!
I HAVE A HUNCH ...
...THAT THIS WATER-TYPE POKÉMON DOESN'T LIVE IN SALTY WATER LIKE THE SEA...
SNFF
SNFF
...BUT IN FRESH-WATER SPRINGS AND SUCH.
YEP ...
...LIKE THIS POOL...
LOOK INTO ITS COOL DEPTHS...
DON'T YOU GET THE FEELING THAT IT MUST BE FILLED WITH CUTE AND BEAUTIFUL POKÉMON?

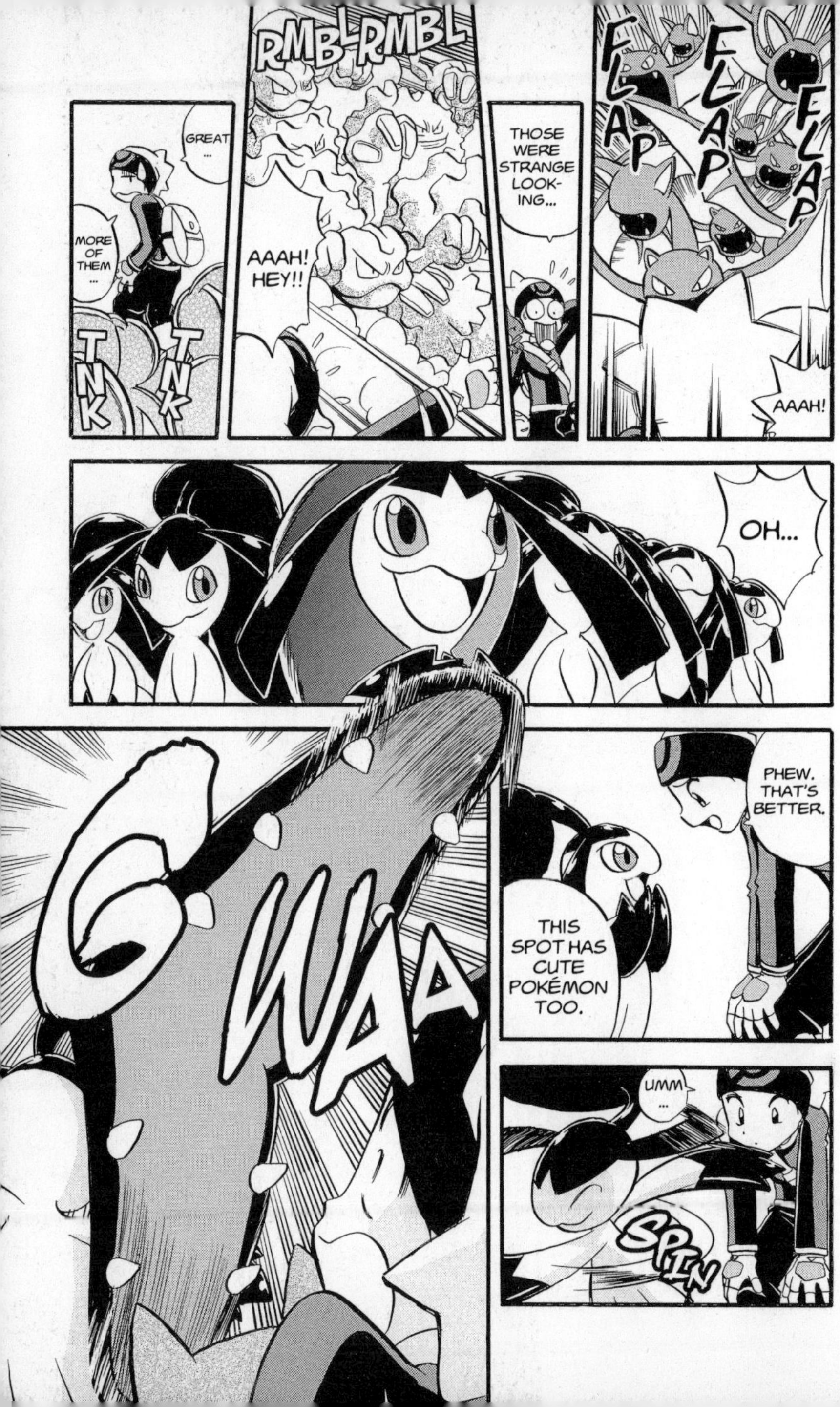
FLAP FLAP FLAP
AAAH!
THOSE WERE STRANGE LOOKING...
RMBLRMBL
AAAH! HEY!!
GREAT...
MORE OF THEM...
TNK TNK
OH...
PHEW. THAT'S BETTER.
THIS SPOT HAS CUTE POKÉMON TOO.
UMM...
SPIN
WAA

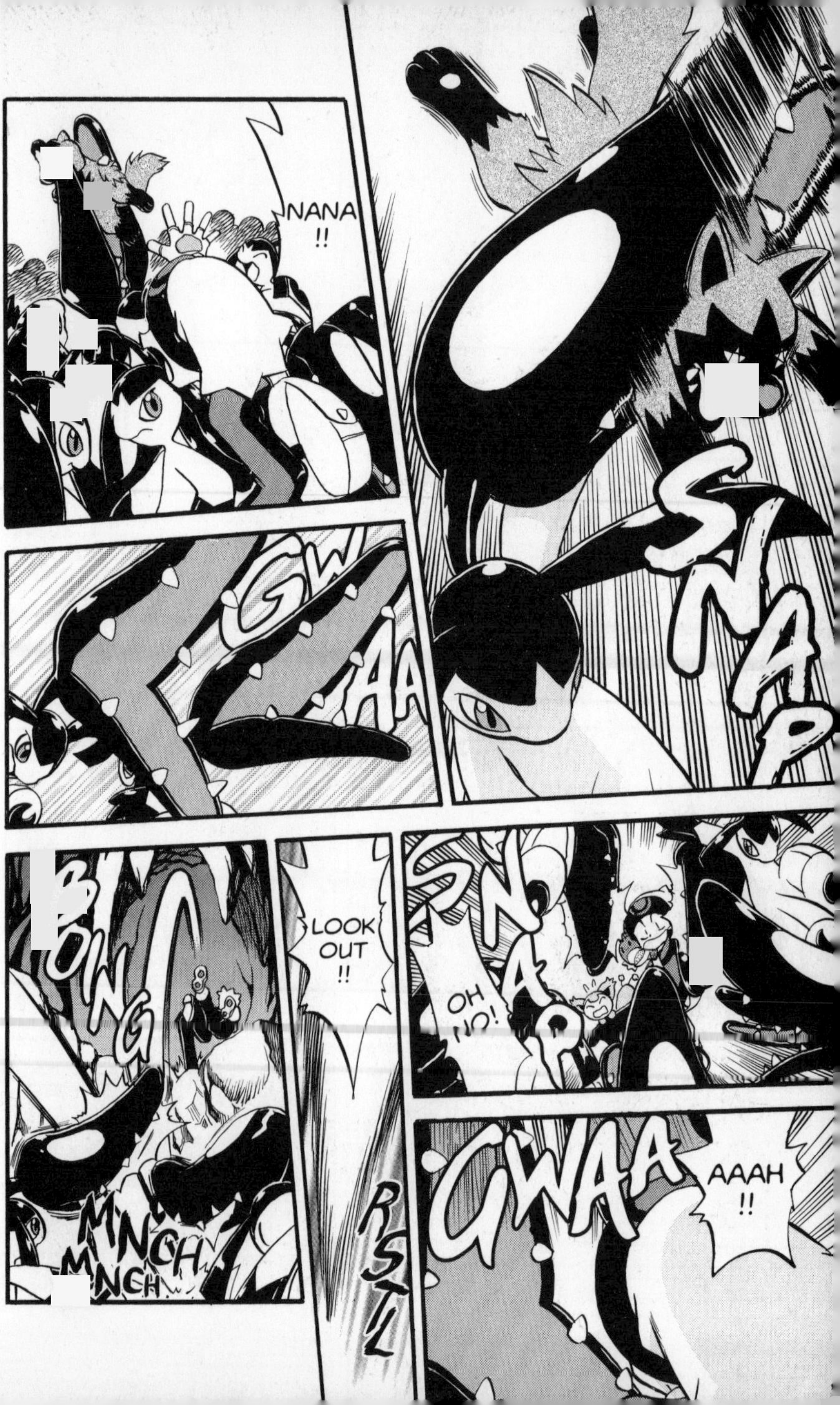
SNAP
NANA!!
GWAA
SNAP
OH NO!
GWAA
AAAH!!
LOOK OUT!!
RSTL
BOING
MNCH MNCH

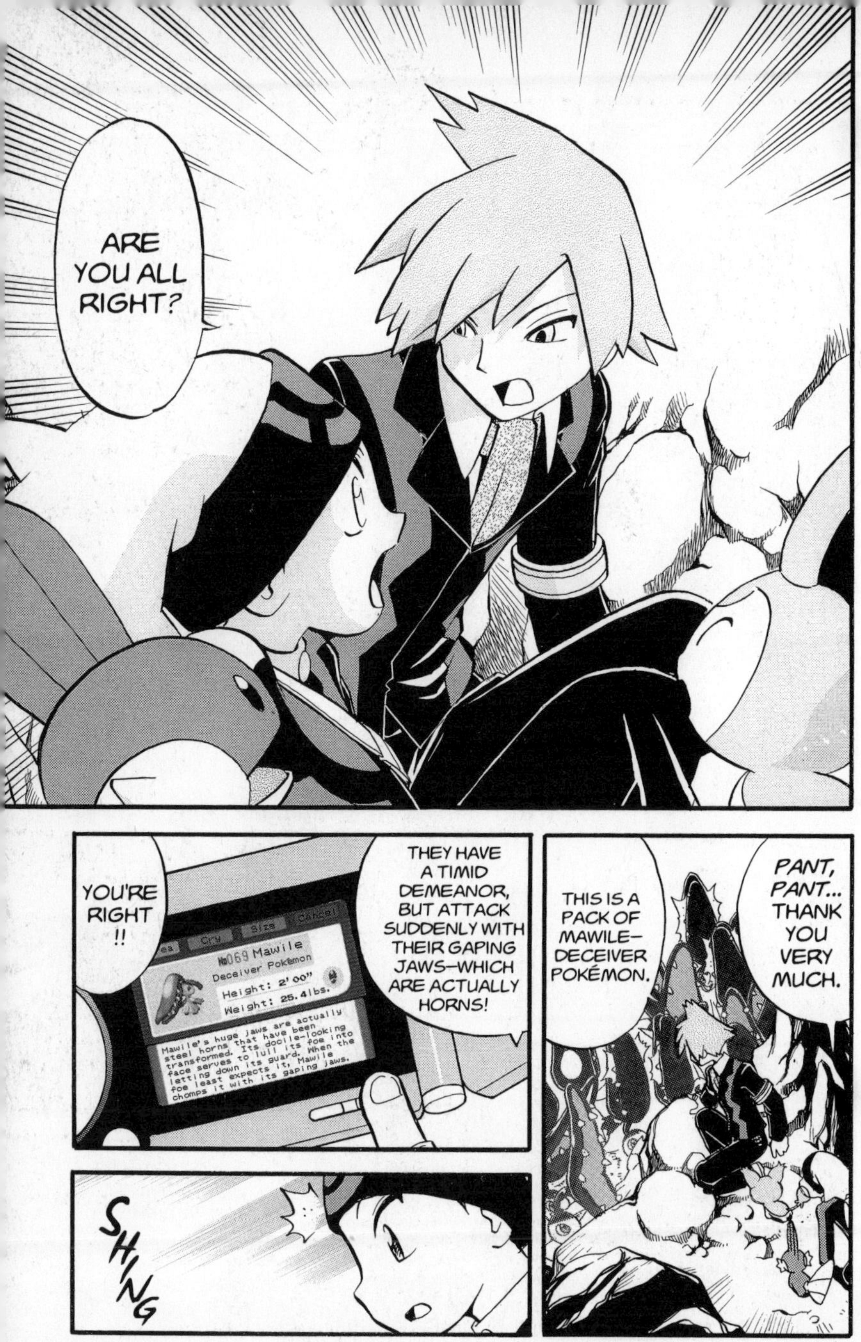
ARE YOU ALL RIGHT?
PANT, PANT... THANK YOU VERY MUCH.
THIS IS A PACK OF MAWILE—DECEIVER POKÉMON.
THEY HAVE A TIMID DEMEANOR, BUT ATTACK SUDDENLY WITH THEIR GAPING JAWS—WHICH ARE ACTUALLY HORNS!
YOU'RE RIGHT !!
Cry Size Cancel
No069 Mawile
Deceiver Pokémon
Height: 2'00"
Weight: 25.4lbs.
Mawile's huge jaws are actually steel horns that have been transformed. Its docile-looking face serves to lull its foe into letting down its guard. When the foe least expects it, Mawile chomps it with its gaping jaws.
SHING

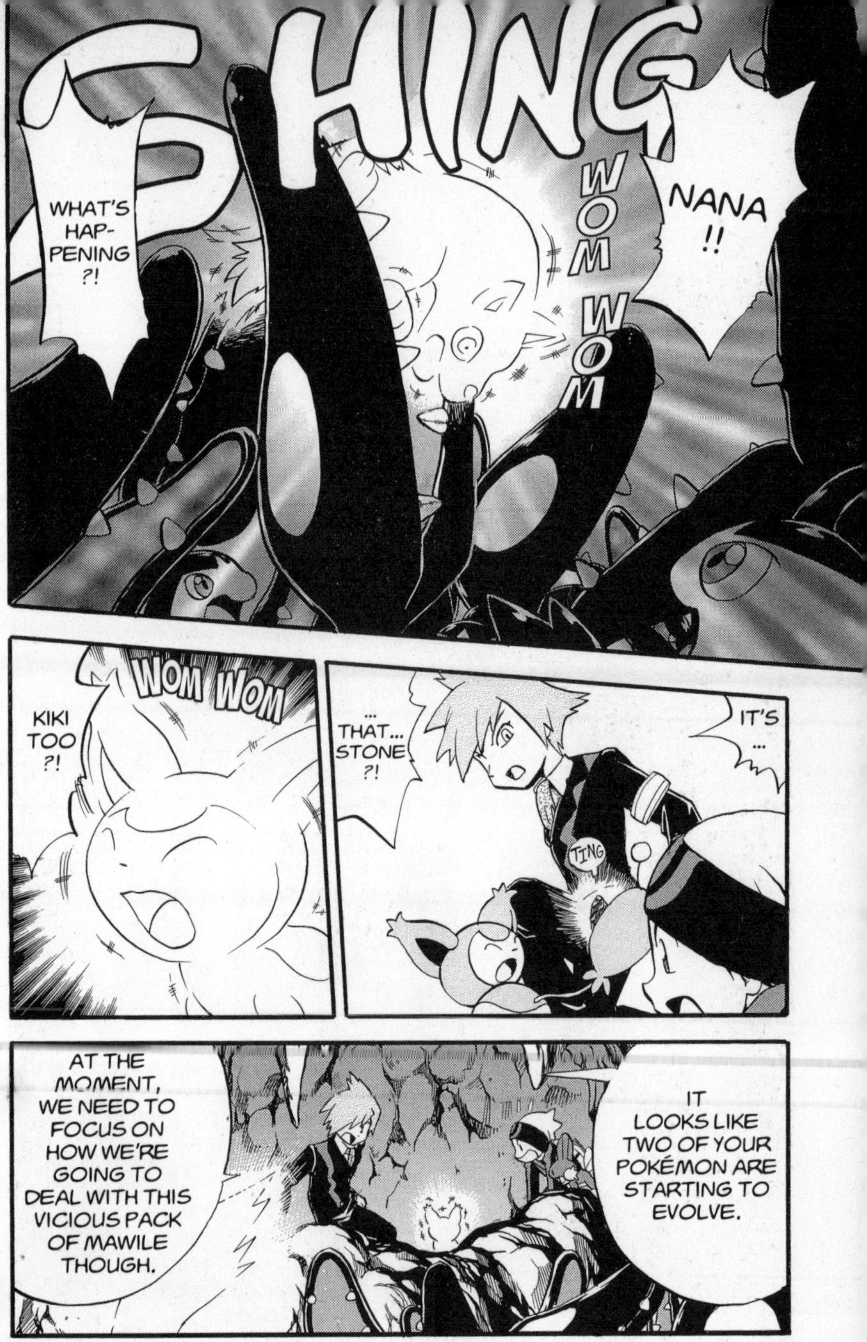
NANA !!
SHING
WOM WOM WOM WOM
WHAT'S HAP-PENING ?!
IT'S ...
... THAT... STONE ?!
TING
WOM WOM
KIKI TOO ?!
IT LOOKS LIKE TWO OF YOUR POKÉMON ARE STARTING TO EVOLVE.
AT THE MOMENT, WE NEED TO FOCUS ON HOW WE'RE GOING TO DEAL WITH THIS VICIOUS PACK OF MAWILE THOUGH.

OF COURSE !!

MY NAME IS STEVEN.

YOU'LL HELP ME, WON'T YOU?

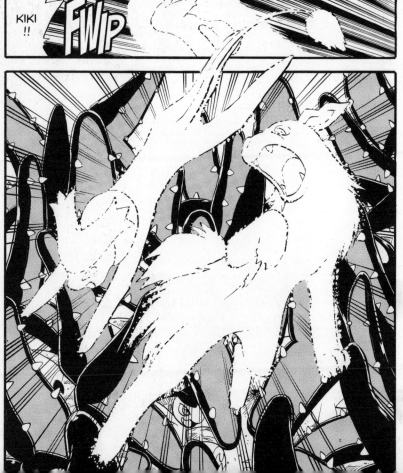

KIKI !!

FWIP

ADVENTURE MAP

SAPPHIRE

RUBY

CHIC
Torchic ♀
Lv15

RONO
Aron ♂
Lv31

LORRY
Wailord ♂
Lv41

Sea Route 105	Sea Route 105
Sea Route 106	Sea Route 106
Dewford Town	
Granite Cave	Granite Cave

NANA
? ♀

KIKI
? ♀

MUMU
Mudkip ♂

SAPPHIRE

RUBY

Stone Badge	Knuckle Badge	Dynamo Badge	Heat Badge
Balance Badge	Feather Badge	Mind Badge	Rain Badge

		Cool	Beauty	Cute	Smart	Tough
Normal		🎀	🎀	🎀	🎀	🎀
Super		🎀	🎀	🎀	🎀	🎀
Hyper						
Master						

● Chapter 195 ●
Mashing Makuhita

POKÉMON™
ADVENTURES
RUBY & SAPPHIRE
The Fourth Chapter

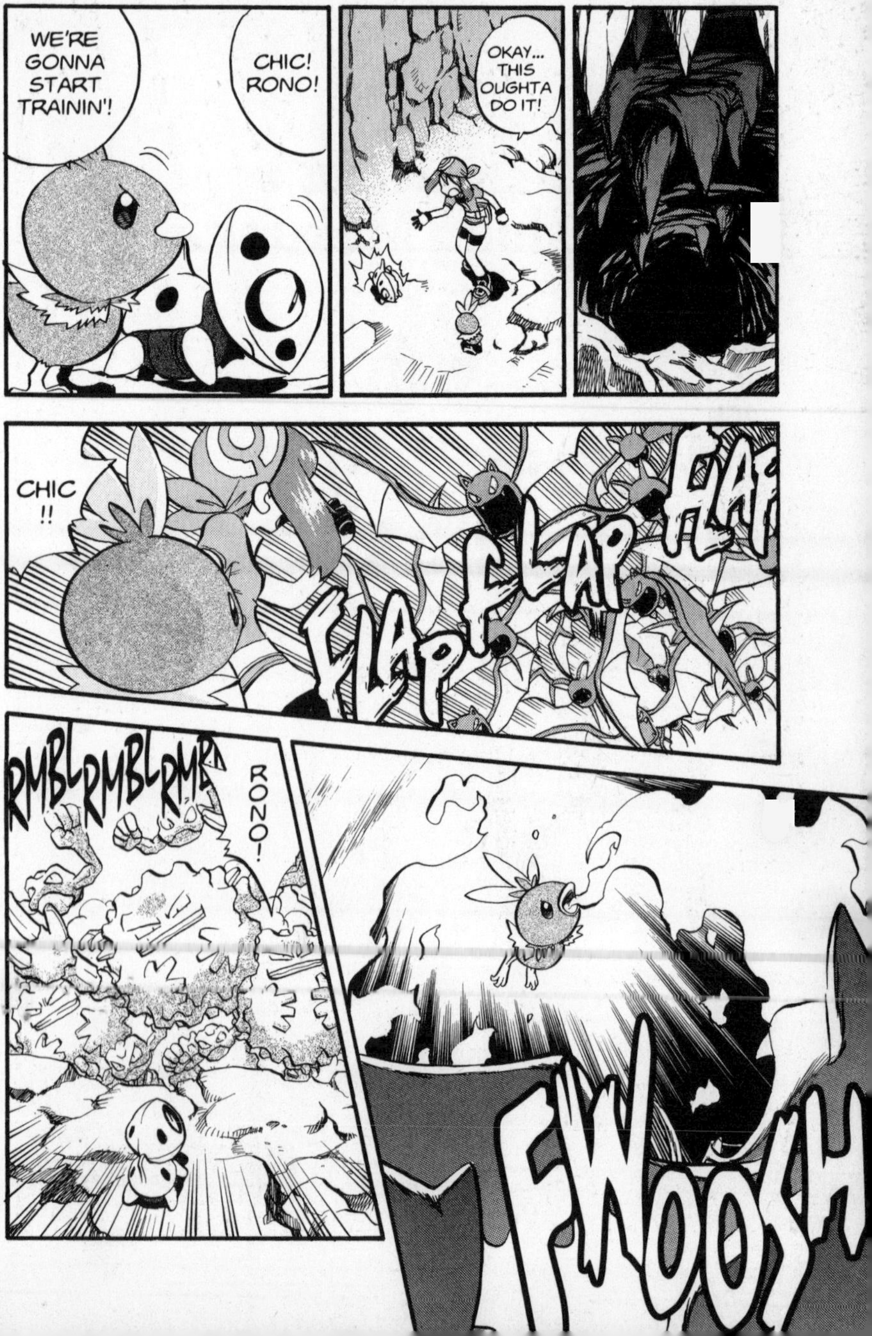
OKAY... THIS OUGHTA DO IT!
CHIC! RONO!
WE'RE GONNA START TRAININ'!
FLAP FLAP FLAP
CHIC !!
FWOOSH
RONO!
RMBL RMBL RMBL

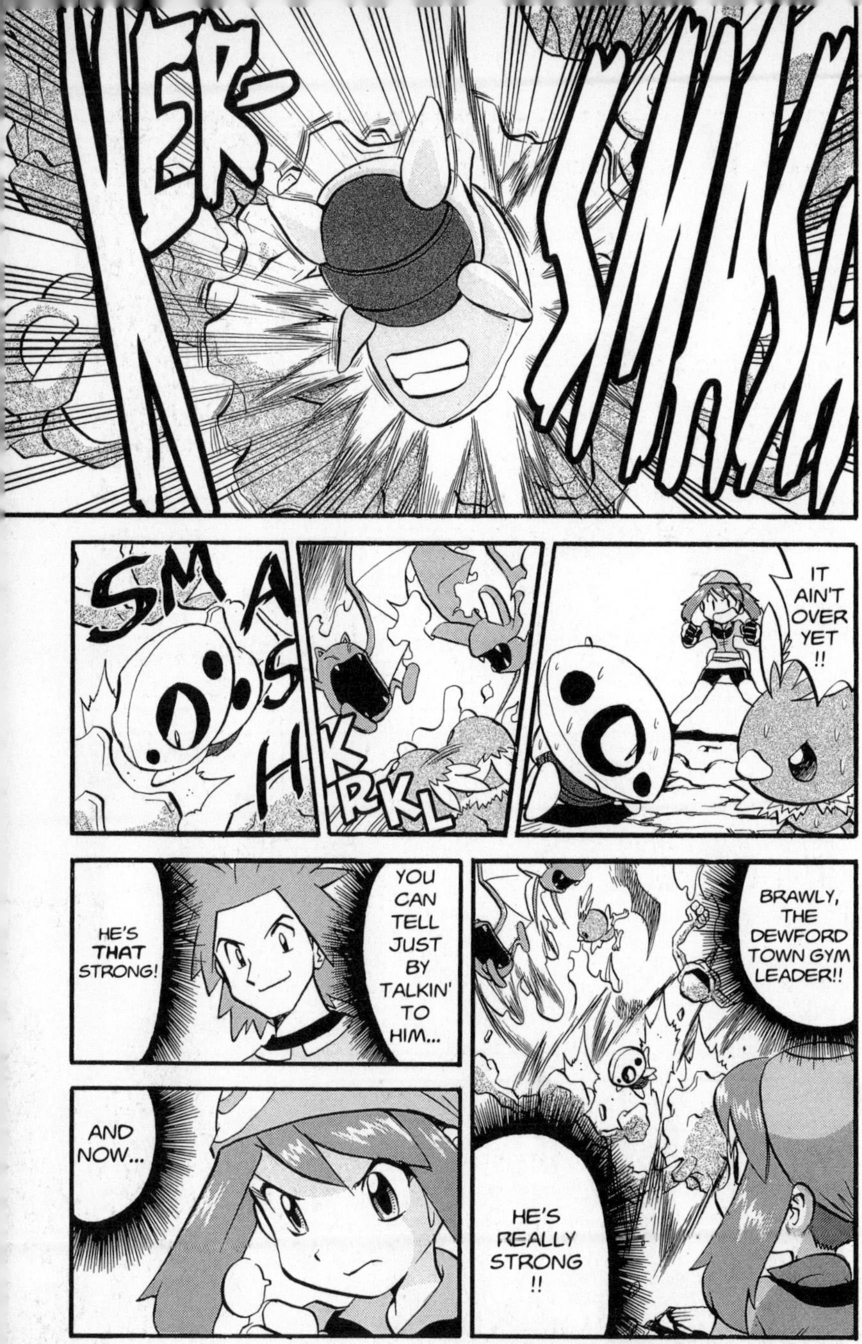
VER-
SMASH
IT AIN'T OVER YET !!
KRKL
SMASH
BRAWLY, THE DEWFORD TOWN GYM LEADER!!
HE'S REALLY STRONG !!
YOU CAN TELL JUST BY TALKIN' TO HIM...
HE'S THAT STRONG!
AND NOW...

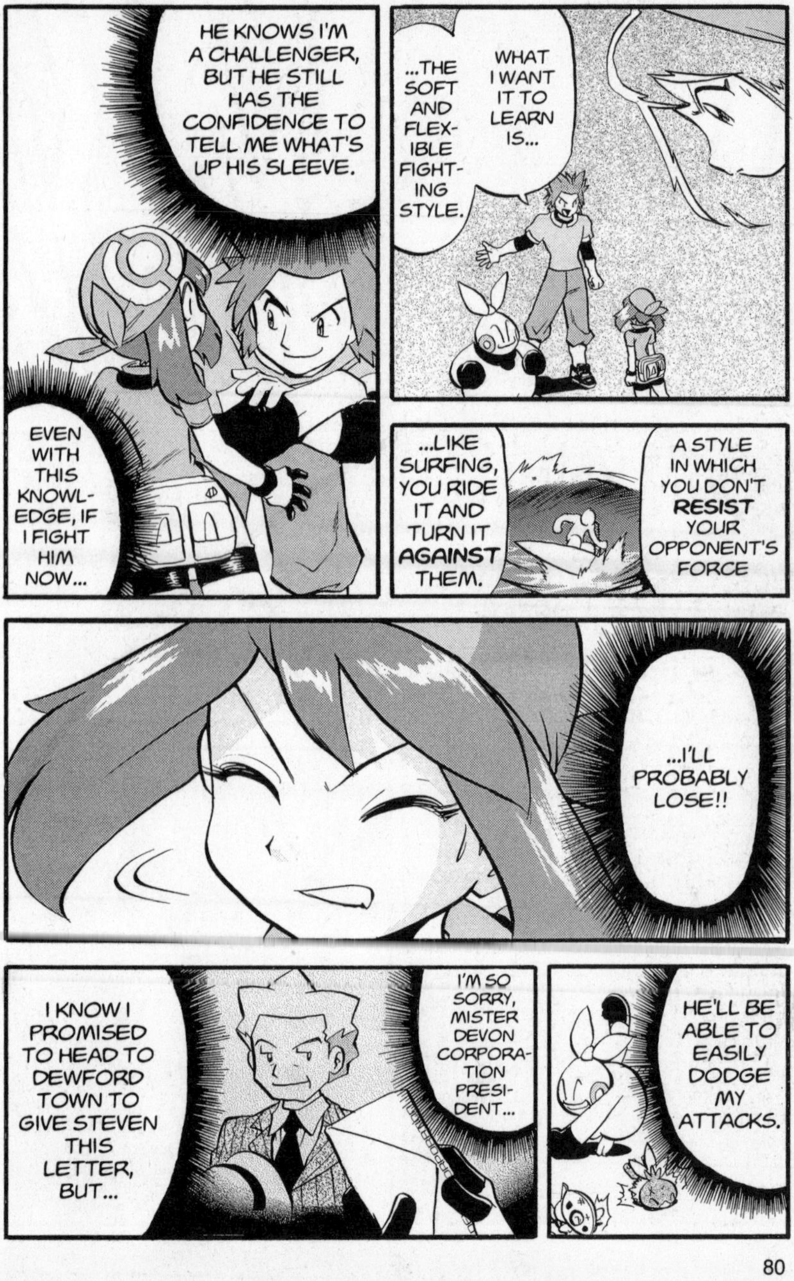
WHAT I WANT IT TO LEARN IS...
...THE SOFT AND FLEXIBLE FIGHTING STYLE.
A STYLE IN WHICH YOU DON'T **RESIST** YOUR OPPONENT'S FORCE
...LIKE SURFING, YOU RIDE IT AND TURN IT **AGAINST** THEM.
HE KNOWS I'M A CHALLENGER, BUT HE STILL HAS THE CONFIDENCE TO TELL ME WHAT'S UP HIS SLEEVE.
EVEN WITH THIS KNOWLEDGE, IF I FIGHT HIM NOW...
...I'LL PROBABLY LOSE!!
HE'LL BE ABLE TO EASILY DODGE MY ATTACKS.
I'M SO SORRY, MISTER DEVON CORPORATION PRESIDENT...
I KNOW I PROMISED TO HEAD TO DEWFORD TOWN TO GIVE STEVEN THIS LETTER, BUT...

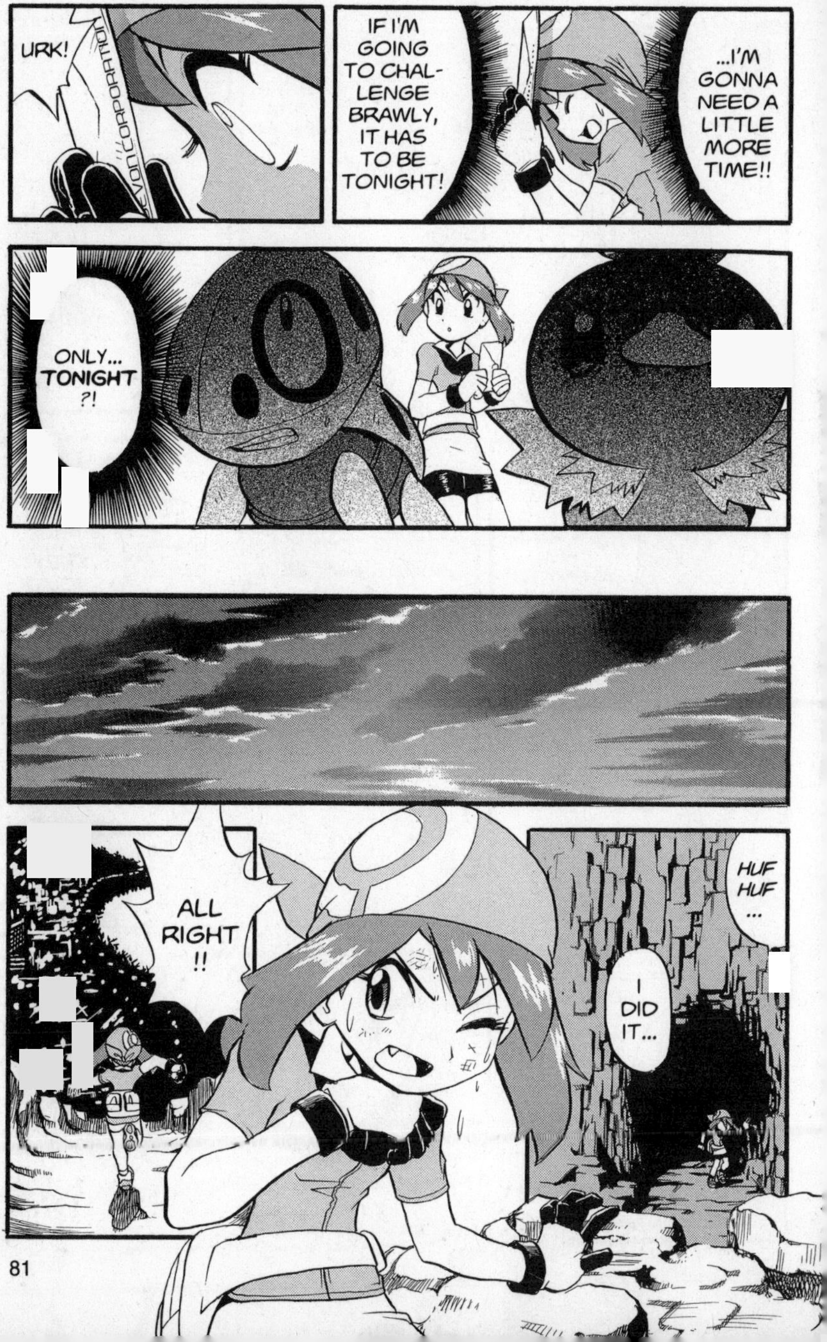
...I'M GONNA NEED A LITTLE MORE TIME!!
IF I'M GOING TO CHAL-LENGE BRAWLY, IT HAS TO BE TONIGHT!
VON CORPORATION
URK!
ONLY... TONIGHT?!
HUF HUF ...
I DID IT...
ALL RIGHT!!

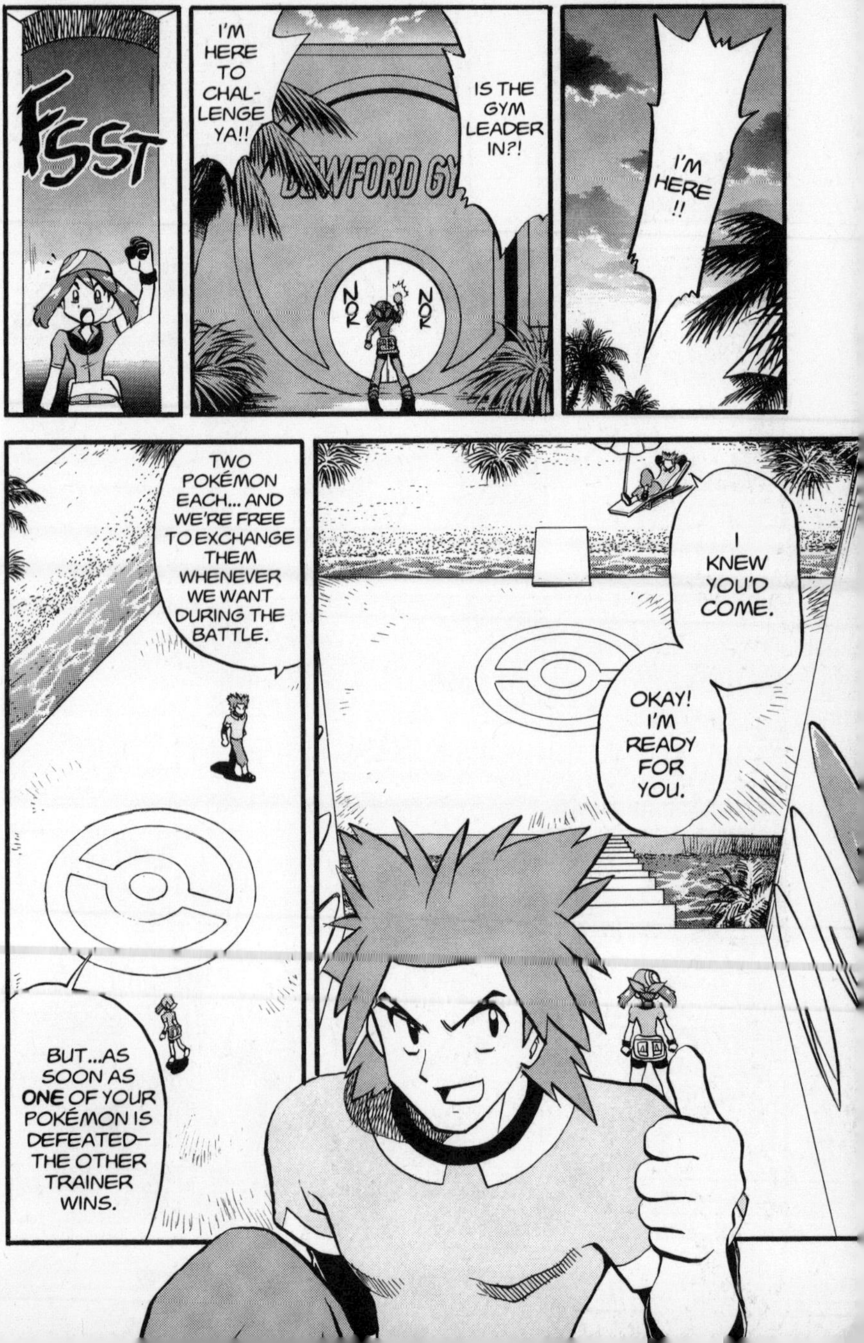
I'M HERE!!
IS THE GYM LEADER IN?!
I'M HERE TO CHAL-LENGE YA!!
NOK NOK
NOK NOK
FSST
I KNEW YOU'D COME.
OKAY! I'M READY FOR YOU.
TWO POKÉMON EACH... AND WE'RE FREE TO EXCHANGE THEM WHENEVER WE WANT DURING THE BATTLE.
BUT...AS SOON AS **ONE** OF YOUR POKÉMON IS DEFEATED— THE OTHER TRAINER WINS.

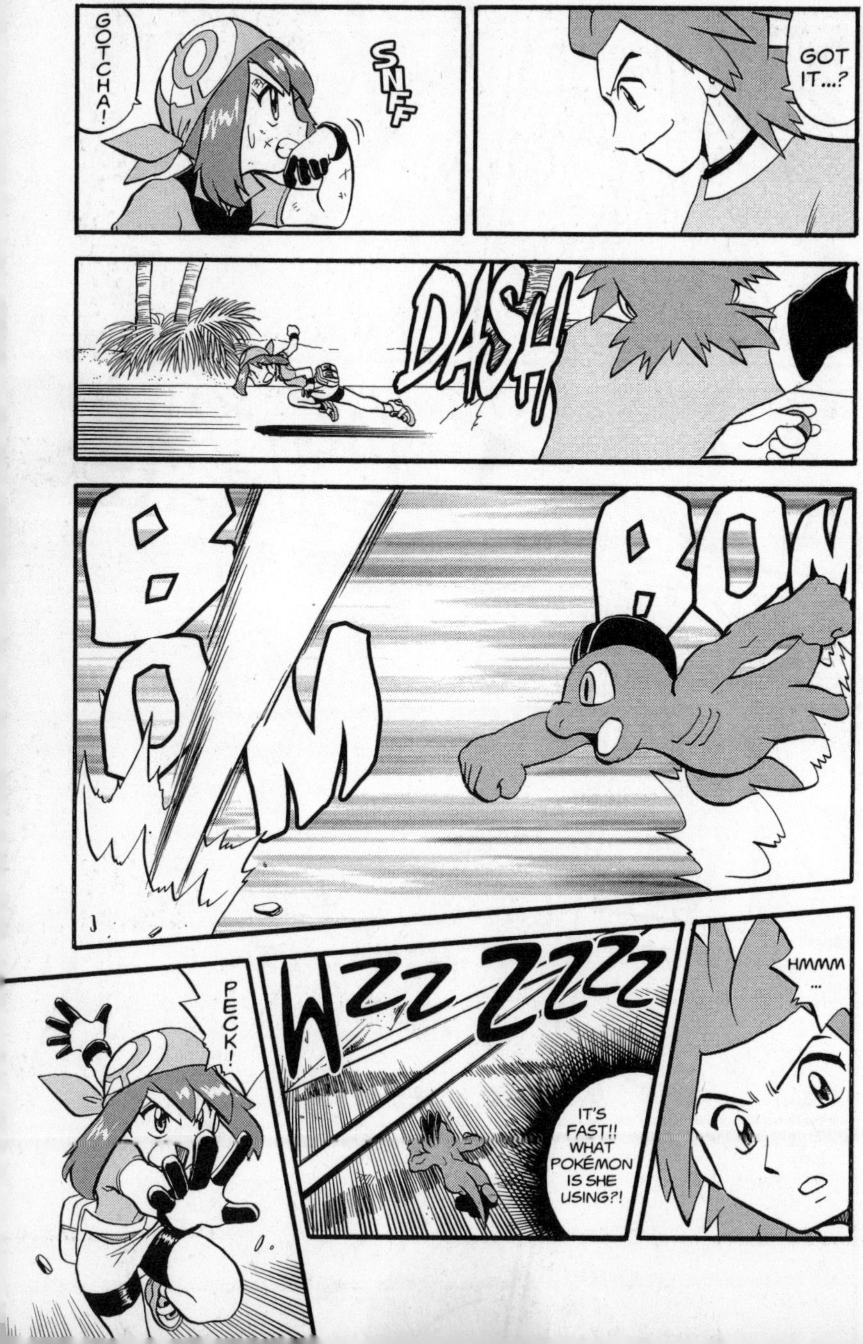
GOT IT...?
SNFF
GOTCHA!
DASH
BOM
BOM
HMMM ...
WZZ ZZZZ
IT'S FAST!! WHAT POKÉMON IS SHE USING?!
PECK!

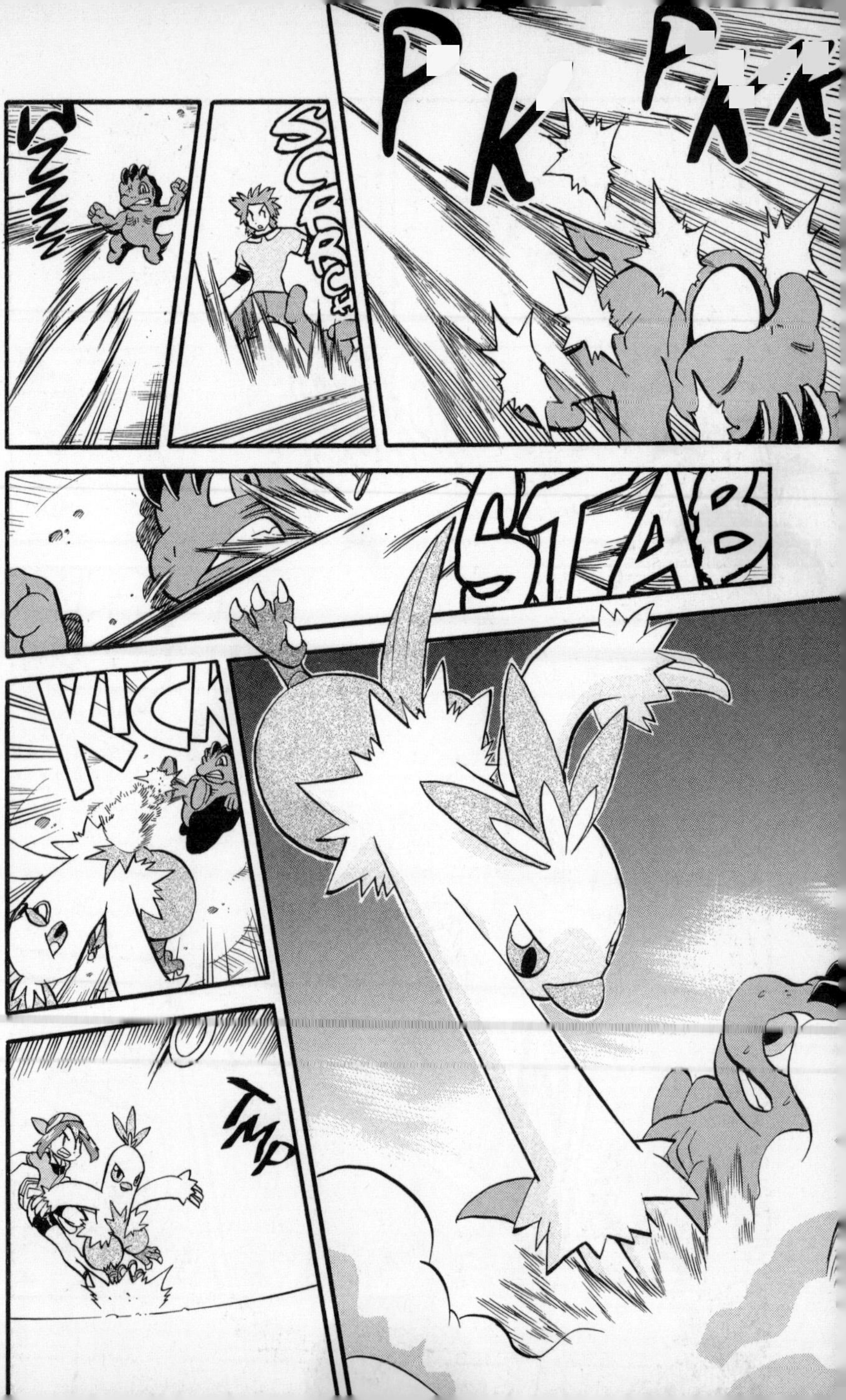
STAB
KICK
TMP

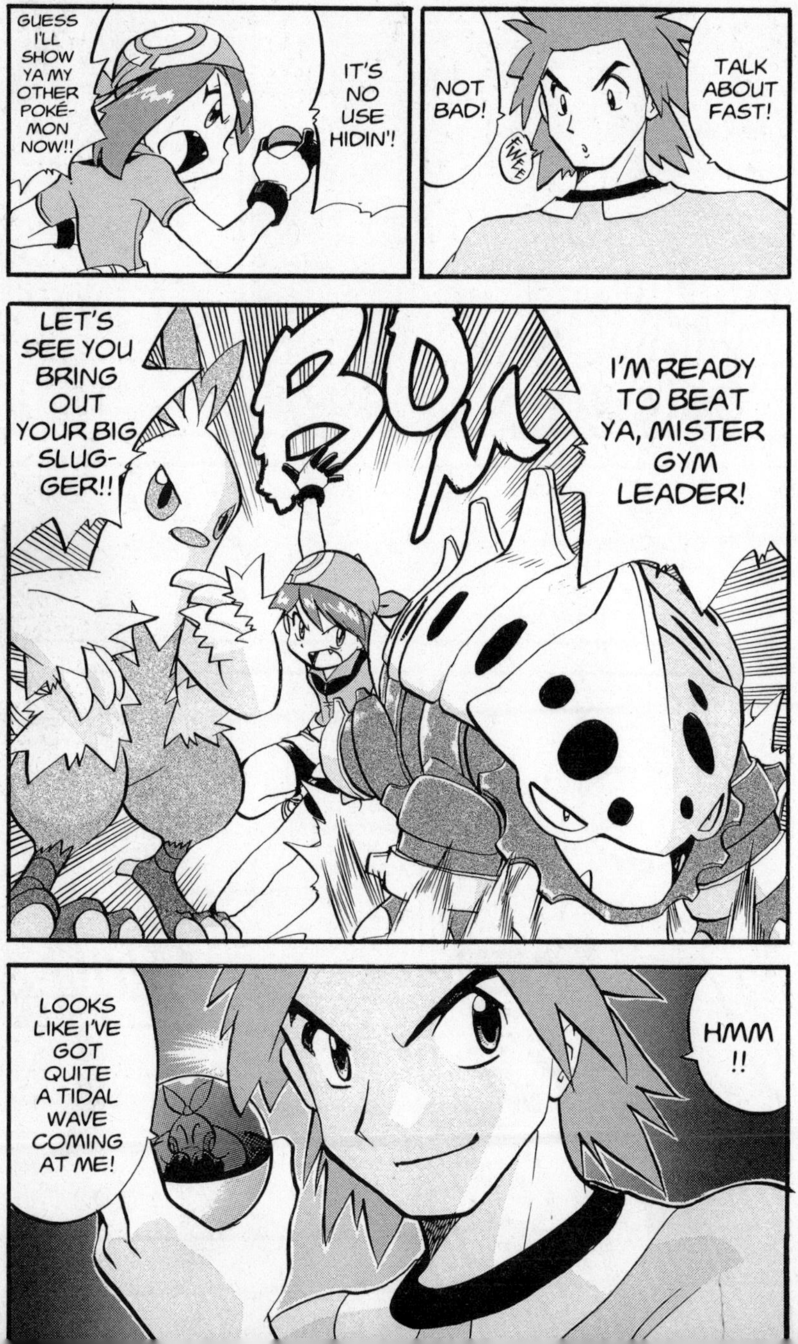
TALK ABOUT FAST!
NOT BAD!
FWEE
IT'S NO USE HIDIN'!
GUESS I'LL SHOW YA MY OTHER POKÉ-MON NOW!!
I'M READY TO BEAT YA, MISTER GYM LEADER!
BOOM
LET'S SEE YOU BRING OUT YOUR BIG SLUG-GER!!
HMM !!
LOOKS LIKE I'VE GOT QUITE A TIDAL WAVE COMING AT ME!

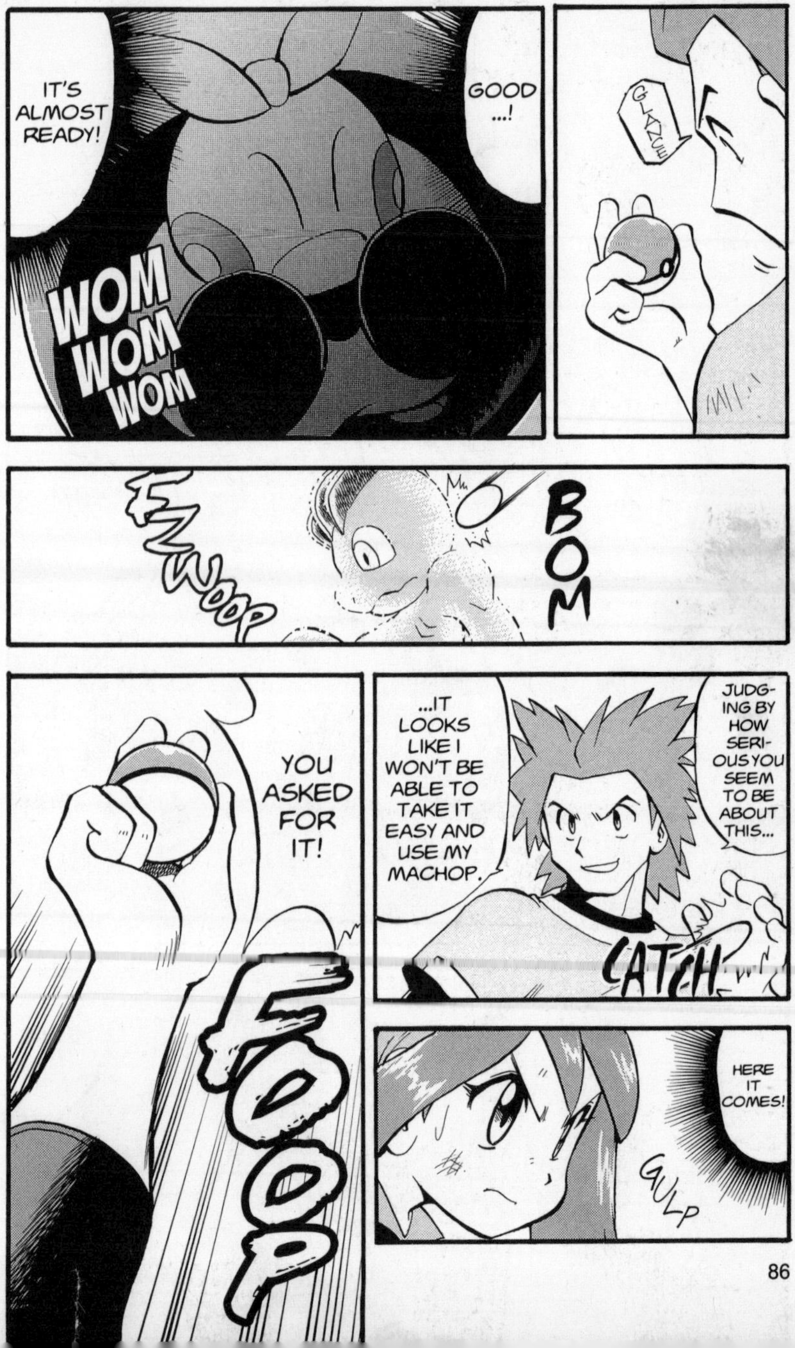
GLANCE
GOOD ...!
IT'S ALMOST READY!
WOM WOM WOM
BOM
FZWOOP
JUDGING BY HOW SERIOUS YOU SEEM TO BE ABOUT THIS...
...IT LOOKS LIKE I WON'T BE ABLE TO TAKE IT EASY AND USE MY MACHOP.
CATCH
HERE IT COMES!
GULP
YOU ASKED FOR IT!
FOOOP

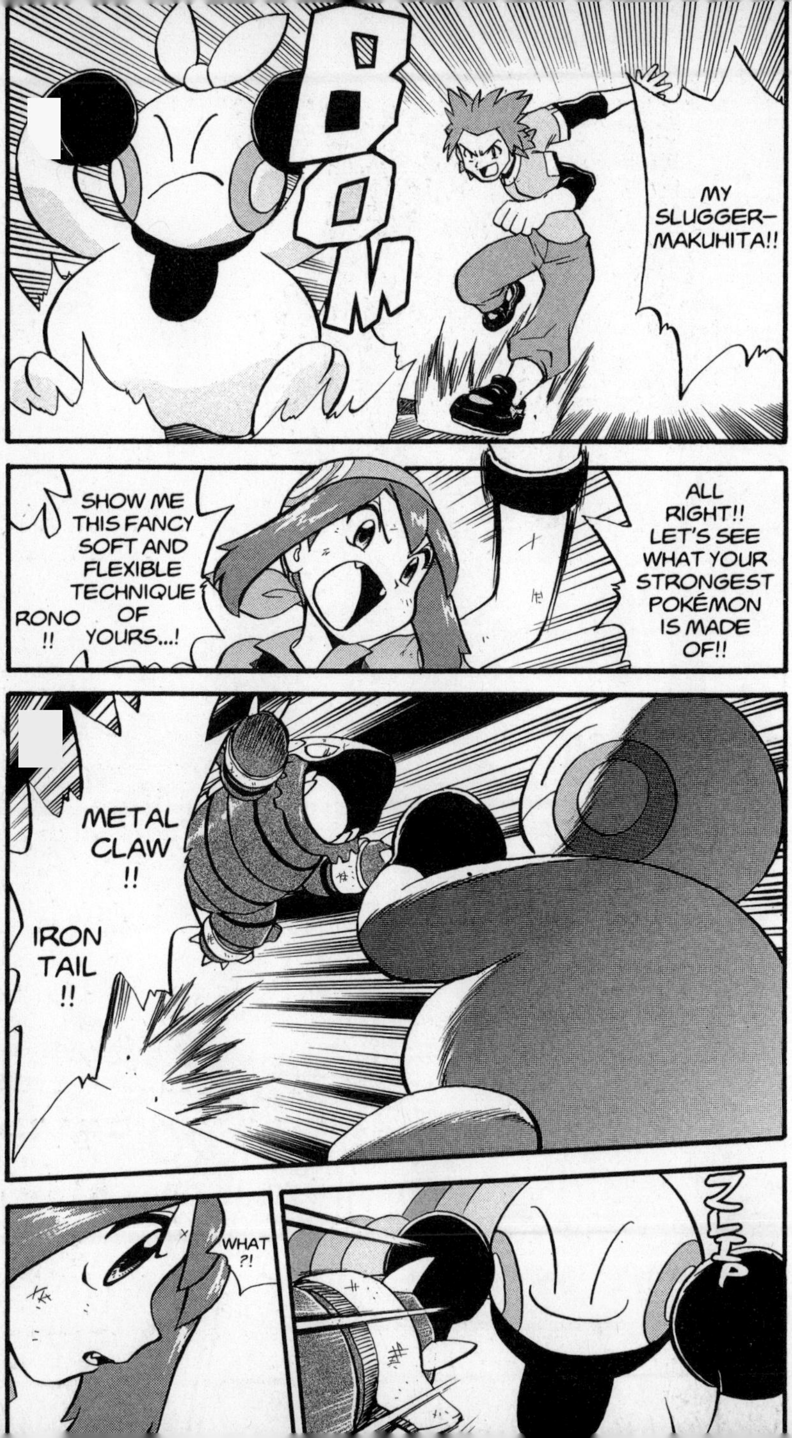
MY SLUGGER–MAKUHITA!!
BOOM
ALL RIGHT!! LET'S SEE WHAT YOUR STRONGEST POKÉMON IS MADE OF!!
SHOW ME THIS FANCY SOFT AND FLEXIBLE TECHNIQUE OF YOURS...!
RONO !!
METAL CLAW !!
IRON TAIL !!
ZLIP
WHAT ?!

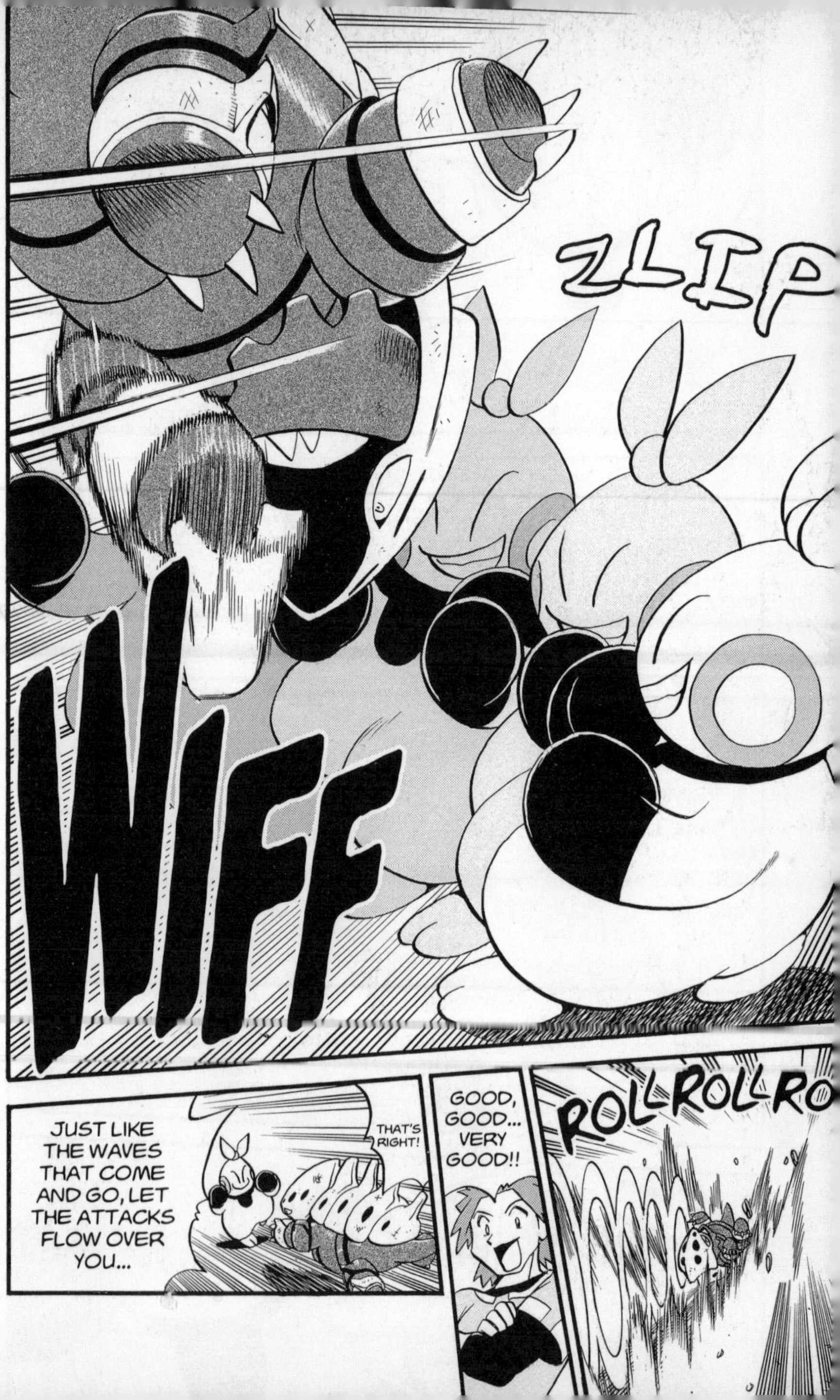
ZLIP
WIFF
ROLLROLLRO
GOOD, GOOD... VERY GOOD!!
THAT'S RIGHT!
JUST LIKE THE WAVES THAT COME AND GO, LET THE ATTACKS FLOW OVER YOU...

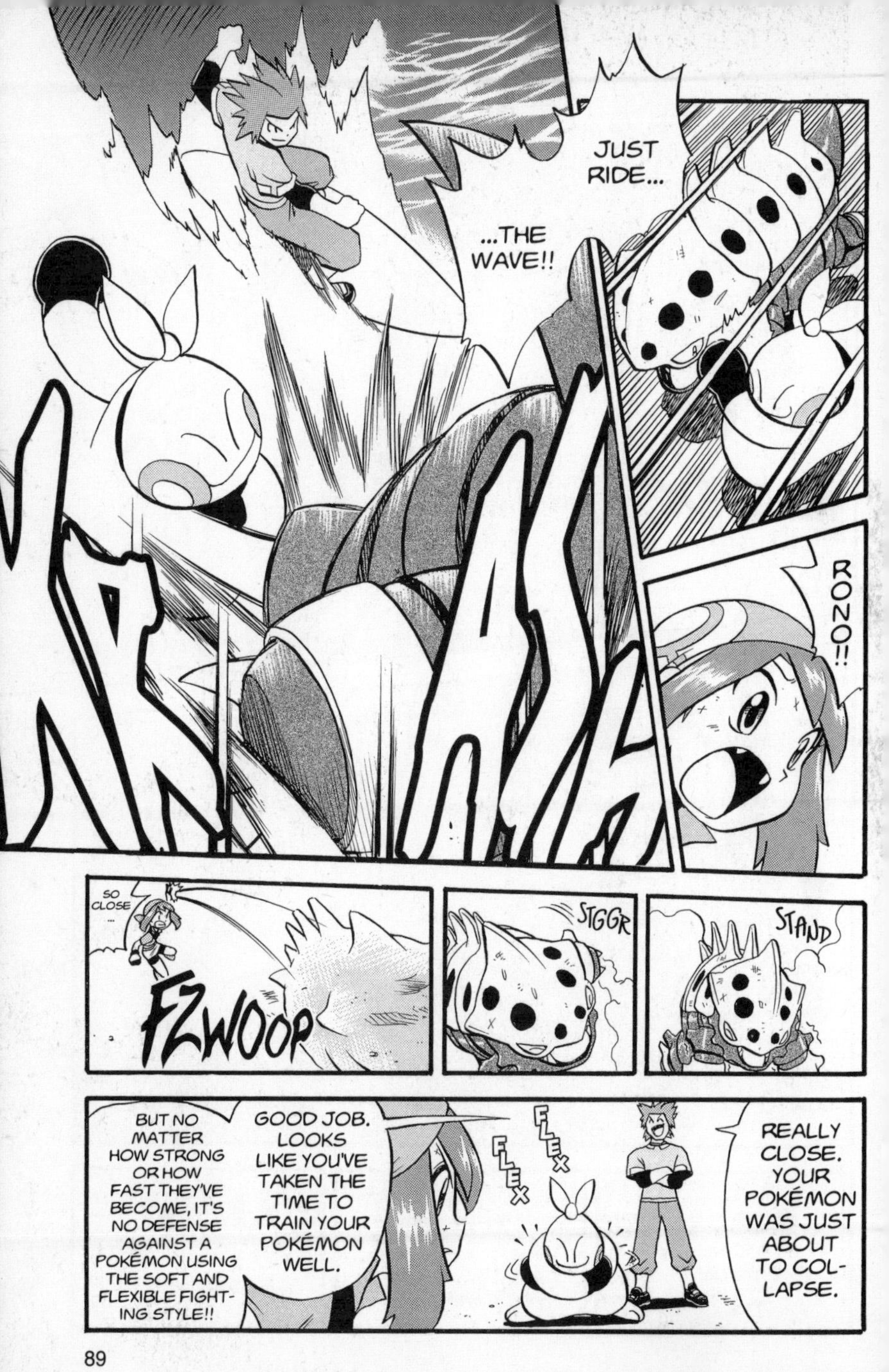
RONO!!
JUST RIDE...
...THE WAVE!!
STAND
STGGR
SO CLOSE ...
FZWOOP
REALLY CLOSE. YOUR POKÉMON WAS JUST ABOUT TO COL-LAPSE.
FLEX
FLEX
GOOD JOB. LOOKS LIKE YOU'VE TAKEN THE TIME TO TRAIN YOUR POKÉMON WELL.
BUT NO MATTER HOW STRONG OR HOW FAST THEY'VE BECOME, IT'S NO DEFENSE AGAINST A POKÉMON USING THE SOFT AND FLEXIBLE FIGHT-ING STYLE!!

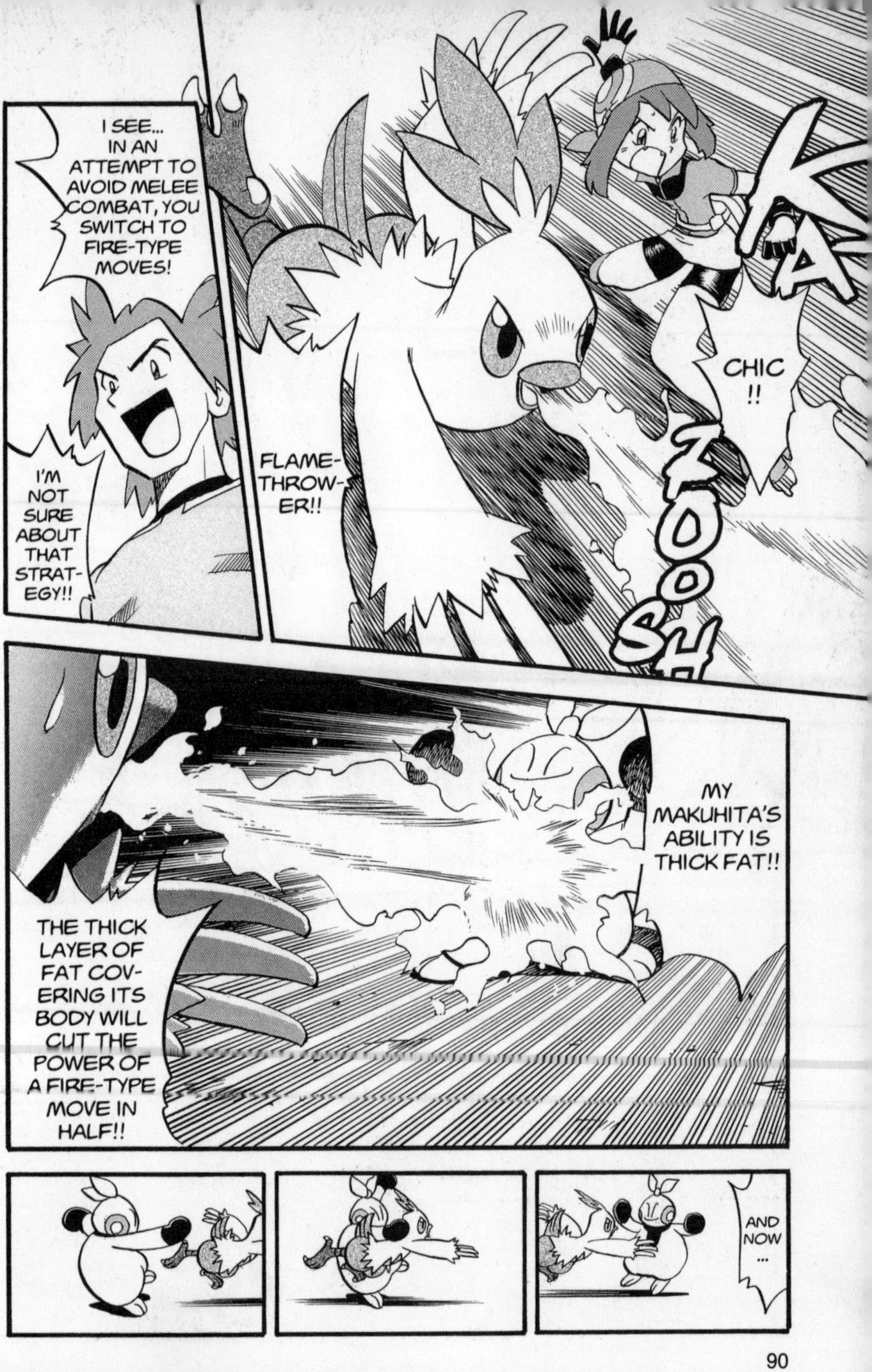
KA
CHIC !!
ZOOSH
FLAME-THROWER!!
I SEE... IN AN ATTEMPT TO AVOID MELEE COMBAT, YOU SWITCH TO FIRE-TYPE MOVES!
I'M NOT SURE ABOUT THAT STRATEGY!!
MY MAKUHITA'S ABILITY IS THICK FAT!!
THE THICK LAYER OF FAT COVERING ITS BODY WILL CUT THE POWER OF A FIRE-TYPE MOVE IN HALF!!
AND NOW ...

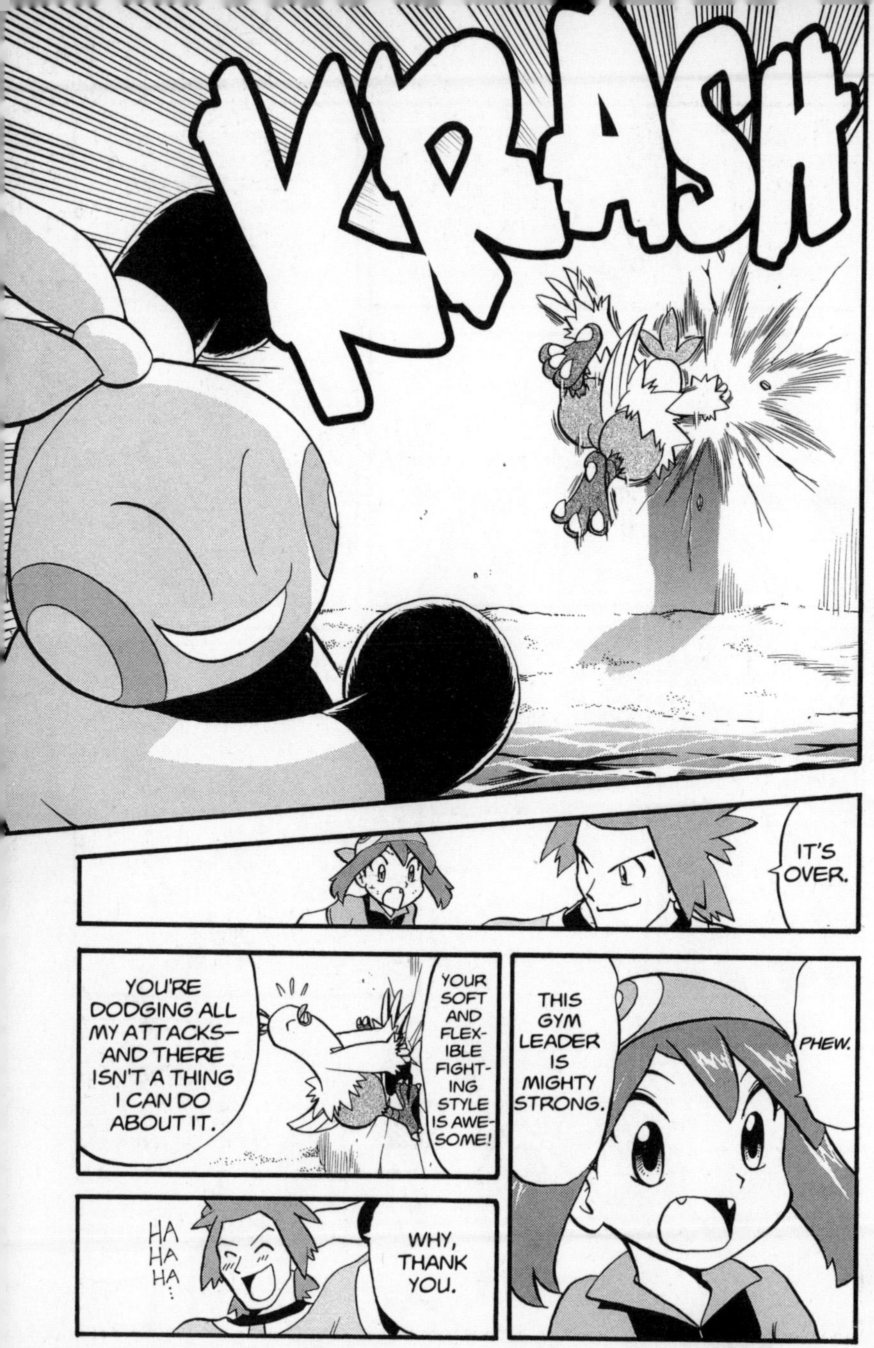
KRASH
IT'S OVER.
PHEW.
THIS GYM LEADER IS MIGHTY STRONG.
YOUR SOFT AND FLEX-IBLE FIGHT-ING STYLE IS AWE-SOME!
YOU'RE DODGING ALL MY ATTACKS—AND THERE ISN'T A THING I CAN DO ABOUT IT.
WHY, THANK YOU.
HA HA HA...

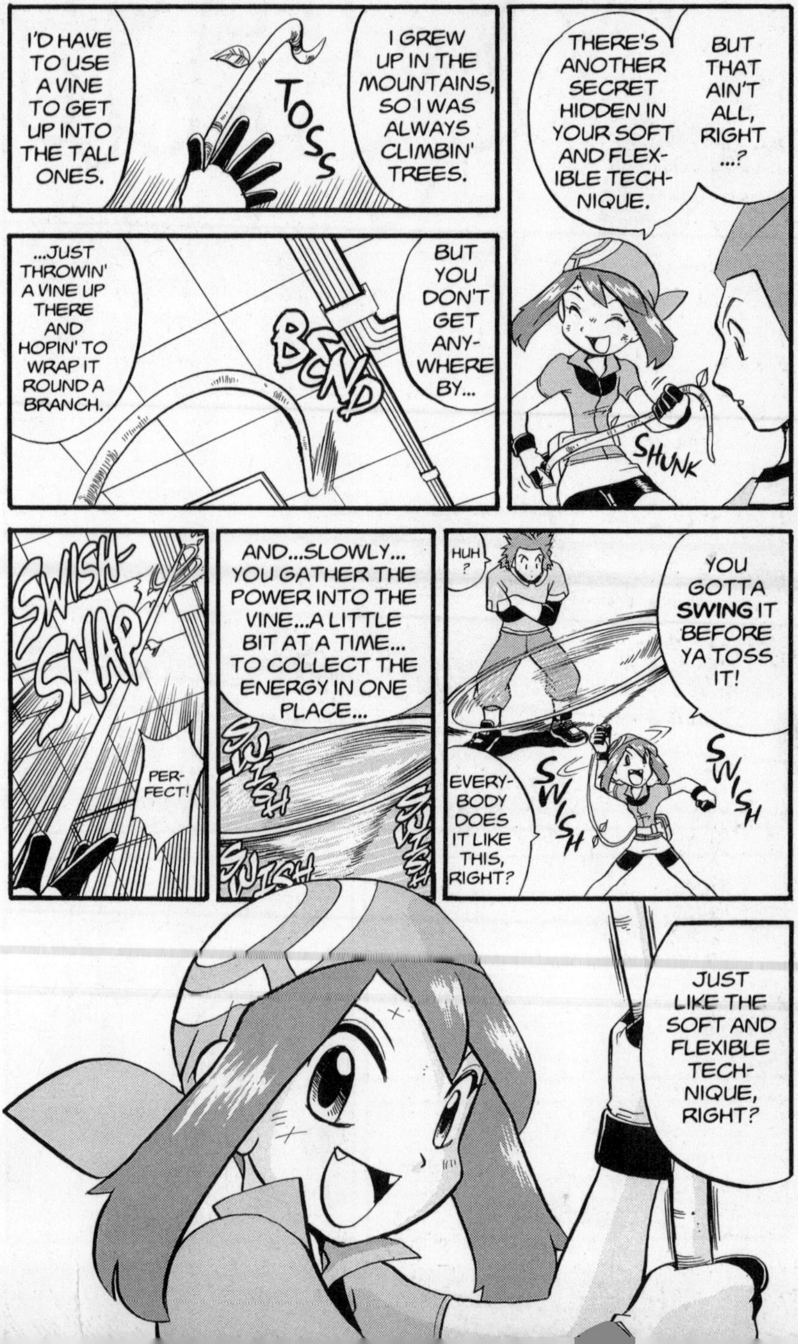
BUT THAT AIN'T ALL, RIGHT ...?
THERE'S ANOTHER SECRET HIDDEN IN YOUR SOFT AND FLEXIBLE TECHNIQUE.
SHUNK
I GREW UP IN THE MOUNTAINS, SO I WAS ALWAYS CLIMBIN' TREES.
TOSS
I'D HAVE TO USE A VINE TO GET UP INTO THE TALL ONES.
BUT YOU DON'T GET ANYWHERE BY...
BEND
...JUST THROWIN' A VINE UP THERE AND HOPIN' TO WRAP IT ROUND A BRANCH.
YOU GOTTA SWING IT BEFORE YA TOSS IT!
HUH?
SWISH
SWISH
EVERYBODY DOES IT LIKE THIS, RIGHT?
AND...SLOWLY... YOU GATHER THE POWER INTO THE VINE...A LITTLE BIT AT A TIME... TO COLLECT THE ENERGY IN ONE PLACE...
SWISH-SNAP
PERFECT!
JUST LIKE THE SOFT AND FLEXIBLE TECHNIQUE, RIGHT?

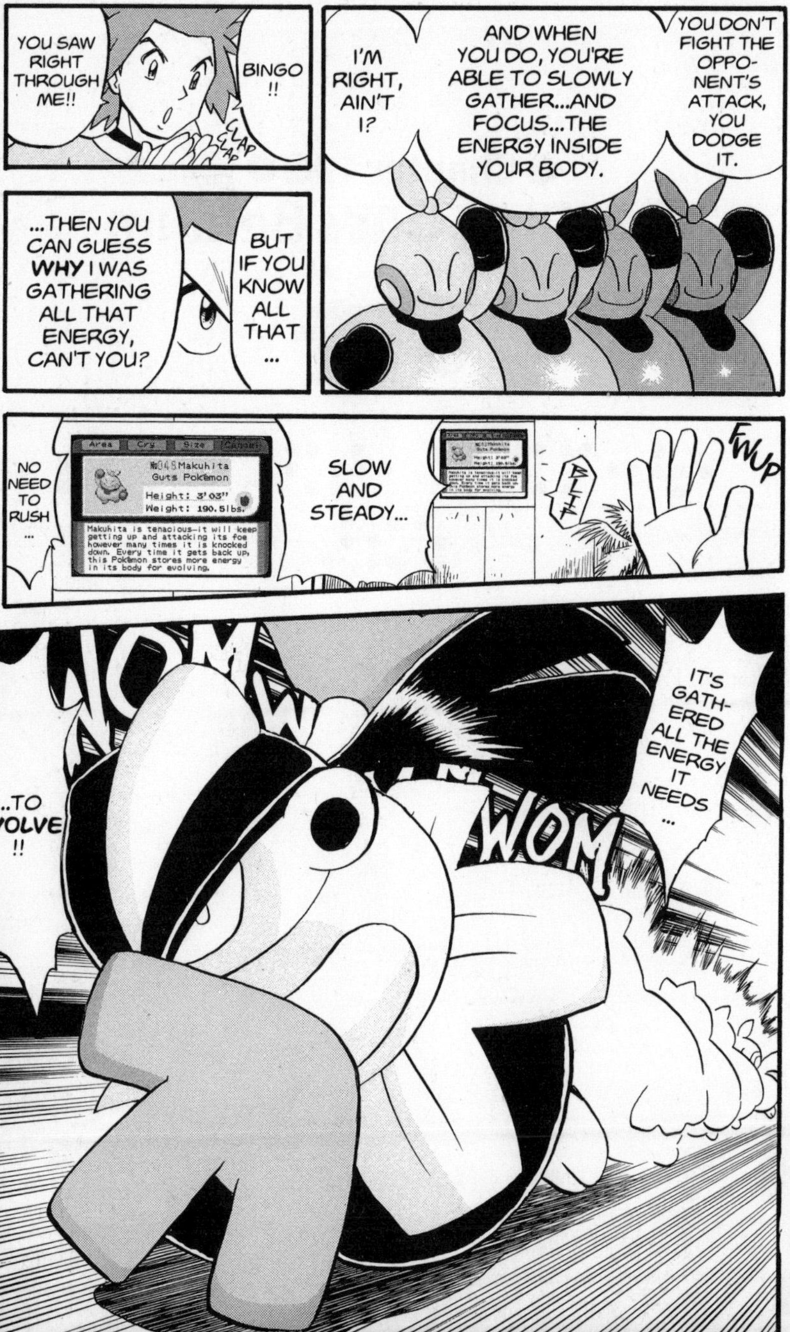
YOU DON'T FIGHT THE OPPO-NENT'S ATTACK, YOU DODGE IT.
AND WHEN YOU DO, YOU'RE ABLE TO SLOWLY GATHER...AND FOCUS...THE ENERGY INSIDE YOUR BODY.
I'M RIGHT, AIN'T I?
BINGO !!
YOU SAW RIGHT THROUGH ME!!
CLAP CLAP
BUT IF YOU KNOW ALL THAT ...
...THEN YOU CAN GUESS **WHY** I WAS GATHERING ALL THAT ENERGY, CAN'T YOU?
FWUP
BLIP
SLOW AND STEADY...
NO NEED TO RUSH ...
Area Cry Size
No048 Makuhita
Guts Pokémon
Height: 3'03"
Weight: 190.5lbs.
Makuhita is tenacious—it will keep getting up and attacking its foe however many times it is knocked down. Every time it gets back up, this Pokémon stores more energy in its body for evolving.
WOM
WOM
WOM
IT'S GATH-ERED ALL THE ENERGY IT NEEDS ...
...TO **EVOLVE** !!

● Chapter 196 ●
Ring Ring Goes Beldum

Pokémon Adventures Ruby & Sapphire
The Fourth Chapter

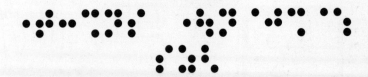

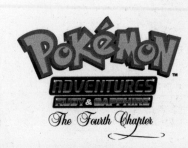

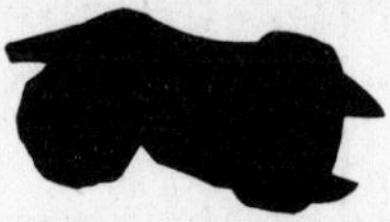

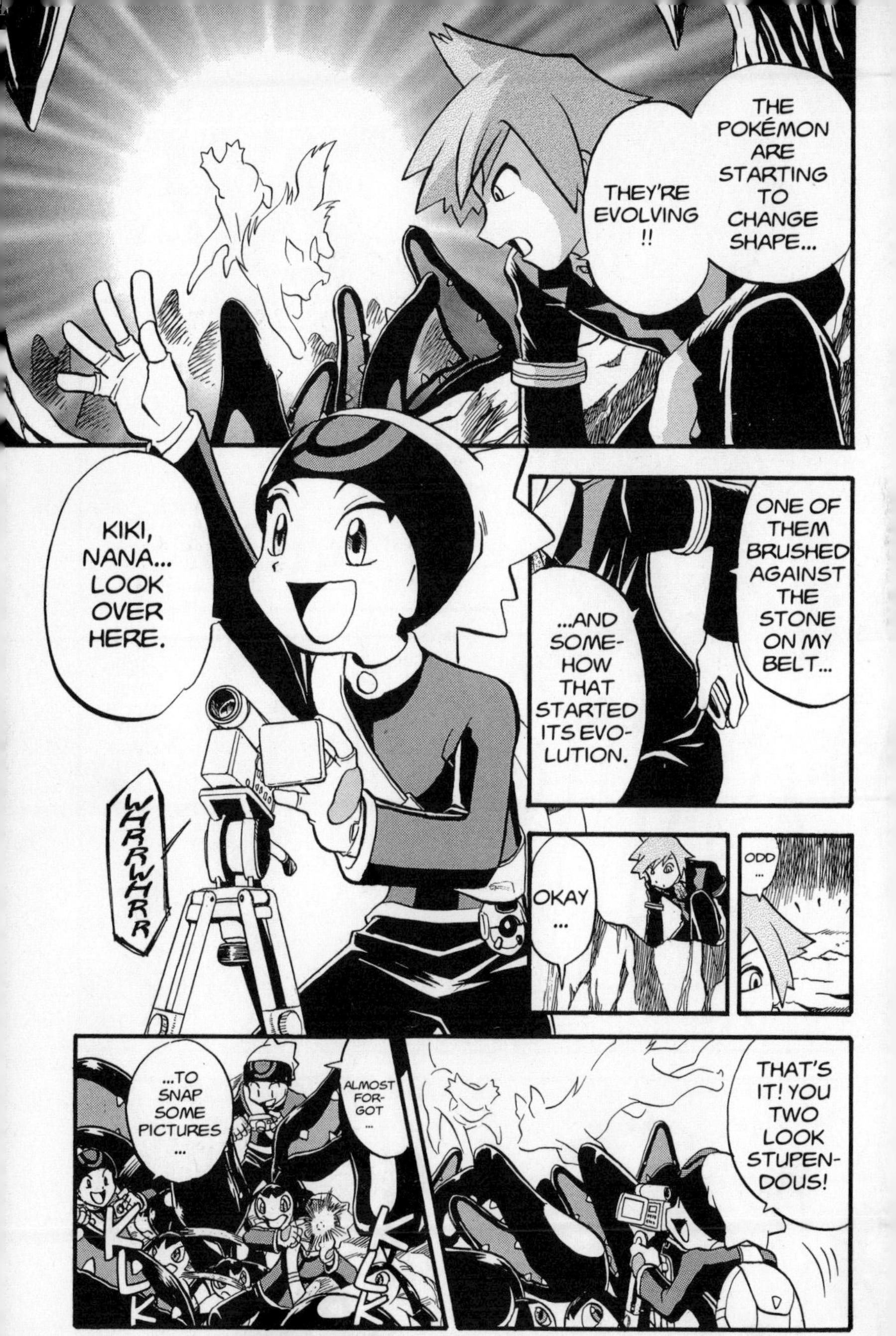
THE POKÉMON ARE STARTING TO CHANGE SHAPE...
THEY'RE EVOLVING !!
ONE OF THEM BRUSHED AGAINST THE STONE ON MY BELT...
...AND SOME-HOW THAT STARTED ITS EVO-LUTION.
ODD ...
OKAY ...
KIKI, NANA... LOOK OVER HERE.
WHRRWHRR
THAT'S IT! YOU TWO LOOK STUPEN-DOUS!
ALMOST FOR-GOT ...
...TO SNAP SOME PICTURES ...
KLIK
KLIK

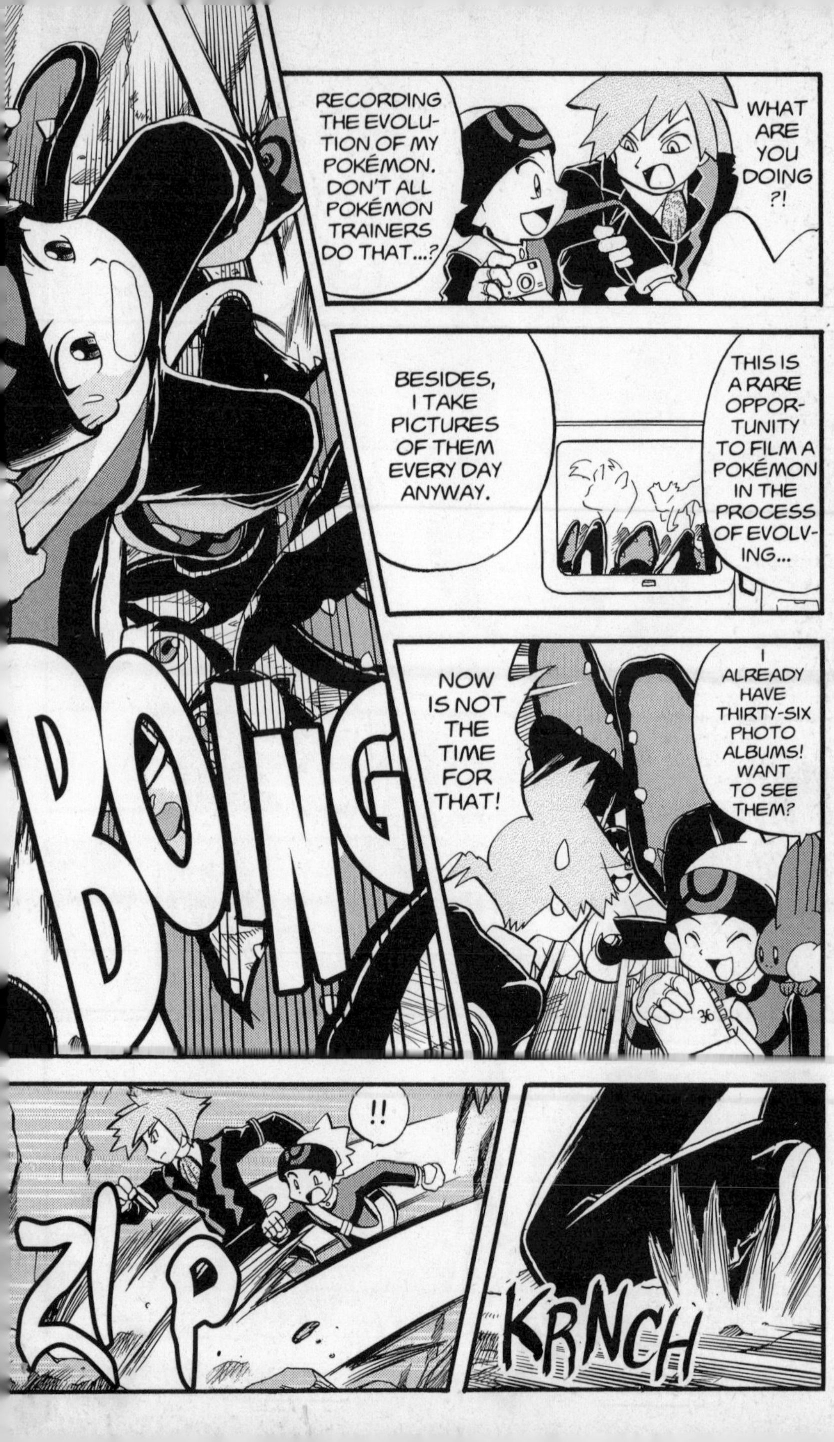
WHAT ARE YOU DOING?!
RECORDING THE EVOLUTION OF MY POKÉMON. DON'T ALL POKÉMON TRAINERS DO THAT...?
THIS IS A RARE OPPORTUNITY TO FILM A POKÉMON IN THE PROCESS OF EVOLVING...
BESIDES, I TAKE PICTURES OF THEM EVERY DAY ANYWAY.
I ALREADY HAVE THIRTY-SIX PHOTO ALBUMS! WANT TO SEE THEM?
36
NOW IS NOT THE TIME FOR THAT!
BOING
KRNCH
!!
ZIP

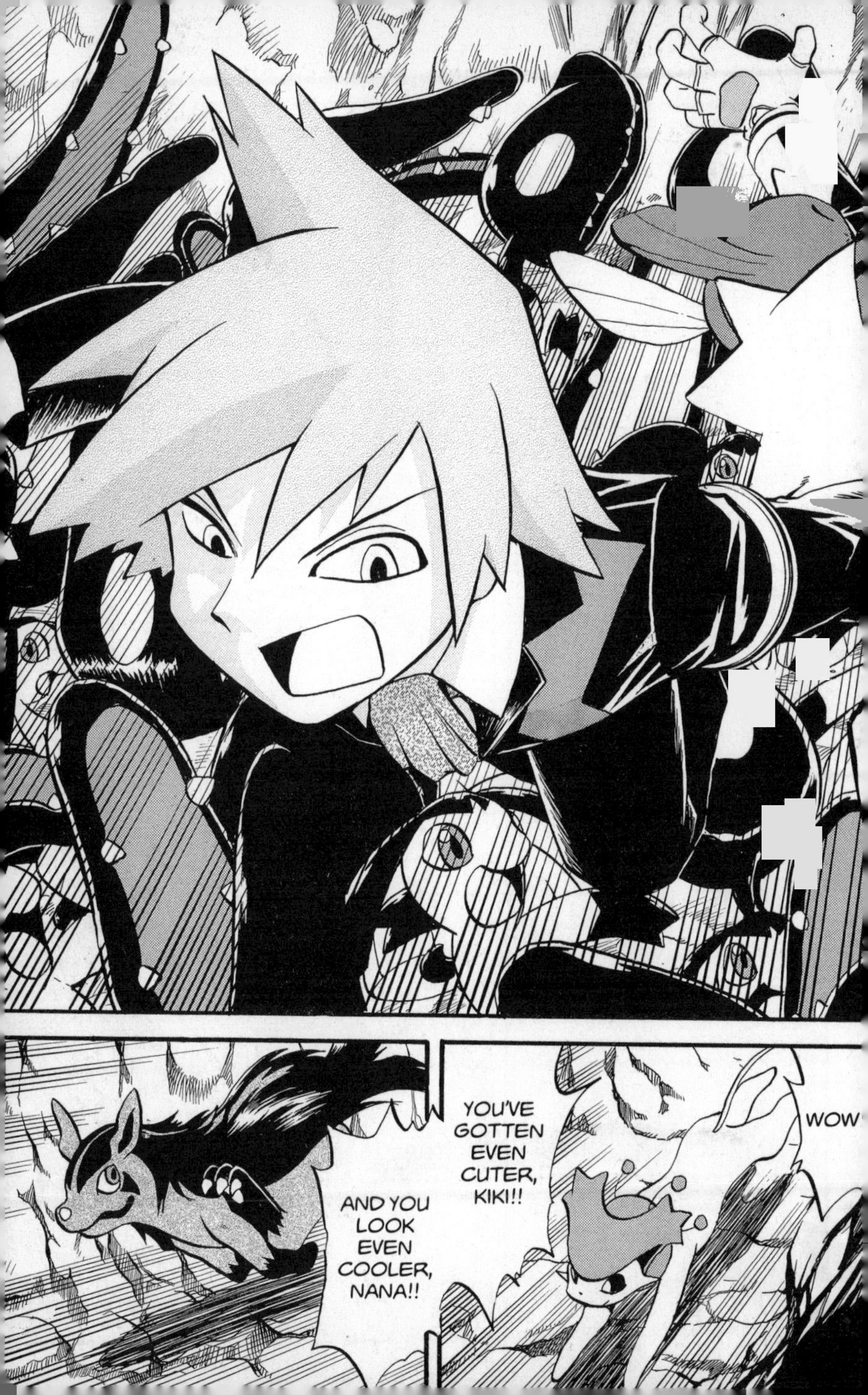
WOW
YOU'VE GOTTEN EVEN CUTER, KIKI!!
AND YOU LOOK EVEN COOLER, NANA!!

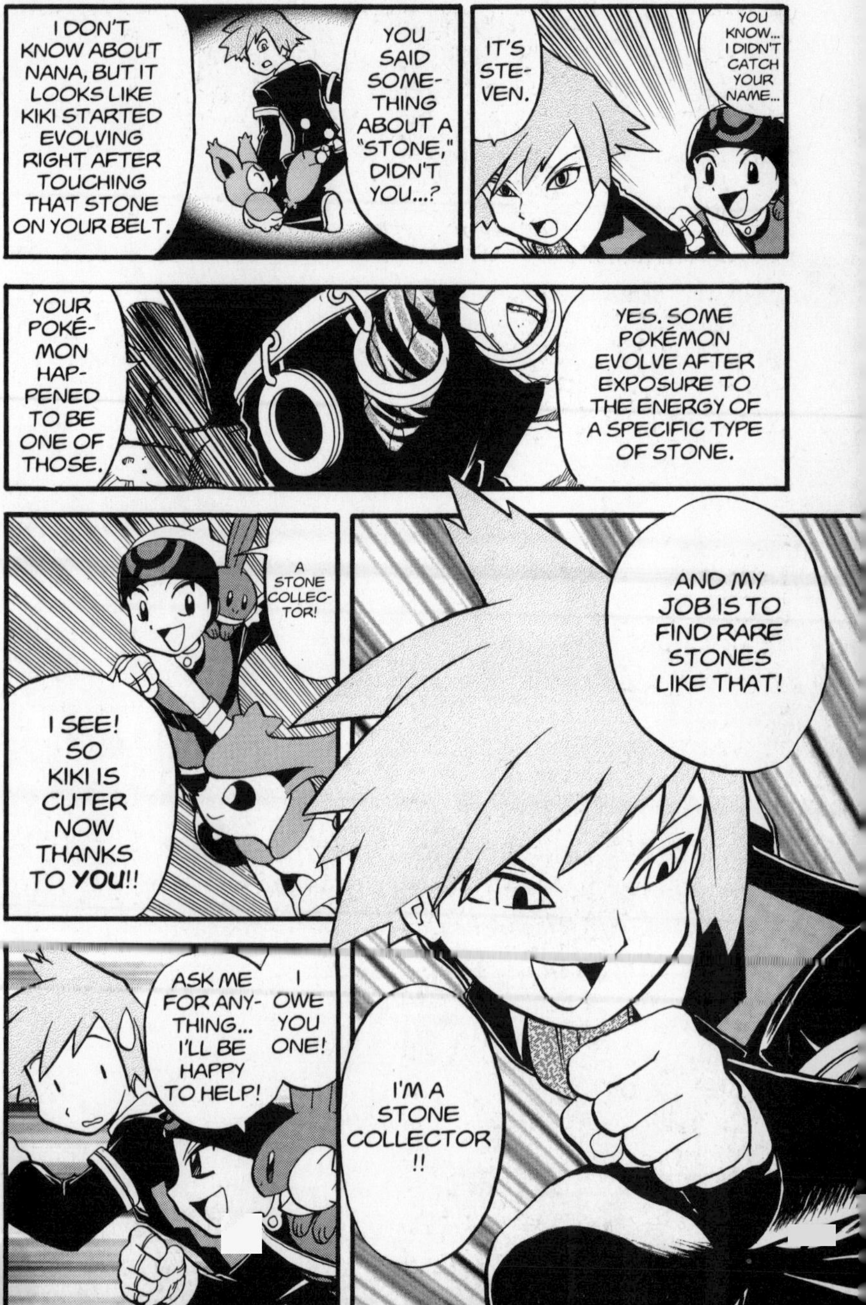
YOU KNOW... I DIDN'T CATCH YOUR NAME...
IT'S STE-VEN.
YOU SAID SOME-THING ABOUT A "STONE," DIDN'T YOU...?
I DON'T KNOW ABOUT NANA, BUT IT LOOKS LIKE KIKI STARTED EVOLVING RIGHT AFTER TOUCHING THAT STONE ON YOUR BELT.
YES. SOME POKÉMON EVOLVE AFTER EXPOSURE TO THE ENERGY OF A SPECIFIC TYPE OF STONE.
YOUR POKÉ-MON HAP-PENED TO BE ONE OF THOSE.
AND MY JOB IS TO FIND RARE STONES LIKE THAT!
I'M A STONE COLLECTOR!!
A STONE COLLEC-TOR!
I SEE! SO KIKI IS CUTER NOW THANKS TO **YOU**!!
I OWE YOU ONE!
ASK ME FOR ANY-THING... I'LL BE HAPPY TO HELP!

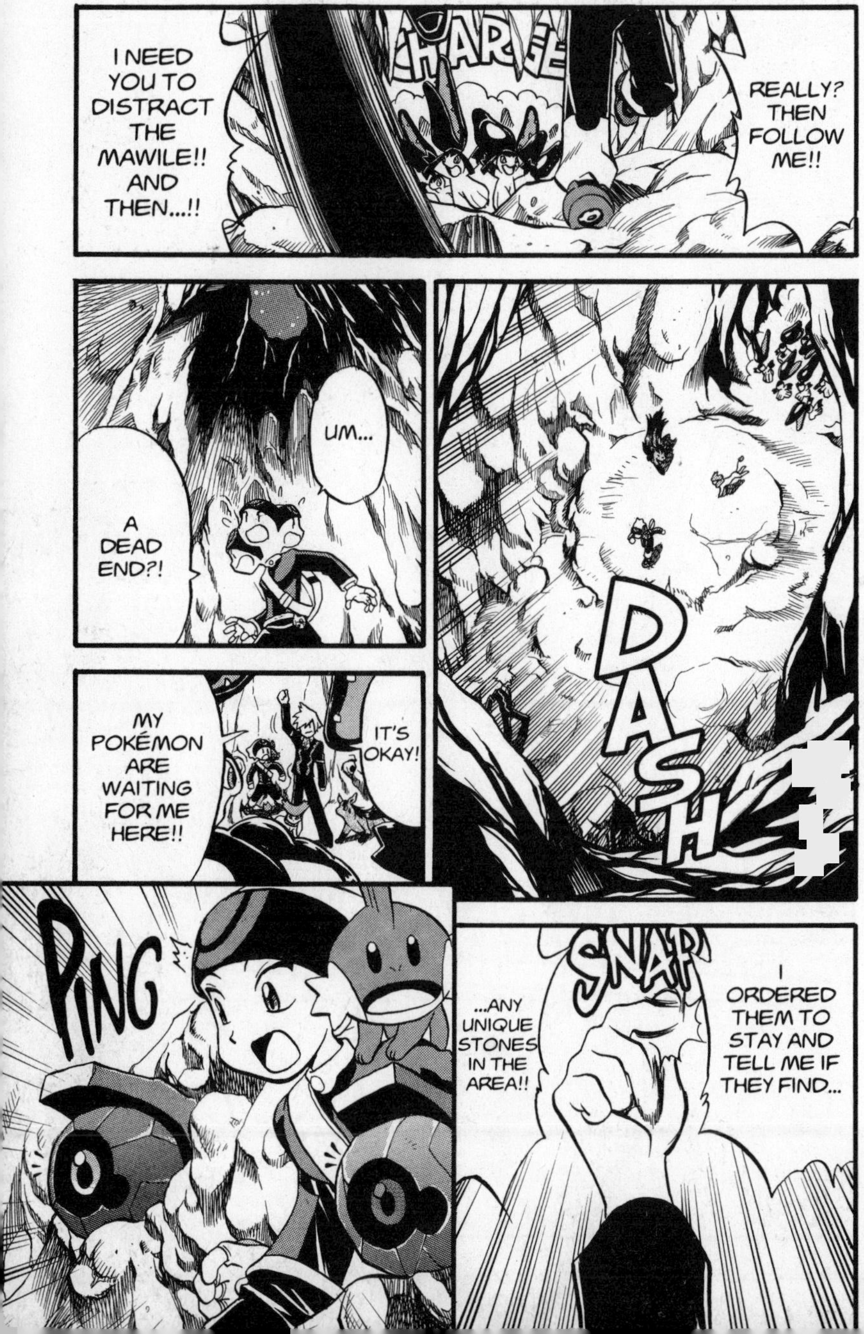
REALLY? THEN FOLLOW ME!!
CHARGE
I NEED YOU TO DISTRACT THE MAWILE!! AND THEN...!!
DASH
UM...
A DEAD END?!
IT'S OKAY!
MY POKÉMON ARE WAITING FOR ME HERE!!
SNAP
I ORDERED THEM TO STAY AND TELL ME IF THEY FIND...
...ANY UNIQUE STONES IN THE AREA!!
PING

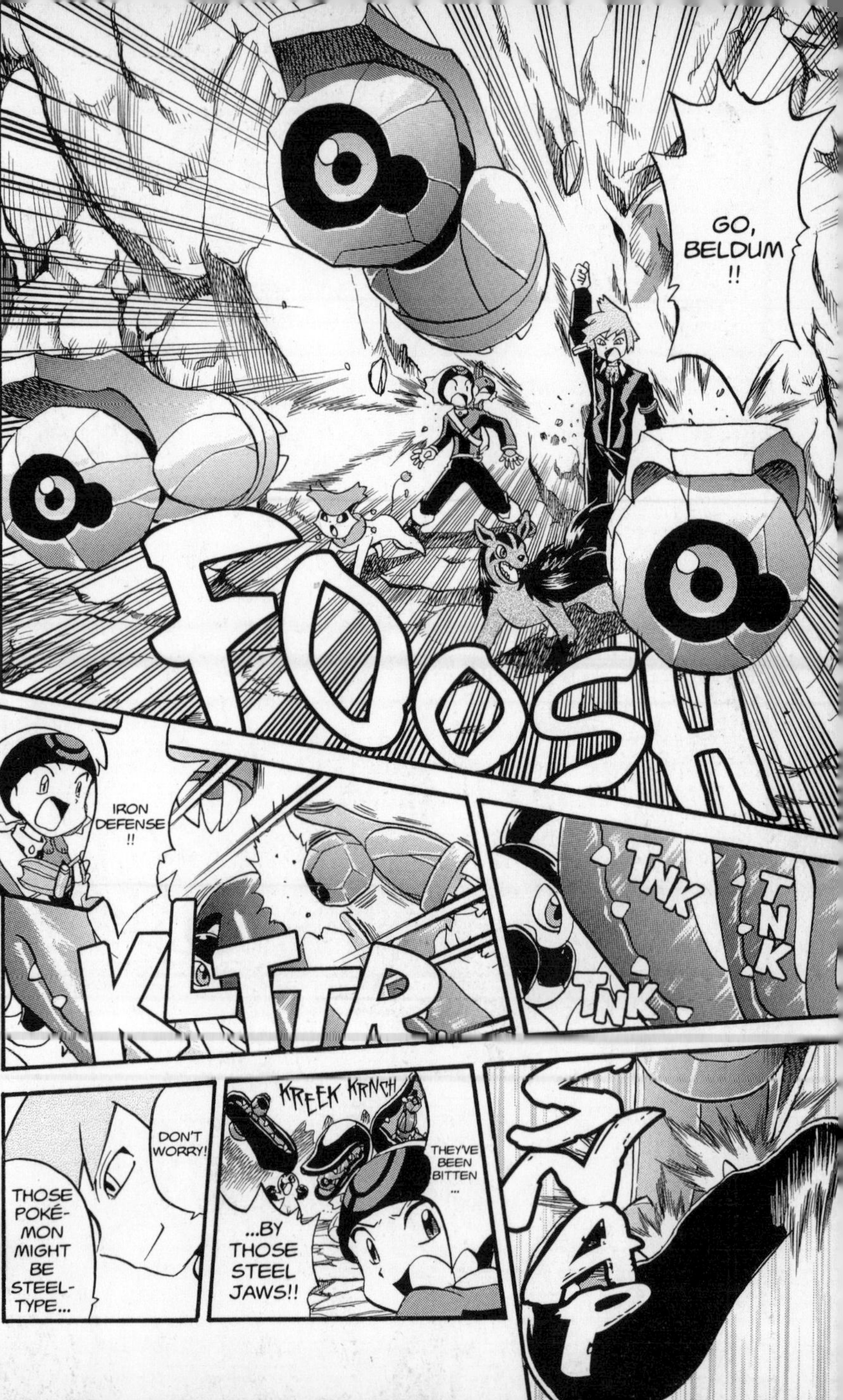
GO, BELDUM!!
FOOSH
TNK TNK TNK
IRON DEFENSE!!
KLTTR
SNAP
KREEK KRNCH
THEY'VE BEEN BITTEN...
...BY THOSE STEEL JAWS!!
DON'T WORRY!
THOSE POKÉMON MIGHT BE STEEL-TYPE...

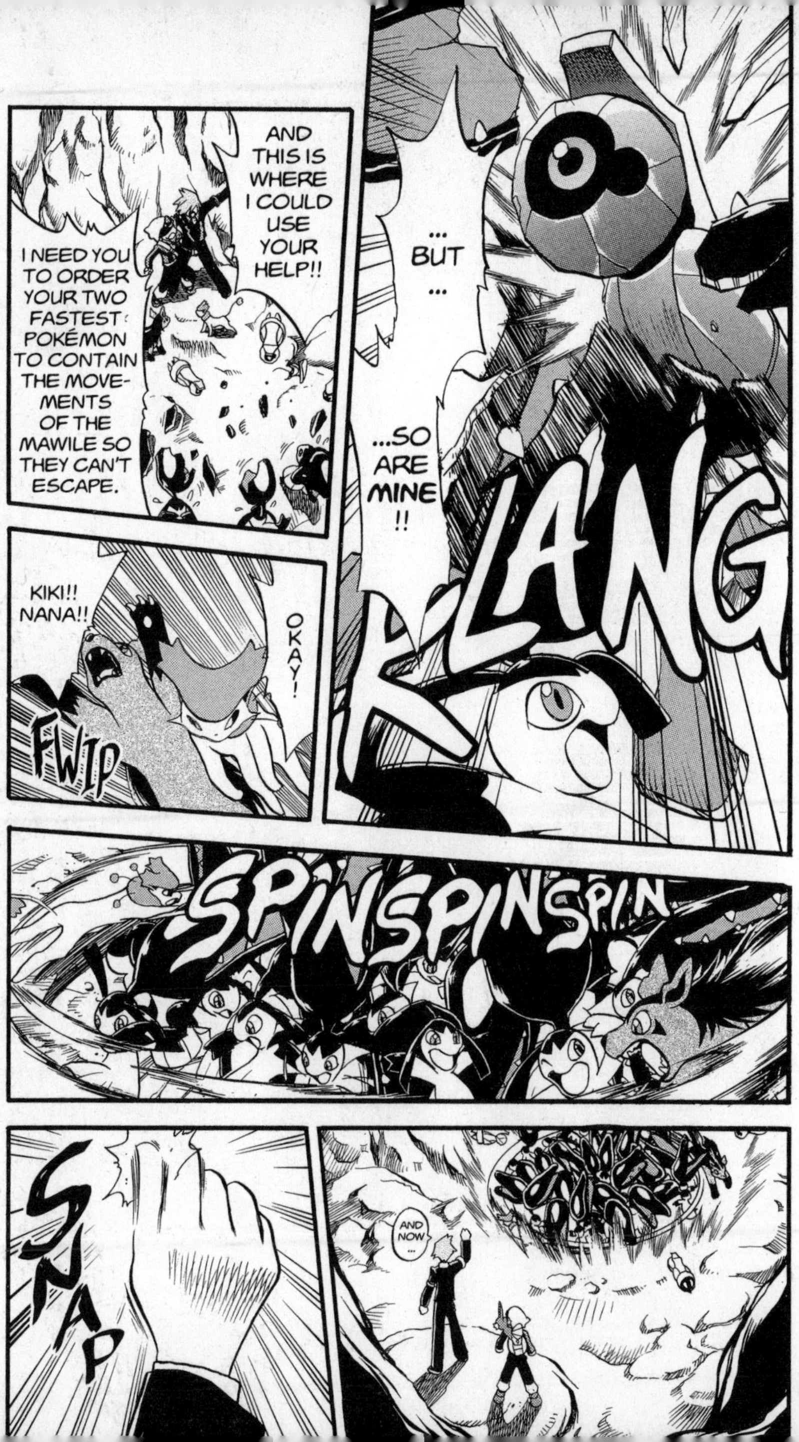
... BUT ...
...SO ARE MINE!!
KLANG
AND THIS IS WHERE I COULD USE YOUR HELP!!
I NEED YOU TO ORDER YOUR TWO FASTEST POKÉMON TO CONTAIN THE MOVEMENTS OF THE MAWILE SO THEY CAN'T ESCAPE.
KIKI!! NANA!!
OKAY!
FWIP
SPINSPINSPIN
AND NOW ...
SNAP

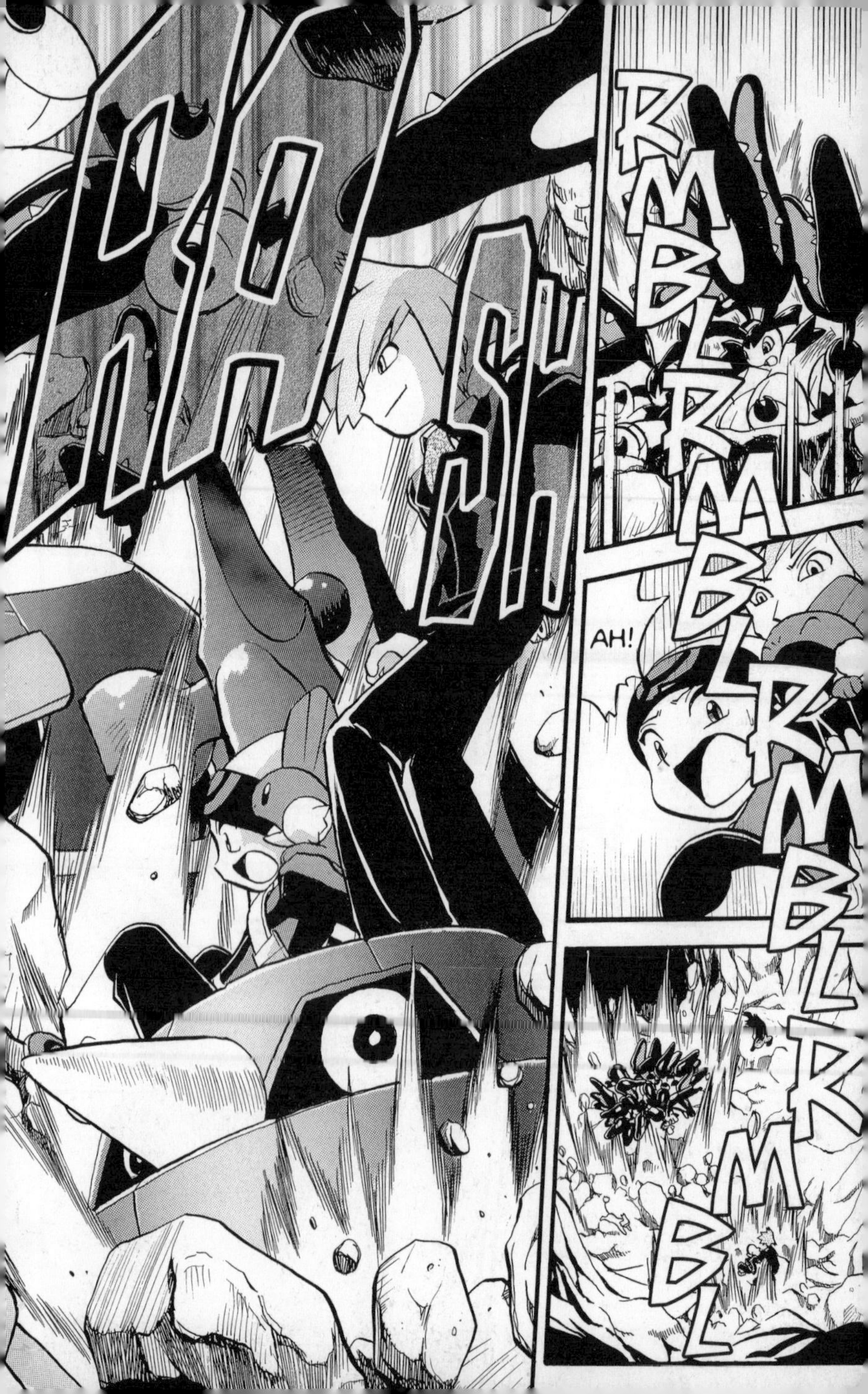
RMBLRMBLRMBLRMBLRMBL
AH!

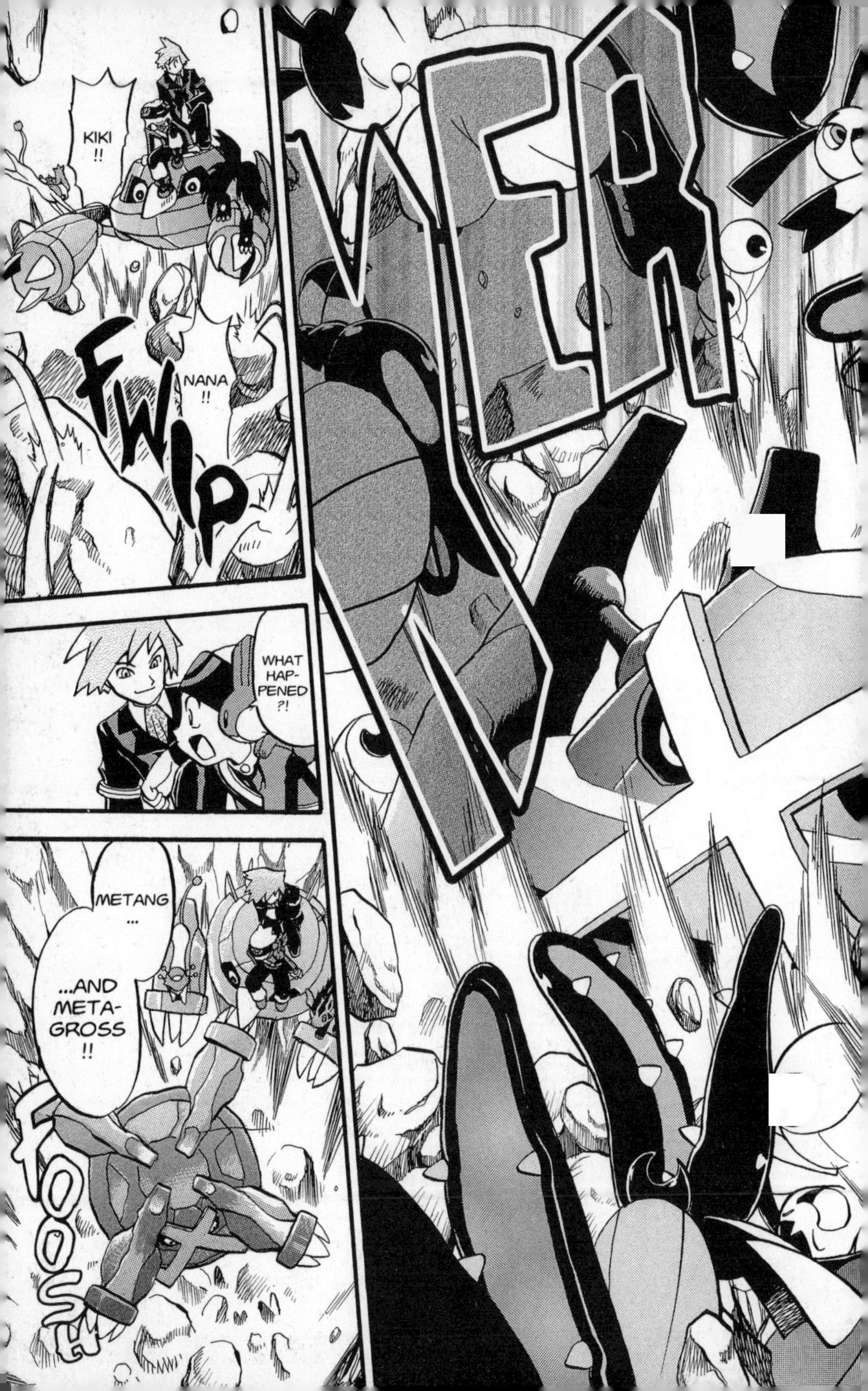
KIKI !!
NANA !!
FWIP
WHAT HAP-PENED ?!
METANG ...
...AND META-GROSS !!
FOOOSH

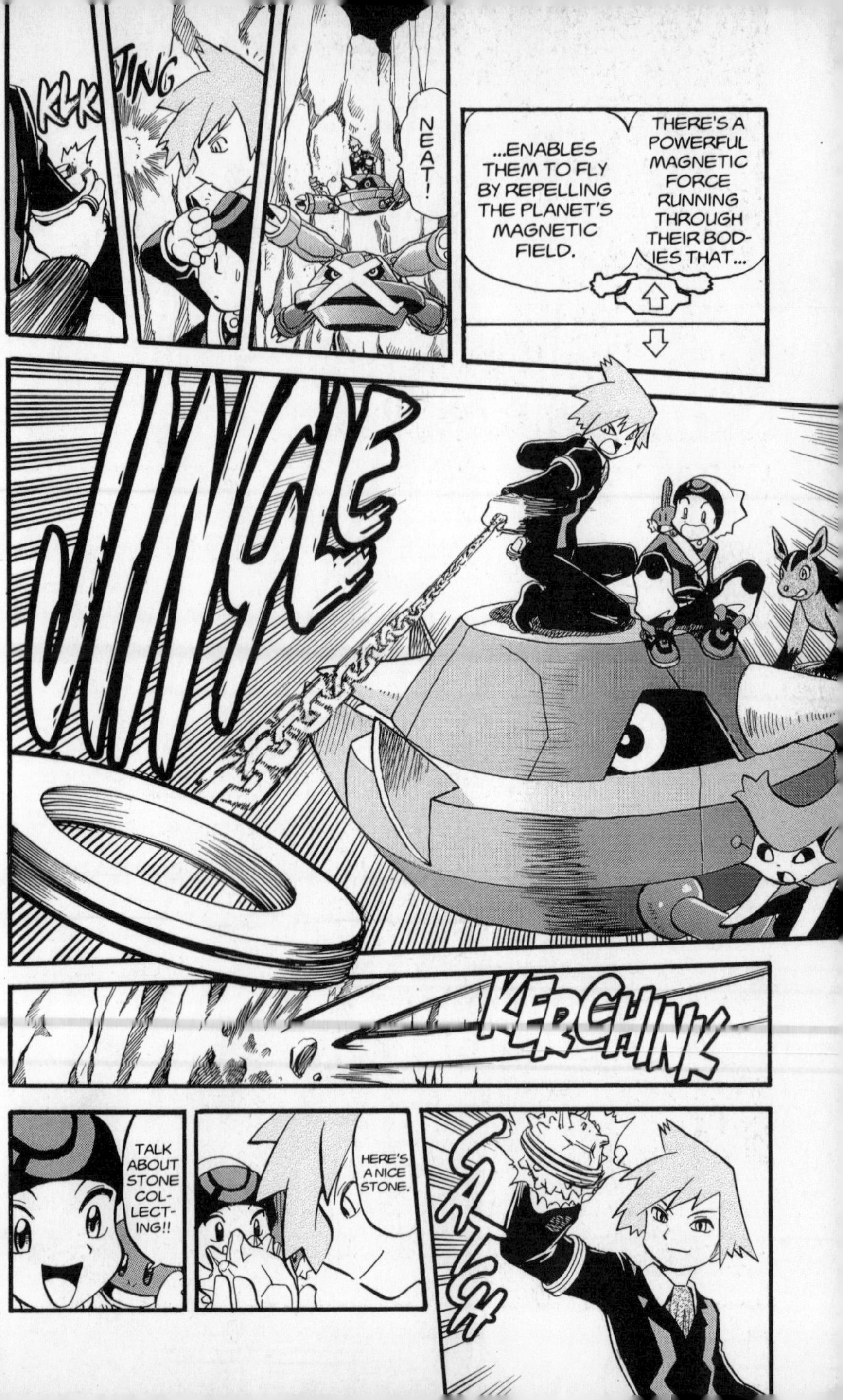
THERE'S A POWERFUL MAGNETIC FORCE RUNNING THROUGH THEIR BODIES THAT...
...ENABLES THEM TO FLY BY REPELLING THE PLANET'S MAGNETIC FIELD.
NEAT!
JING
KLK
JINGLE
KERCHINK
CATCH
HERE'S A NICE STONE.
TALK ABOUT STONE COLLECTING!!

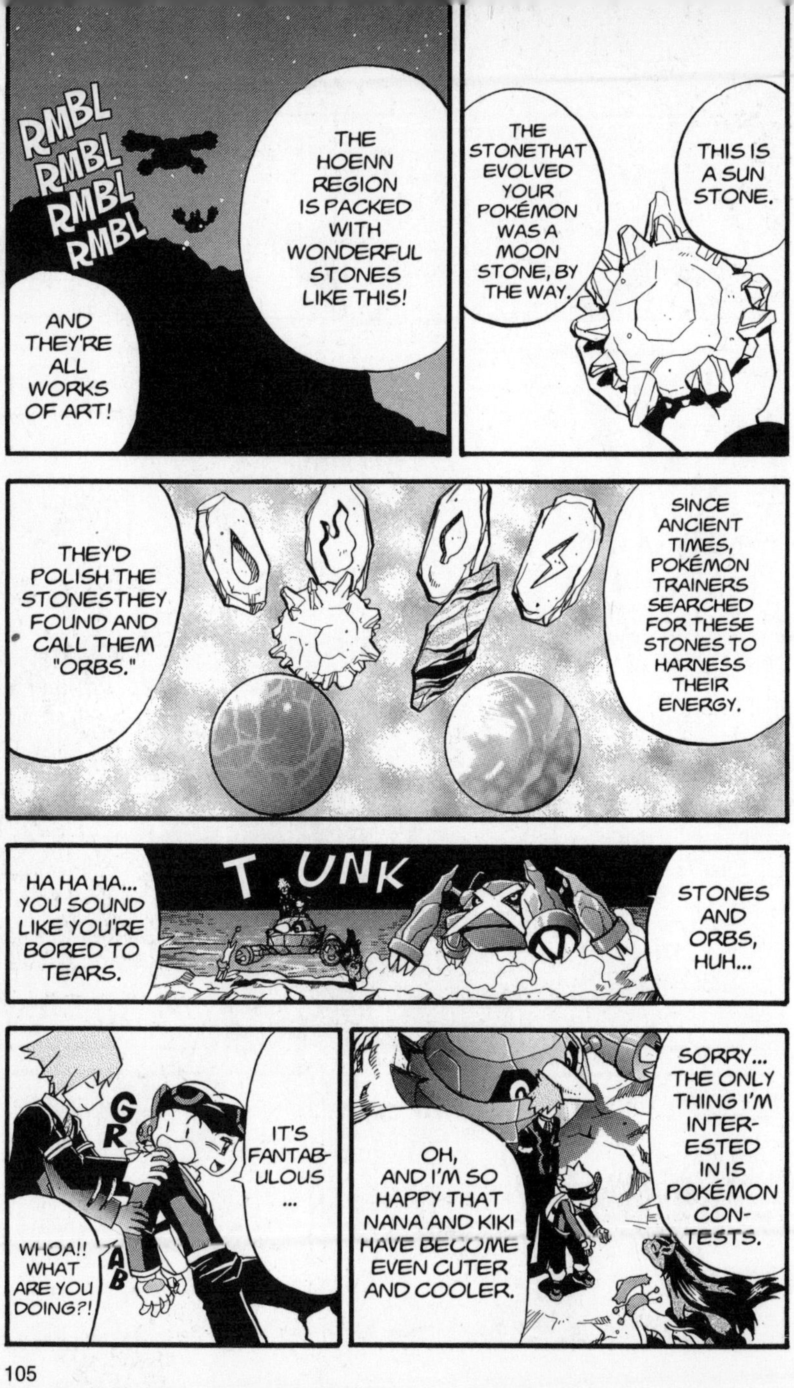
THIS IS A SUN STONE.
THE STONE THAT EVOLVED YOUR POKÉMON WAS A MOON STONE, BY THE WAY.
RMBL RMBL RMBL RMBL
THE HOENN REGION IS PACKED WITH WONDERFUL STONES LIKE THIS!
AND THEY'RE ALL WORKS OF ART!
SINCE ANCIENT TIMES, POKÉMON TRAINERS SEARCHED FOR THESE STONES TO HARNESS THEIR ENERGY.
THEY'D POLISH THE STONES THEY FOUND AND CALL THEM "ORBS."
STONES AND ORBS, HUH...
TUNK
HA HA HA... YOU SOUND LIKE YOU'RE BORED TO TEARS.
SORRY... THE ONLY THING I'M INTERESTED IN IS POKÉMON CONTESTS.
OH, AND I'M SO HAPPY THAT NANA AND KIKI HAVE BECOME EVEN CUTER AND COOLER.
IT'S FANTABULOUS...
GRAB
WHOA!! WHAT ARE YOU DOING?!

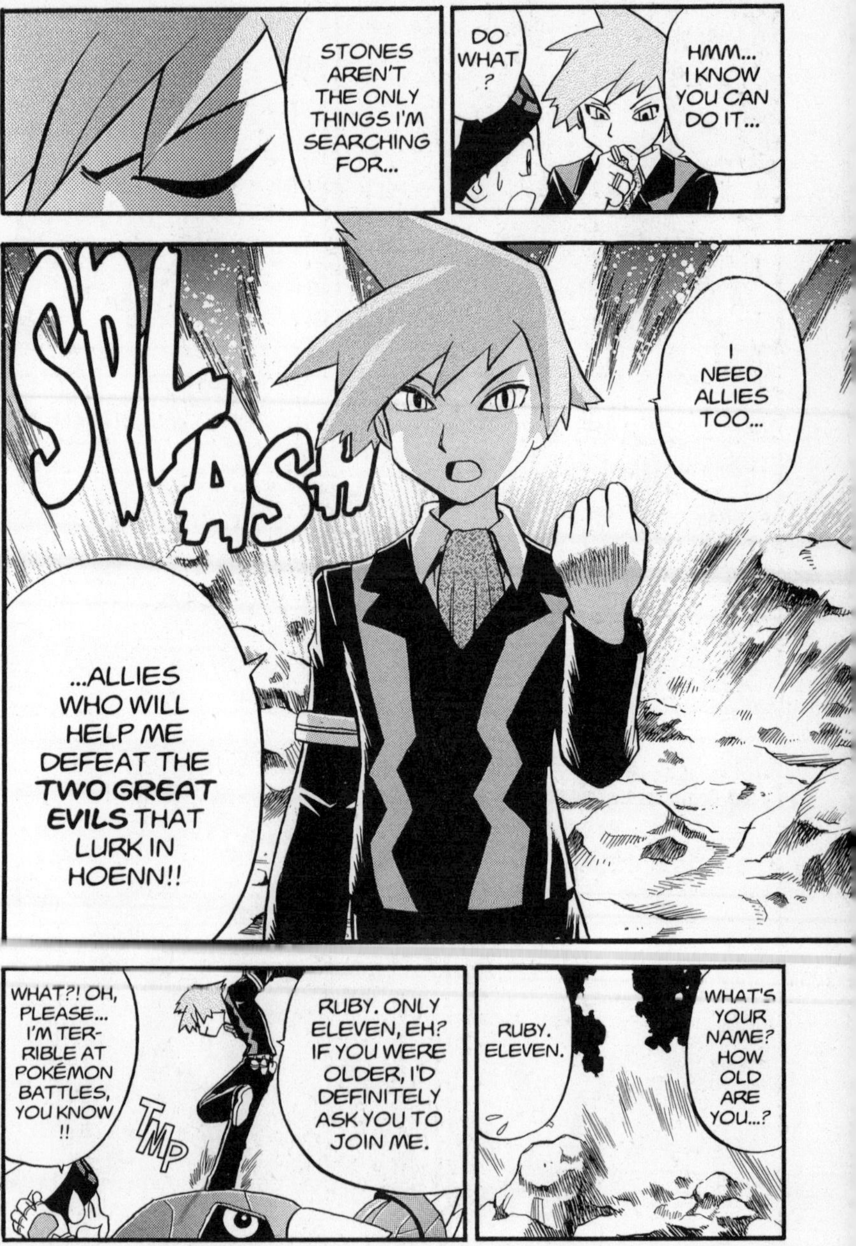
HMM... I KNOW YOU CAN DO IT...
DO WHAT?
STONES AREN'T THE ONLY THINGS I'M SEARCHING FOR...
I NEED ALLIES TOO...
SPLASH
...ALLIES WHO WILL HELP ME DEFEAT THE **TWO GREAT EVILS** THAT LURK IN HOENN!!
WHAT'S YOUR NAME? HOW OLD ARE YOU...?
RUBY. ELEVEN.
RUBY. ONLY ELEVEN, EH? IF YOU WERE OLDER, I'D DEFINITELY ASK YOU TO JOIN ME.
TMP
WHAT?! OH, PLEASE... I'M TER-RIBLE AT POKÉMON BATTLES, YOU KNOW!!

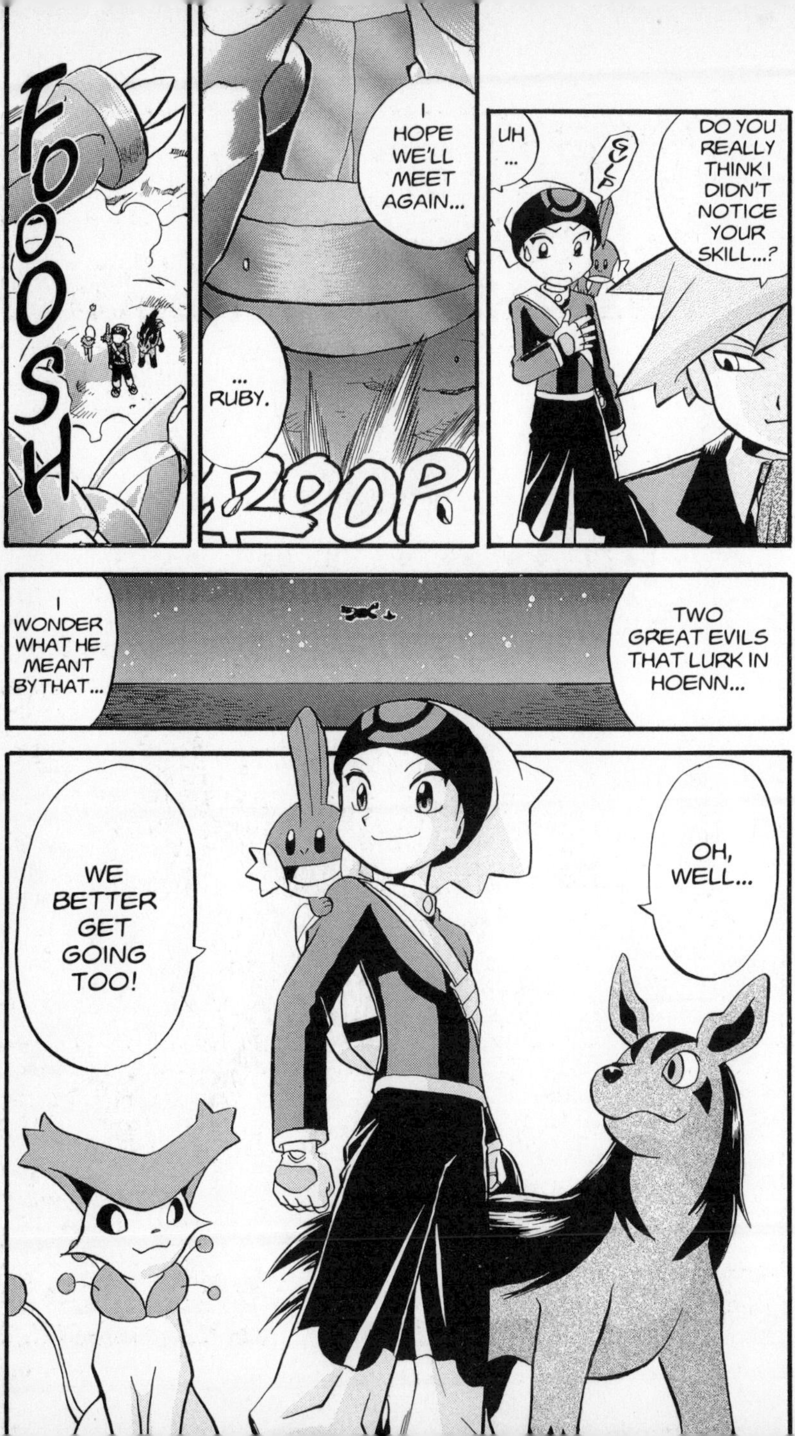
DO YOU REALLY THINK I DIDN'T NOTICE YOUR SKILL...?
UH ...
GULP
I HOPE WE'LL MEET AGAIN...
... RUBY.
ZOOP
FOOOSH
TWO GREAT EVILS THAT LURK IN HOENN...
I WONDER WHAT HE MEANT BY THAT...
OH, WELL...
WE BETTER GET GOING TOO!

● Chapter 197 ●
Heavy Hitting Hariyama

Pokémon™ Adventures Ruby & Sapphire
The Fourth Chapter

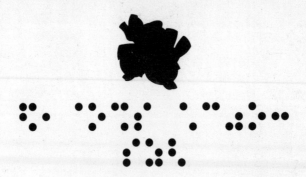

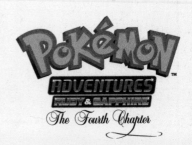

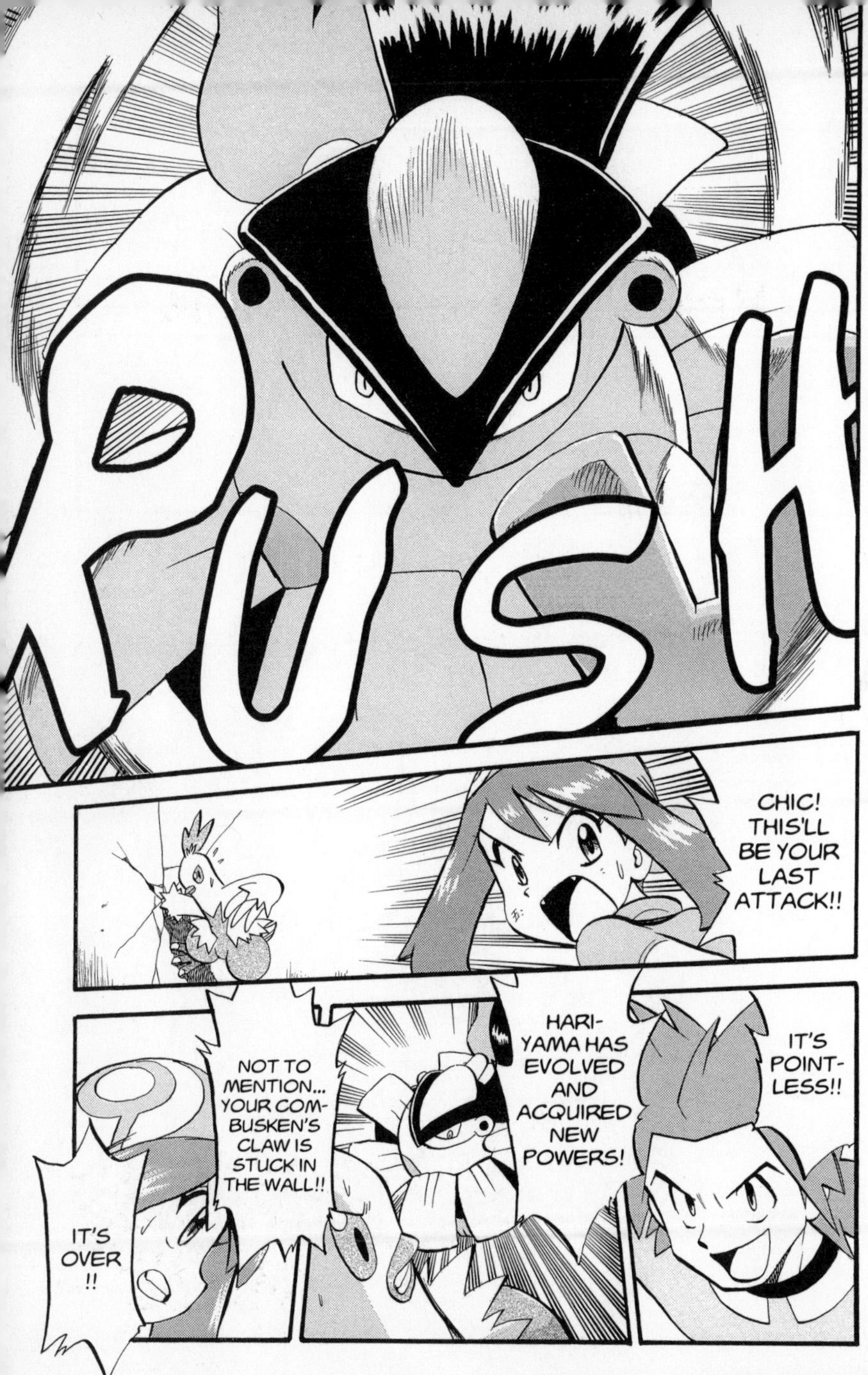
RUSH
CHIC! THIS'LL BE YOUR LAST ATTACK!!
IT'S POINTLESS!!
HARIYAMA HAS EVOLVED AND ACQUIRED NEW POWERS!
NOT TO MENTION... YOUR COMBUSKEN'S CLAW IS STUCK IN THE WALL!!
IT'S OVER!!

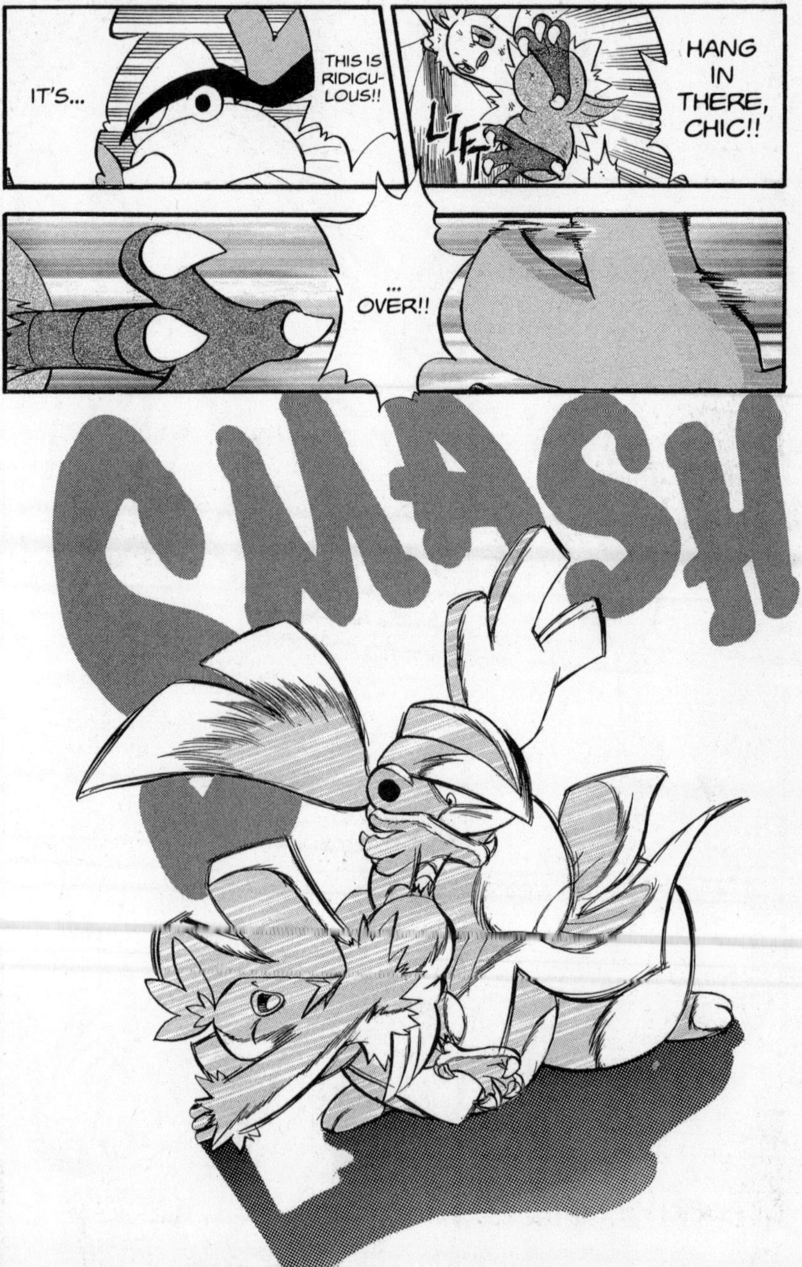
HANG IN THERE, CHIC!!
LIFT
THIS IS RIDICULOUS!!
IT'S...
...OVER!!
SMASH

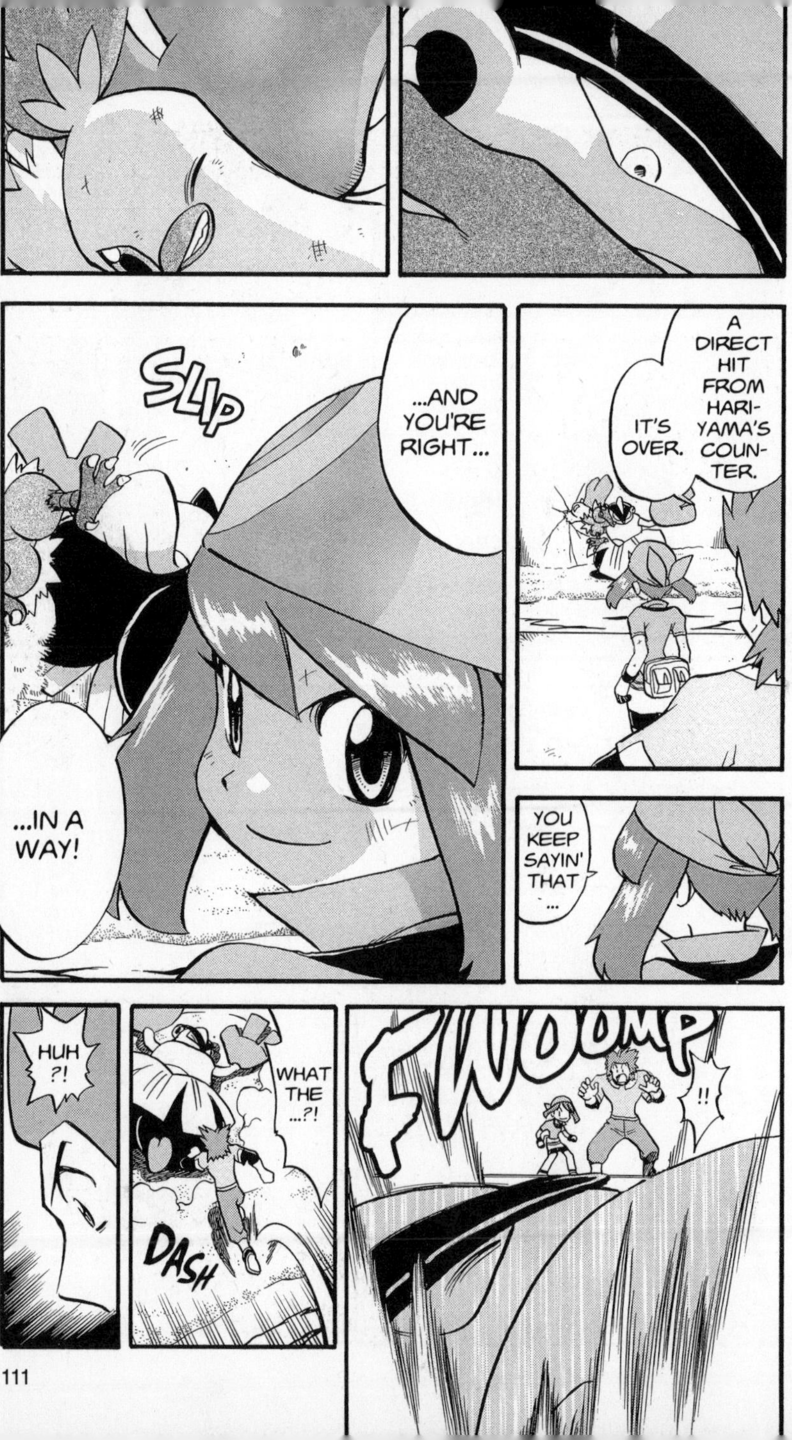
A DIRECT HIT FROM HARIYAMA'S COUNTER.
IT'S OVER.
YOU KEEP SAYIN' THAT...
...AND YOU'RE RIGHT...
SLIP
...IN A WAY!
FWOOMP
!!
WHAT THE ...?!
DASH
HUH ?!

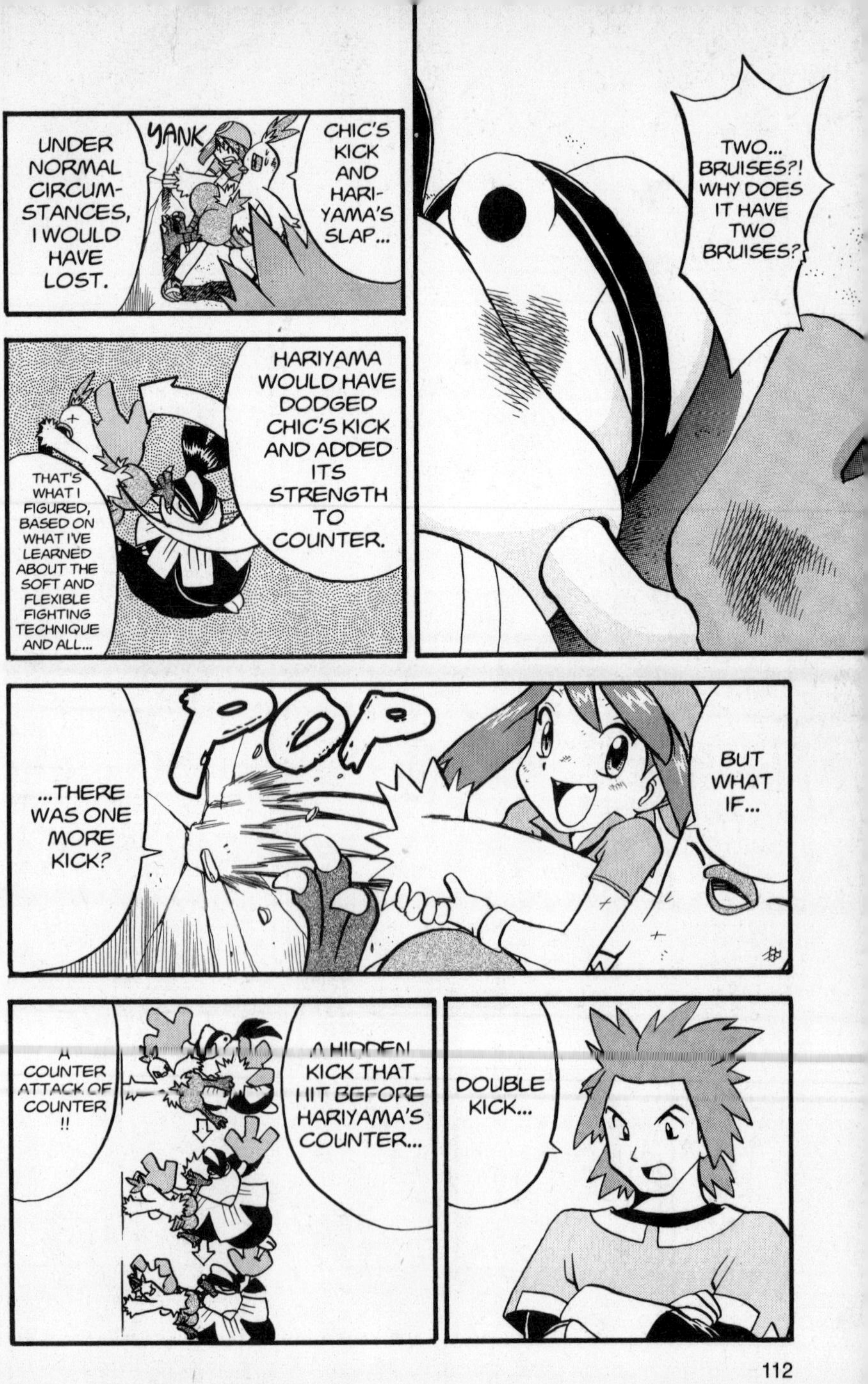
TWO... BRUISES?! WHY DOES IT HAVE TWO BRUISES?
CHIC'S KICK AND HARI-YAMA'S SLAP...
YANK
UNDER NORMAL CIRCUM-STANCES, I WOULD HAVE LOST.
HARIYAMA WOULD HAVE DODGED CHIC'S KICK AND ADDED ITS STRENGTH TO COUNTER.
THAT'S WHAT I FIGURED, BASED ON WHAT I'VE LEARNED ABOUT THE SOFT AND FLEXIBLE FIGHTING TECHNIQUE AND ALL...
BUT WHAT IF...
POP
...THERE WAS ONE MORE KICK?
DOUBLE KICK...
A HIDDEN KICK THAT HIT BEFORE HARIYAMA'S COUNTER...
A COUNTER ATTACK OF COUNTER !!

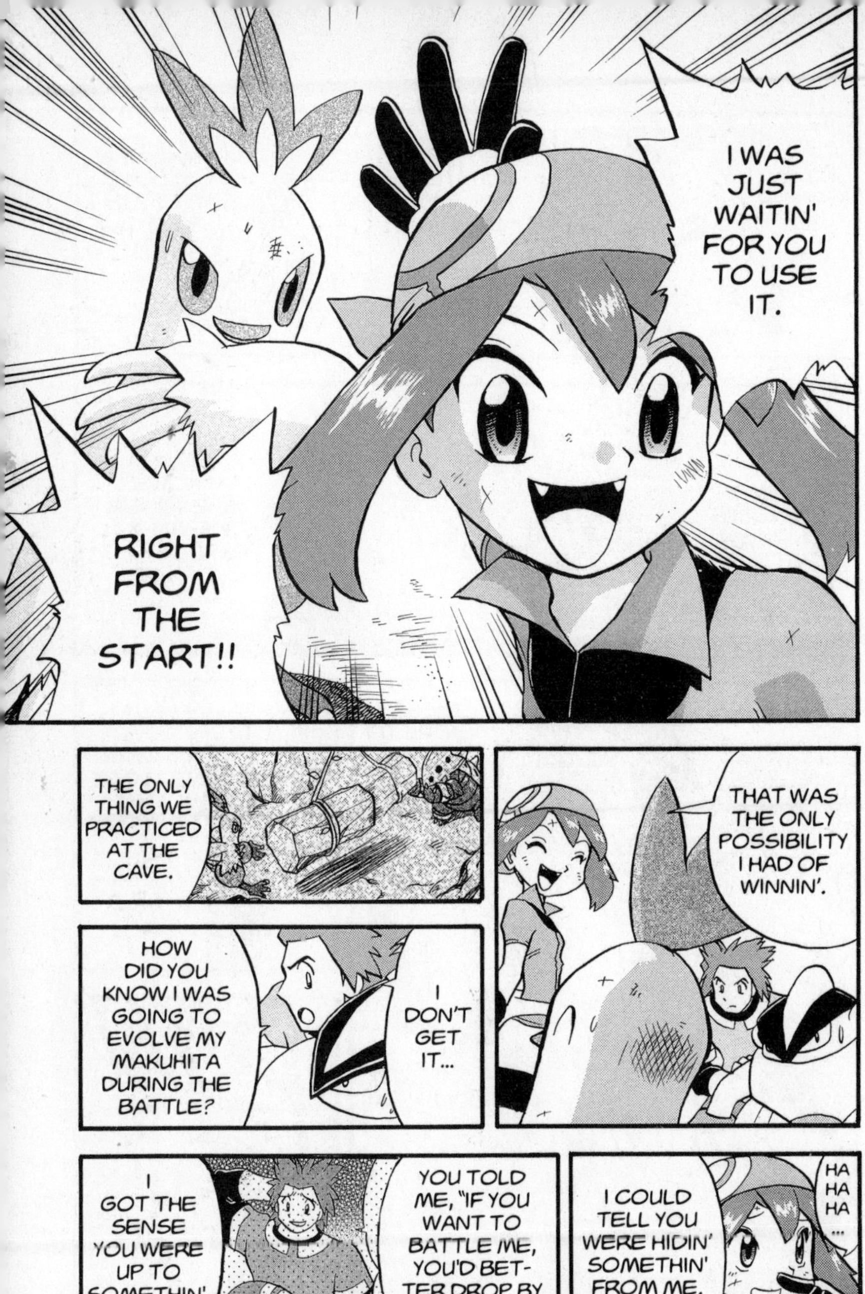
I WAS JUST WAITIN' FOR YOU TO USE IT.
RIGHT FROM THE START!!
THAT WAS THE ONLY POSSIBILITY I HAD OF WINNIN'.
THE ONLY THING WE PRACTICED AT THE CAVE.
I DON'T GET IT...
HOW DID YOU KNOW I WAS GOING TO EVOLVE MY MAKUHITA DURING THE BATTLE?
HA HA HA...
I COULD TELL YOU WERE HIDIN' SOMETHIN' FROM ME.
YOU TOLD ME, "IF YOU WANT TO BATTLE ME, YOU'D BET-TER DROP BY TONIGHT..."
I GOT THE SENSE YOU WERE UP TO SOMETHIN'.

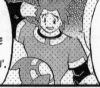

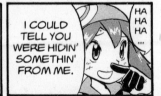

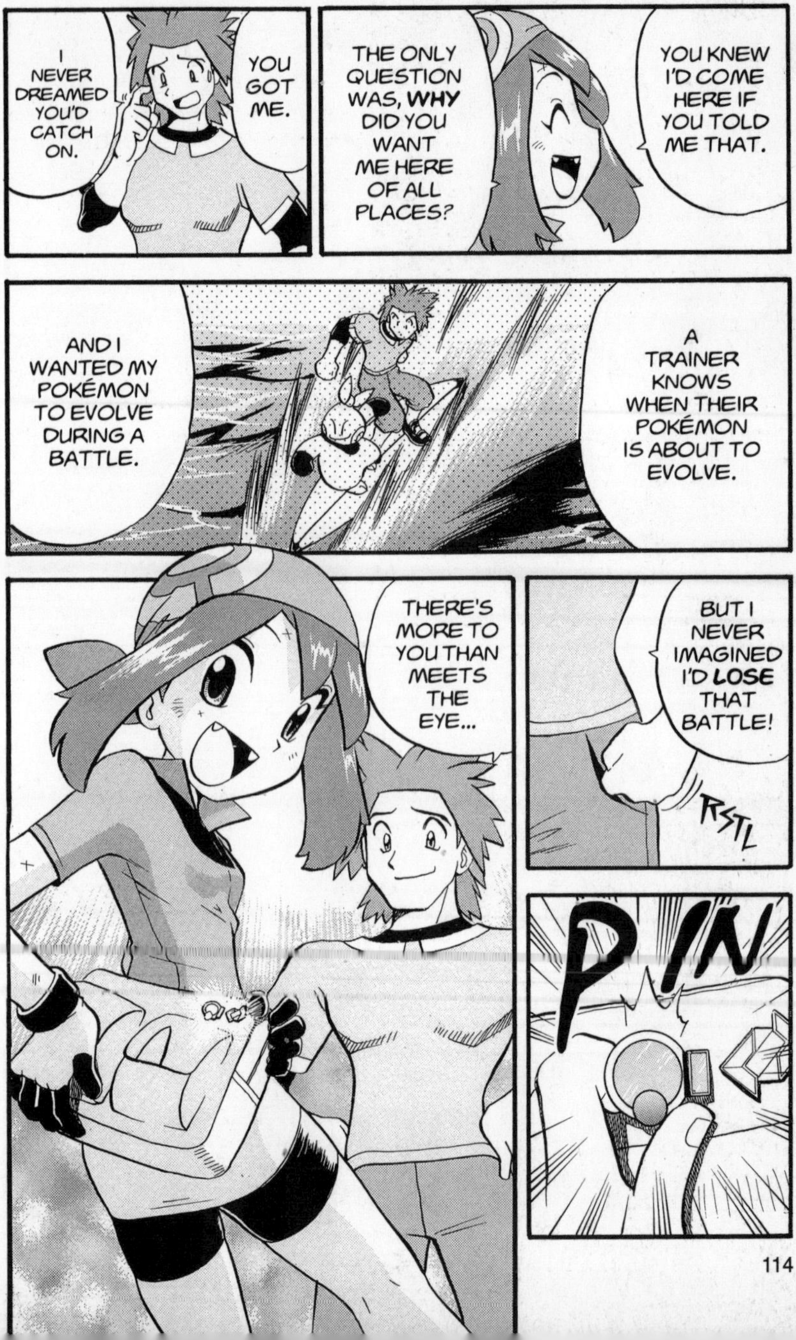
YOU KNEW I'D COME HERE IF YOU TOLD ME THAT.
THE ONLY QUESTION WAS, **WHY** DID YOU WANT ME HERE OF ALL PLACES?
YOU GOT ME.
I NEVER DREAMED YOU'D CATCH ON.
A TRAINER KNOWS WHEN THEIR POKÉMON IS ABOUT TO EVOLVE.
AND I WANTED MY POKÉMON TO EVOLVE DURING A BATTLE.
BUT I NEVER IMAGINED I'D **LOSE** THAT BATTLE!
RSTL
PIN
THERE'S MORE TO YOU THAN MEETS THE EYE...

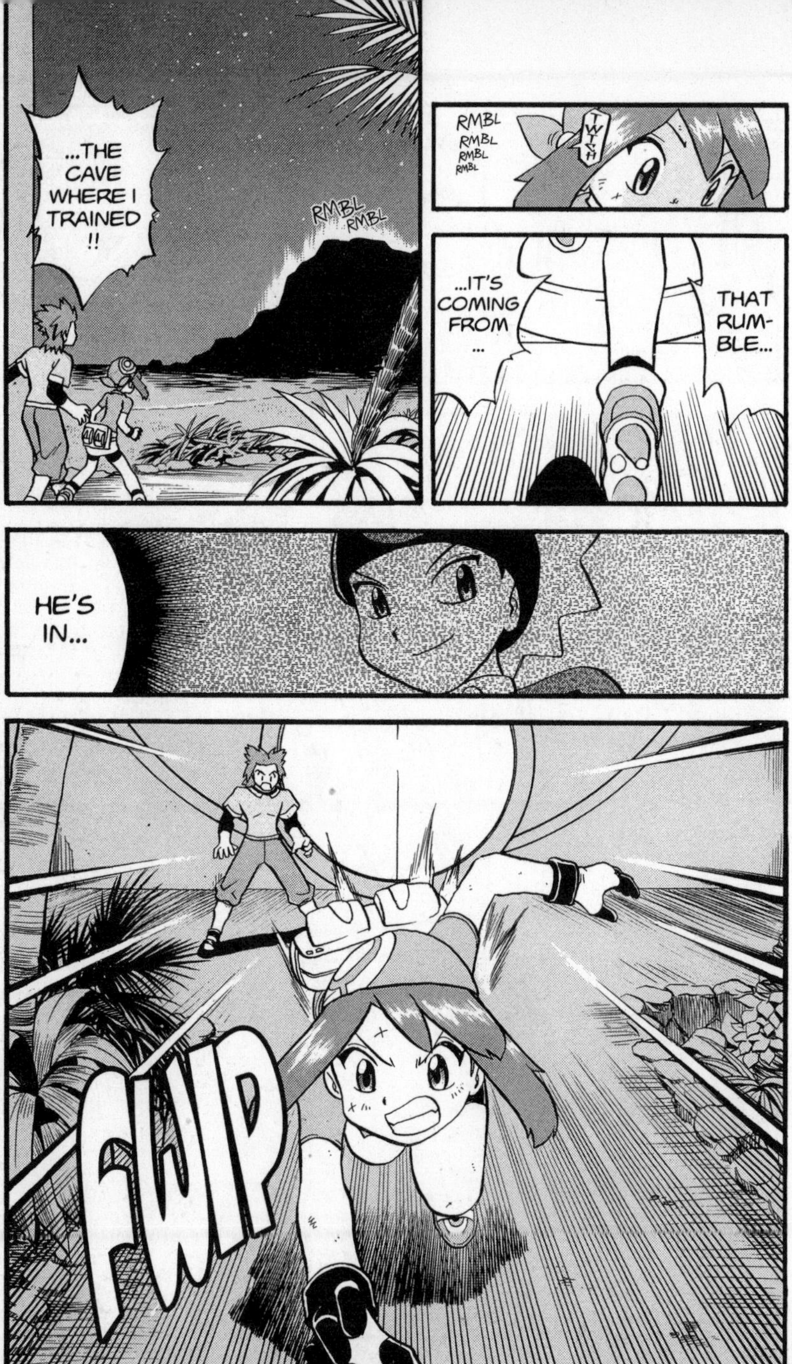
RMBL RMBL RMBL RMBL
TWITCH
THAT RUMBLE...
...IT'S COMING FROM ...
...THE CAVE WHERE I TRAINED !!
RMBL RMBL
HE'S IN...
FWIP

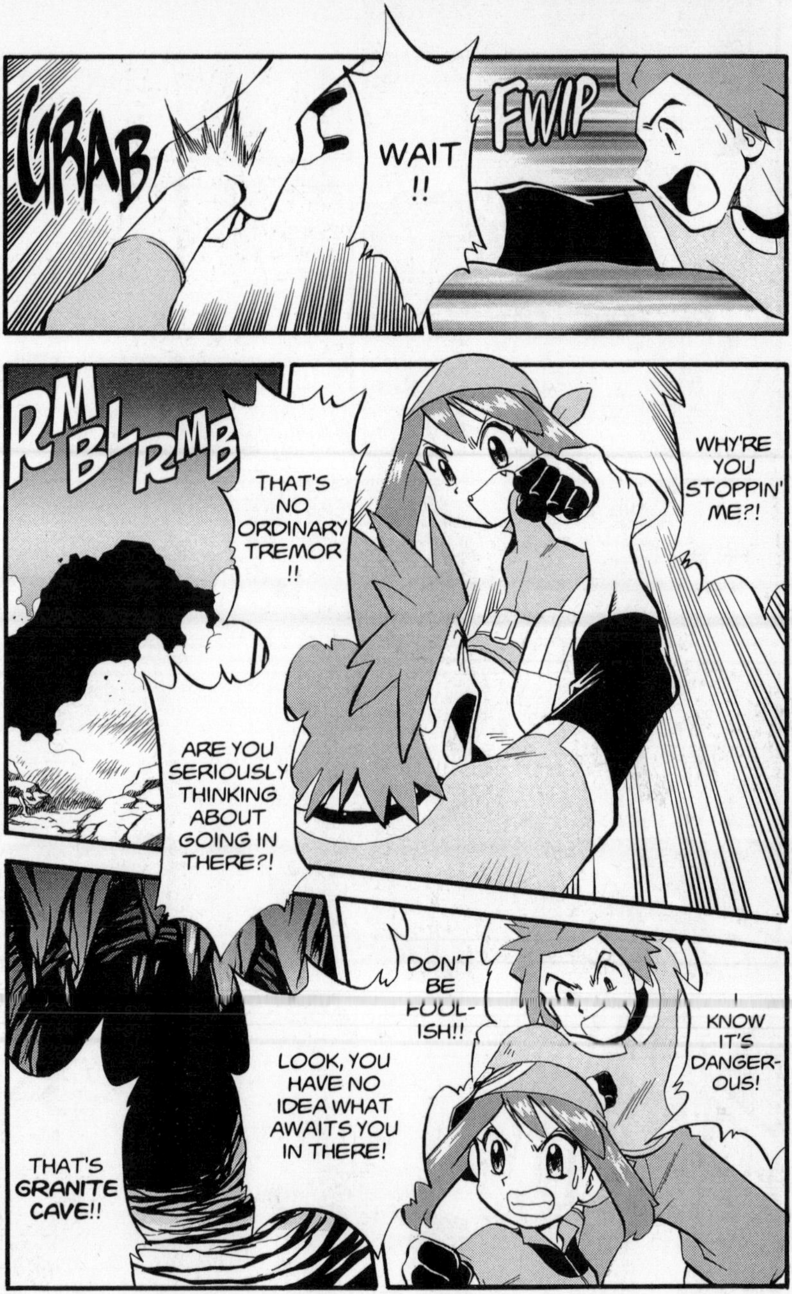
FWIP
WAIT!!
GRAB
WHY'RE YOU STOPPIN' ME?!
RMBLRMB
THAT'S NO ORDINARY TREMOR!!
ARE YOU SERIOUSLY THINKING ABOUT GOING IN THERE?!
DON'T BE FOOL-ISH!!
I KNOW IT'S DANGER-OUS!
LOOK, YOU HAVE NO IDEA WHAT AWAITS YOU IN THERE!
THAT'S GRANITE CAVE!!

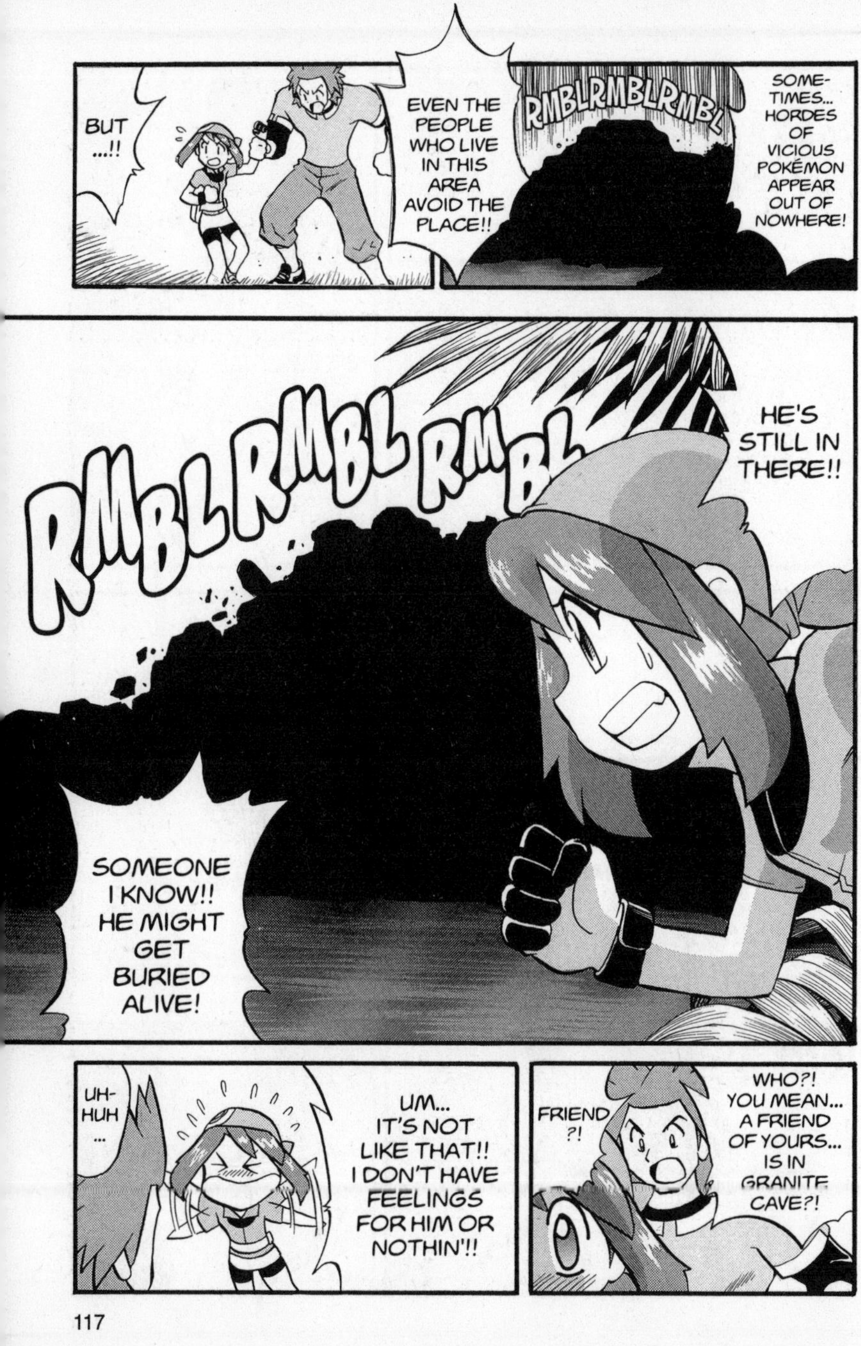
SOME-TIMES... HORDES OF VICIOUS POKÉMON APPEAR OUT OF NOWHERE!
RMBLRMBLRMBL
EVEN THE PEOPLE WHO LIVE IN THIS AREA AVOID THE PLACE!!
BUT ...!!
HE'S STILL IN THERE!!
RMBLRMBLRMBL
SOMEONE I KNOW!! HE MIGHT GET BURIED ALIVE!
WHO?! YOU MEAN... A FRIEND OF YOURS... IS IN GRANITE CAVE?!
FRIEND ?!
UM... IT'S NOT LIKE THAT!! I DON'T HAVE FEELINGS FOR HIM OR NOTHIN'!!
UH-HUH ...

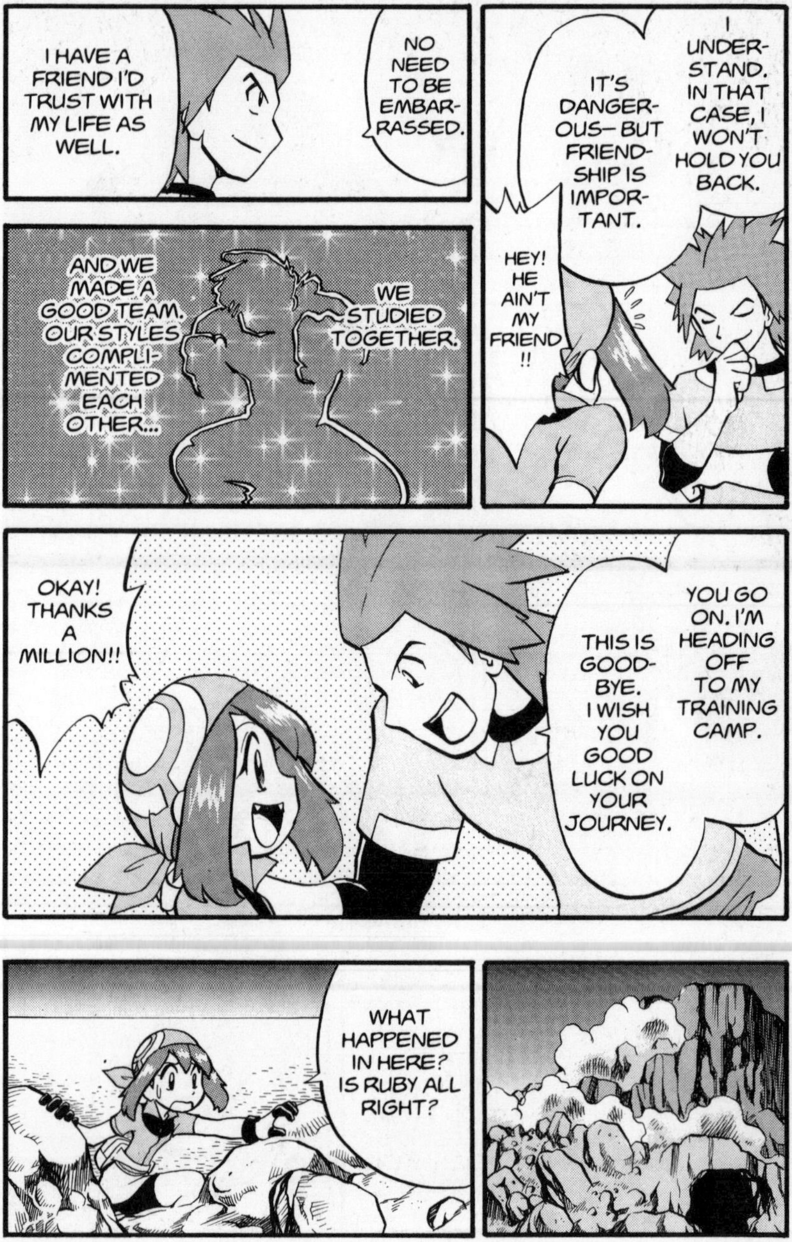
I UNDERSTAND. IN THAT CASE, I WON'T HOLD YOU BACK.
IT'S DANGEROUS— BUT FRIENDSHIP IS IMPORTANT.
HEY! HE AIN'T MY FRIEND!!
NO NEED TO BE EMBARRASSED.
I HAVE A FRIEND I'D TRUST WITH MY LIFE AS WELL.
WE STUDIED TOGETHER.
AND WE MADE A GOOD TEAM. OUR STYLES COMPLIMENTED EACH OTHER...
YOU GO ON. I'M HEADING OFF TO MY TRAINING CAMP.
THIS IS GOODBYE. I WISH YOU GOOD LUCK ON YOUR JOURNEY.
OKAY! THANKS A MILLION!!
WHAT HAPPENED IN HERE? IS RUBY ALL RIGHT?

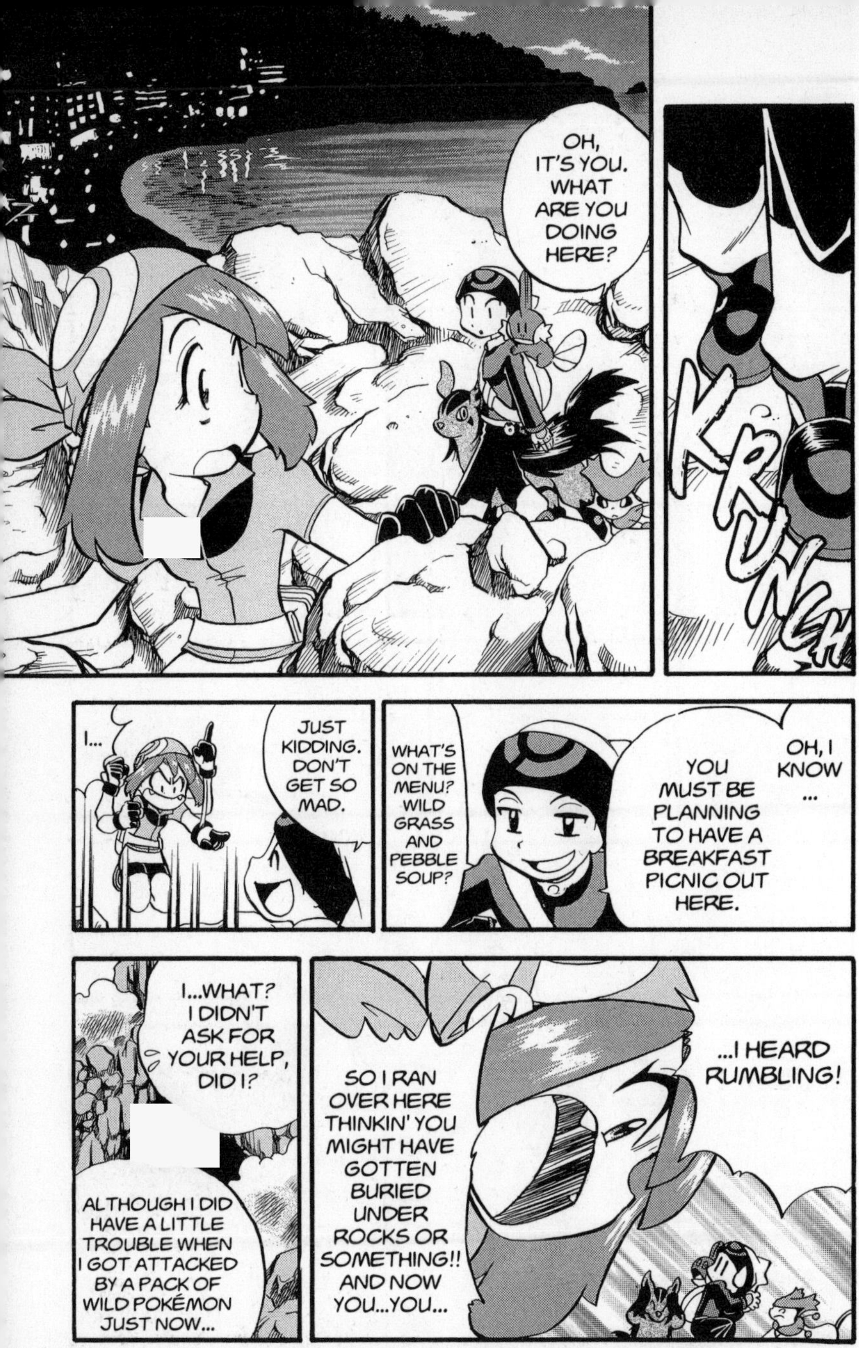
KRUNCH
OH, IT'S YOU. WHAT ARE YOU DOING HERE?
OH, I KNOW ...
YOU MUST BE PLANNING TO HAVE A BREAKFAST PICNIC OUT HERE.
WHAT'S ON THE MENU? WILD GRASS AND PEBBLE SOUP?
JUST KIDDING. DON'T GET SO MAD.
I...
...I HEARD RUMBLING!
SO I RAN OVER HERE THINKIN' YOU MIGHT HAVE GOTTEN BURIED UNDER ROCKS OR SOMETHING!! AND NOW YOU...YOU...
I...WHAT? I DIDN'T ASK FOR YOUR HELP, DID I?
ALTHOUGH I DID HAVE A LITTLE TROUBLE WHEN I GOT ATTACKED BY A PACK OF WILD POKÉMON JUST NOW...

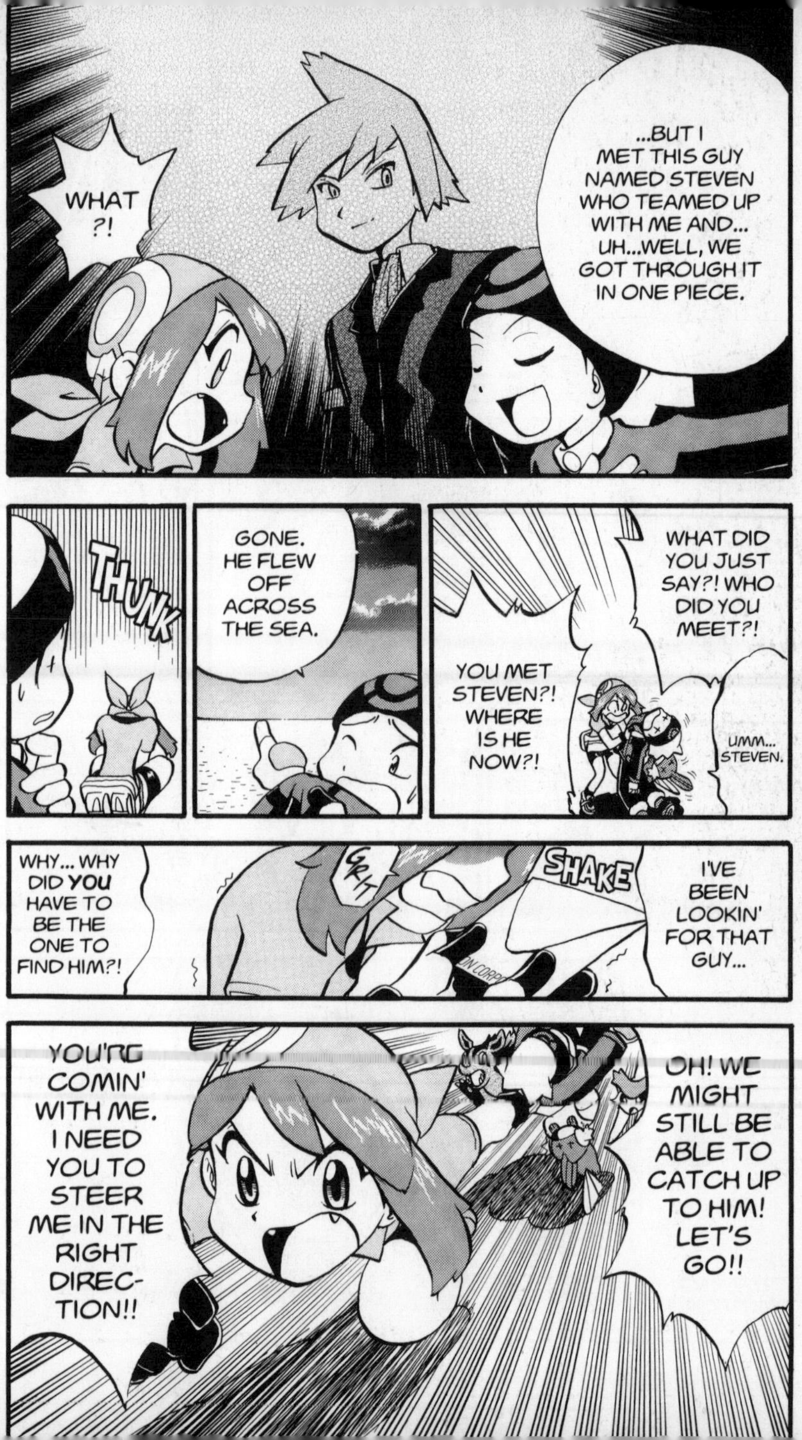
...BUT I MET THIS GUY NAMED STEVEN WHO TEAMED UP WITH ME AND... UH...WELL, WE GOT THROUGH IT IN ONE PIECE.
WHAT ?!
WHAT DID YOU JUST SAY?! WHO DID YOU MEET?!
UMM... STEVEN.
YOU MET STEVEN?! WHERE IS HE NOW?!
GONE. HE FLEW OFF ACROSS THE SEA.
THUNK
I'VE BEEN LOOKIN' FOR THAT GUY...
SHAKE
GRIT
WHY... WHY DID YOU HAVE TO BE THE ONE TO FIND HIM?!
OH! WE MIGHT STILL BE ABLE TO CATCH UP TO HIM! LET'S GO!!
YOU'RE COMIN' WITH ME. I NEED YOU TO STEER ME IN THE RIGHT DIREC-TION!!

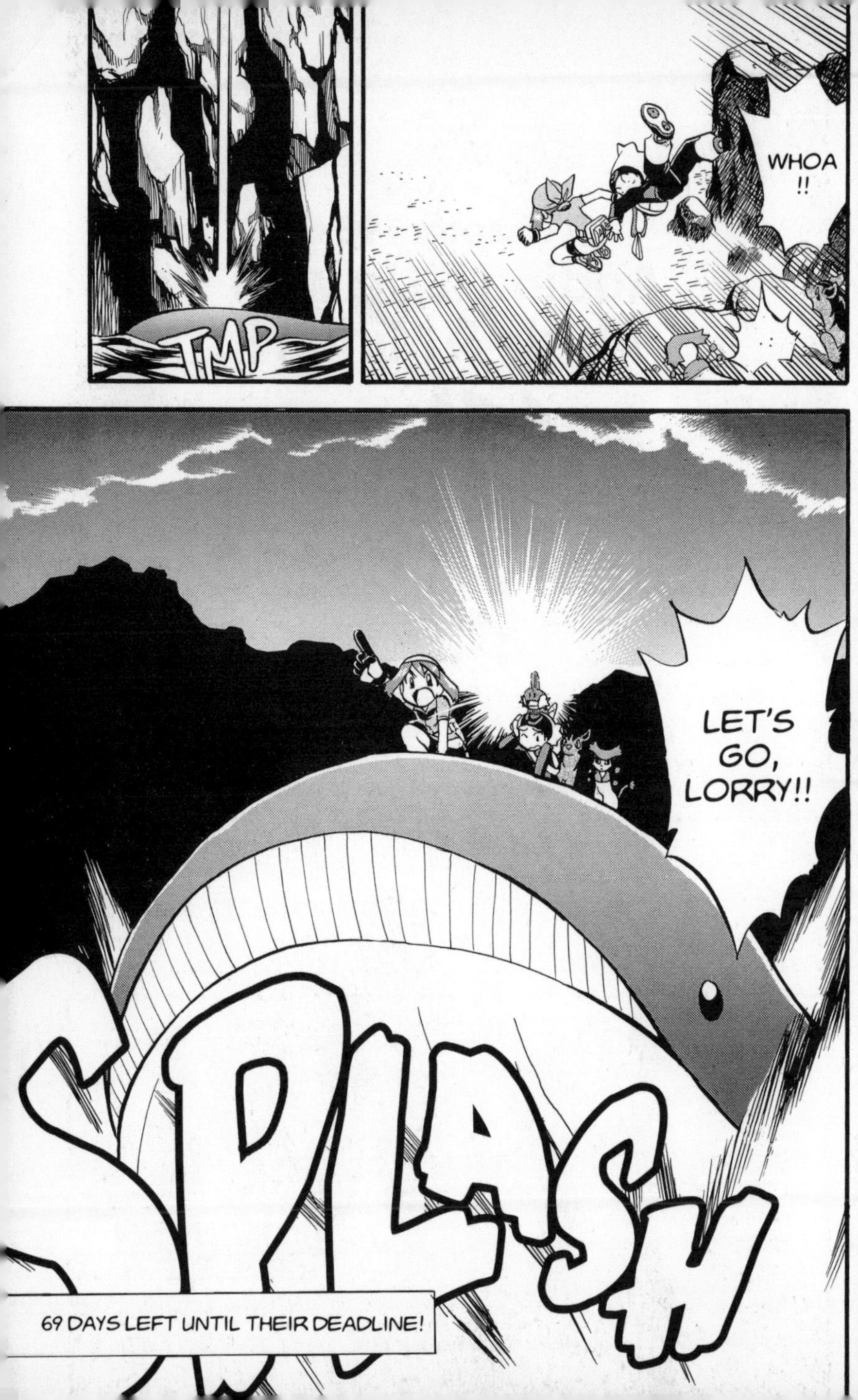
WHOA !!
TMP
LET'S GO, LORRY!!
SPLASH
69 DAYS LEFT UNTIL THEIR DEADLINE!

● Chapter 198 ●
Adding It Up with
Plusle & Minun I

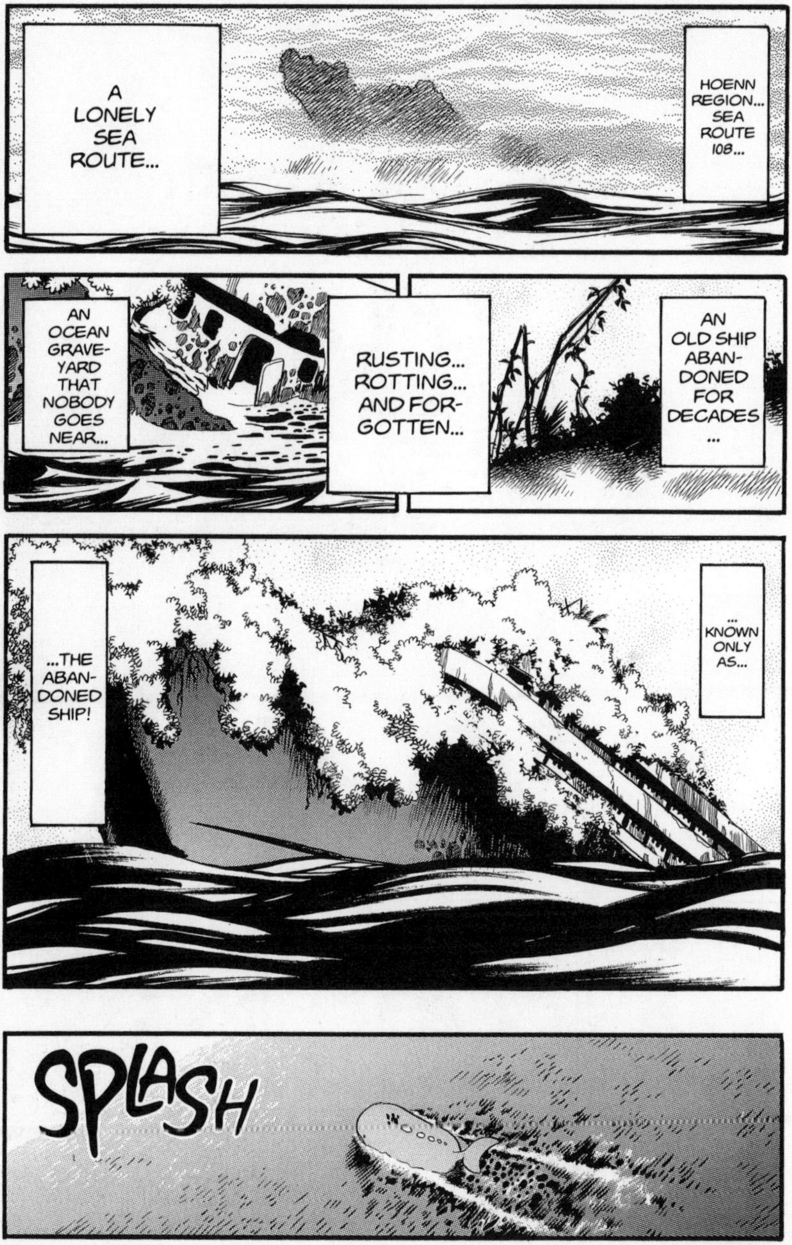
HOENN REGION... SEA ROUTE 108...
A LONELY SEA ROUTE...
AN OLD SHIP ABAN-DONED FOR DECADES...
RUSTING... ROTTING... AND FOR-GOTTEN...
AN OCEAN GRAVE-YARD THAT NOBODY GOES NEAR...
...KNOWN ONLY AS...
...THE ABAN-DONED SHIP!
SPLASH

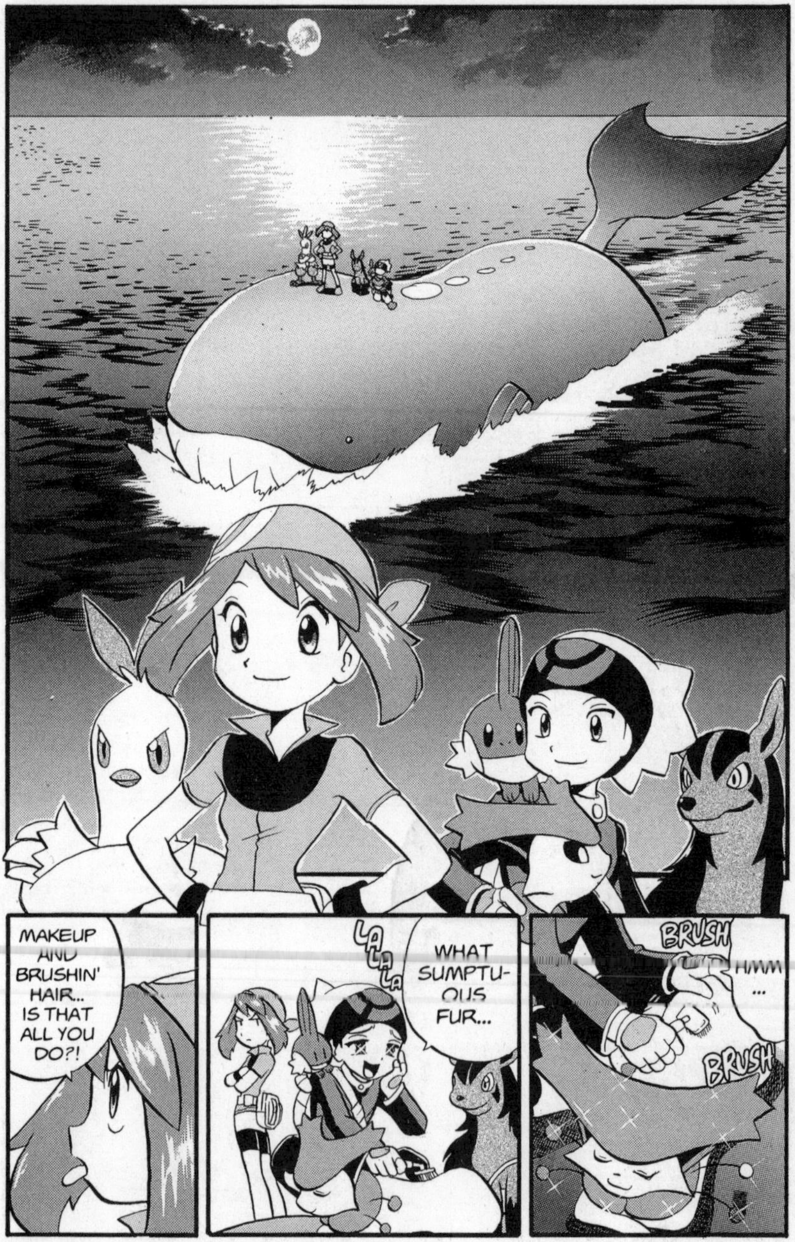
BRUSH
HMM ...
BRUSH
LA LA LA
WHAT SUMPTU-OUS FUR...
MAKEUP AND BRUSHIN' HAIR... IS THAT ALL YOU DO?!

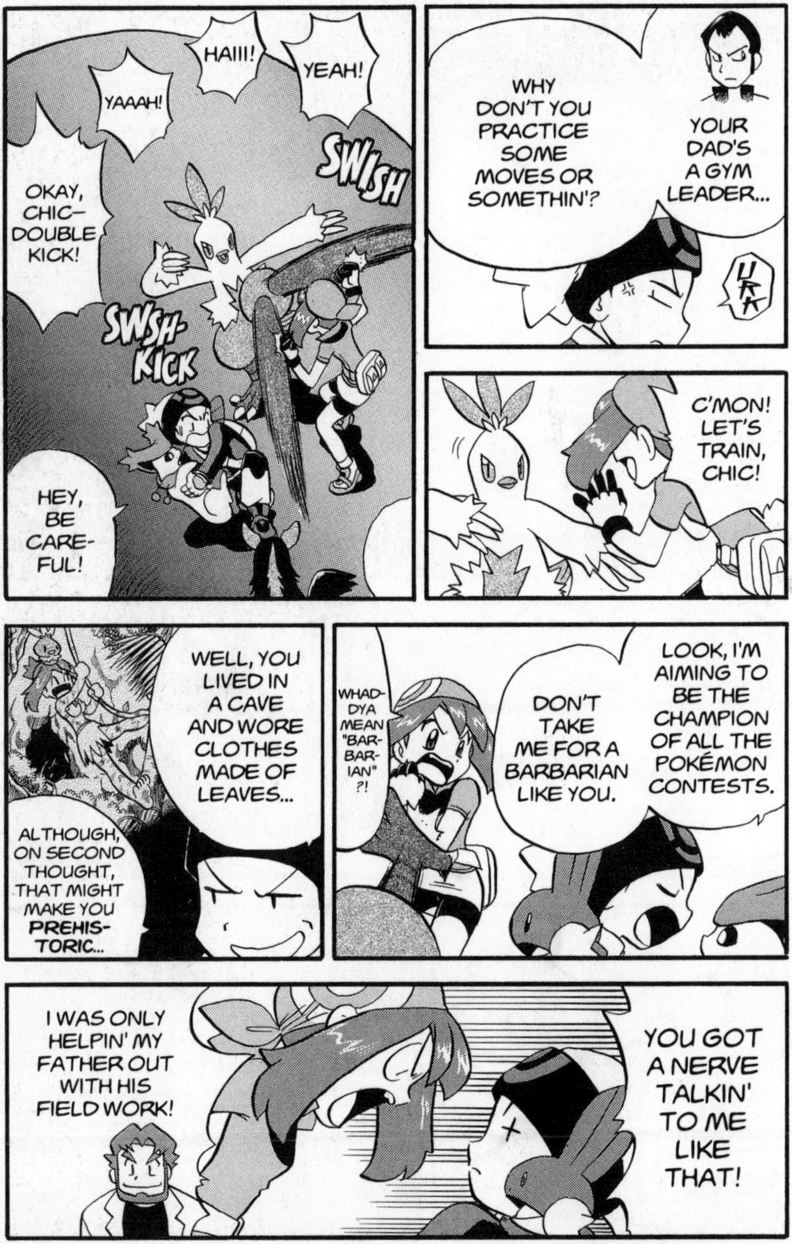
YOUR DAD'S A GYM LEADER...
WHY DON'T YOU PRACTICE SOME MOVES OR SOMETHIN'?
URK
C'MON! LET'S TRAIN, CHIC!
YEAH!
HAIII!
YAAAH!
SWISH
OKAY, CHIC— DOUBLE KICK!
SWSH-KICK
HEY, BE CARE-FUL!
LOOK, I'M AIMING TO BE THE CHAMPION OF ALL THE POKÉMON CONTESTS.
DON'T TAKE ME FOR A BARBARIAN LIKE YOU.
WHADDYA MEAN "BARBARIAN"?!
WELL, YOU LIVED IN A CAVE AND WORE CLOTHES MADE OF LEAVES...
ALTHOUGH, ON SECOND THOUGHT, THAT MIGHT MAKE YOU PREHIS-TORIC...
YOU GOT A NERVE TALKIN' TO ME LIKE THAT!
I WAS ONLY HELPIN' MY FATHER OUT WITH HIS FIELD WORK!

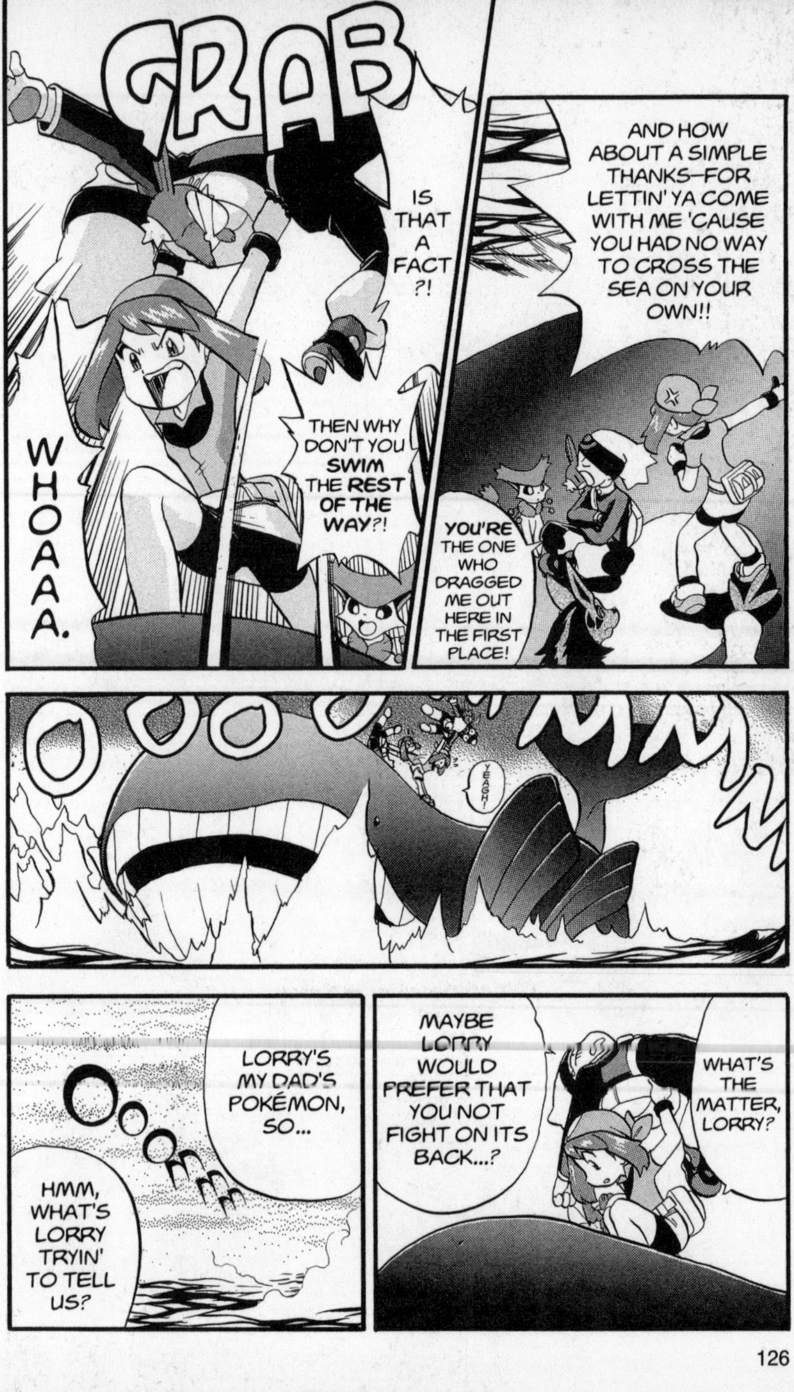
AND HOW ABOUT A SIMPLE THANKS—FOR LETTIN' YA COME WITH ME 'CAUSE YOU HAD NO WAY TO CROSS THE SEA ON YOUR OWN!!
YOU'RE THE ONE WHO DRAGGED ME OUT HERE IN THE FIRST PLACE!
GRAB
IS THAT A FACT?!
THEN WHY DON'T YOU SWIM THE REST OF THE WAY?!
WHOAAAA.
YEAGH!
WHAT'S THE MATTER, LORRY?
MAYBE LORRY WOULD PREFER THAT YOU NOT FIGHT ON ITS BACK...?
LORRY'S MY DAD'S POKÉMON, SO...
HMM, WHAT'S LORRY TRYIN' TO TELL US?

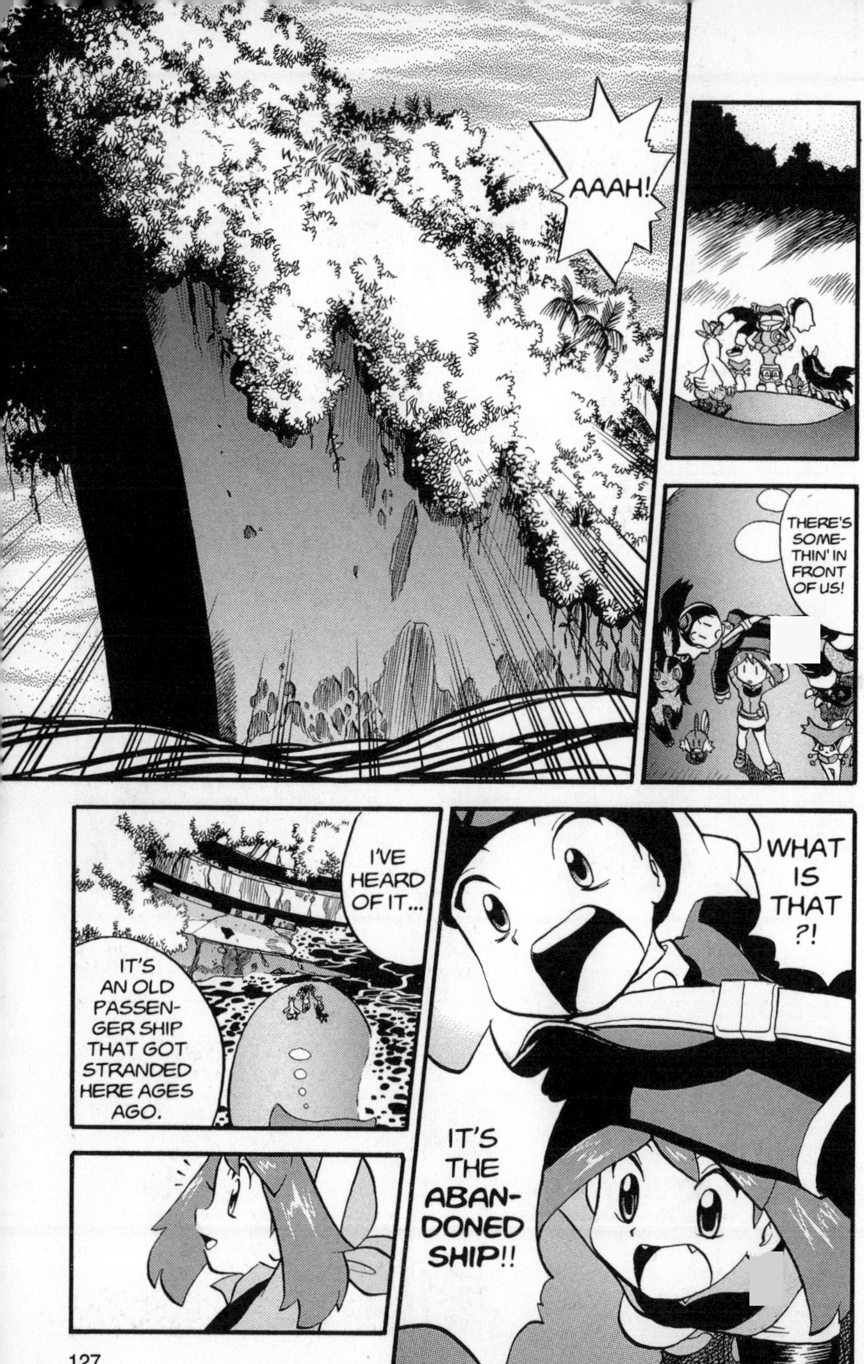
THERE'S SOMETHIN' IN FRONT OF US!
AAAH!
WHAT IS THAT?!
IT'S THE ABANDONED SHIP!!
I'VE HEARD OF IT...
IT'S AN OLD PASSENGER SHIP THAT GOT STRANDED HERE AGES AGO.

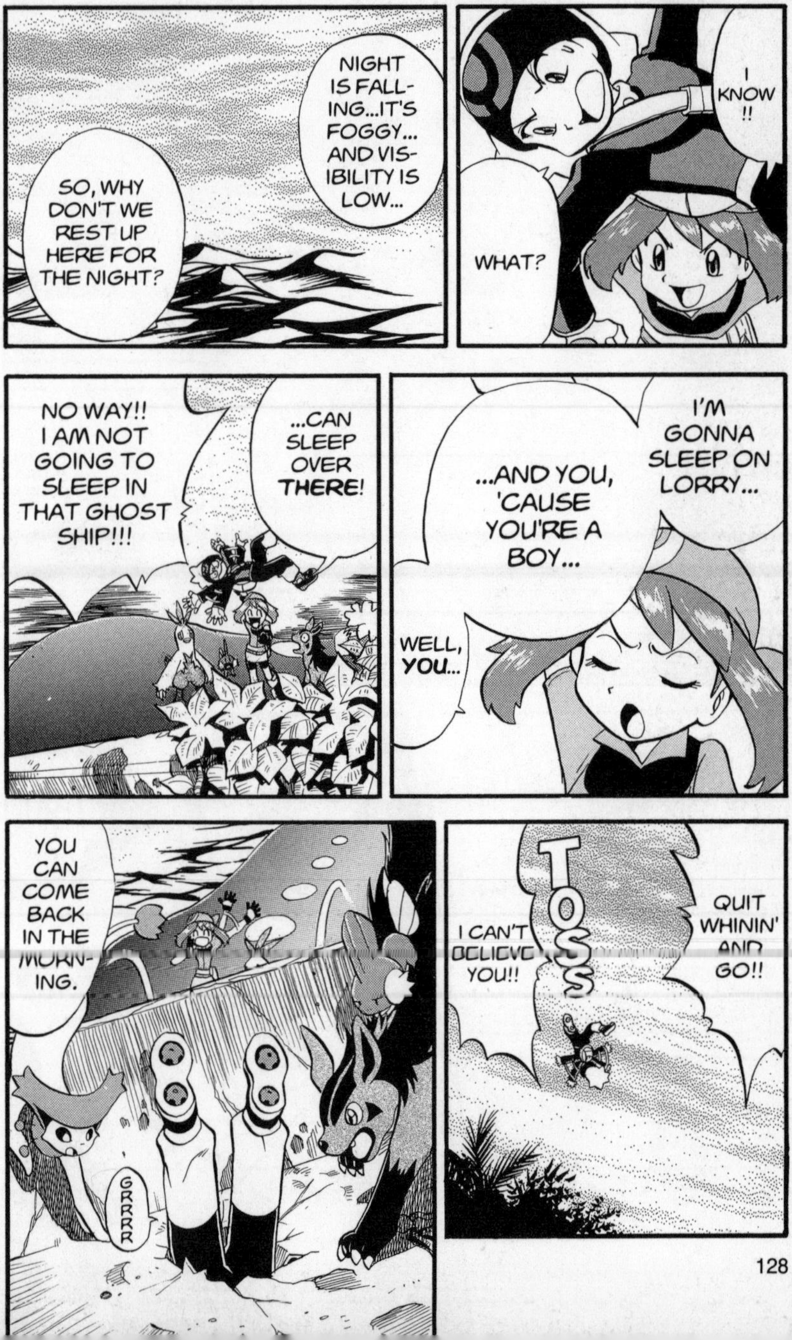
I KNOW!!
WHAT?
NIGHT IS FALLING...IT'S FOGGY... AND VISIBILITY IS LOW...
SO, WHY DON'T WE REST UP HERE FOR THE NIGHT?
I'M GONNA SLEEP ON LORRY...
...AND YOU, 'CAUSE YOU'RE A BOY...
WELL, **YOU**...
...CAN SLEEP OVER **THERE**!
NO WAY!! I AM NOT GOING TO SLEEP IN THAT GHOST SHIP!!!
QUIT WHININ' AND GO!!
TOSS
I CAN'T BELIEVE YOU!!
YOU CAN COME BACK IN THE MORNING.
GRRRR

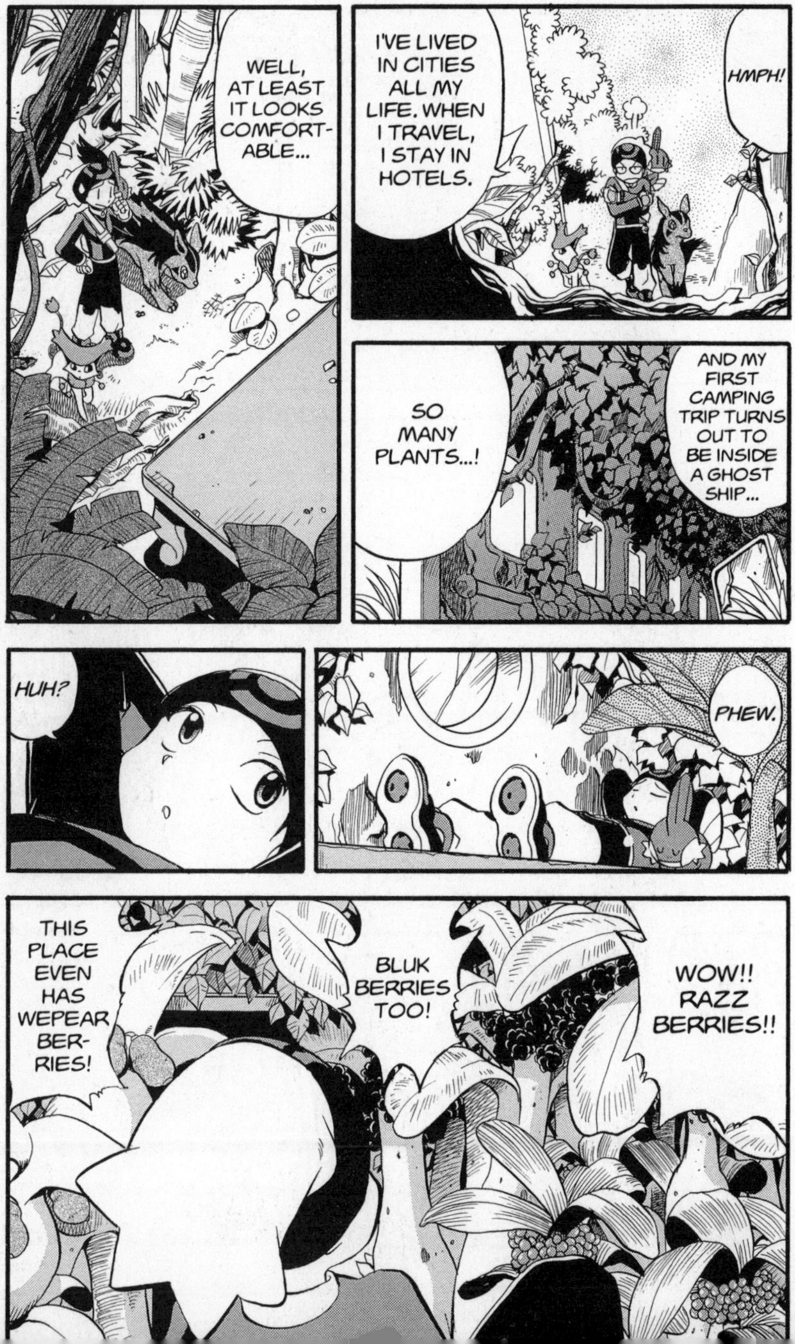
HMPH!
I'VE LIVED IN CITIES ALL MY LIFE. WHEN I TRAVEL, I STAY IN HOTELS.
AND MY FIRST CAMPING TRIP TURNS OUT TO BE INSIDE A GHOST SHIP...
SO MANY PLANTS...!
WELL, AT LEAST IT LOOKS COMFORT-ABLE...
PHEW.
HUH?
WOW!! RAZZ BERRIES!!
BLUK BERRIES TOO!
THIS PLACE EVEN HAS WEPEAR BER-RIES!

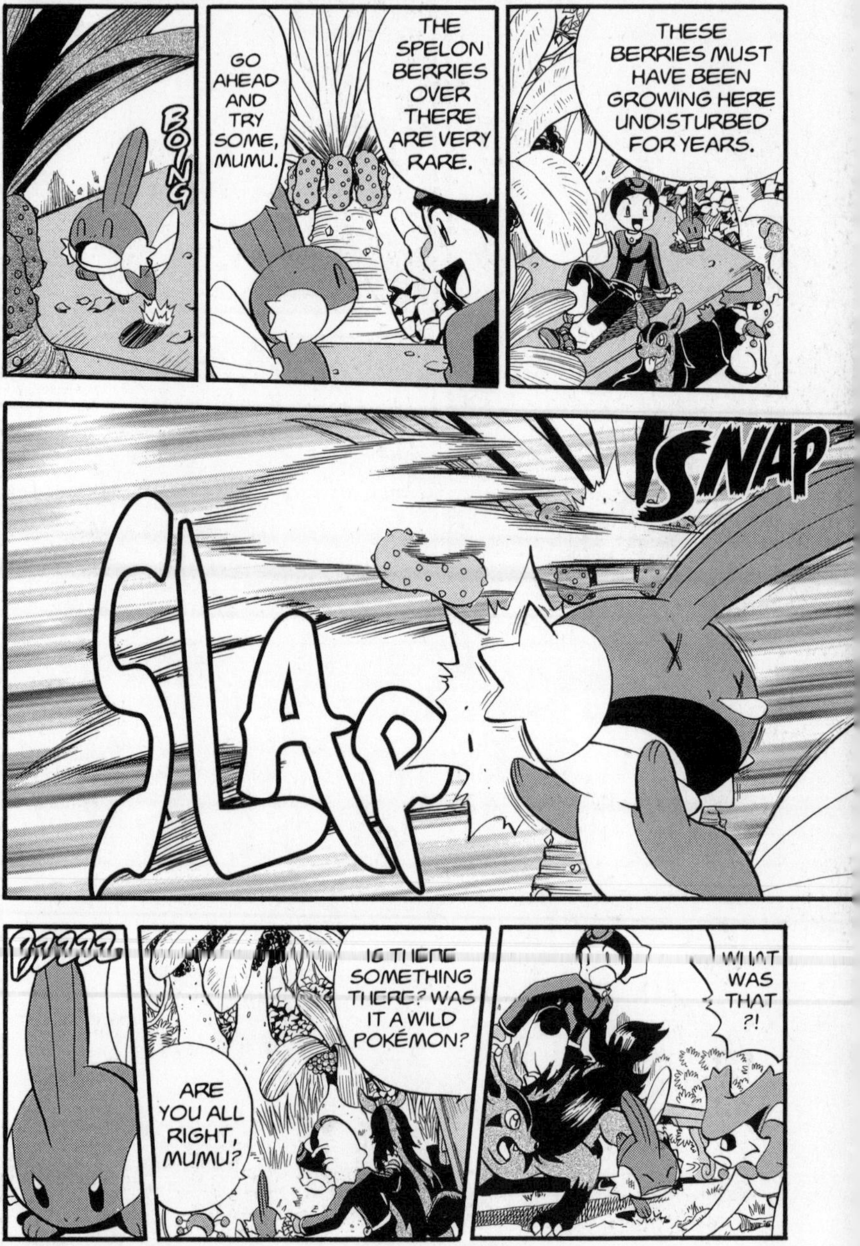
THESE BERRIES MUST HAVE BEEN GROWING HERE UNDISTURBED FOR YEARS.
THE SPELON BERRIES OVER THERE ARE VERY RARE.
GO AHEAD AND TRY SOME, MUMU.
BOING
SNAP
SLAP
WHAT WAS THAT?!
IS THERE SOMETHING THERE? WAS IT A WILD POKÉMON?
ARE YOU ALL RIGHT, MUMU?

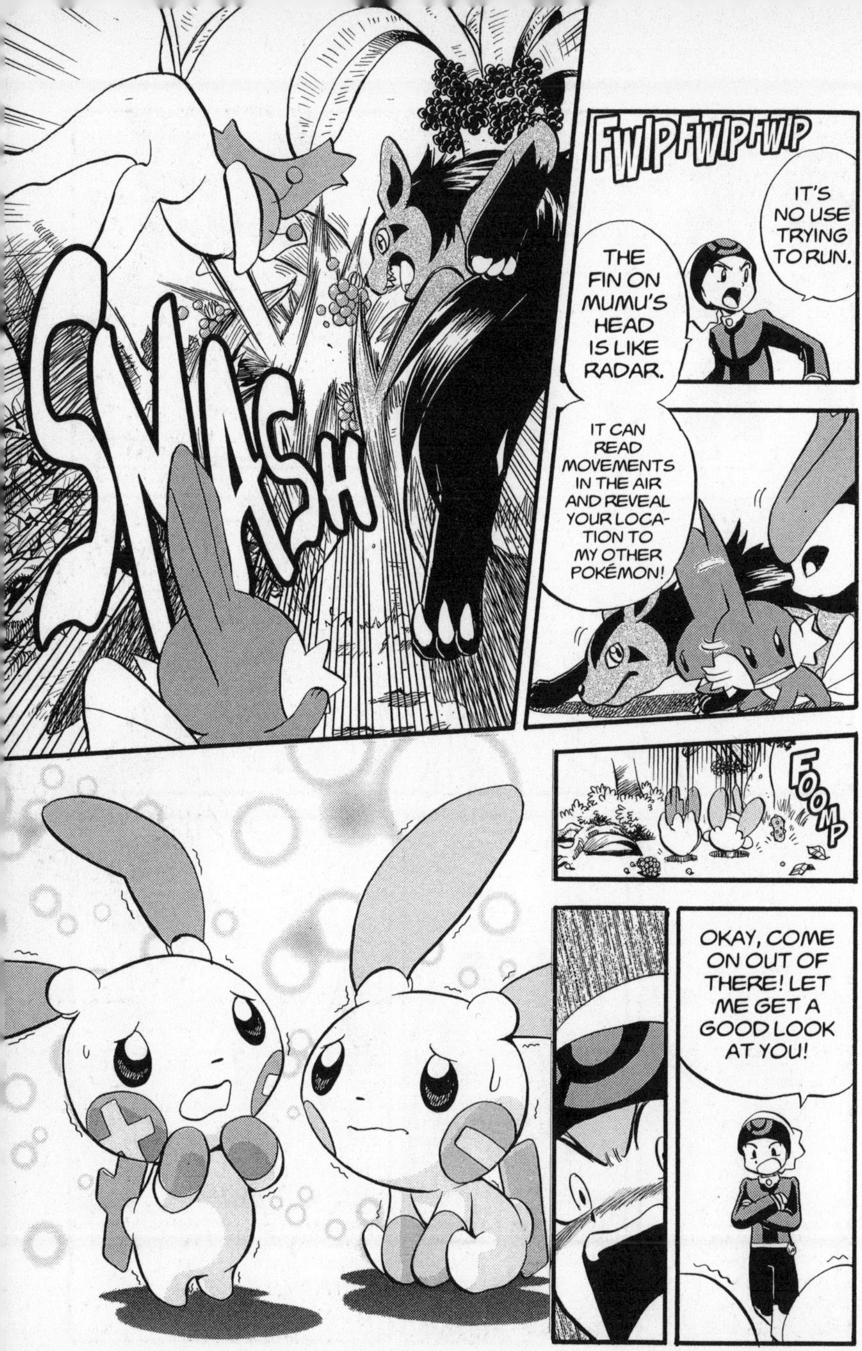
FWIP FWIP FWIP
IT'S NO USE TRYING TO RUN.
THE FIN ON MUMU'S HEAD IS LIKE RADAR.
IT CAN READ MOVEMENTS IN THE AIR AND REVEAL YOUR LOCATION TO MY OTHER POKÉMON!
SMASH
FOOMP
OKAY, COME ON OUT OF THERE! LET ME GET A GOOD LOOK AT YOU!

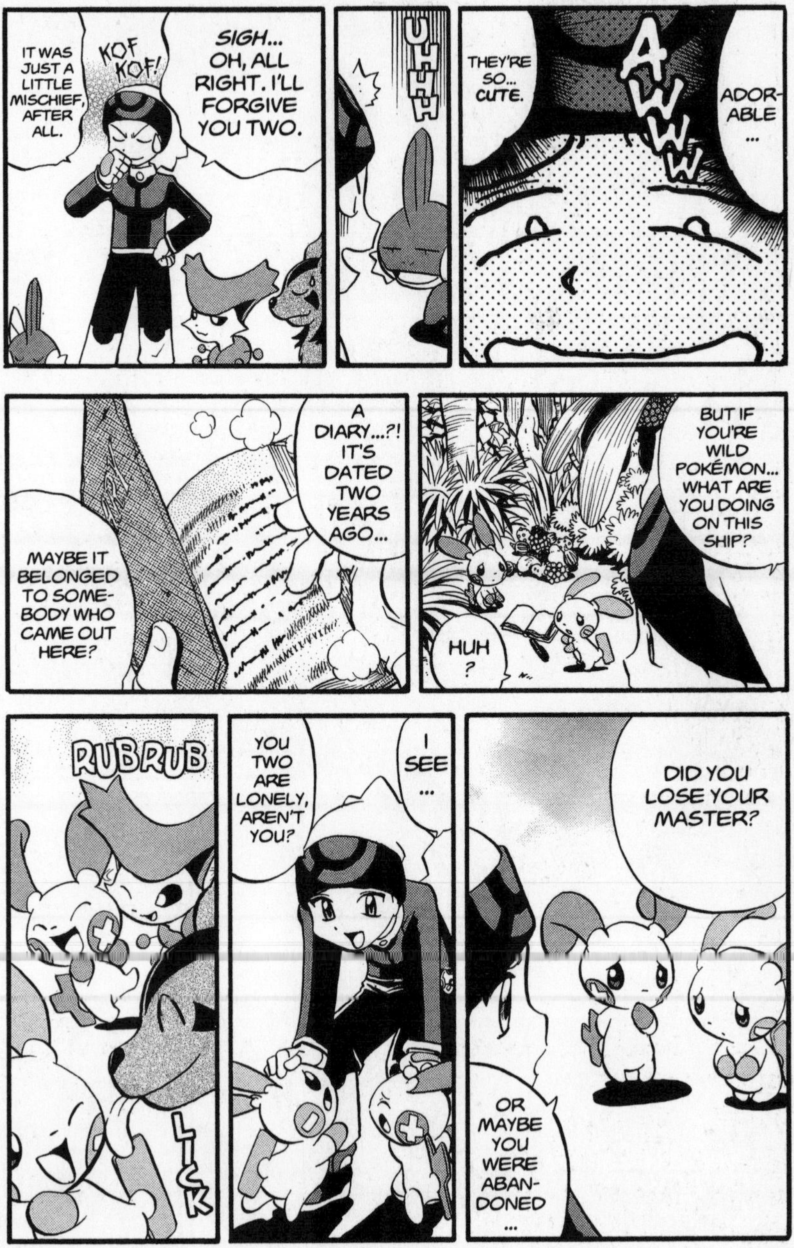
ADOR-ABLE...
AWWW
THEY'RE SO... CUTE.
UHHH
SIGH... OH, ALL RIGHT. I'LL FORGIVE YOU TWO.
KOF KOF!
IT WAS JUST A LITTLE MISCHIEF, AFTER ALL.
BUT IF YOU'RE WILD POKÉMON... WHAT ARE YOU DOING ON THIS SHIP?
HUH?
A DIARY...?! IT'S DATED TWO YEARS AGO...
MAYBE IT BELONGED TO SOMEBODY WHO CAME OUT HERE?
DID YOU LOSE YOUR MASTER?
OR MAYBE YOU WERE ABANDONED...
I SEE...
YOU TWO ARE LONELY, AREN'T YOU?
RUBRUB
LICK

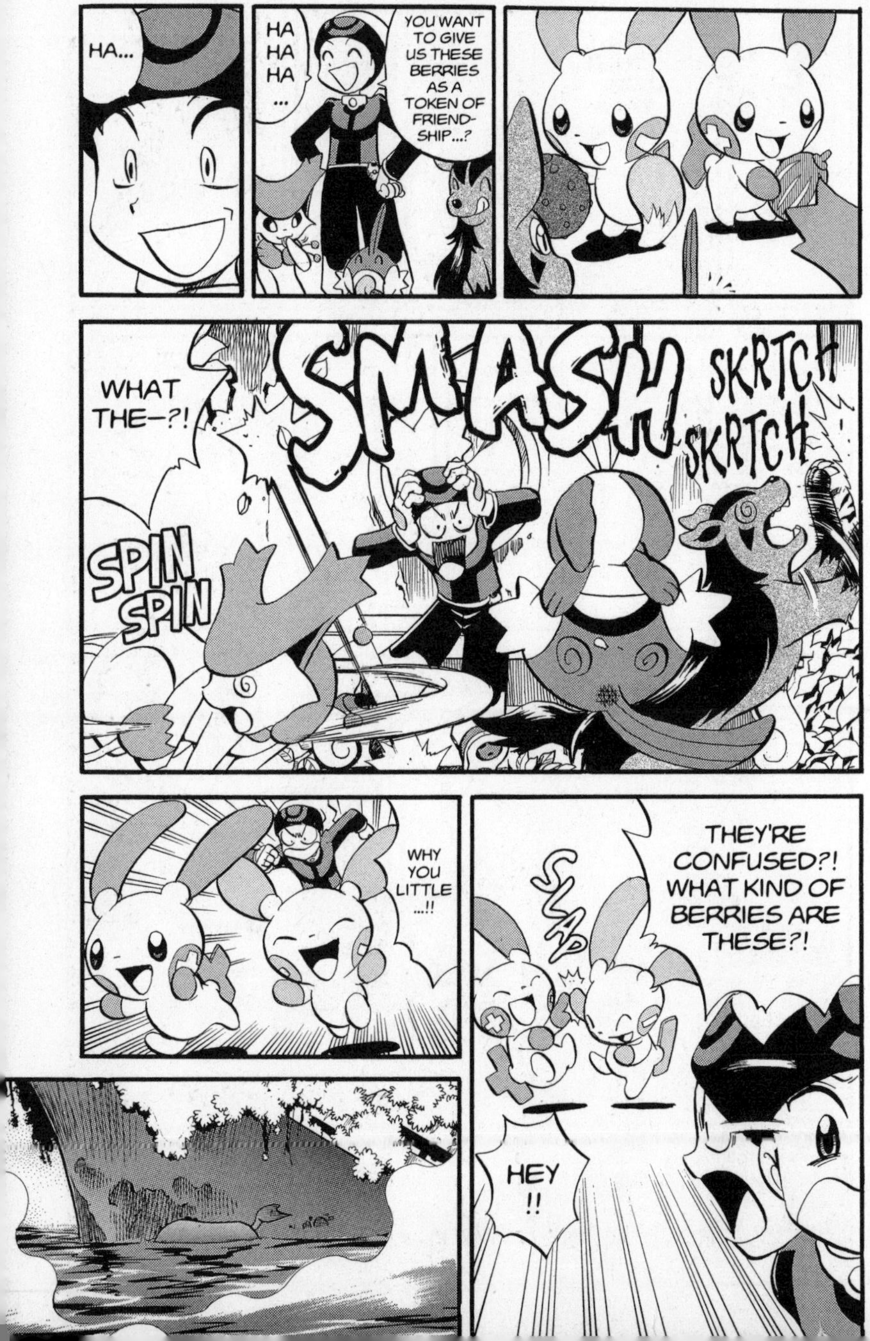
YOU WANT TO GIVE US THESE BERRIES AS A TOKEN OF FRIEND-SHIP...?
HA HA HA ...
HA...
SKRTCH SKRTCH
SMASH
WHAT THE-?!
SPIN SPIN
THEY'RE CONFUSED?! WHAT KIND OF BERRIES ARE THESE?!
SLAP
HEY !!
WHY YOU LITTLE ...!!

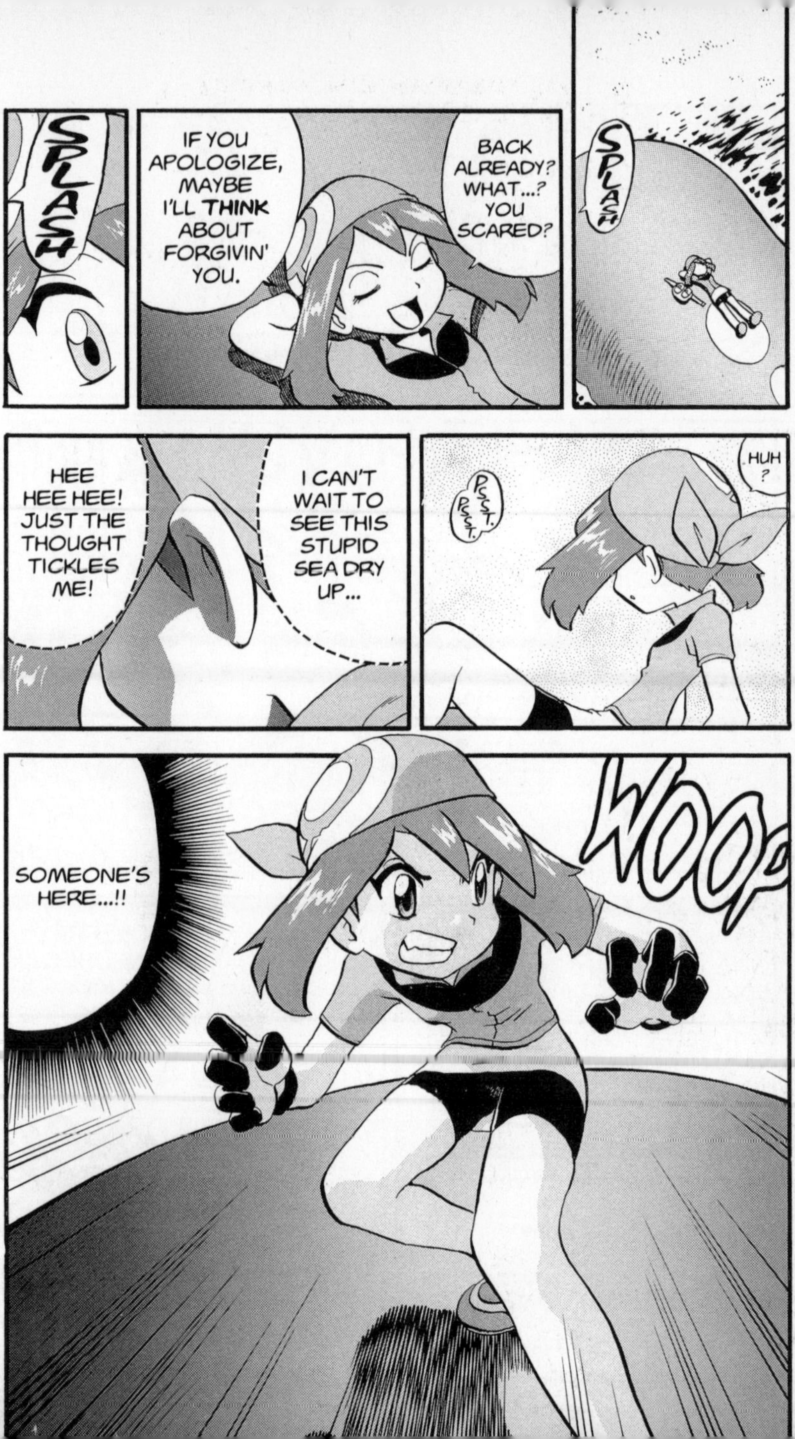
SPLASH
BACK ALREADY? WHAT...? YOU SCARED?
IF YOU APOLOGIZE, MAYBE I'LL **THINK** ABOUT FORGIVIN' YOU.
SPLASH
HUH?
PSST. PSST.
I CAN'T WAIT TO SEE THIS STUPID SEA DRY UP...
HEE HEE HEE! JUST THE THOUGHT TICKLES ME!
WOOP
SOMEONE'S HERE...!!

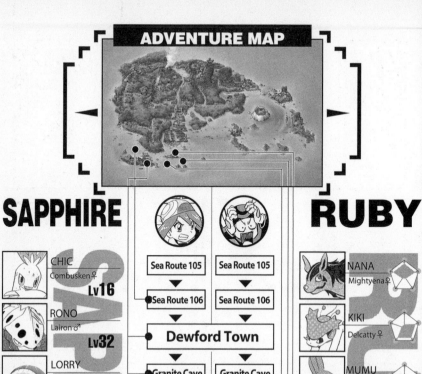

ADVENTURE MAP

SAPPHIRE

CHIC
Combusken ♀
Lv16

RONO
Lairon ♂
Lv32

LORRY
Wailord ♂
Lv41

RUBY

NANA
Mightyena ♀

KIKI
Delcatty ♀

MUMU
Mudkip ♂

SAPPHIRE		RUBY
Sea Route 105	Sea Route 105	
Sea Route 106	Sea Route 106	
Dewford Town	Dewford Town	
Granite Cave	Granite Cave	
Sea Route 107		
Sea Route 108		
Abandoned Ship		

Stone Badge	Knuckle Badge	Dynamo Badge	Heat Badge
Balance Badge	Feather Badge	Mind Badge	Rain Badge

	Cool	Beauty	Cute	Smart	Tough
Normal					
Super					
Hyper					
Master					

● Chapter 199 ●

Adding It Up with Plusle & Minun II

Pokémon Adventures Ruby & Sapphire
The Fourth Chapter

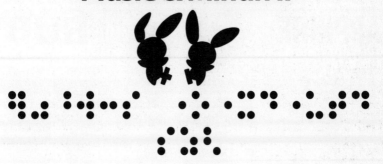

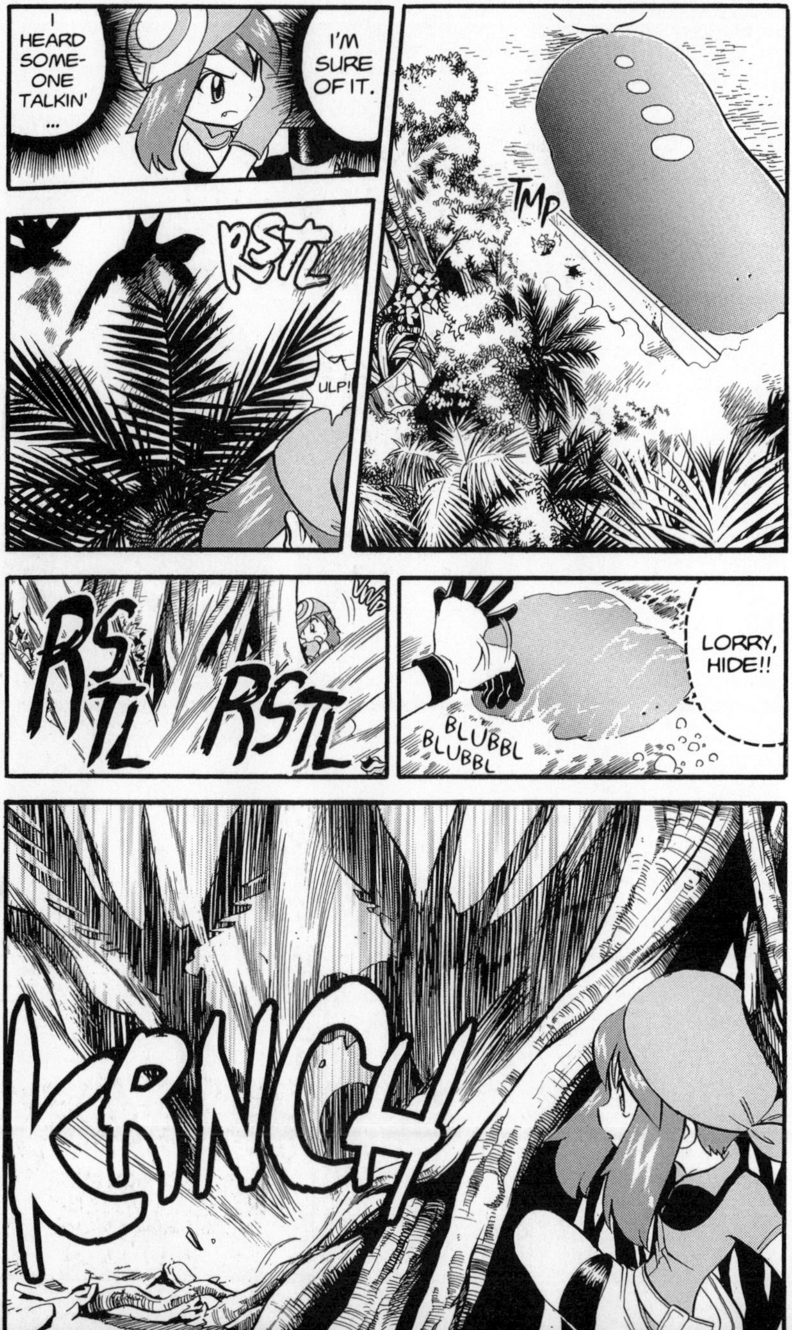
TMP
I'M SURE OF IT.
I HEARD SOME-ONE TALKIN' ...
RSTL
ULP!
LORRY, HIDE!!
BLUBBL BLUBBL
RSTL
RSTL
KRNCH

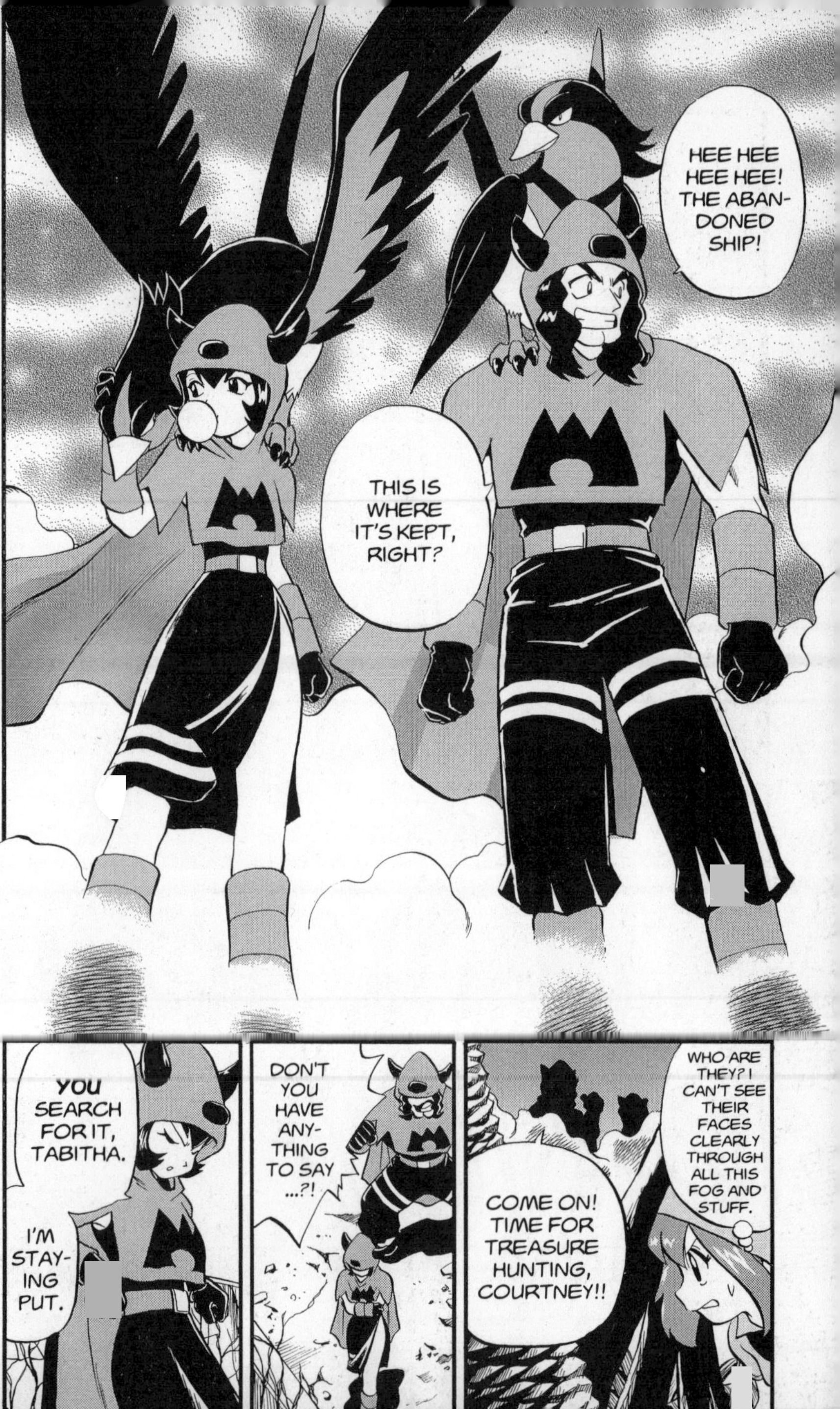
HEE HEE HEE HEE! THE ABAN-DONED SHIP!
THIS IS WHERE IT'S KEPT, RIGHT?
WHO ARE THEY? I CAN'T SEE THEIR FACES CLEARLY THROUGH ALL THIS FOG AND STUFF.
COME ON! TIME FOR TREASURE HUNTING, COURTNEY!!
DON'T YOU HAVE ANY-THING TO SAY ...?!
...
YOU SEARCH FOR IT, TABITHA.
I'M STAY-ING PUT.

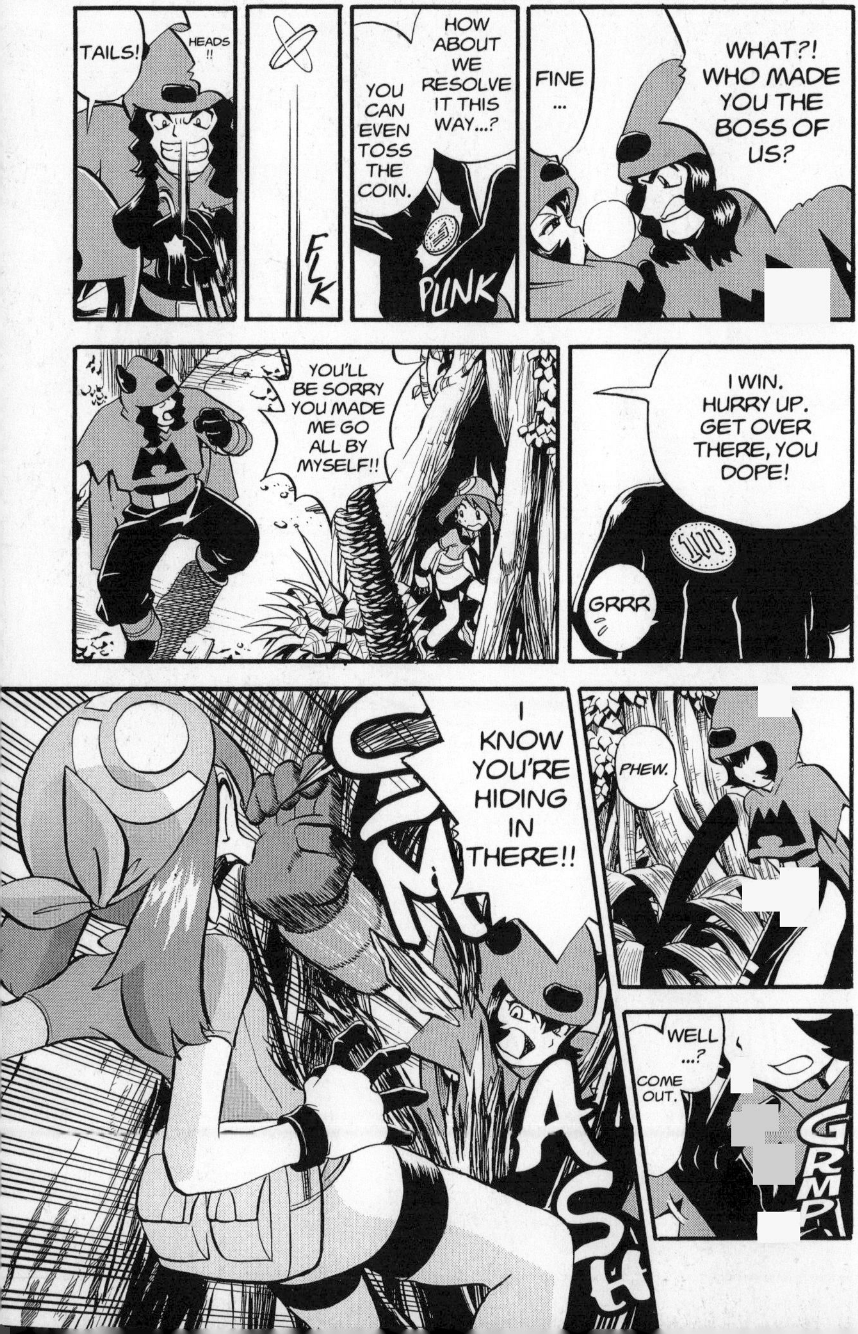
WHAT?! WHO MADE YOU THE BOSS OF US?
FINE ...
HOW ABOUT WE RESOLVE IT THIS WAY...?
YOU CAN EVEN TOSS THE COIN.
PLINK
FLK
HEADS !!
TAILS!
I WIN. HURRY UP. GET OVER THERE, YOU DOPE!
GRRR
YOU'LL BE SORRY YOU MADE ME GO ALL BY MYSELF!!
PHEW.
WELL ...?
COME OUT.
GRMP
I KNOW YOU'RE HIDING IN THERE!!
CRASH

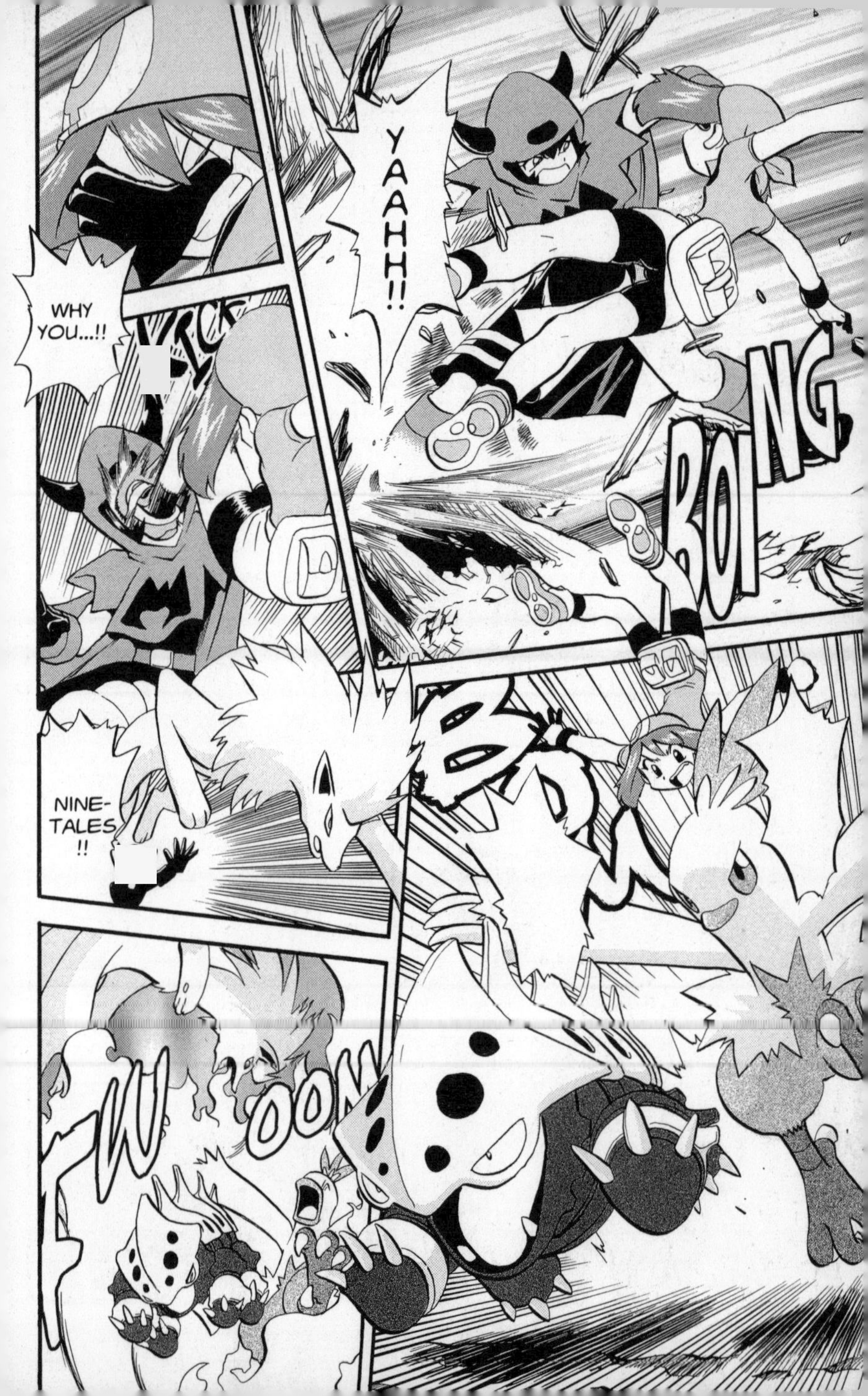
YAAHH!!
BOING
WHY YOU...!!
NINE-TALES !!

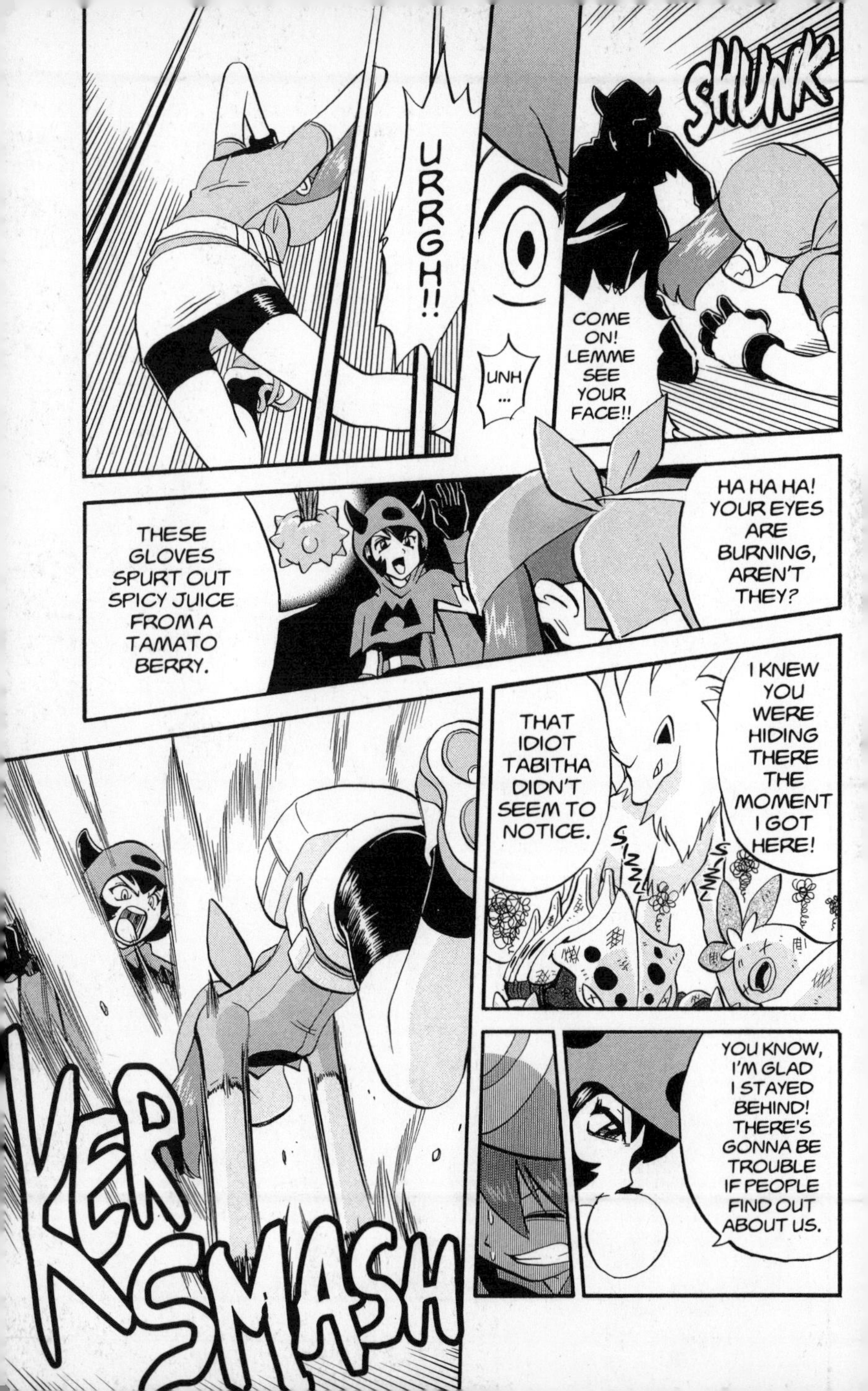
SHUNK
COME ON! LEMME SEE YOUR FACE!!
UNH ...
URRGH!!
HA HA HA! YOUR EYES ARE BURNING, AREN'T THEY?
THESE GLOVES SPURT OUT SPICY JUICE FROM A TAMATO BERRY.
I KNEW YOU WERE HIDING THERE THE MOMENT I GOT HERE!
THAT IDIOT TABITHA DIDN'T SEEM TO NOTICE.
SIZZZ
SIZZZ
YOU KNOW, I'M GLAD I STAYED BEHIND! THERE'S GONNA BE TROUBLE IF PEOPLE FIND OUT ABOUT US.
KER SMASH

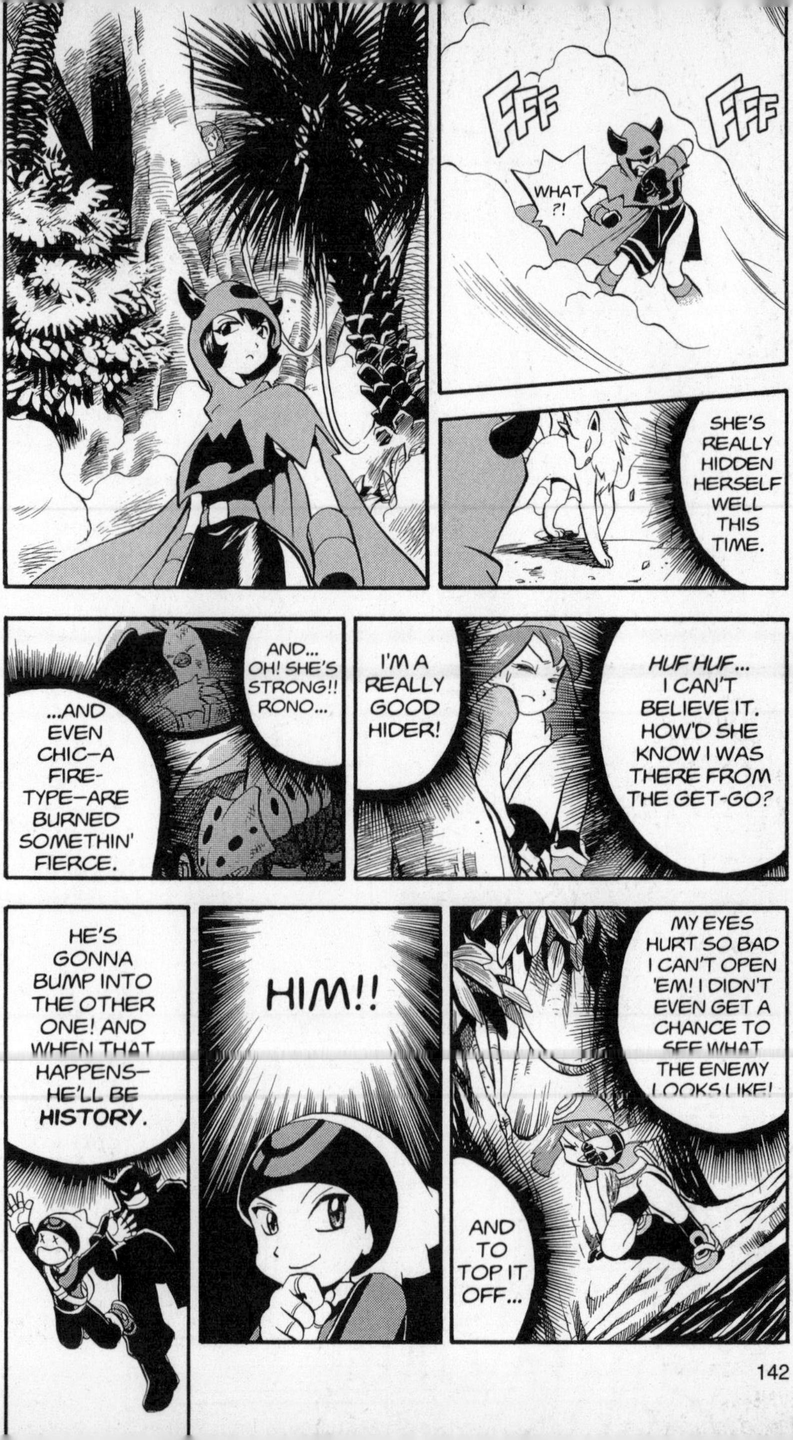
FFF
FFF
WHAT ?!
SHE'S REALLY HIDDEN HERSELF WELL THIS TIME.
HUF HUF...
I CAN'T BELIEVE IT. HOW'D SHE KNOW I WAS THERE FROM THE GET-GO?
I'M A REALLY GOOD HIDER!
AND... OH! SHE'S STRONG!! RONO...
...AND EVEN CHIC—A FIRE-TYPE—ARE BURNED SOMETHIN' FIERCE.
MY EYES HURT SO BAD I CAN'T OPEN 'EM! I DIDN'T EVEN GET A CHANCE TO SEE WHAT THE ENEMY LOOKS LIKE!
AND TO TOP IT OFF...
HIM!!
HE'S GONNA BUMP INTO THE OTHER ONE! AND WHEN THAT HAPPENS— HE'LL BE **HISTORY**.

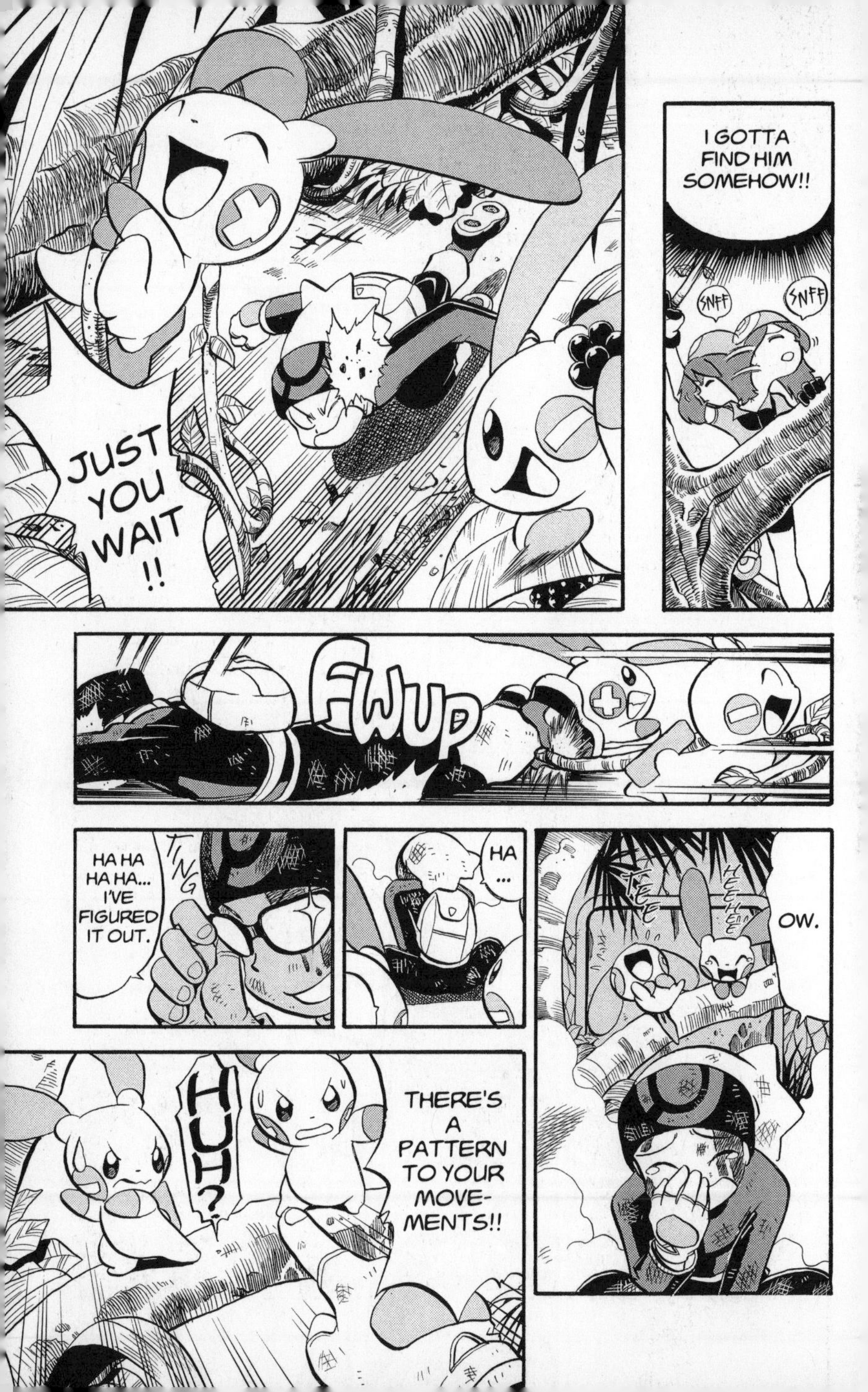
I GOTTA FIND HIM SOMEHOW!!
SNFF
SNFF
JUST YOU WAIT!!
FWUP
OW.
HA ...
HA HA HA HA... I'VE FIGURED IT OUT.
TING
THERE'S A PATTERN TO YOUR MOVE-MENTS!!
HUH?

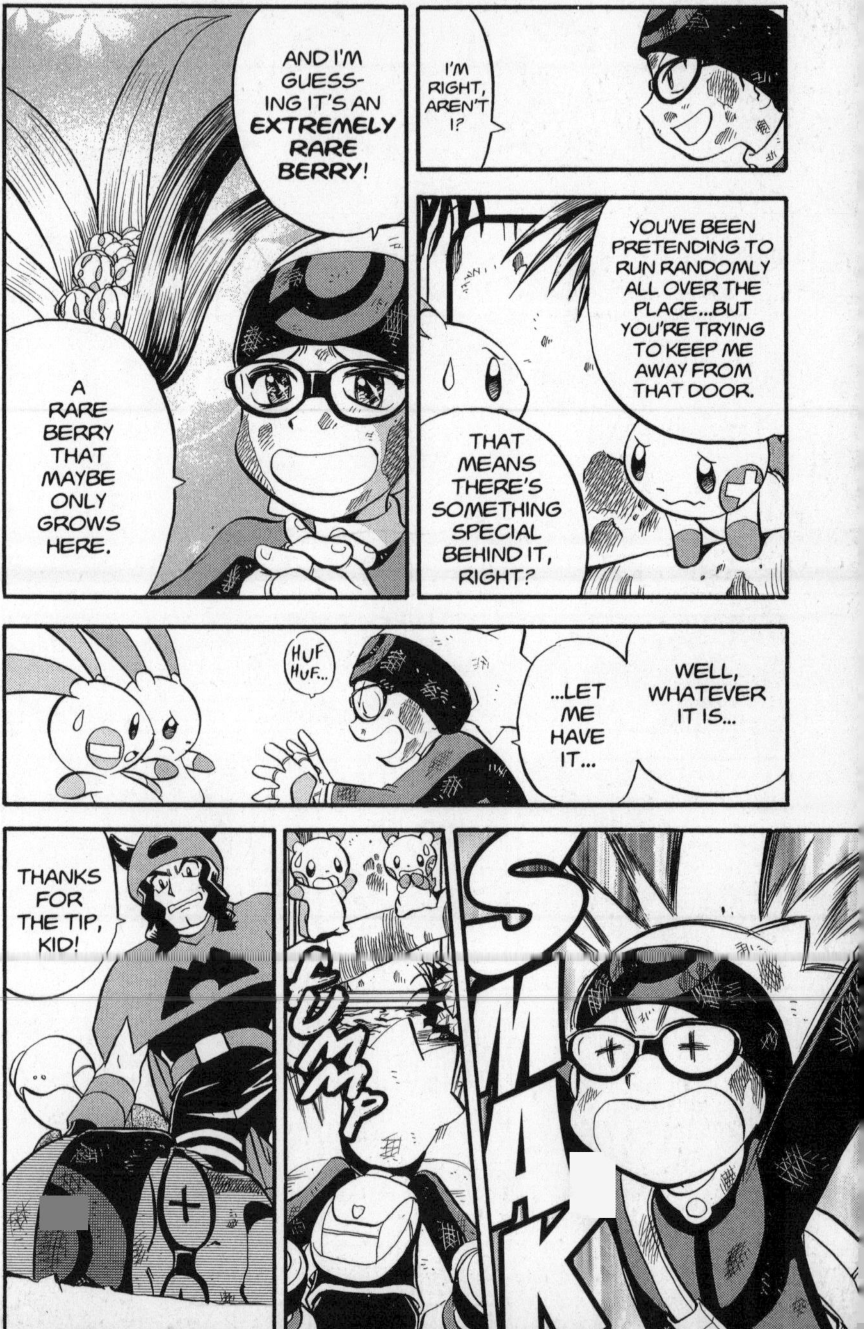
I'M RIGHT, AREN'T I?
YOU'VE BEEN PRETENDING TO RUN RANDOMLY ALL OVER THE PLACE...BUT YOU'RE TRYING TO KEEP ME AWAY FROM THAT DOOR.
THAT MEANS THERE'S SOMETHING SPECIAL BEHIND IT, RIGHT?
AND I'M GUESSING IT'S AN **EXTREMELY RARE BERRY**!
A RARE BERRY THAT MAYBE ONLY GROWS HERE.
WELL, WHATEVER IT IS...
...LET ME HAVE IT...
HUF HUF...
SMAK
THUMP
THANKS FOR THE TIP, KID!

S M A S H

I SAID, BEAT IT!!

MOVE ASIDE NOW!!

SPROING

HEE HEE HEE! BINGO!

I don't have much time left. My only concern is the scanner and my Plusle and Minun.

HUH?

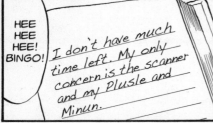

STRCCH

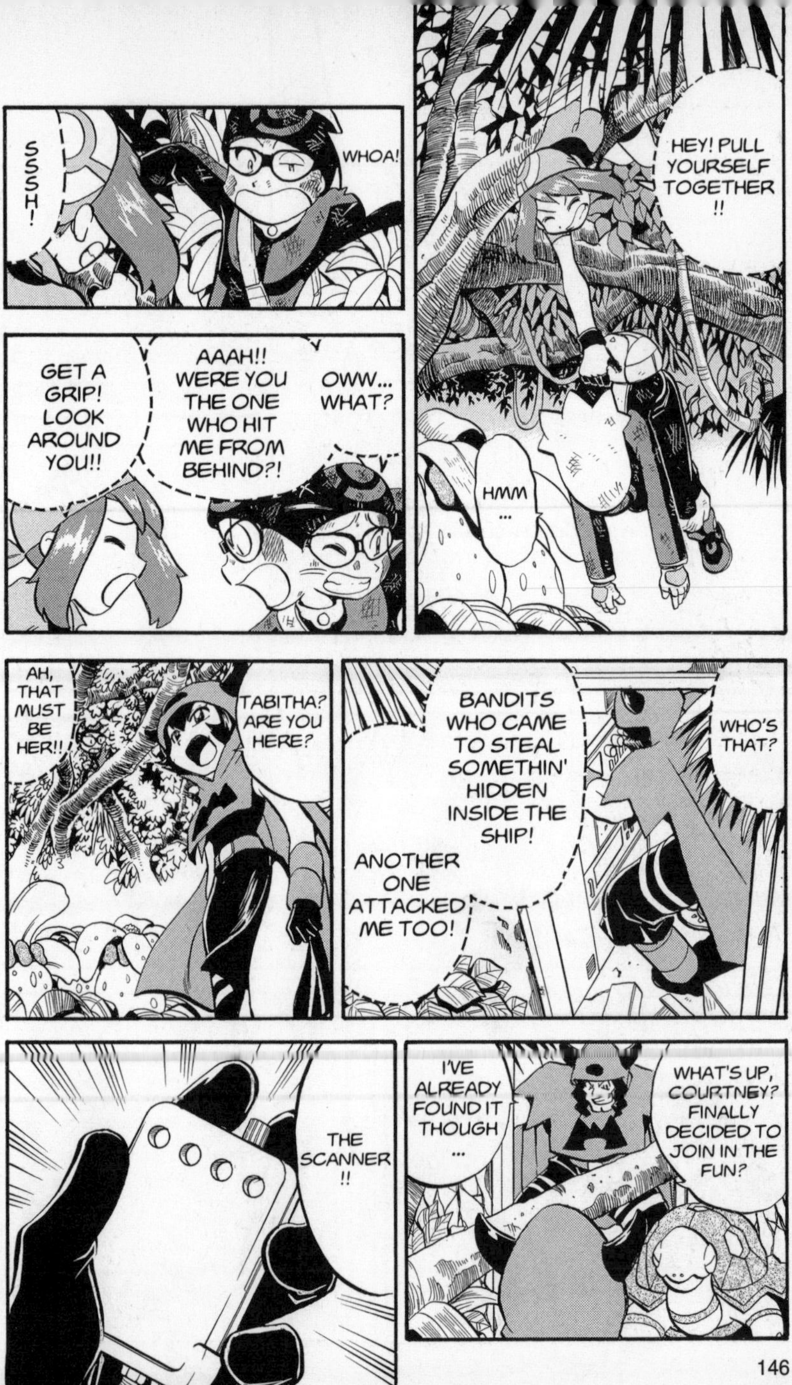
HEY! PULL YOURSELF TOGETHER !!
HMM ...
WHOA!
SSSH!
OWW... WHAT?
AAAH!! WERE YOU THE ONE WHO HIT ME FROM BEHIND?!
GET A GRIP! LOOK AROUND YOU!!
WHO'S THAT?
BANDITS WHO CAME TO STEAL SOMETHIN' HIDDEN INSIDE THE SHIP!
ANOTHER ONE ATTACKED ME TOO!
TABITHA? ARE YOU HERE?
AH, THAT MUST BE HER!!
WHAT'S UP, COURTNEY? FINALLY DECIDED TO JOIN IN THE FUN?
I'VE ALREADY FOUND IT THOUGH ...
THE SCANNER !!

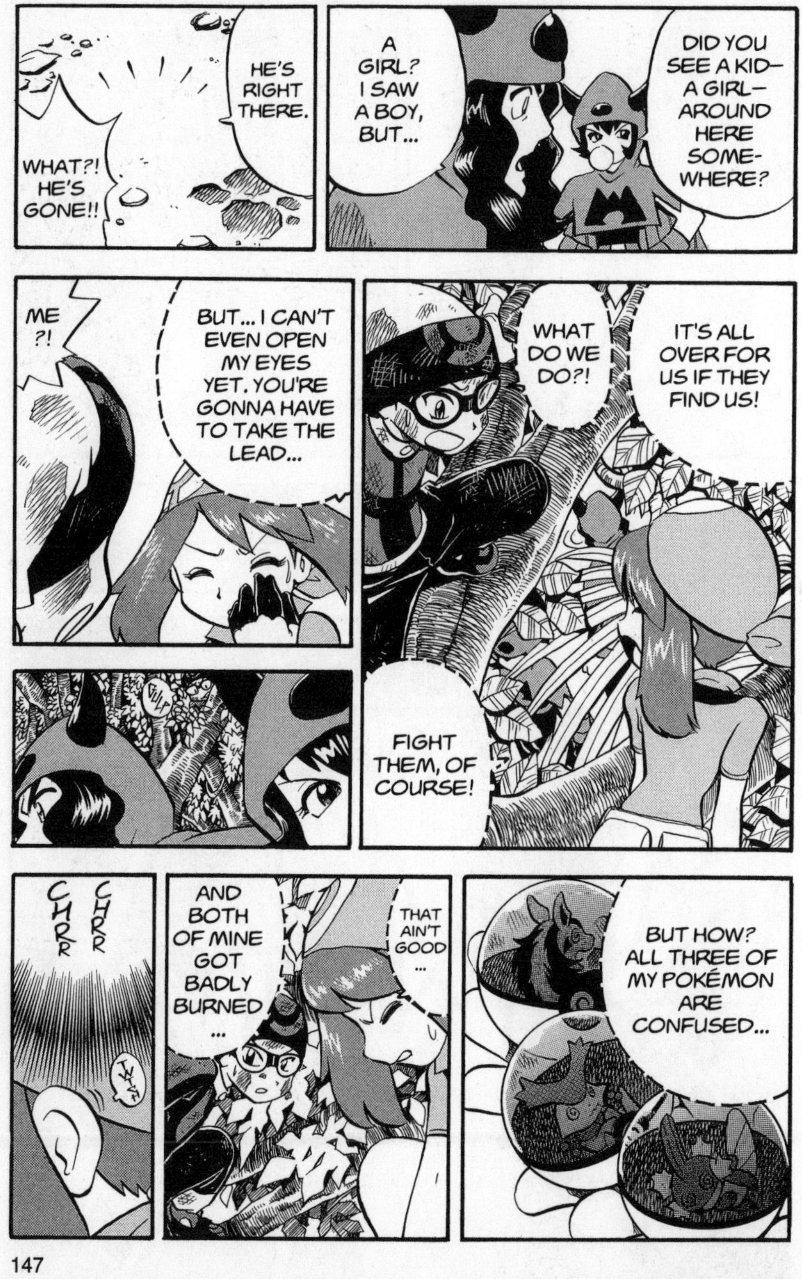
DID YOU SEE A KID— A GIRL— AROUND HERE SOMEWHERE?
A GIRL? I SAW A BOY, BUT...
HE'S RIGHT THERE.
WHAT?! HE'S GONE!!
IT'S ALL OVER FOR US IF THEY FIND US!
WHAT DO WE DO?!
FIGHT THEM, OF COURSE!
BUT... I CAN'T EVEN OPEN MY EYES YET. YOU'RE GONNA HAVE TO TAKE THE LEAD...
ME ?!
GULP
BUT HOW? ALL THREE OF MY POKÉMON ARE CONFUSED...
THAT AIN'T GOOD ...
AND BOTH OF MINE GOT BADLY BURNED ...
CHRR
CHRR
TWISH

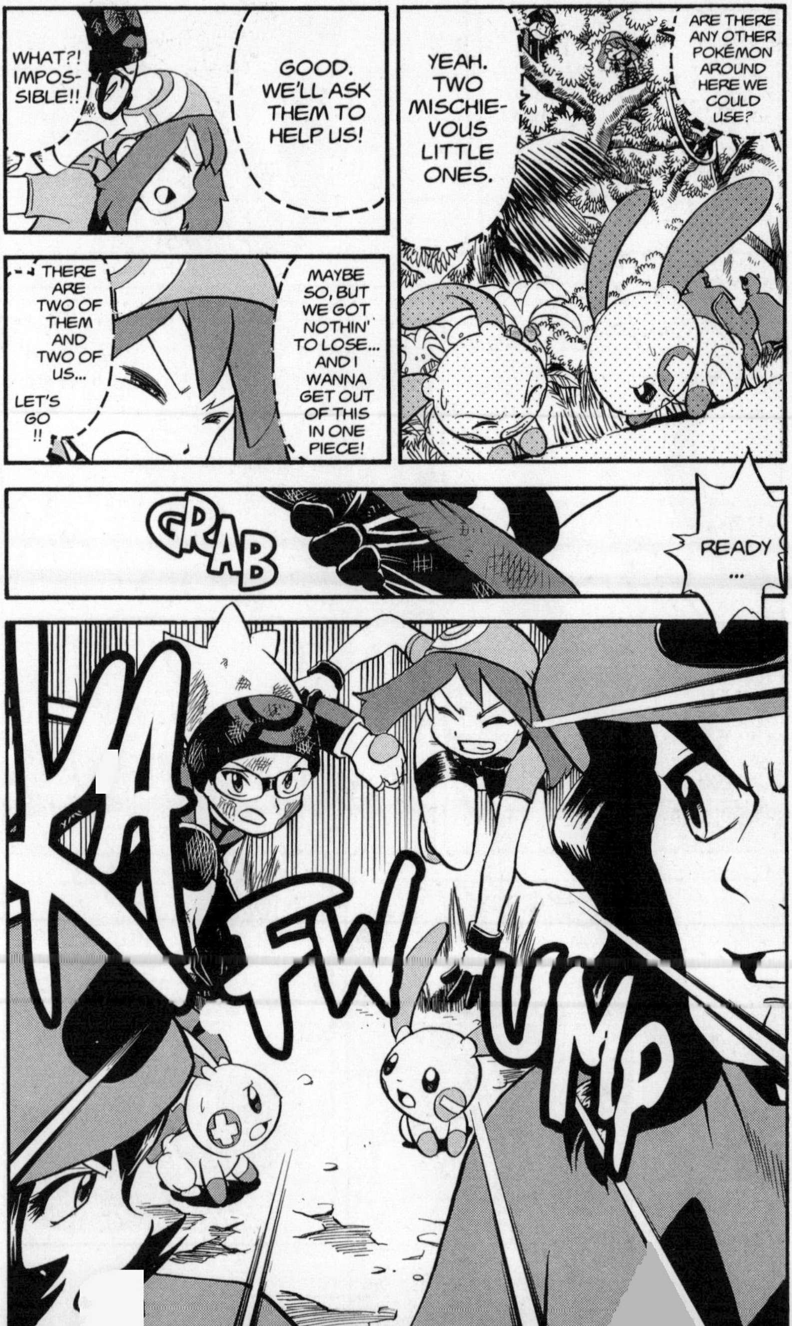
ARE THERE ANY OTHER POKÉMON AROUND HERE WE COULD USE?
YEAH. TWO MISCHIEVOUS LITTLE ONES.
GOOD. WE'LL ASK THEM TO HELP US!
WHAT?! IMPOSSIBLE!!
MAYBE SO, BUT WE GOT NOTHIN' TO LOSE... AND I WANNA GET OUT OF THIS IN ONE PIECE!
THERE ARE TWO OF THEM AND TWO OF US...
LET'S GO!!
READY...
GRAB
FWUMP

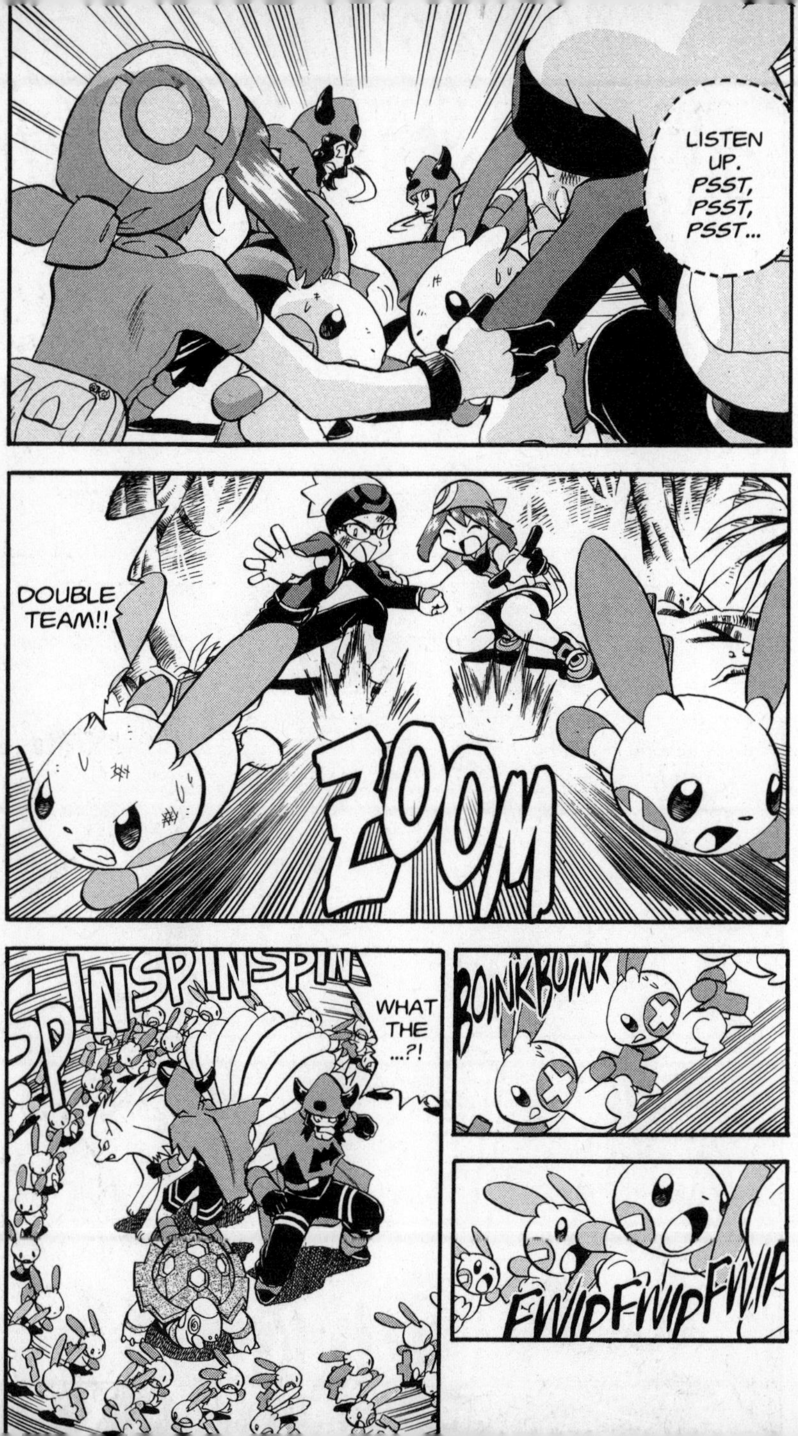
LISTEN UP. PSST, PSST, PSST...
DOUBLE TEAM!!
ZOOM
BOINK BOINK
FWIP FWIP FWIP
SPIN SPIN SPIN SPIN
WHAT THE ...?!

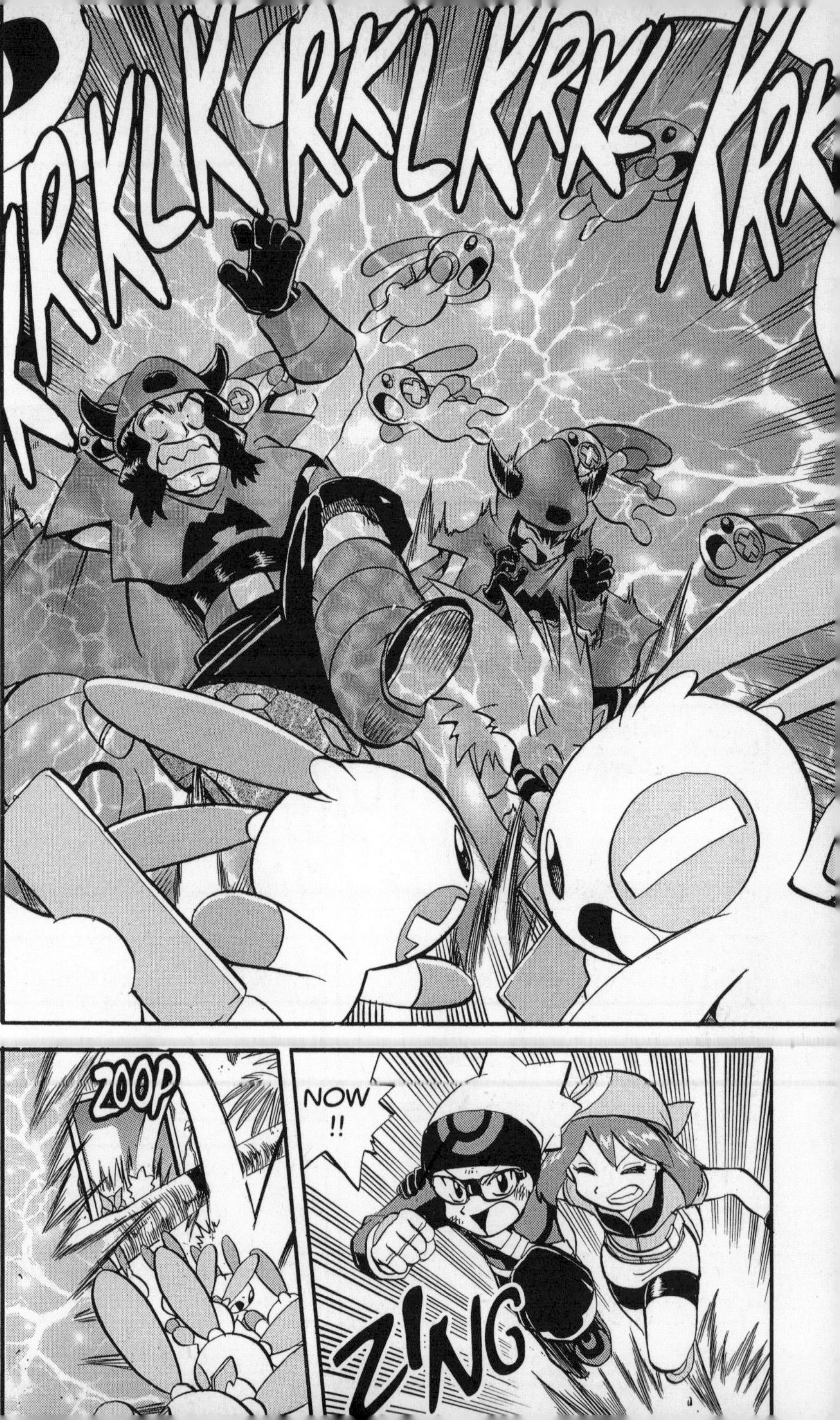
KRKLK KRKL KRKL KRK
NOW!!
ZING
ZOOP

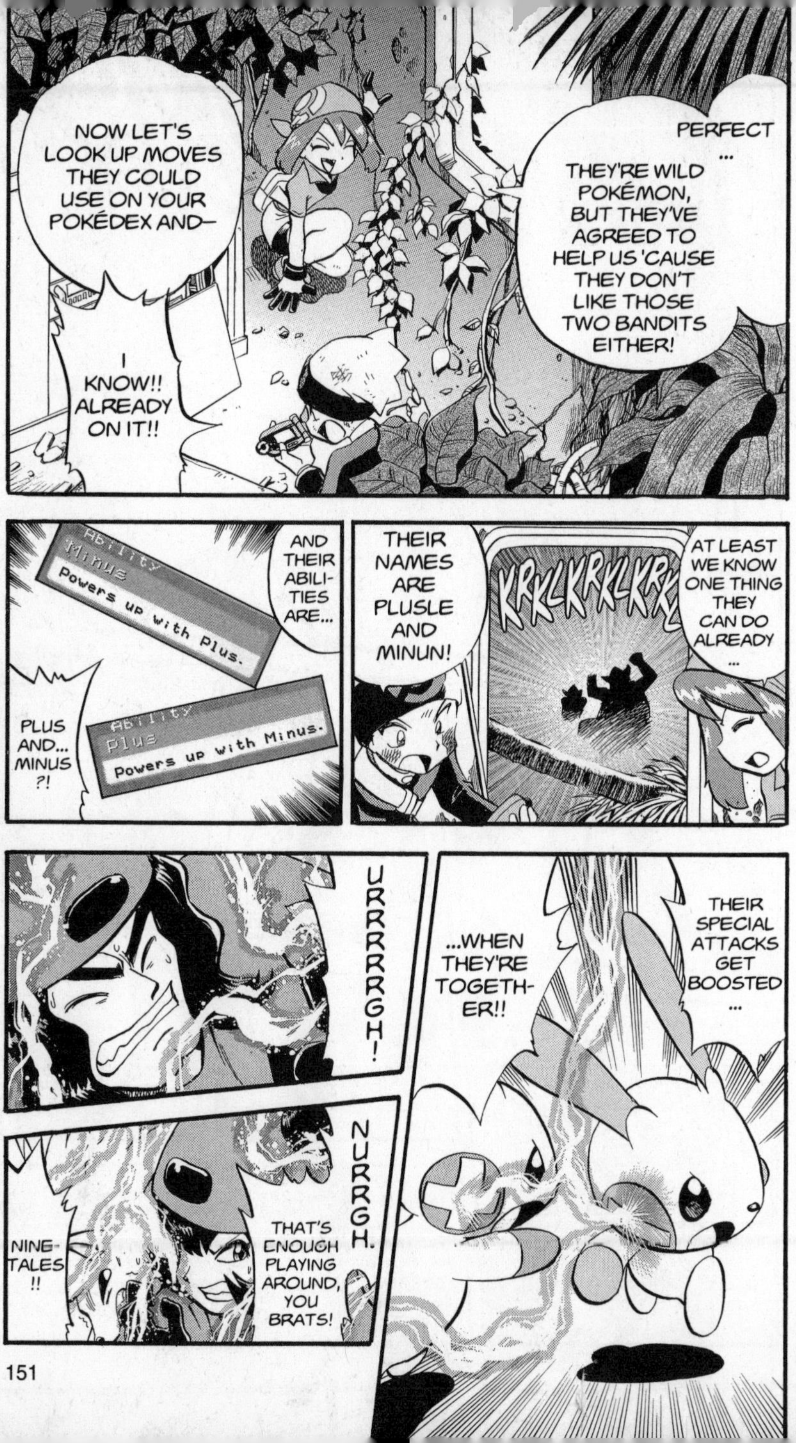
PERFECT ... THEY'RE WILD POKÉMON, BUT THEY'VE AGREED TO HELP US 'CAUSE THEY DON'T LIKE THOSE TWO BANDITS EITHER!
NOW LET'S LOOK UP MOVES THEY COULD USE ON YOUR POKÉDEX AND—
I KNOW!! ALREADY ON IT!!
AT LEAST WE KNOW ONE THING THEY CAN DO ALREADY ...
KRKLKRKLKR
THEIR NAMES ARE PLUSLE AND MINUN!
AND THEIR ABILITIES ARE...
Ability Minus Powers up with Plus.
Ability Plus Powers up with Minus.
PLUS AND... MINUS ?!
THEIR SPECIAL ATTACKS GET BOOSTED ...
...WHEN THEY'RE TOGETHER!!
URRRRRGH!
NURRGH.
THAT'S ENOUGH PLAYING AROUND, YOU BRATS!
NINETALES!!

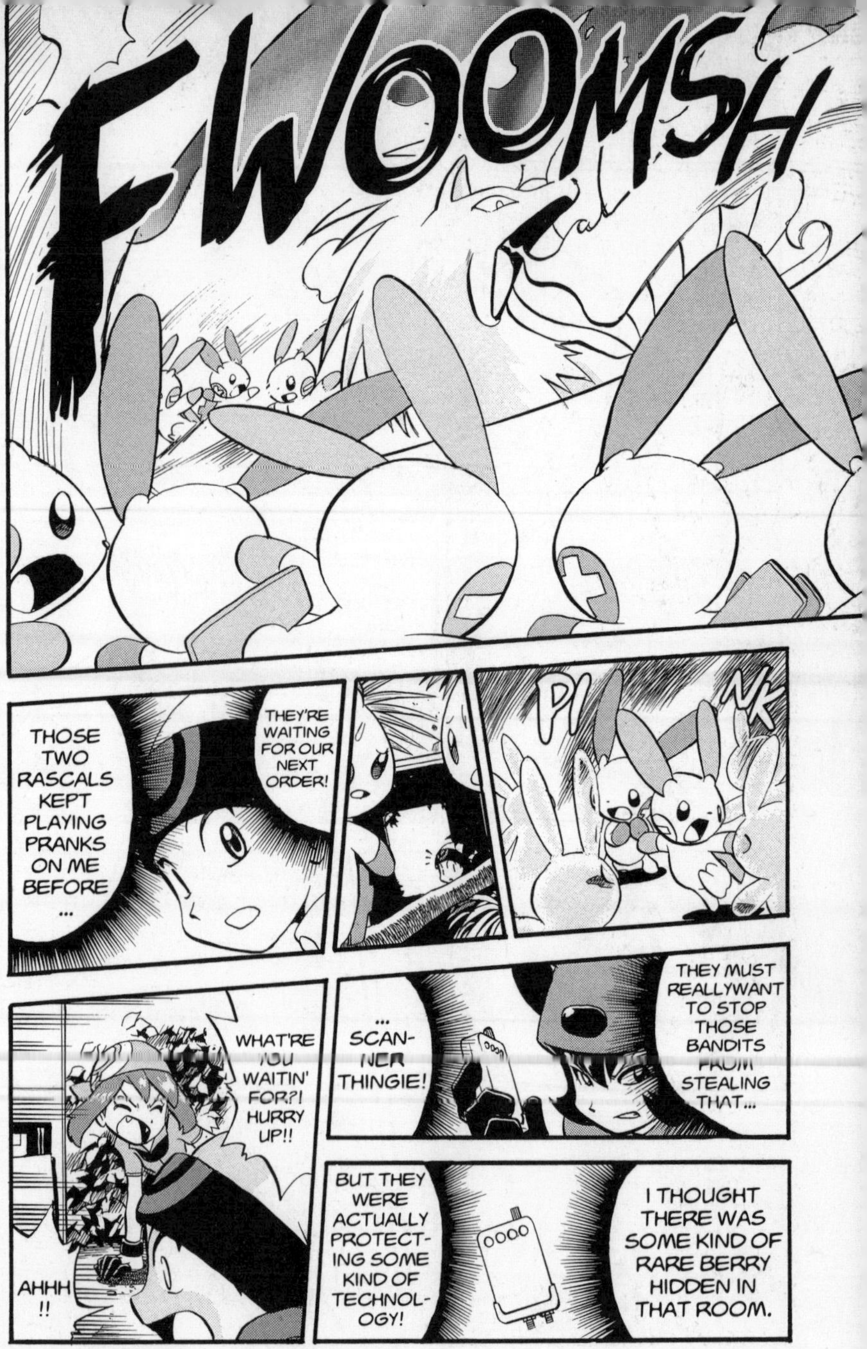
FWOOMSH
PI NK
THEY'RE WAITING FOR OUR NEXT ORDER!
THOSE TWO RASCALS KEPT PLAYING PRANKS ON ME BEFORE ...
THEY MUST REALLY WANT TO STOP THOSE BANDITS FROM STEALING THAT...
... SCANNER THINGIE!
I THOUGHT THERE WAS SOME KIND OF RARE BERRY HIDDEN IN THAT ROOM.
BUT THEY WERE ACTUALLY PROTECTING SOME KIND OF TECHNOLOGY!
WHAT'RE YOU WAITIN' FOR?! HURRY UP!!
AHHH!!

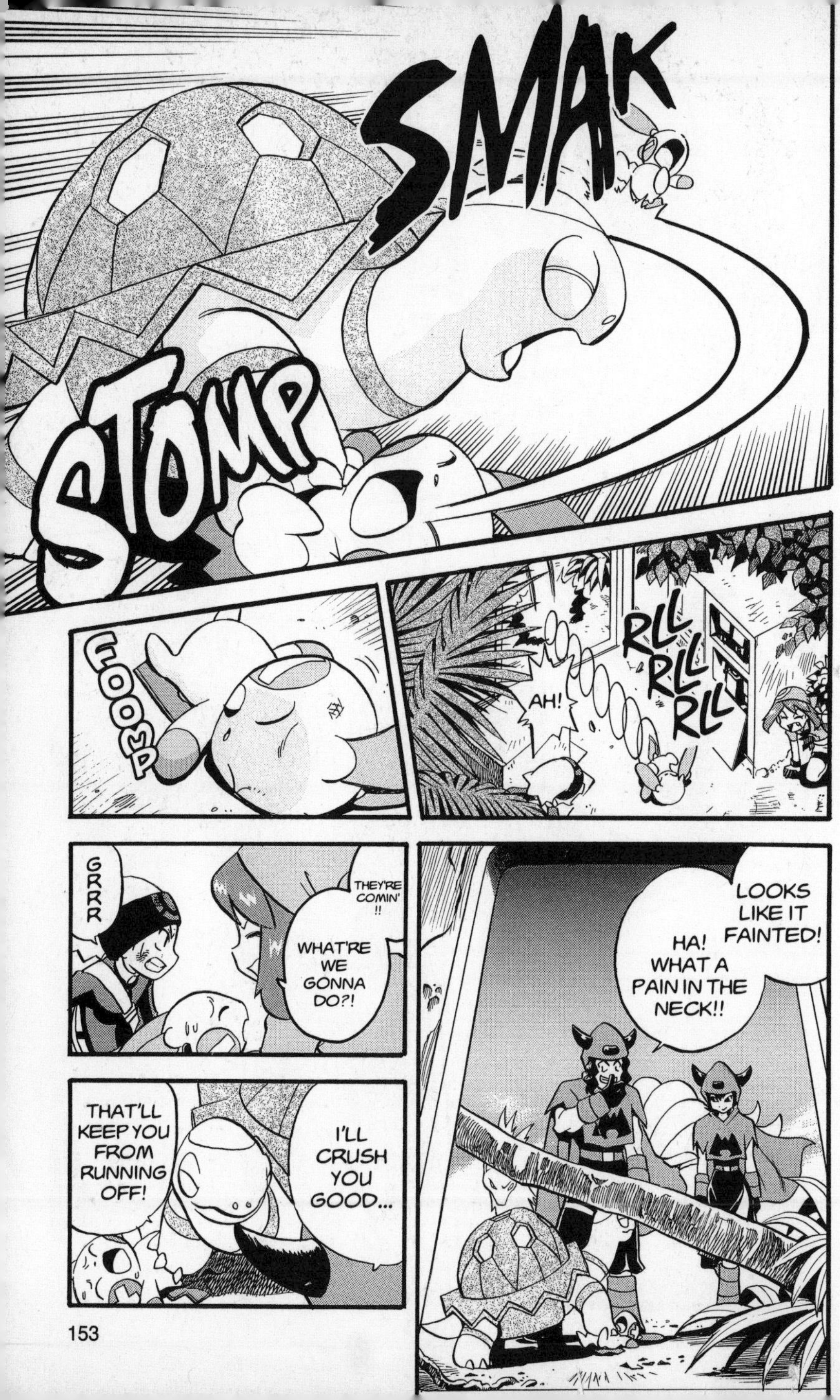
SMAK
STOMP
AH!
RLL RLL RLL
FOOMP
LOOKS LIKE IT FAINTED!
HA! WHAT A PAIN IN THE NECK!!
THEY'RE COMIN'!!
WHAT'RE WE GONNA DO?!
GRRR
I'LL CRUSH YOU GOOD...
THAT'LL KEEP YOU FROM RUNNING OFF!

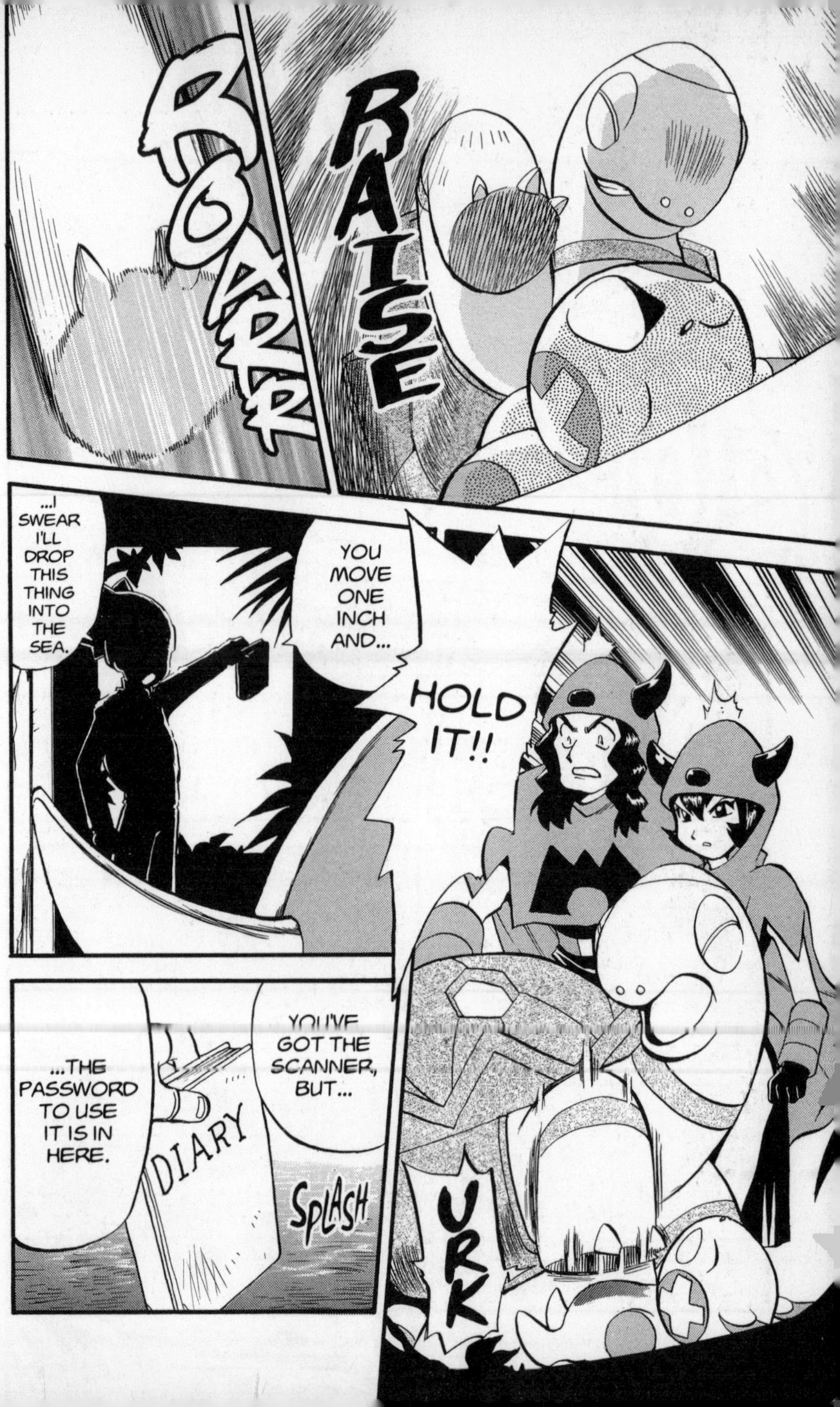
RAISE
ROARRR
HOLD IT!!
YOU MOVE ONE INCH AND...
...I SWEAR I'LL DROP THIS THING INTO THE SEA.
URK
YOU'VE GOT THE SCANNER, BUT...
...THE PASSWORD TO USE IT IS IN HERE.
DIARY
SPLASH

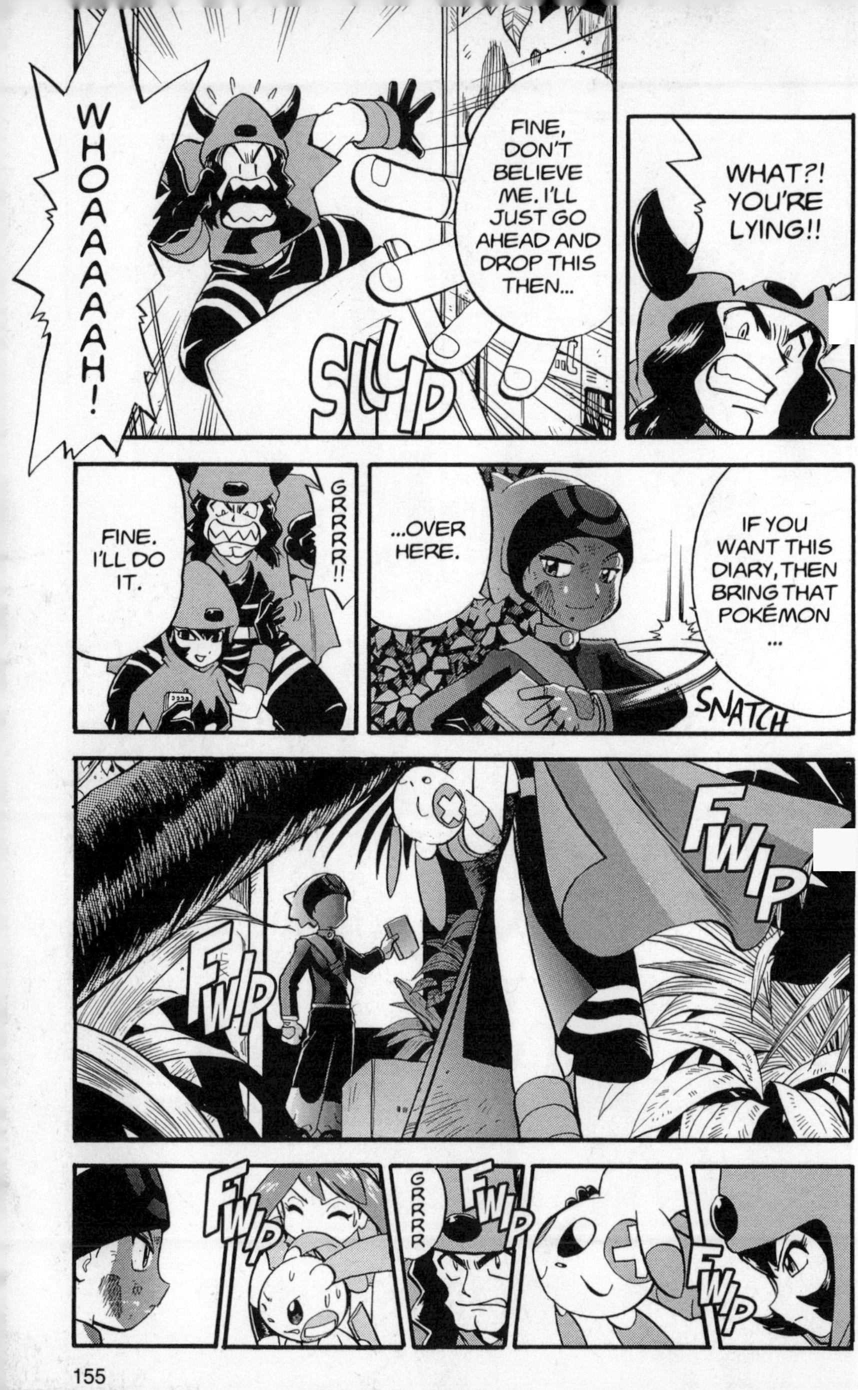
WHAT?! YOU'RE LYING!!
FINE, DON'T BELIEVE ME. I'LL JUST GO AHEAD AND DROP THIS THEN...
SLLIP
WHOAAAAAAAH!
IF YOU WANT THIS DIARY, THEN BRING THAT POKÉMON ...
SNATCH
...OVER HERE.
GRRRRR!!
FINE. I'LL DO IT.
FWIP
FWIP
FWIP
FWIP
GRRRR
FWIP

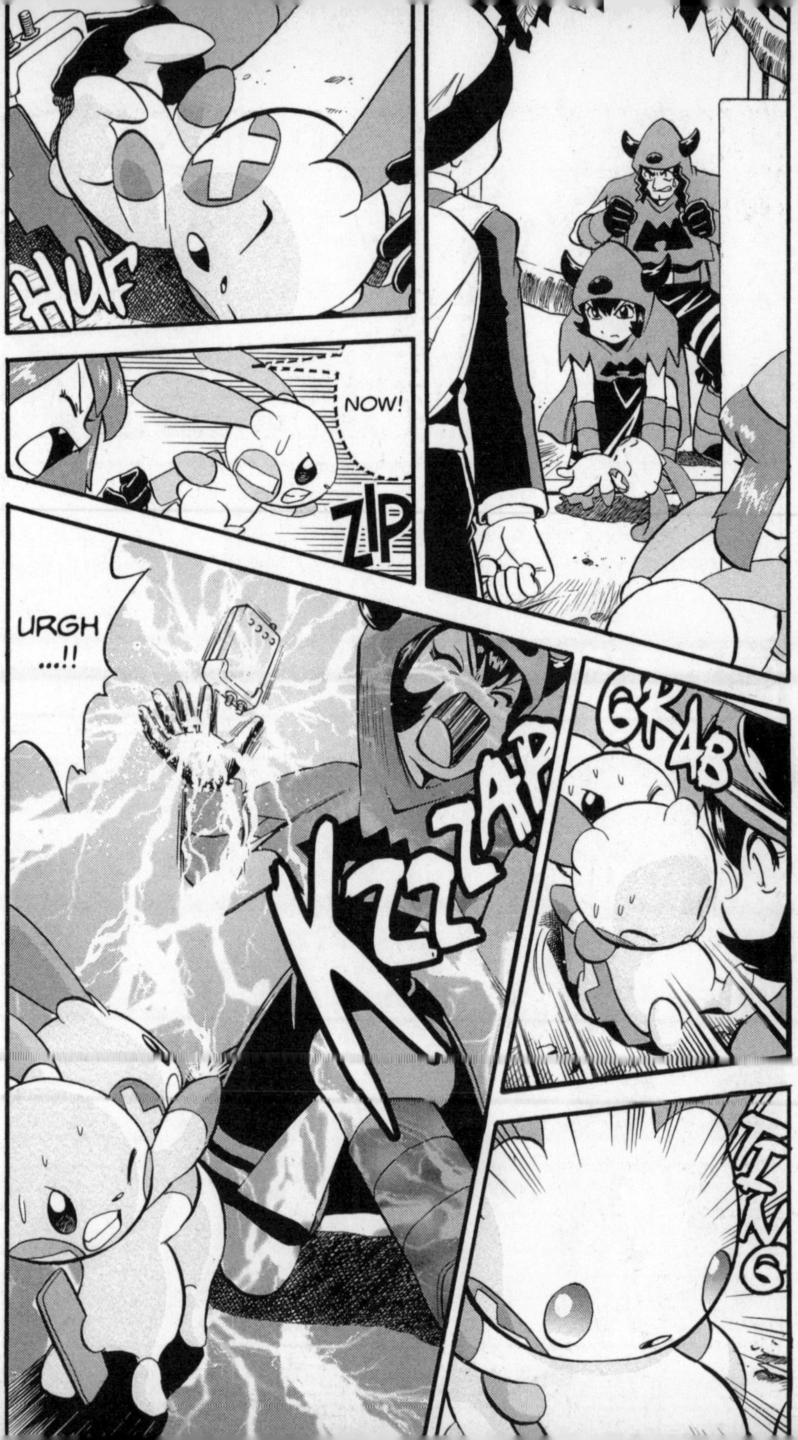
HUF
NOW!
ZIP
GRAB
TING
URGH ...!!
XZZZAP

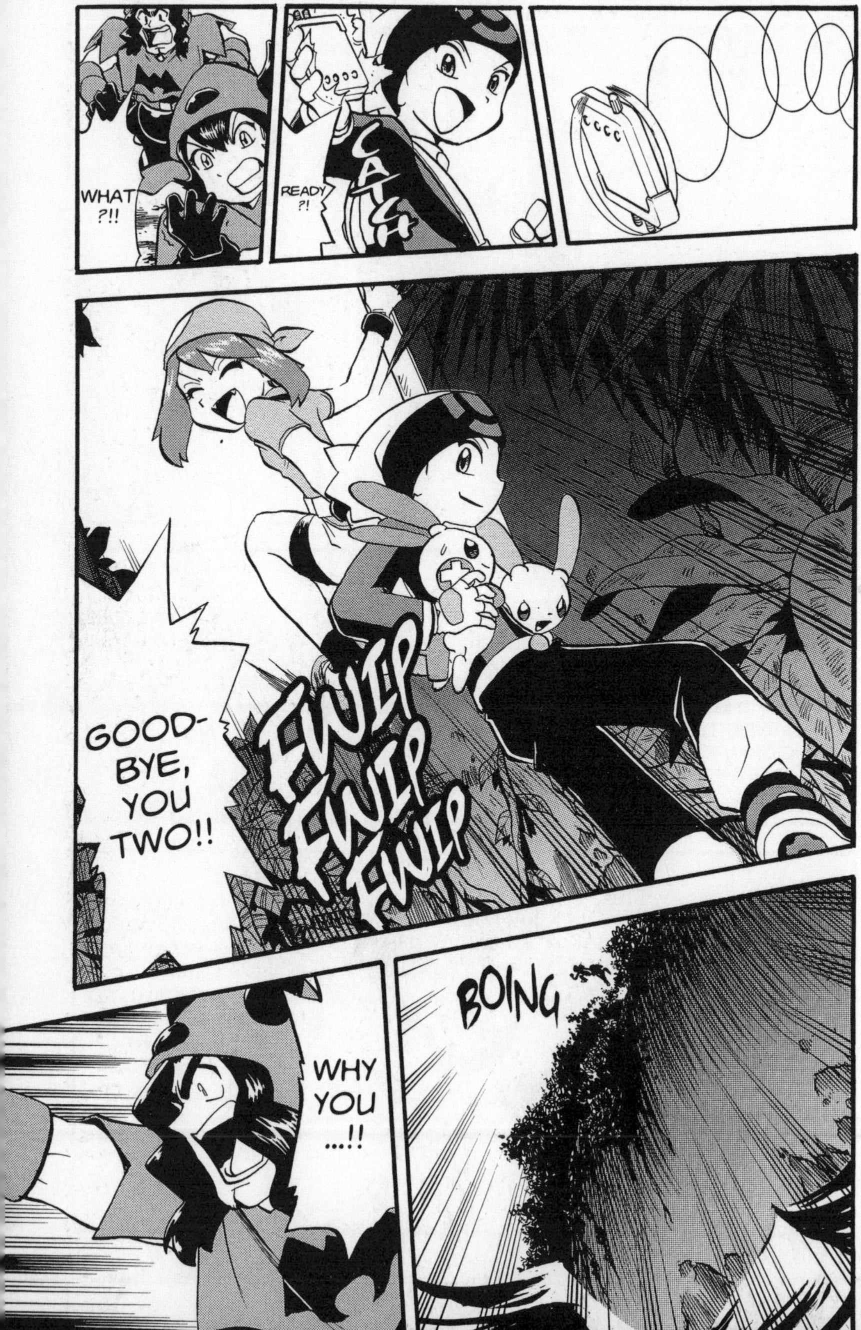
CATCH
READY ?!
WHAT ?!!
FWIP FWIP FWIP
GOOD-BYE, YOU TWO!!
BOING
WHY YOU ...!!

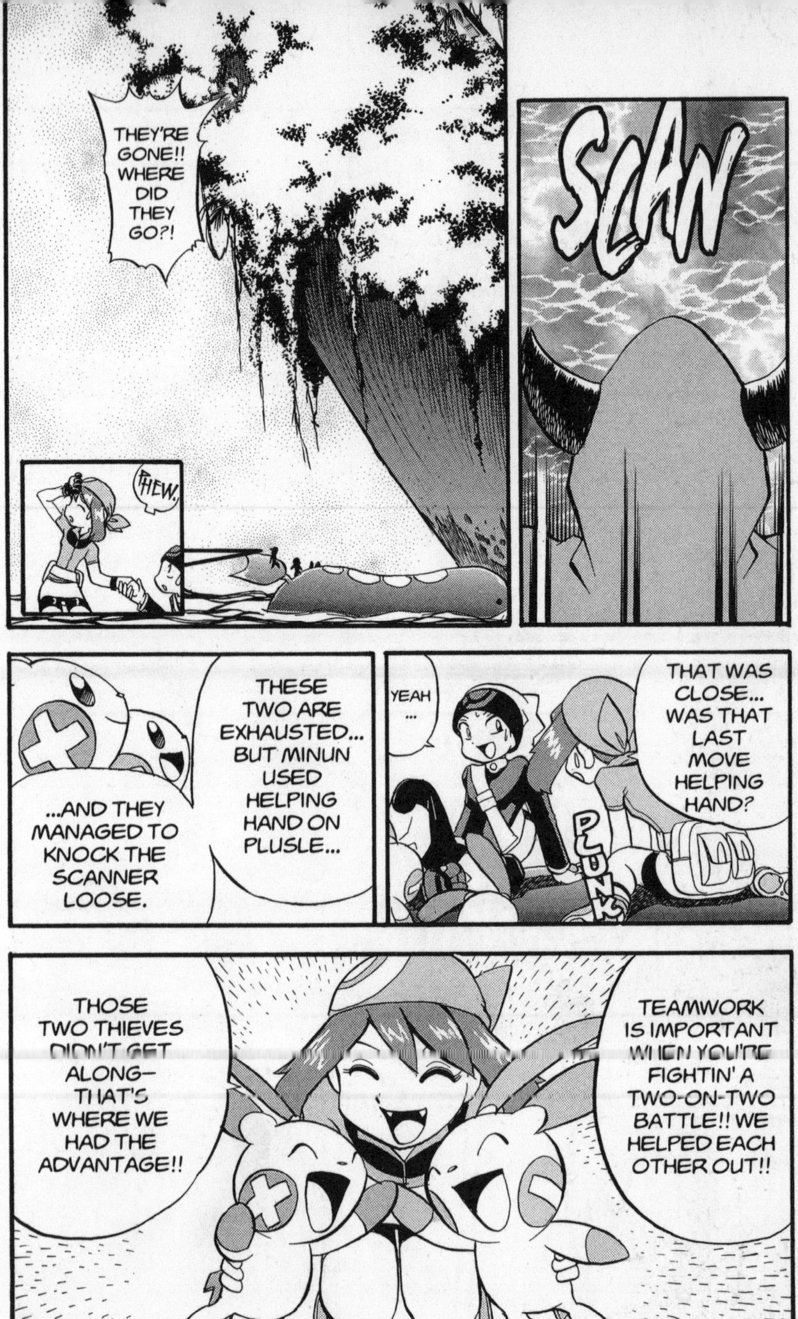
SCAN
THEY'RE GONE!! WHERE DID THEY GO?!
PHEW.
THAT WAS CLOSE... WAS THAT LAST MOVE HELPING HAND?
YEAH ...
PLUNK
THESE TWO ARE EXHAUSTED... BUT MINUN USED HELPING HAND ON PLUSLE...
...AND THEY MANAGED TO KNOCK THE SCANNER LOOSE.
TEAMWORK IS IMPORTANT WHEN YOU'RE FIGHTIN' A TWO-ON-TWO BATTLE!! WE HELPED EACH OTHER OUT!!
THOSE TWO THIEVES DIDN'T GET ALONG—THAT'S WHERE WE HAD THE ADVANTAGE!!

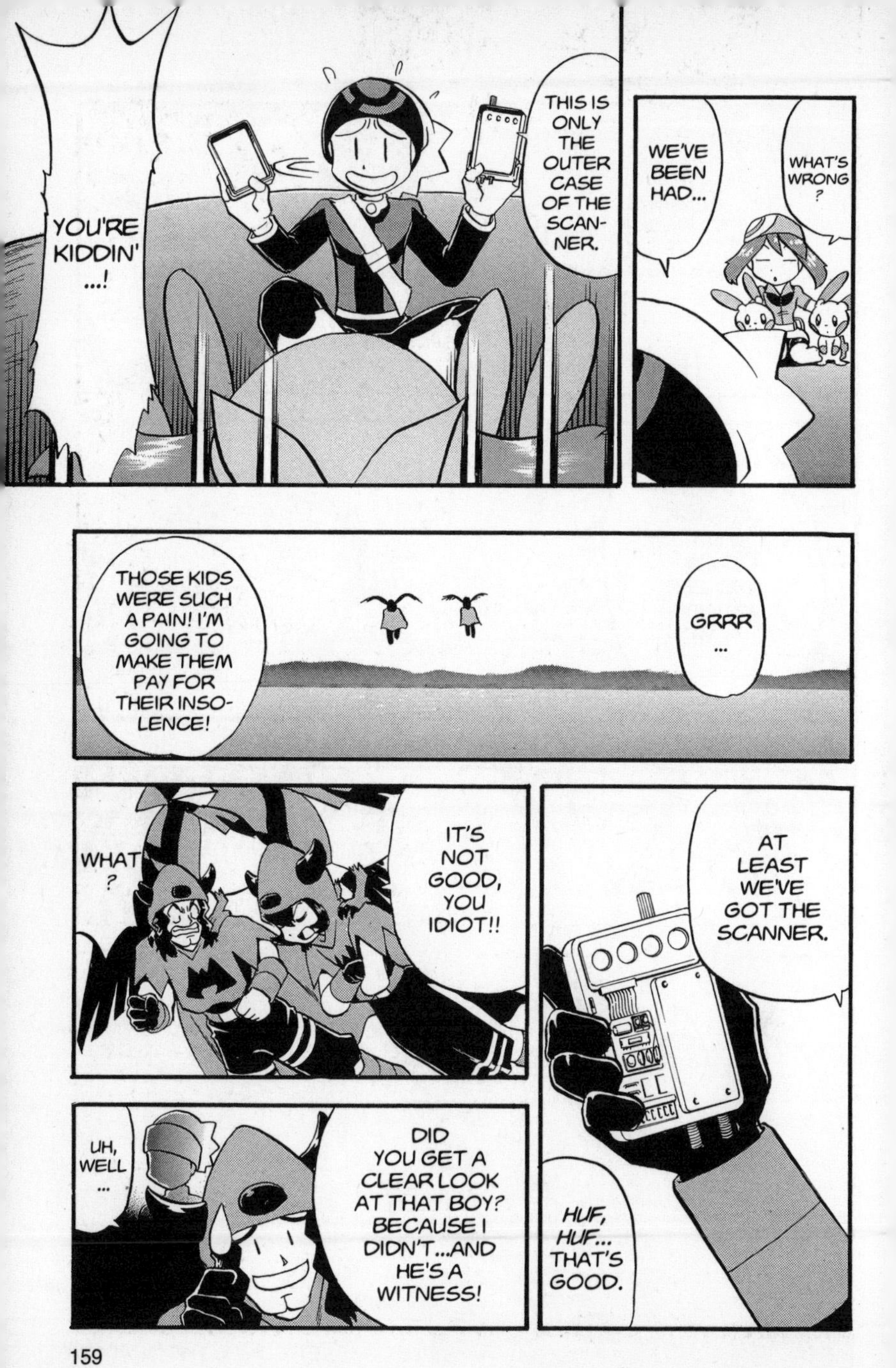
WHAT'S WRONG?
WE'VE BEEN HAD...
THIS IS ONLY THE OUTER CASE OF THE SCAN-NER.
YOU'RE KIDDIN' ...!
GRRR...
THOSE KIDS WERE SUCH A PAIN! I'M GOING TO MAKE THEM PAY FOR THEIR INSO-LENCE!
AT LEAST WE'VE GOT THE SCANNER.
HUF, HUF... THAT'S GOOD.
IT'S NOT GOOD, YOU IDIOT!!
WHAT?
DID YOU GET A CLEAR LOOK AT THAT BOY? BECAUSE I DIDN'T...AND HE'S A WITNESS!
UH, WELL...

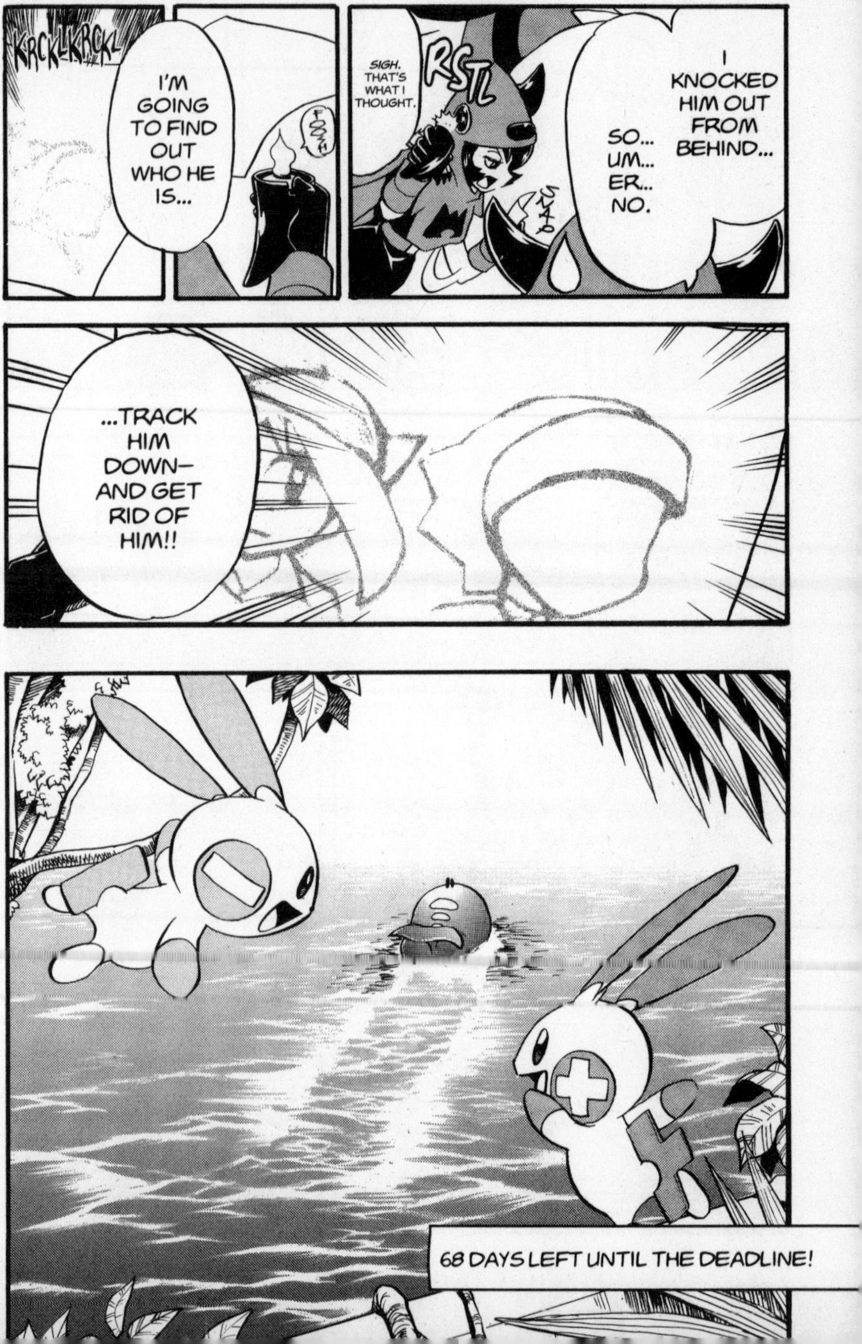
I KNOCKED HIM OUT FROM BEHIND...
SO... UM... ER... NO.
SNAP
RSTL
SIGH. THAT'S WHAT I THOUGHT.
I'M GOING TO FIND OUT WHO HE IS...
FOOSH
KRCKLKRCKL
...TRACK HIM DOWN—AND GET RID OF HIM!!
68 DAYS LEFT UNTIL THE DEADLINE!

● Chapter 200 ●
Tripped Up by Torkoal

Pokémon Adventures Ruby & Sapphire The Fourth Chapter

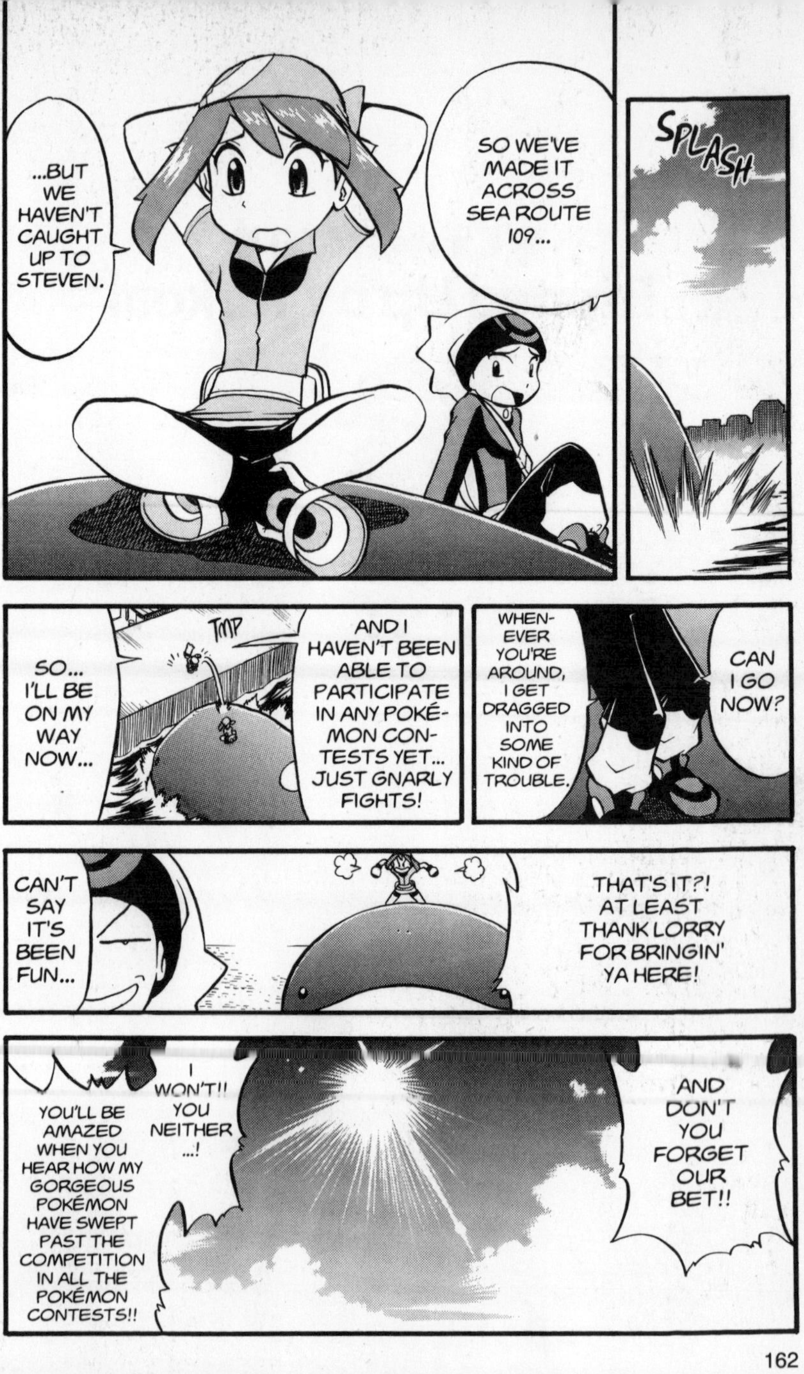
SPLASH
SO WE'VE MADE IT ACROSS SEA ROUTE 109...
...BUT WE HAVEN'T CAUGHT UP TO STEVEN.
CAN I GO NOW?
WHEN-EVER YOU'RE AROUND, I GET DRAGGED INTO SOME KIND OF TROUBLE.
AND I HAVEN'T BEEN ABLE TO PARTICIPATE IN ANY POKÉ-MON CON-TESTS YET... JUST GNARLY FIGHTS!
TMP
SO... I'LL BE ON MY WAY NOW...
THAT'S IT?! AT LEAST THANK LORRY FOR BRINGIN' YA HERE!
CAN'T SAY IT'S BEEN FUN...
AND DON'T YOU FORGET OUR BET!!
I WON'T!! YOU NEITHER ...!
YOU'LL BE AMAZED WHEN YOU HEAR HOW MY GORGEOUS POKÉMON HAVE SWEPT PAST THE COMPETITION IN ALL THE POKÉMON CONTESTS!!

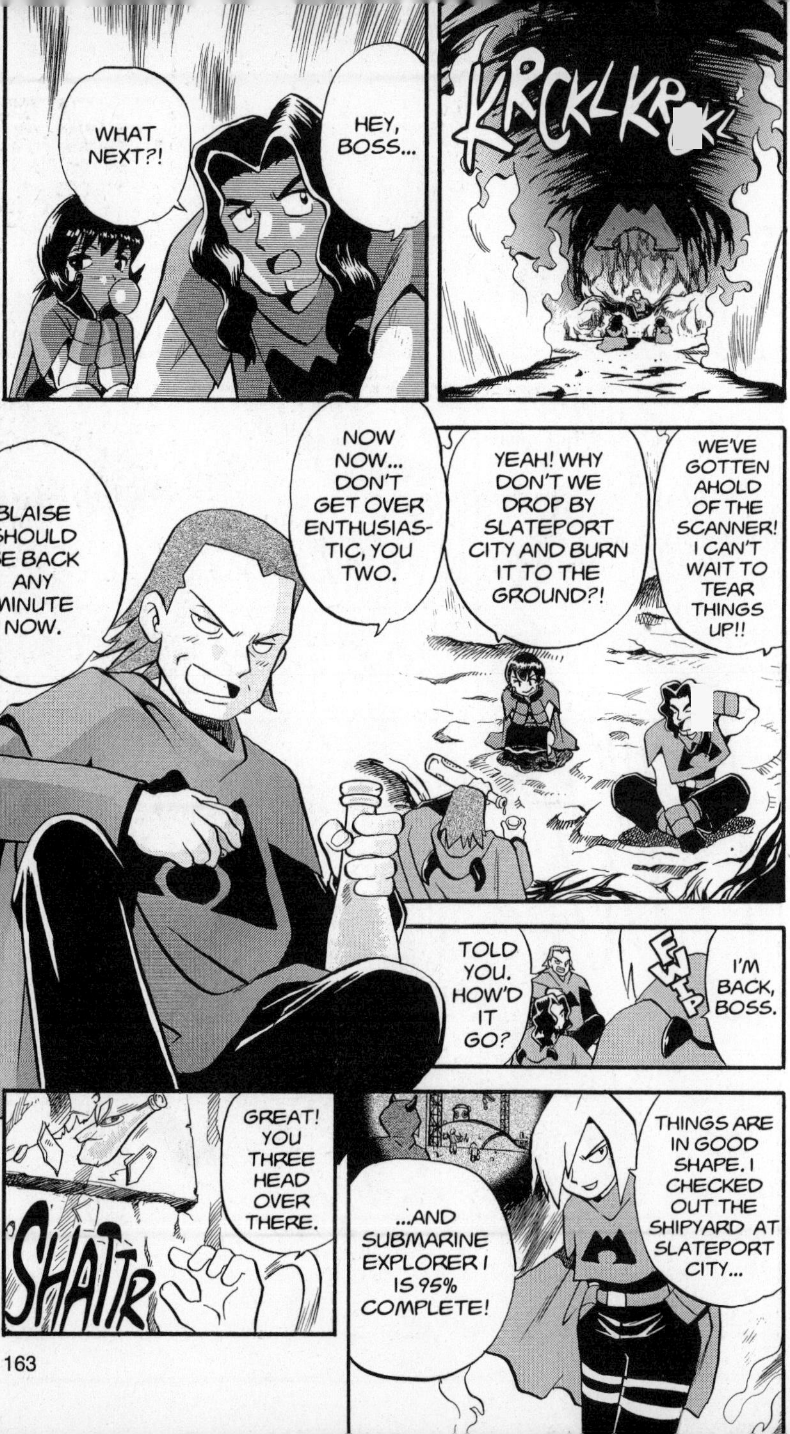
KRCKLKR KL
HEY, BOSS...
WHAT NEXT?!
WE'VE GOTTEN AHOLD OF THE SCANNER! I CAN'T WAIT TO TEAR THINGS UP!!
YEAH! WHY DON'T WE DROP BY SLATEPORT CITY AND BURN IT TO THE GROUND?!
NOW NOW... DON'T GET OVER ENTHUSIAS-TIC, YOU TWO.
BLAISE SHOULD BE BACK ANY MINUTE NOW.
I'M BACK, BOSS.
FWIP
TOLD YOU. HOW'D IT GO?
THINGS ARE IN GOOD SHAPE. I CHECKED OUT THE SHIPYARD AT SLATEPORT CITY...
...AND SUBMARINE EXPLORER 1 IS 95% COMPLETE!
GREAT! YOU THREE HEAD OVER THERE.
SHATTR

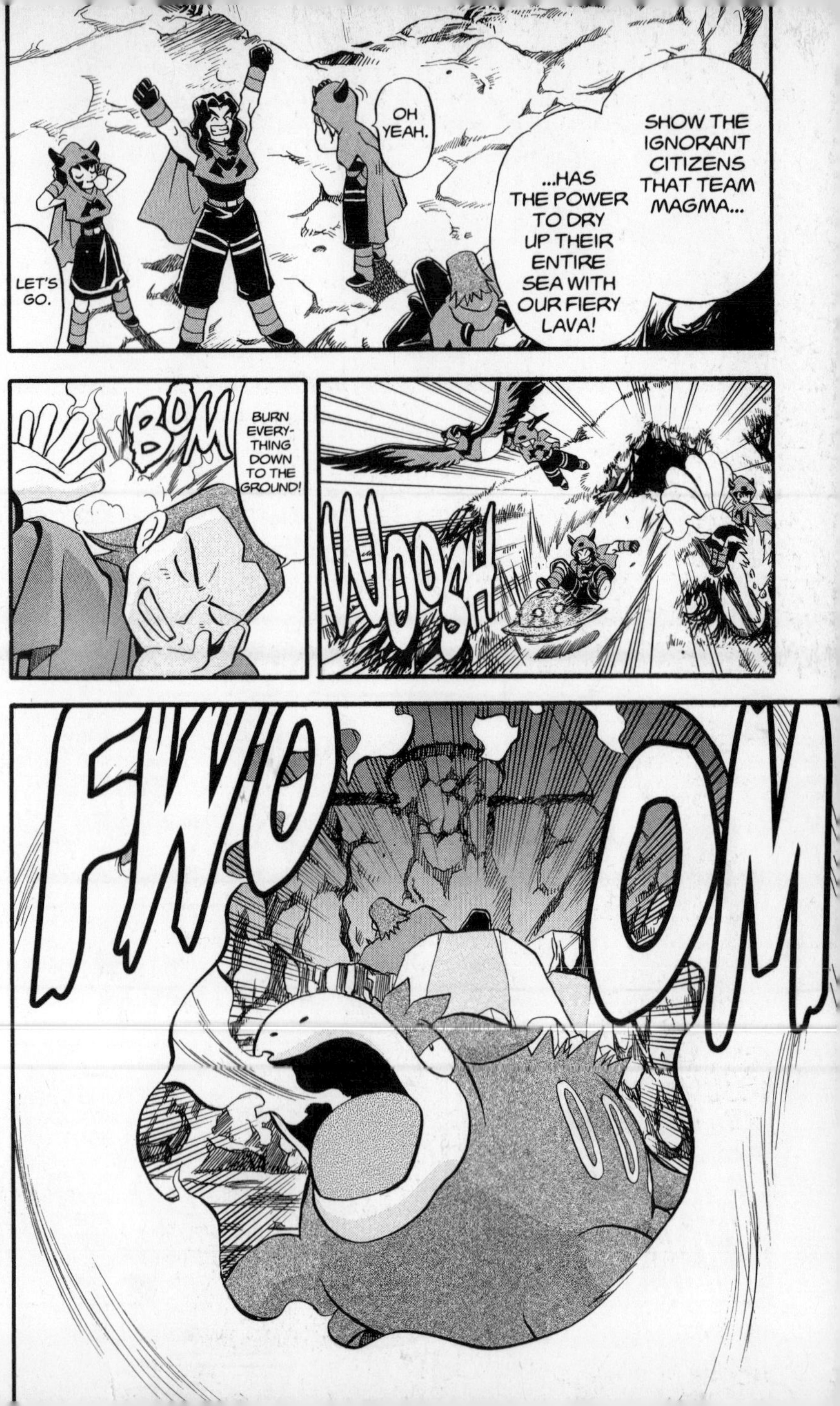
SHOW THE IGNORANT CITIZENS THAT TEAM MAGMA...
...HAS THE POWER TO DRY UP THEIR ENTIRE SEA WITH OUR FIERY LAVA!
OH YEAH.
LET'S GO.
WOOSH
BURN EVERY-THING DOWN TO THE GROUND!
BOM
FWOOM

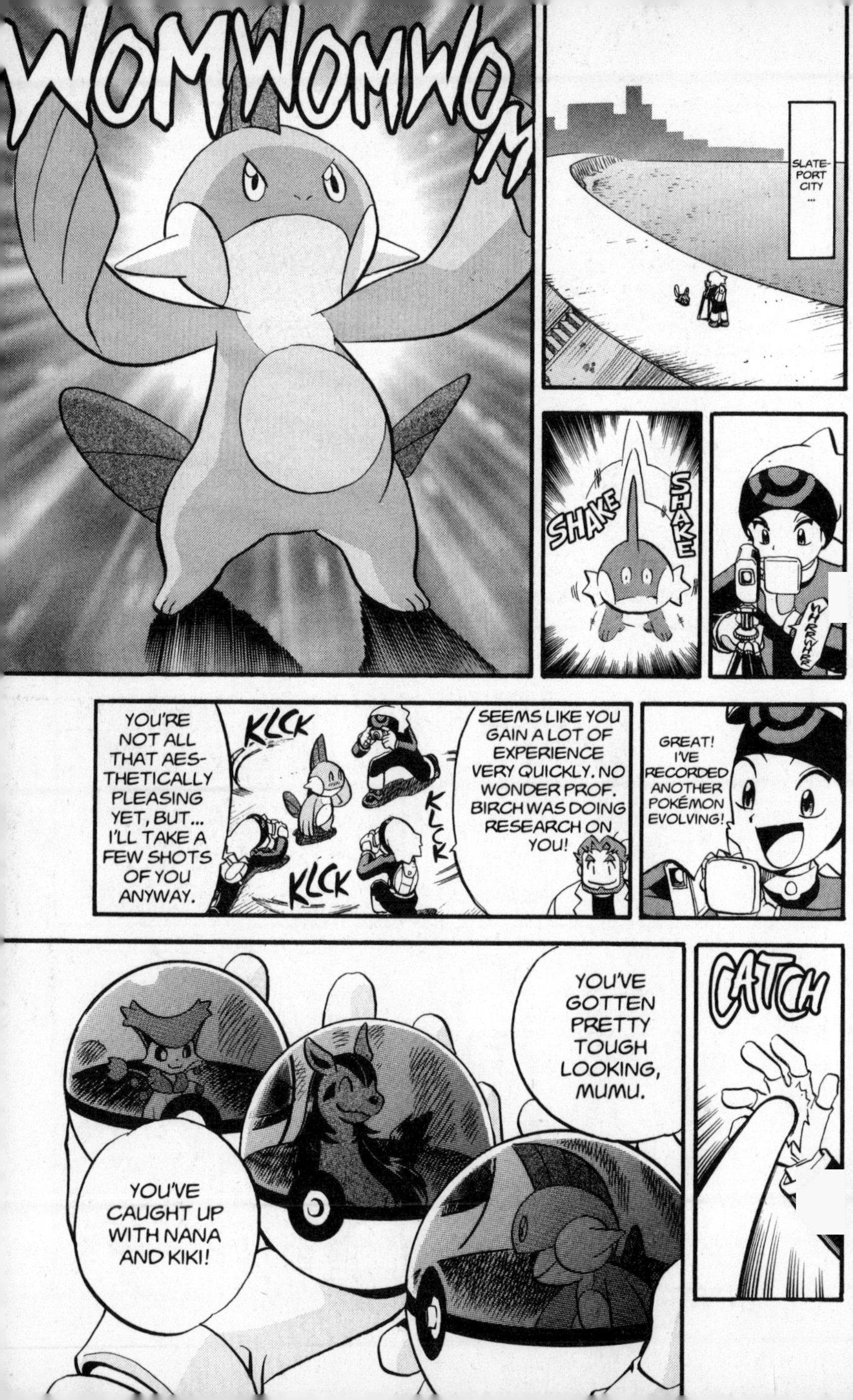
SLATEPORT CITY ...
WHRRWHRR
SHAKE SHAKE
WOMWOMWOM
GREAT! I'VE RECORDED ANOTHER POKÉMON EVOLVING!
SEEMS LIKE YOU GAIN A LOT OF EXPERIENCE VERY QUICKLY. NO WONDER PROF. BIRCH WAS DOING RESEARCH ON YOU!
KLICK
KLICK
KLICK
YOU'RE NOT ALL THAT AESTHETICALLY PLEASING YET, BUT... I'LL TAKE A FEW SHOTS OF YOU ANYWAY.
CATCH
YOU'VE GOTTEN PRETTY TOUGH LOOKING, MUMU.
YOU'VE CAUGHT UP WITH NANA AND KIKI!

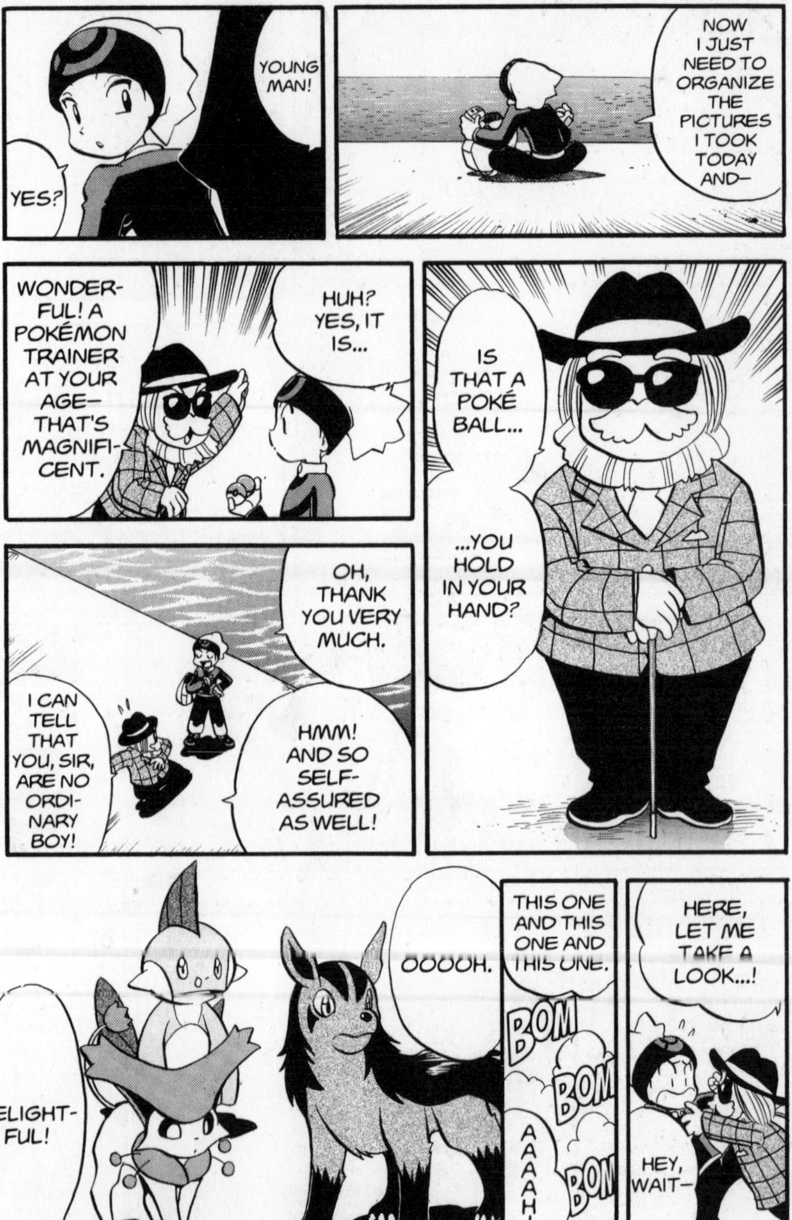
NOW I JUST NEED TO ORGANIZE THE PICTURES I TOOK TODAY AND—
YOUNG MAN!
YES?
IS THAT A POKÉ BALL...
...YOU HOLD IN YOUR HAND?
HUH? YES, IT IS...
WONDER-FUL! A POKÉMON TRAINER AT YOUR AGE— THAT'S MAGNIFI-CENT.
OH, THANK YOU VERY MUCH.
HMM! AND SO SELF-ASSURED AS WELL!
I CAN TELL THAT YOU, SIR, ARE NO ORDI-NARY BOY!
HERE, LET ME TAKE A LOOK...!
HEY, WAIT—
THIS ONE AND THIS ONE AND THIS ONE.
BOM
BOM
BOM
AAAAH!
OOOOH.
DELIGHT-FUL!

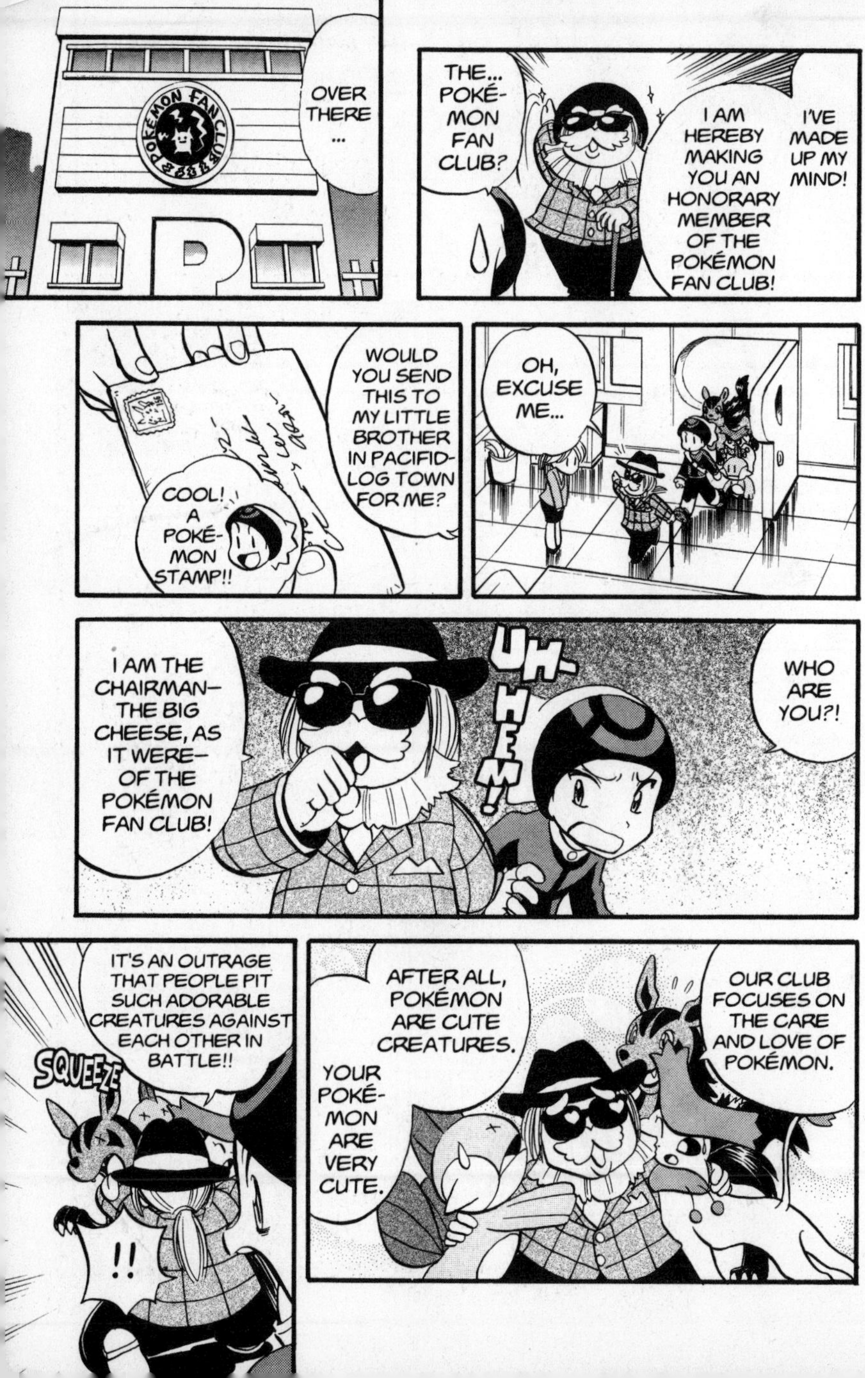
I'VE MADE UP MY MIND!
I AM HEREBY MAKING YOU AN HONORARY MEMBER OF THE POKÉMON FAN CLUB!
THE... POKÉ-MON FAN CLUB?
OVER THERE...
POKÉMON FAN CLUB
OH, EXCUSE ME...
WOULD YOU SEND THIS TO MY LITTLE BROTHER IN PACIFID-LOG TOWN FOR ME?
COOL! A POKÉ-MON STAMP!!
WHO ARE YOU?!
UH-HEM!
I AM THE CHAIRMAN—THE BIG CHEESE, AS IT WERE—OF THE POKÉMON FAN CLUB!
OUR CLUB FOCUSES ON THE CARE AND LOVE OF POKÉMON.
AFTER ALL, POKÉMON ARE CUTE CREATURES.
YOUR POKÉ-MON ARE VERY CUTE.
IT'S AN OUTRAGE THAT PEOPLE PIT SUCH ADORABLE CREATURES AGAINST EACH OTHER IN BATTLE!!
SQUEEZE
!!

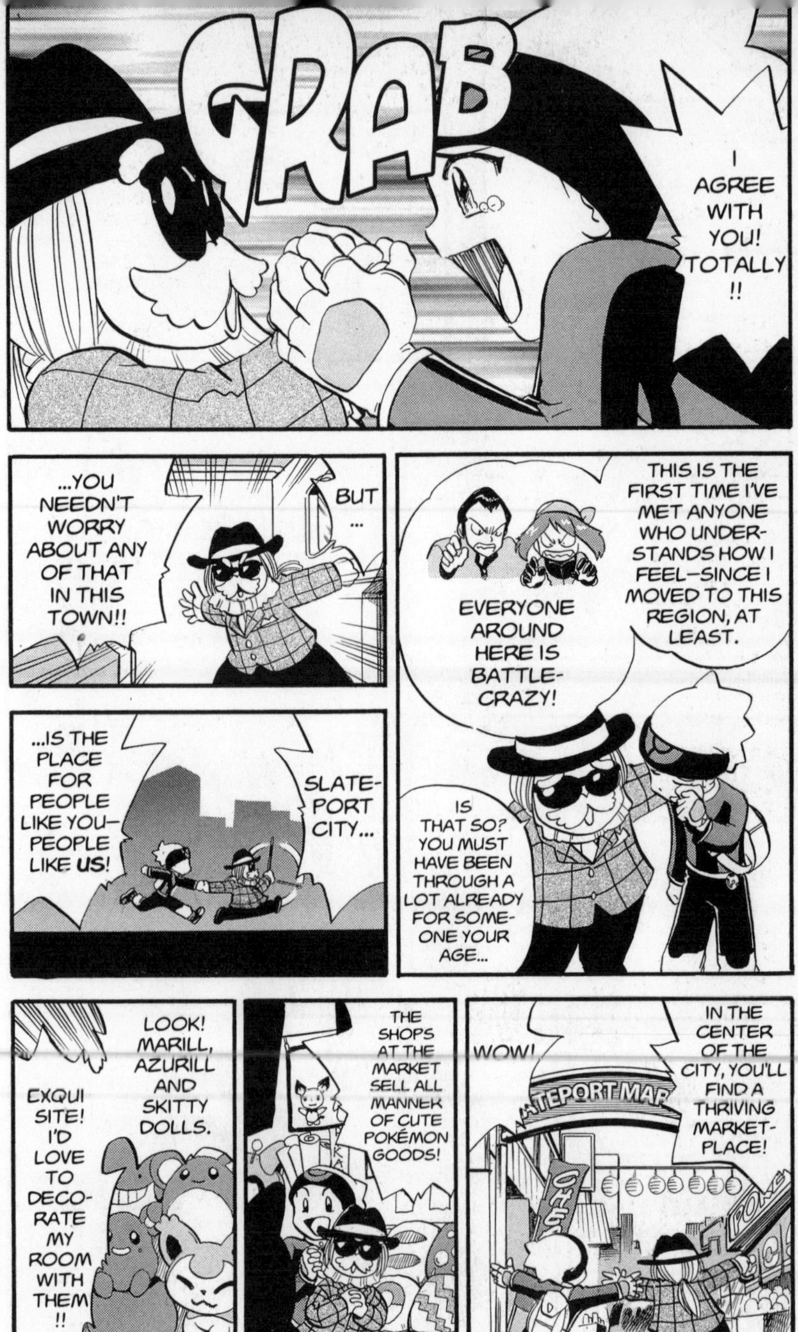
GRAB
I AGREE WITH YOU! TOTALLY!!
THIS IS THE FIRST TIME I'VE MET ANYONE WHO UNDER-STANDS HOW I FEEL—SINCE I MOVED TO THIS REGION, AT LEAST.
EVERYONE AROUND HERE IS BATTLE-CRAZY!
IS THAT SO? YOU MUST HAVE BEEN THROUGH A LOT ALREADY FOR SOME-ONE YOUR AGE...
BUT ...
...YOU NEEDN'T WORRY ABOUT ANY OF THAT IN THIS TOWN!!
SLATE-PORT CITY...
...IS THE PLACE FOR PEOPLE LIKE YOU—PEOPLE LIKE **US**!
IN THE CENTER OF THE CITY, YOU'LL FIND A THRIVING MARKET-PLACE!
WOW!
TEPORT MAR
THE SHOPS AT THE MARKET SELL ALL MANNER OF CUTE POKÉMON GOODS!
LOOK! MARILL, AZURILL AND SKITTY DOLLS.
EXQUI SITE! I'D LOVE TO DECO-RATE MY ROOM WITH THEM!!

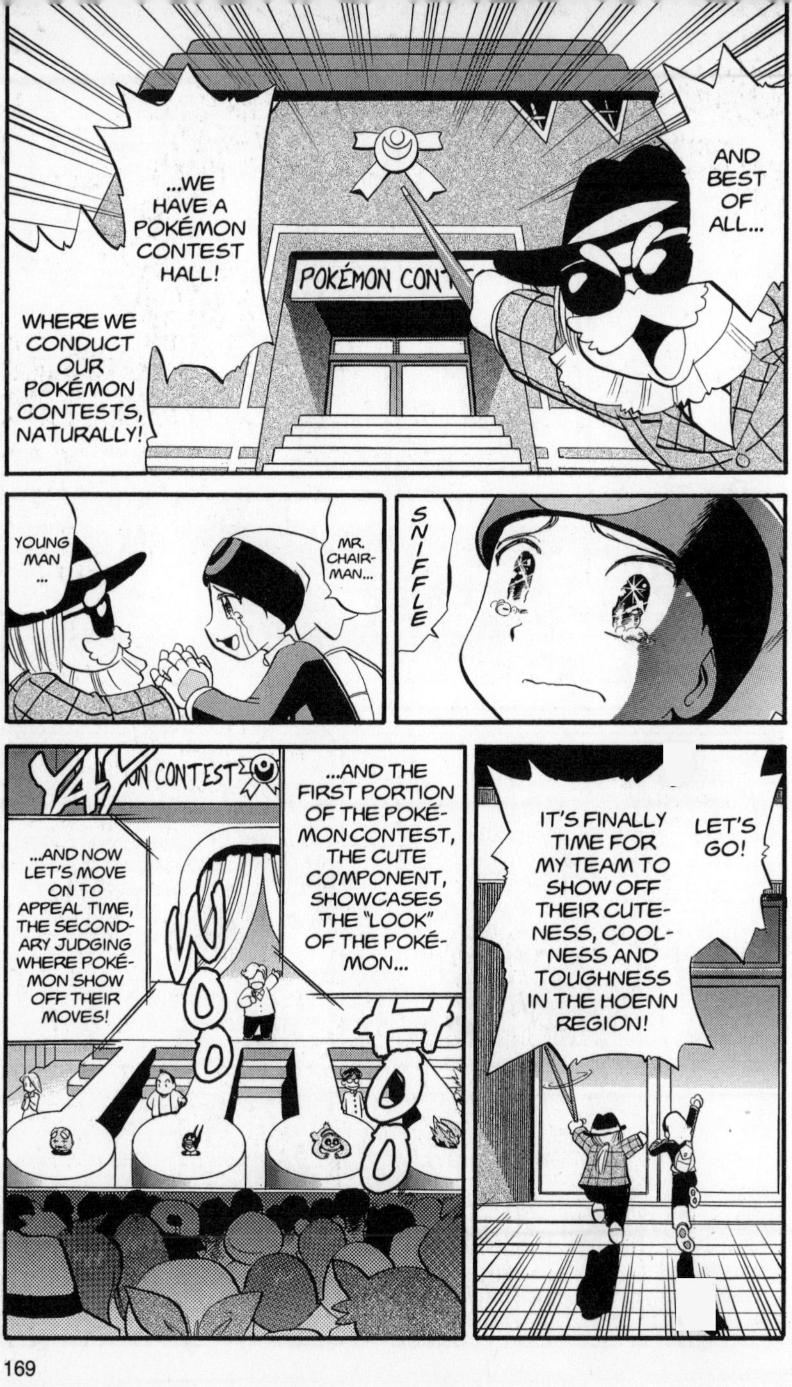
AND BEST OF ALL...
...WE HAVE A POKÉMON CONTEST HALL!
POKÉMON CONT
WHERE WE CONDUCT OUR POKÉMON CONTESTS, NATURALLY!
SNIFFLE
MR. CHAIR-MAN...
YOUNG MAN ...
LET'S GO!
IT'S FINALLY TIME FOR MY TEAM TO SHOW OFF THEIR CUTE-NESS, COOL-NESS AND TOUGHNESS IN THE HOENN REGION!
YAY
ON CONTEST
...AND THE FIRST PORTION OF THE POKÉ-MON CONTEST, THE CUTE COMPONENT, SHOWCASES THE "LOOK" OF THE POKÉ-MON...
...AND NOW LET'S MOVE ON TO APPEAL TIME, THE SECOND-ARY JUDGING WHERE POKÉ-MON SHOW OFF THEIR MOVES!
WOO
HOO

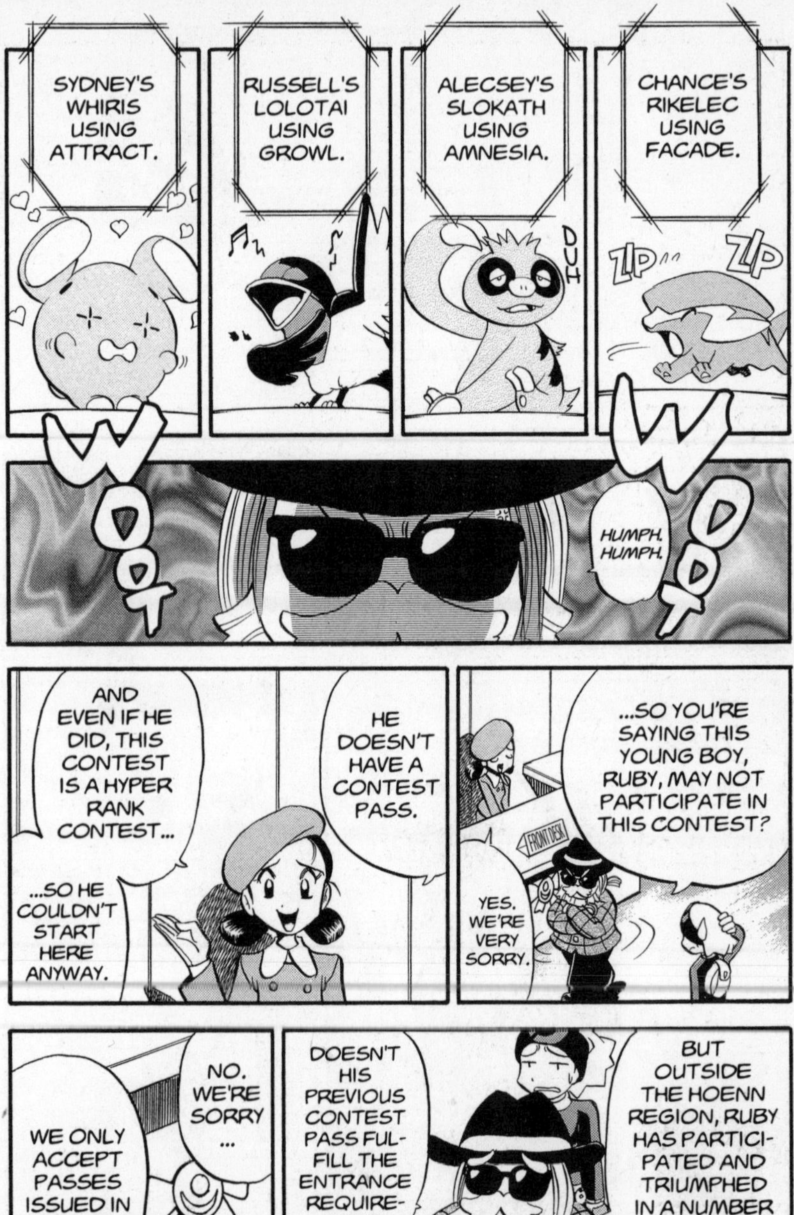
CHANCE'S RIKELEC USING FACADE.
ZIP
ZIP
ALECSEY'S SLOKATH USING AMNESIA.
DUH
RUSSELL'S LOLOTAI USING GROWL.
SYDNEY'S WHIRIS USING ATTRACT.
WOOT
WOOT
HUMPH. HUMPH.
...SO YOU'RE SAYING THIS YOUNG BOY, RUBY, MAY NOT PARTICIPATE IN THIS CONTEST?
FRONT DESK
YES. WE'RE VERY SORRY.
HE DOESN'T HAVE A CONTEST PASS.
AND EVEN IF HE DID, THIS CONTEST IS A HYPER RANK CONTEST...
...SO HE COULDN'T START HERE ANYWAY.
BUT OUTSIDE THE HOENN REGION, RUBY HAS PARTICI-PATED AND TRIUMPHED IN A NUMBER OF COMPETI-TIONS!
DOESN'T HIS PREVIOUS CONTEST PASS FUL-FILL THE ENTRANCE REQUIRE-MENT?
NO. WE'RE SORRY ...
WE ONLY ACCEPT PASSES ISSUED IN HOENN.

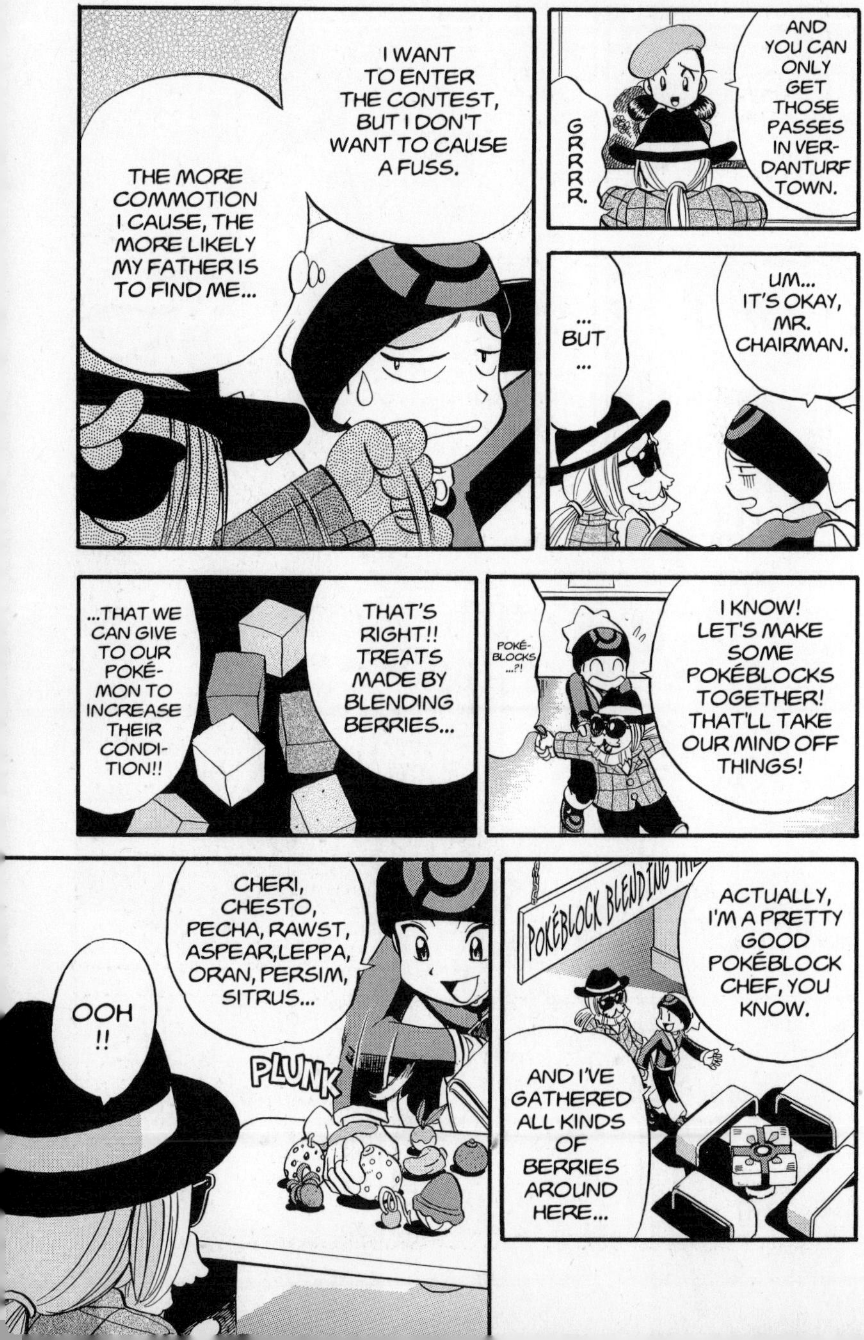
AND YOU CAN ONLY GET THOSE PASSES IN VERDANTURF TOWN.
GRRRR.
UM... IT'S OKAY, MR. CHAIRMAN.
...BUT...
I WANT TO ENTER THE CONTEST, BUT I DON'T WANT TO CAUSE A FUSS.
THE MORE COMMOTION I CAUSE, THE MORE LIKELY MY FATHER IS TO FIND ME...
I KNOW! LET'S MAKE SOME POKÉBLOCKS TOGETHER! THAT'LL TAKE OUR MIND OFF THINGS!
POKÉBLOCKS...?!
THAT'S RIGHT!! TREATS MADE BY BLENDING BERRIES...
...THAT WE CAN GIVE TO OUR POKÉMON TO INCREASE THEIR CONDITION!!
ACTUALLY, I'M A PRETTY GOOD POKÉBLOCK CHEF, YOU KNOW.
AND I'VE GATHERED ALL KINDS OF BERRIES AROUND HERE...
CHERI, CHESTO, PECHA, RAWST, ASPEAR, LEPPA, ORAN, PERSIM, SITRUS...
OOH!!
PLUNK

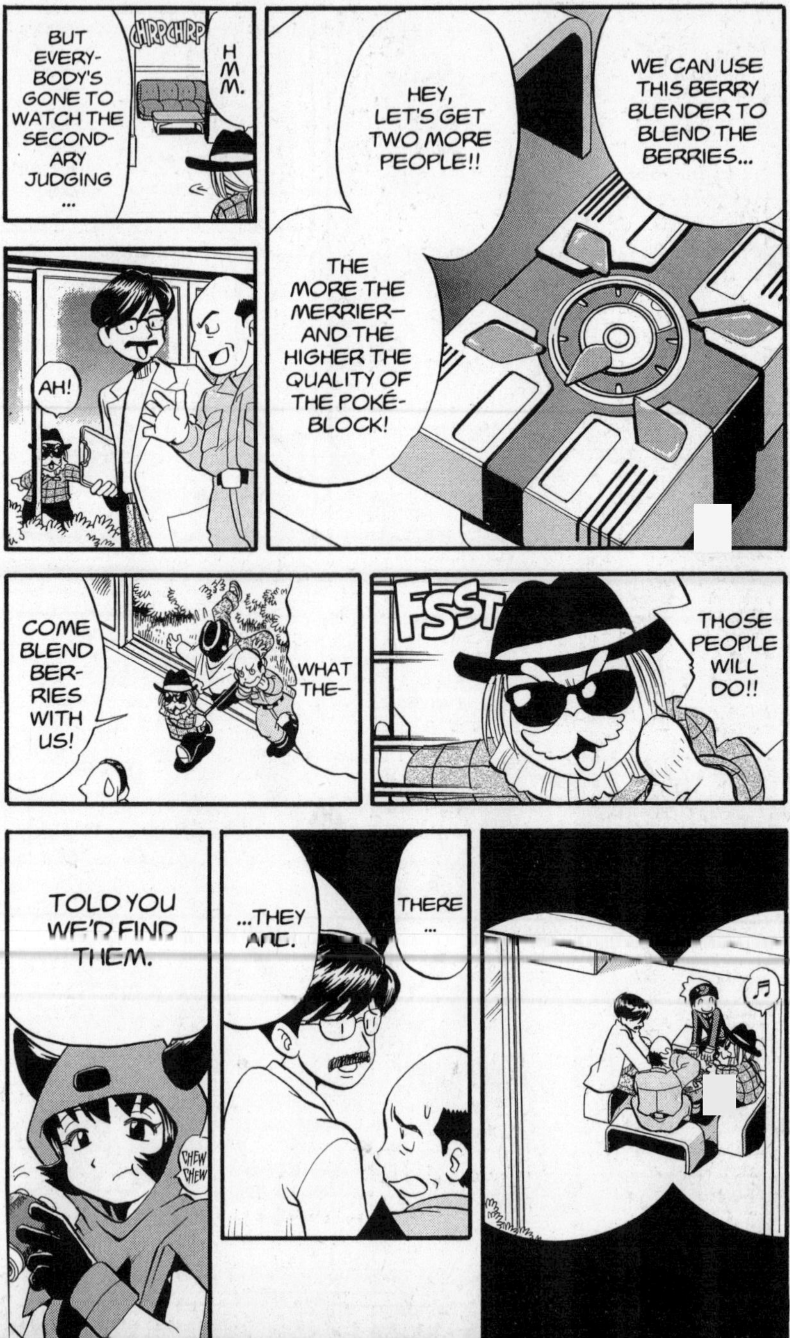
WE CAN USE THIS BERRY BLENDER TO BLEND THE BERRIES...
HEY, LET'S GET TWO MORE PEOPLE!!
THE MORE THE MERRIER— AND THE HIGHER THE QUALITY OF THE POKÉ-BLOCK!
HMM.
CHIRP CHIRP
BUT EVERY-BODY'S GONE TO WATCH THE SECOND-ARY JUDGING ...
AH!
FSST
THOSE PEOPLE WILL DO!!
WHAT THE—
COME BLEND BER-RIES WITH US!
♪
THERE ...
...THEY ARE.
TOLD YOU WE'D FIND THEM.
CHEW CHEW

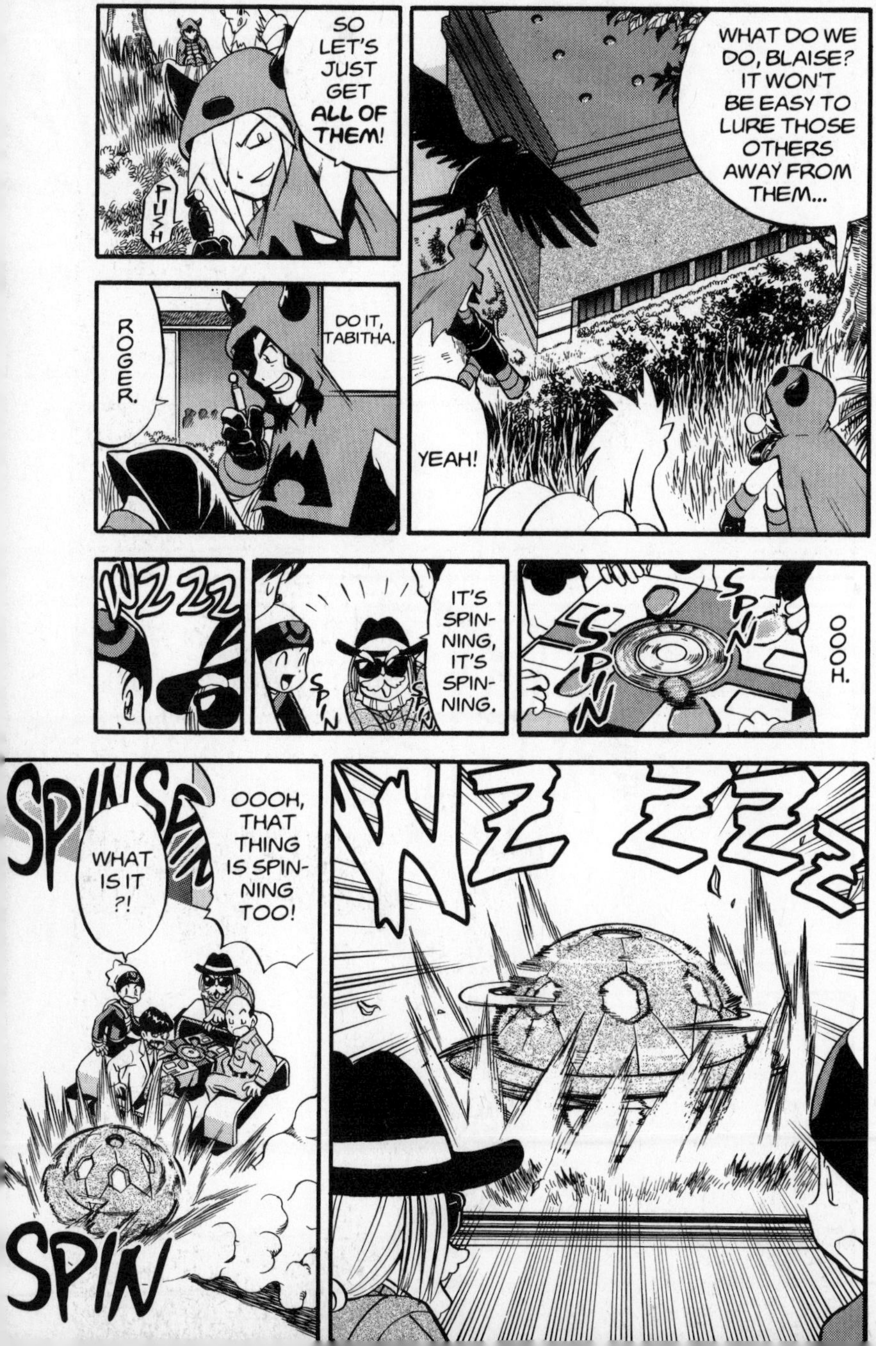
WHAT DO WE DO, BLAISE? IT WON'T BE EASY TO LURE THOSE OTHERS AWAY FROM THEM...
YEAH!
SO LET'S JUST GET ALL OF THEM!
PUSH
DO IT, TABITHA.
ROGER.
OOOH.
SPIN
SPIN
IT'S SPINNING, IT'S SPINNING.
SPIN
SPIN
WZZZ
WZ ZZZ
SPIN SPIN
OOOH, THAT THING IS SPINNING TOO!
WHAT IS IT ?!
SPIN

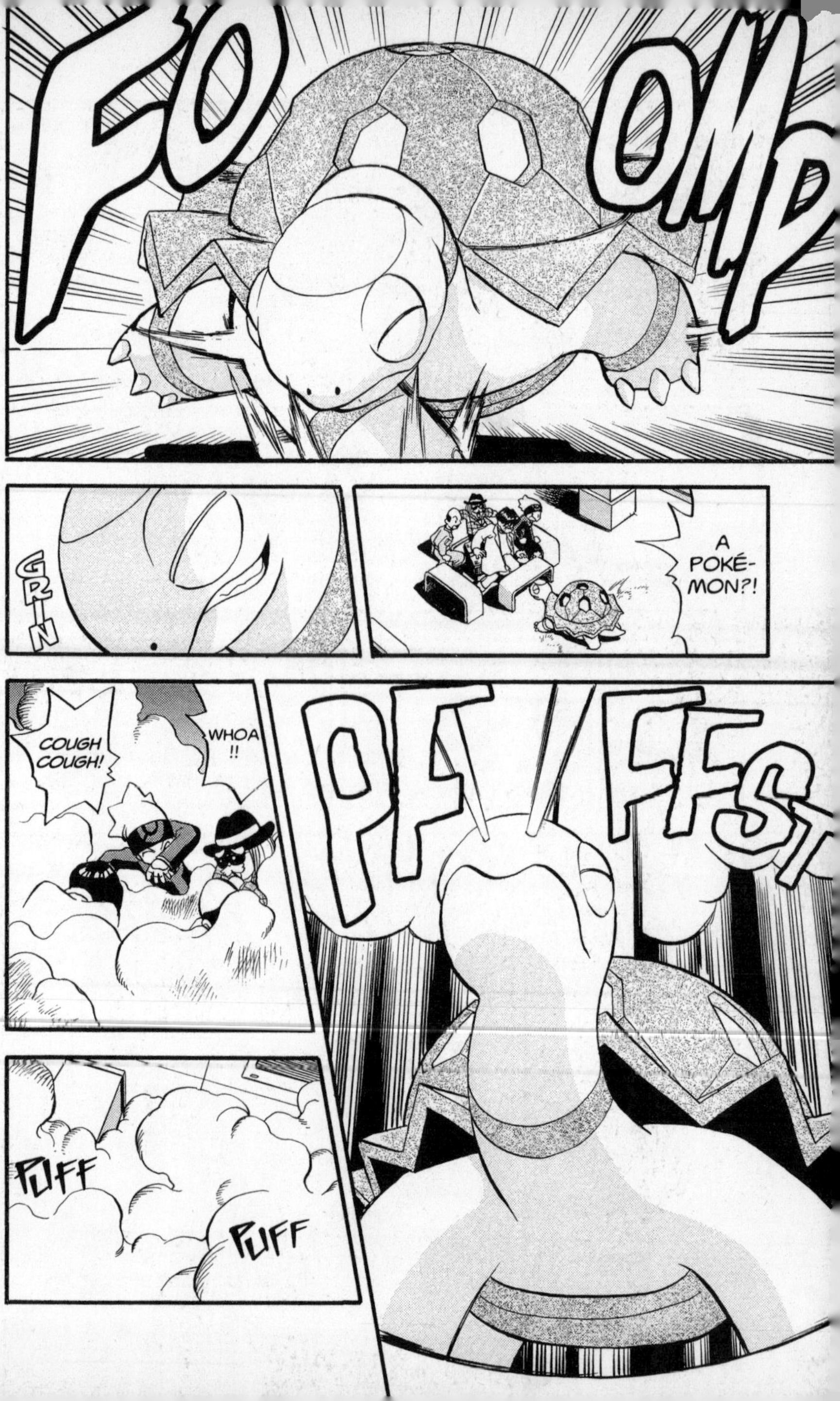
FOOMP
A POKÉ-MON?!
GRIN
PFFFST
WHOA !!
COUGH COUGH!
PUFF
PUFF

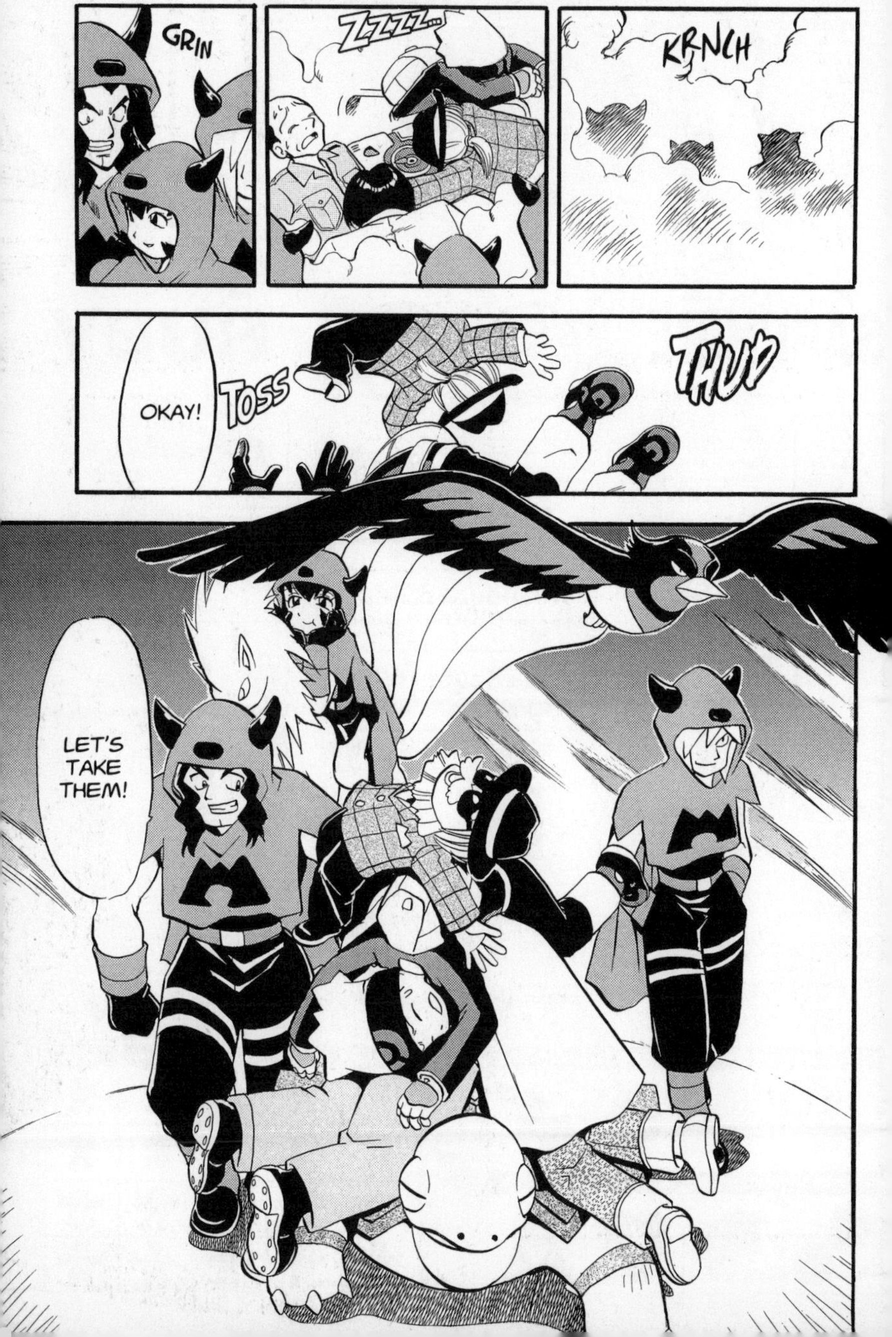
KRNCH
ZZZZ...
GRIN
THUD
TOSS
OKAY!
LET'S TAKE THEM!

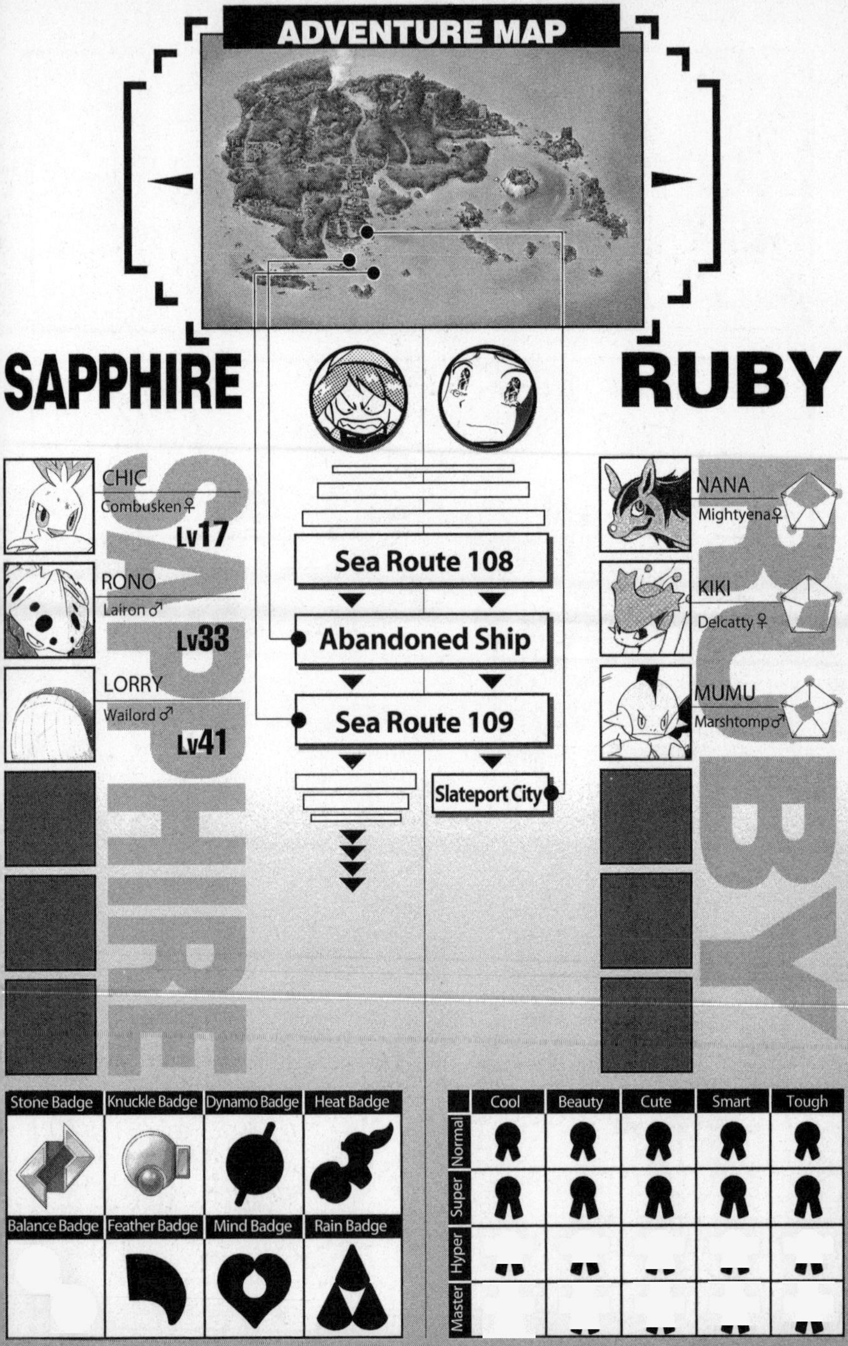

ADVENTURE MAP

SAPPHIRE

CHIC
Combusken ♀
Lv**17**

RONO
Lairon ♂
Lv**33**

LORRY
Wailord ♂
Lv**41**

RUBY

NANA
Mightyena♀

KIKI
Delcatty ♀

MUMU
Marshtomp♂

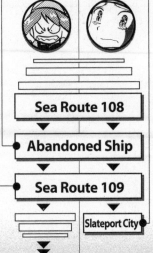

Sea Route 108

▼ ▼

Abandoned Ship

▼ ▼

Sea Route 109

Slateport City

▼
▼
▼

Stone Badge	Knuckle Badge	Dynamo Badge	Heat Badge
Balance Badge	Feather Badge	Mind Badge	Rain Badge

		Cool	Beauty	Cute	Smart	Tough
Normal						
Super						
Hyper						
Master						

● Chapter 201 ●
Slugging It Out with Slugma

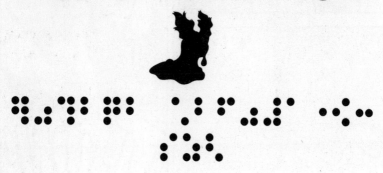

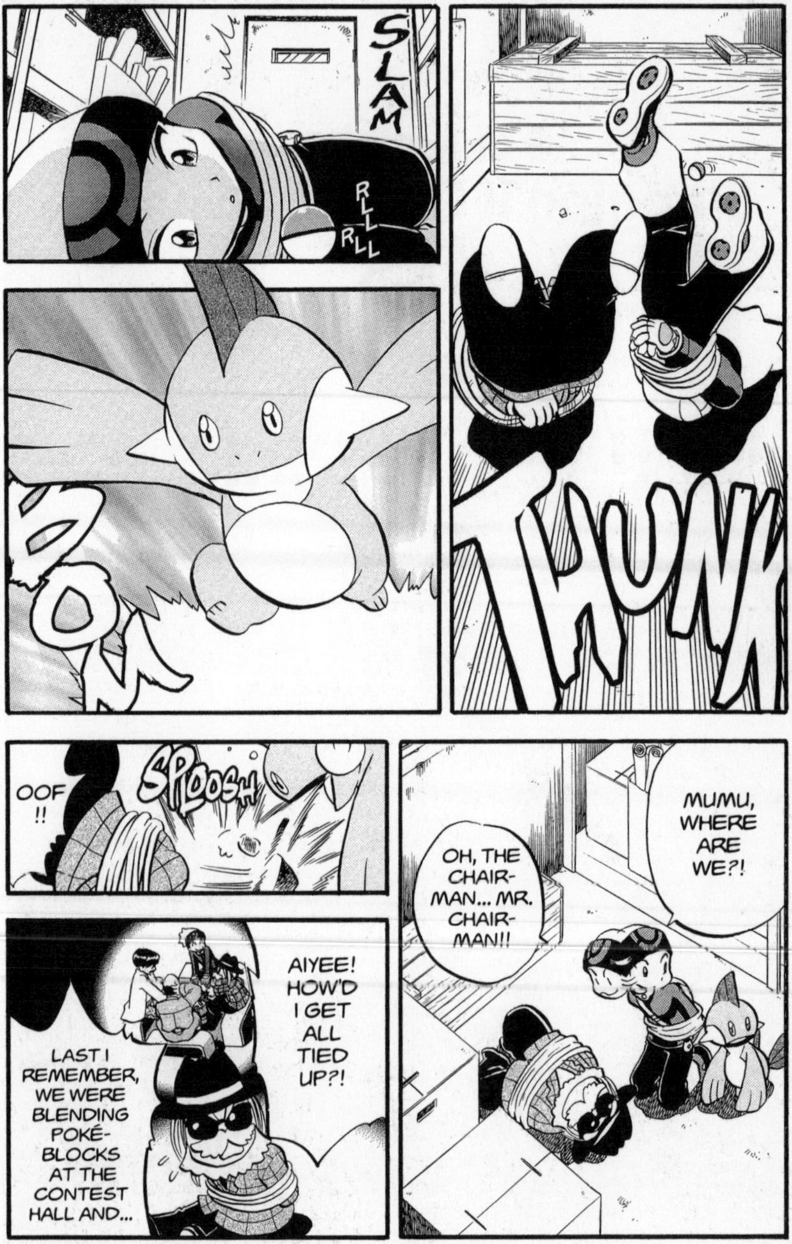
THUNK
SLAM
RLLL
RLLL
MUMU, WHERE ARE WE?!
OH, THE CHAIR-MAN... MR. CHAIR-MAN!!
SPLOOSH
OOF!!
AIYEE! HOW'D I GET ALL TIED UP?!
LAST I REMEMBER, WE WERE BLENDING POKÉ-BLOCKS AT THE CONTEST HALL AND...

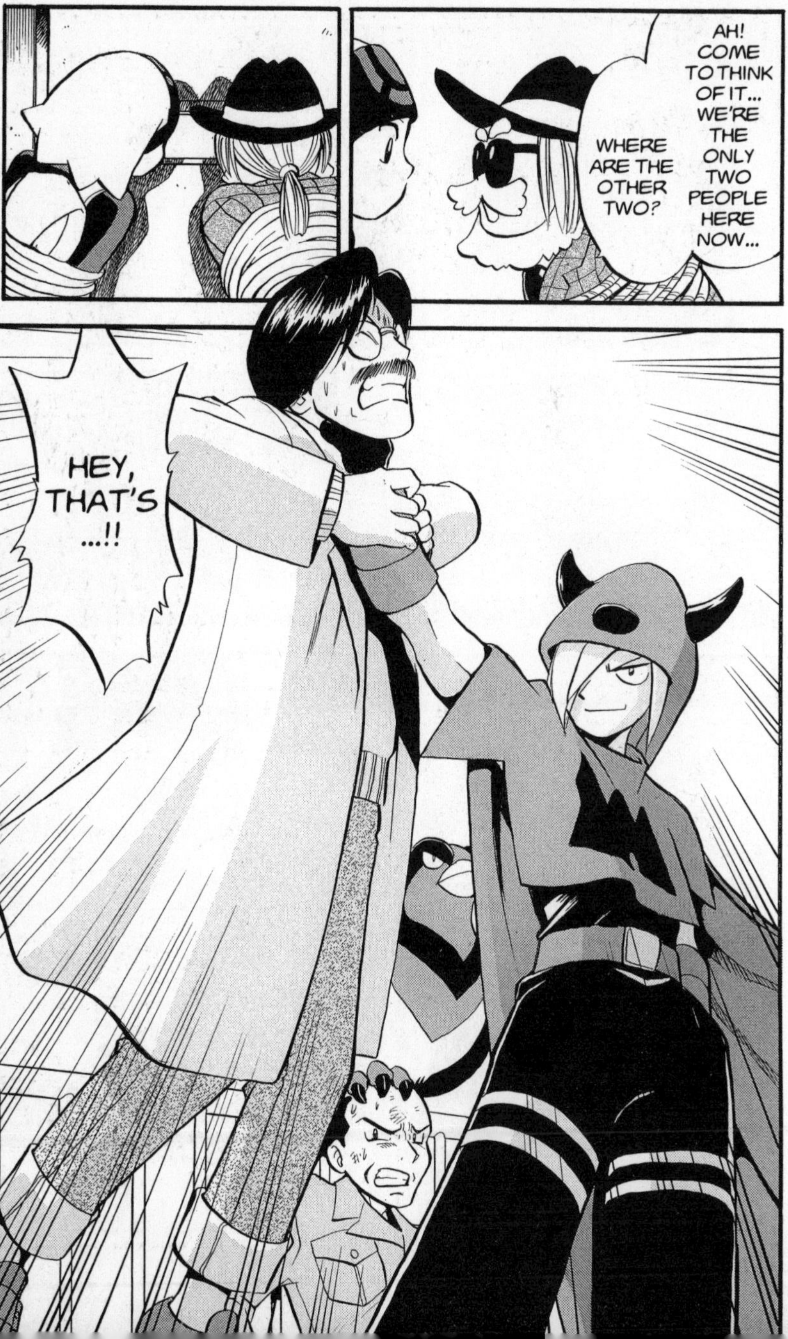
AH! COME TO THINK OF IT... WE'RE THE ONLY TWO PEOPLE HERE NOW...
WHERE ARE THE OTHER TWO?
HEY, THAT'S ...!!

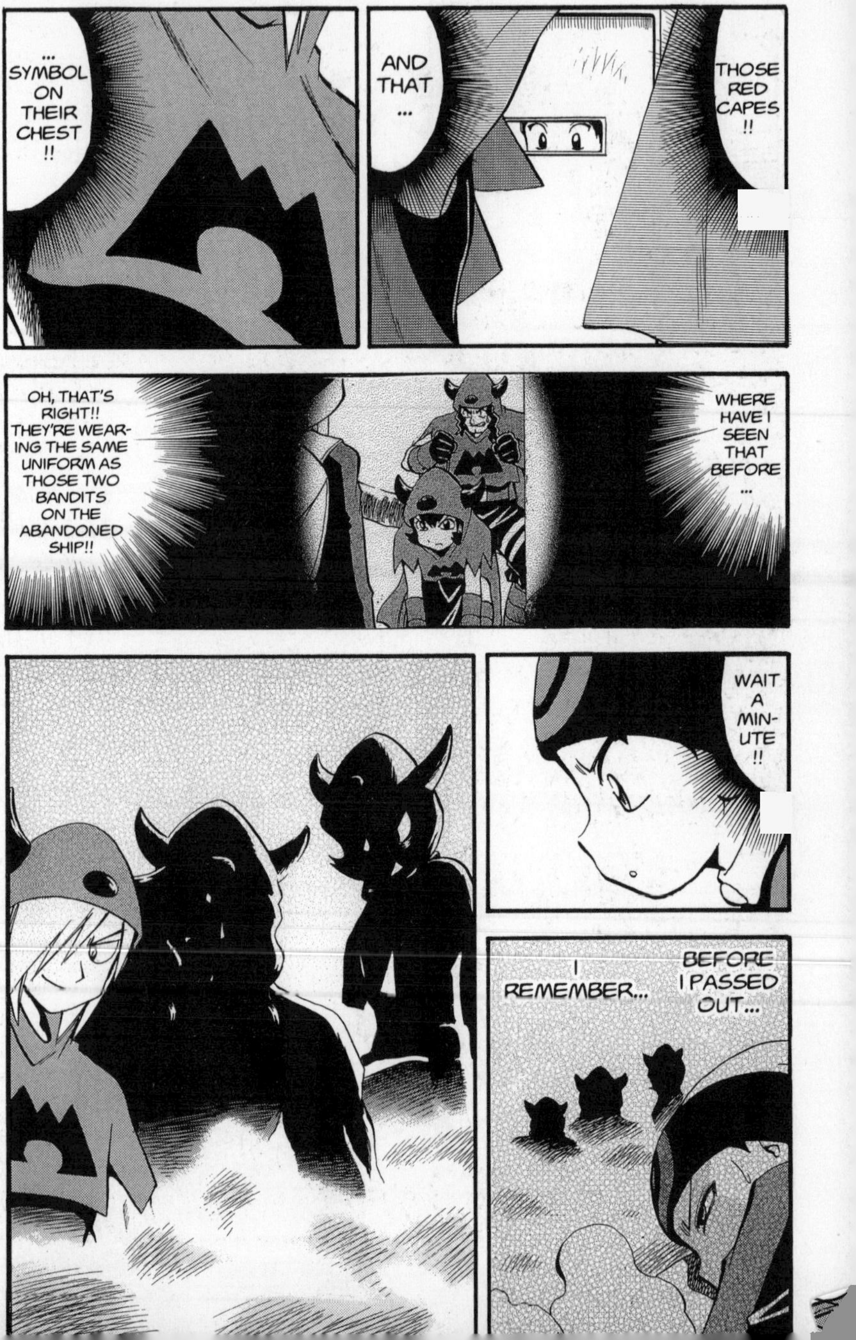
THOSE RED CAPES !!
AND THAT ...
... SYMBOL ON THEIR CHEST !!
WHERE HAVE I SEEN THAT BEFORE ...
OH, THAT'S RIGHT!! THEY'RE WEAR-ING THE SAME UNIFORM AS THOSE TWO BANDITS ON THE ABANDONED SHIP!!
WAIT A MIN-UTE !!
BEFORE I PASSED OUT...
I REMEMBER...

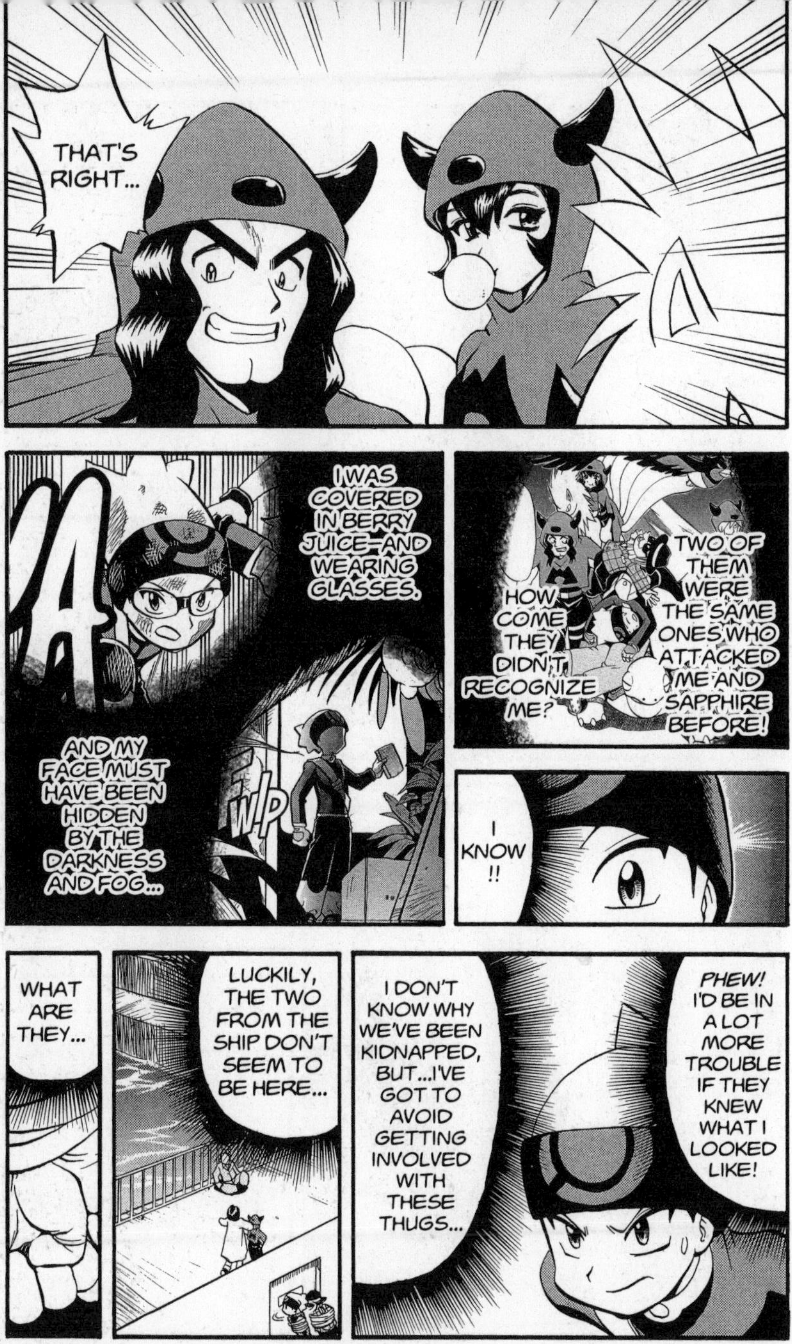
THAT'S RIGHT...
TWO OF THEM WERE THE SAME ONES WHO ATTACKED ME AND SAPPHIRE BEFORE!
HOW COME THEY DIDN'T RECOGNIZE ME?
I KNOW!!
I WAS COVERED IN BERRY JUICE—AND WEARING GLASSES.
A
FWIP
AND MY FACE MUST HAVE BEEN HIDDEN BY THE DARKNESS AND FOG...
PHEW! I'D BE IN A LOT MORE TROUBLE IF THEY KNEW WHAT I LOOKED LIKE!
I DON'T KNOW WHY WE'VE BEEN KIDNAPPED, BUT...I'VE GOT TO AVOID GETTING INVOLVED WITH THESE THUGS...
LUCKILY, THE TWO FROM THE SHIP DON'T SEEM TO BE HERE...
WHAT ARE THEY...

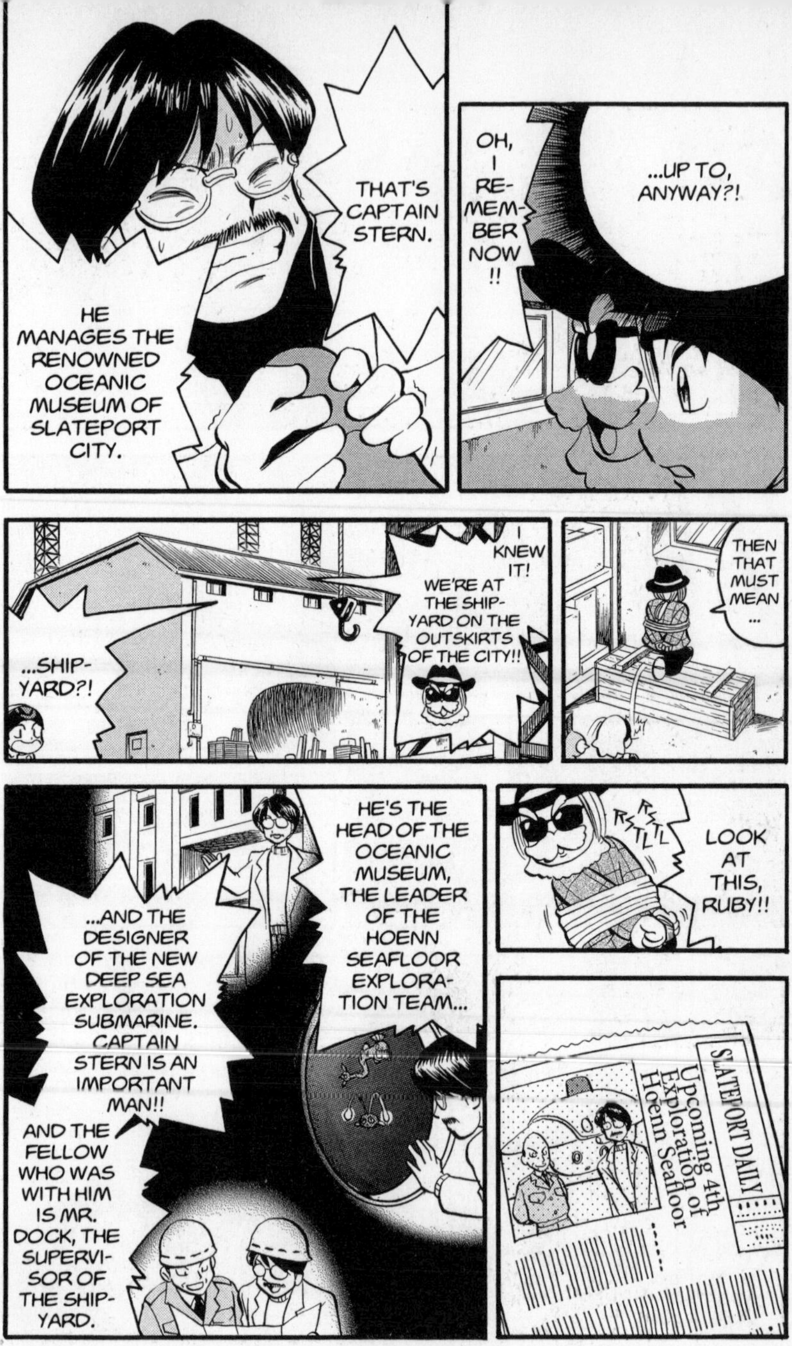
...UP TO, ANYWAY?!
OH, I RE-MEM-BER NOW!!
THAT'S CAPTAIN STERN.
HE MANAGES THE RENOWNED OCEANIC MUSEUM OF SLATEPORT CITY.
THEN THAT MUST MEAN...
I KNEW IT!
WE'RE AT THE SHIP-YARD ON THE OUTSKIRTS OF THE CITY!!
...SHIP-YARD?!
RSTL RSTL
LOOK AT THIS, RUBY!!
SLATEPORT DAILY
Upcoming 4th Exploration of Hoenn Seafloor
......
HE'S THE HEAD OF THE OCEANIC MUSEUM, THE LEADER OF THE HOENN SEAFLOOR EXPLORA-TION TEAM...
...AND THE DESIGNER OF THE NEW DEEP SEA EXPLORATION SUBMARINE. CAPTAIN STERN IS AN IMPORTANT MAN!!
AND THE FELLOW WHO WAS WITH HIM IS MR. DOCK, THE SUPERVI-SOR OF THE SHIP-YARD.

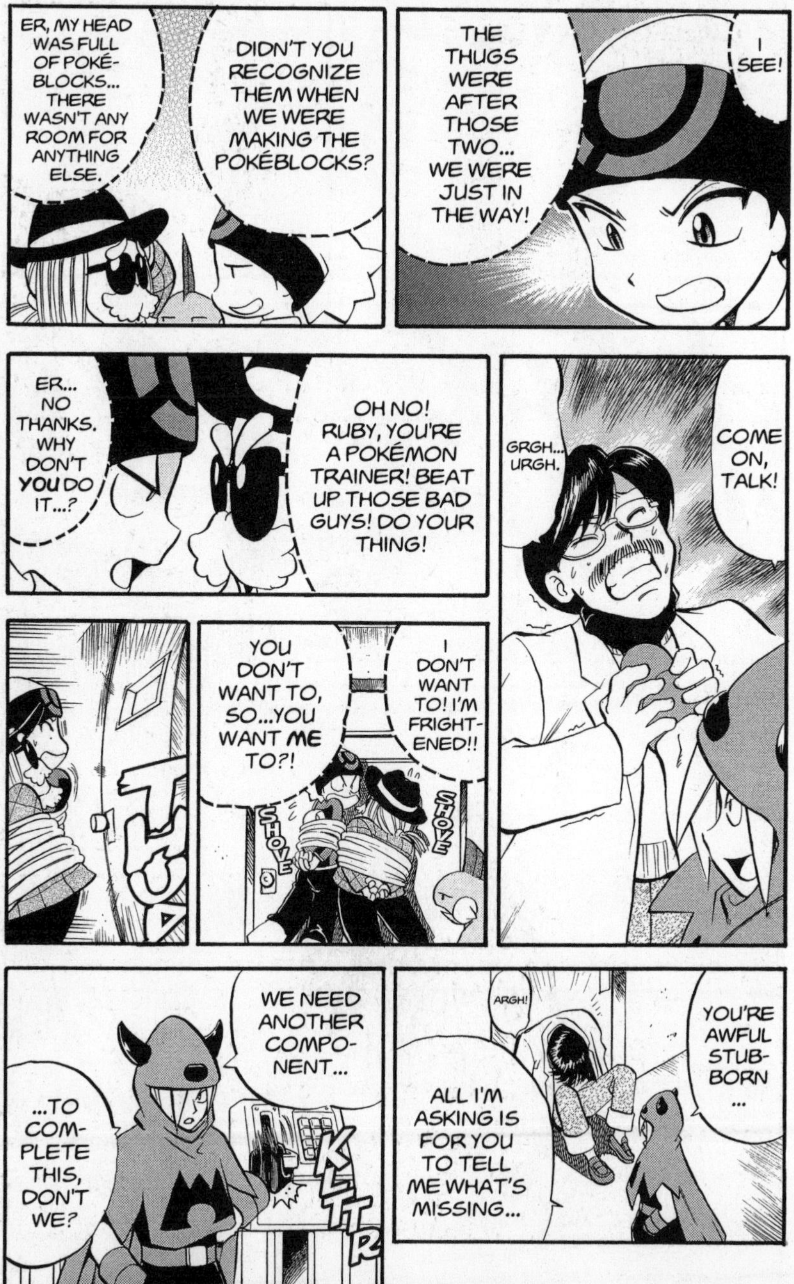
I SEE!
THE THUGS WERE AFTER THOSE TWO... WE WERE JUST IN THE WAY!
DIDN'T YOU RECOGNIZE THEM WHEN WE WERE MAKING THE POKÉBLOCKS?
ER, MY HEAD WAS FULL OF POKÉ-BLOCKS... THERE WASN'T ANY ROOM FOR ANYTHING ELSE.
COME ON, TALK!
GRGH... URGH.
OH NO! RUBY, YOU'RE A POKÉMON TRAINER! BEAT UP THOSE BAD GUYS! DO YOUR THING!
ER... NO THANKS. WHY DON'T **YOU** DO IT...?
I DON'T WANT TO! I'M FRIGHT-ENED!!
YOU DON'T WANT TO, SO...YOU WANT **ME** TO?!
SHOVE
SHOVE
THUD
YOU'RE AWFUL STUB-BORN ...
ARGH!
ALL I'M ASKING IS FOR YOU TO TELL ME WHAT'S MISSING...
WE NEED ANOTHER COMPO-NENT...
...TO COM-PLETE THIS, DON'T WE?
KLTTR

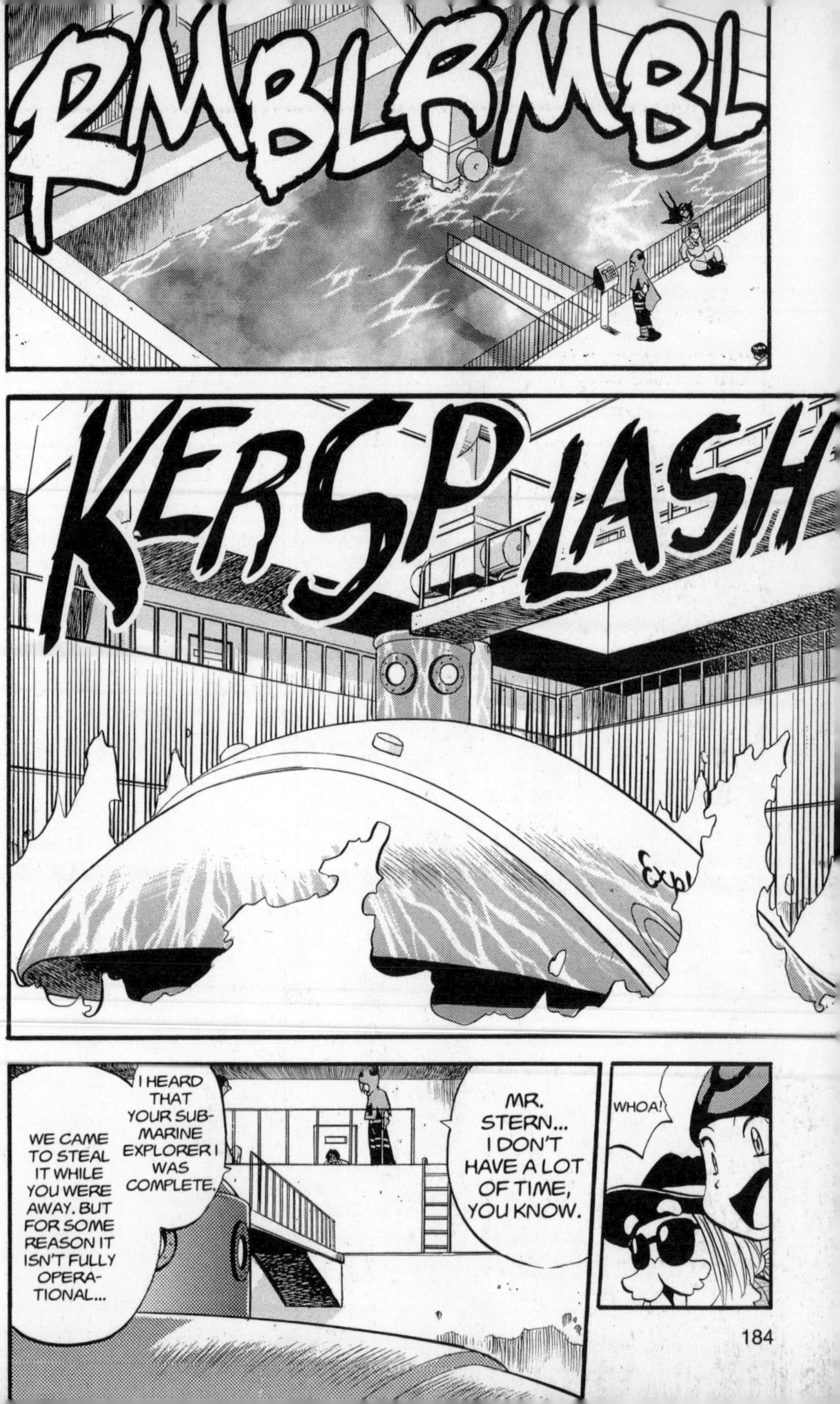
RMBLRMBL
KERSPLASH
WHOA!
MR. STERN... I DON'T HAVE A LOT OF TIME, YOU KNOW.
I HEARD THAT YOUR SUB-MARINE EXPLORER WAS COMPLETE.
WE CAME TO STEAL IT WHILE YOU WERE AWAY. BUT FOR SOME REASON IT ISN'T FULLY OPERA-TIONAL...

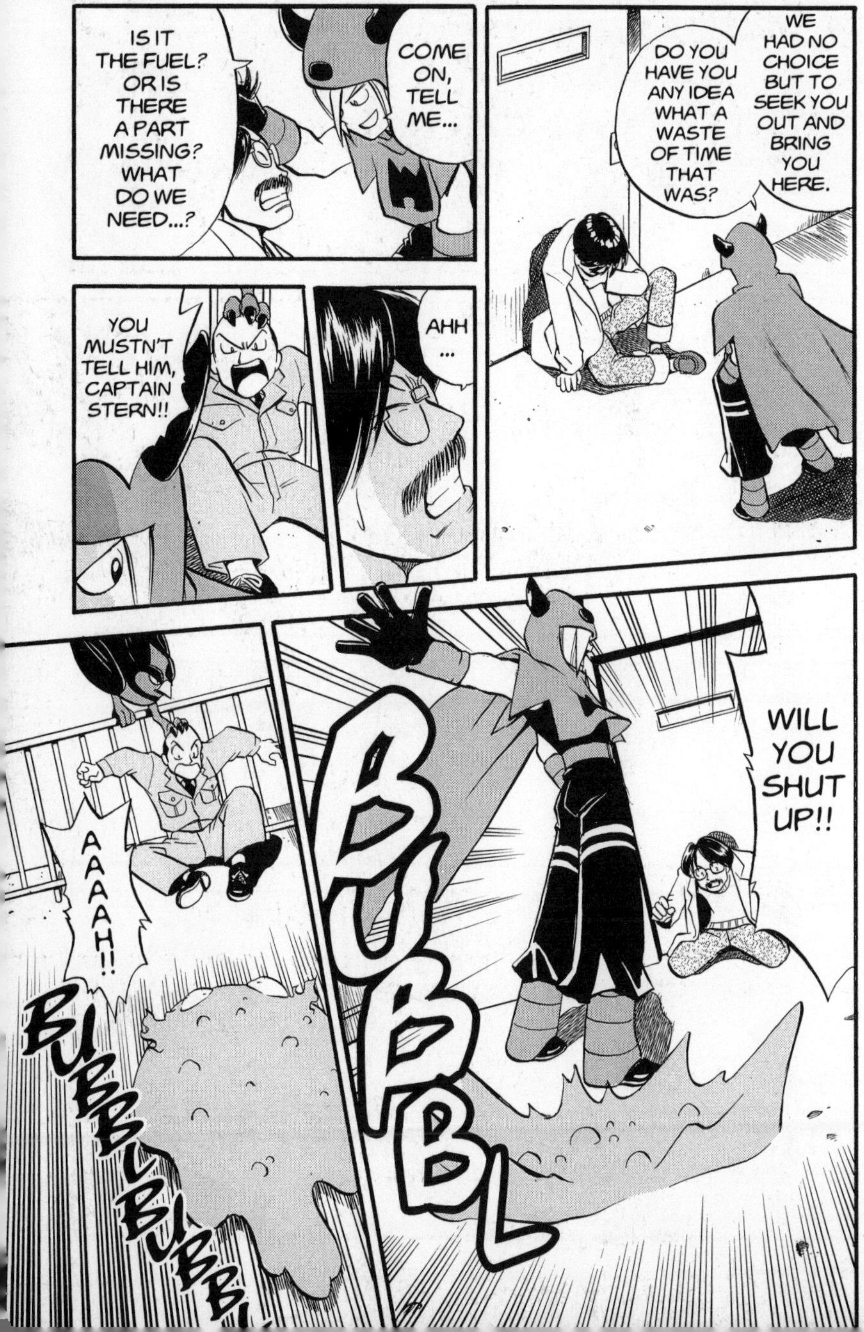
WE HAD NO CHOICE BUT TO SEEK YOU OUT AND BRING YOU HERE.
DO YOU HAVE YOU ANY IDEA WHAT A WASTE OF TIME THAT WAS?
COME ON, TELL ME...
IS IT THE FUEL? OR IS THERE A PART MISSING? WHAT DO WE NEED...?
AHH ...
YOU MUSTN'T TELL HIM, CAPTAIN STERN!!
WILL YOU SHUT UP!!
BUBBL
AAAAH!!
BUBBBLUBBUBBBI

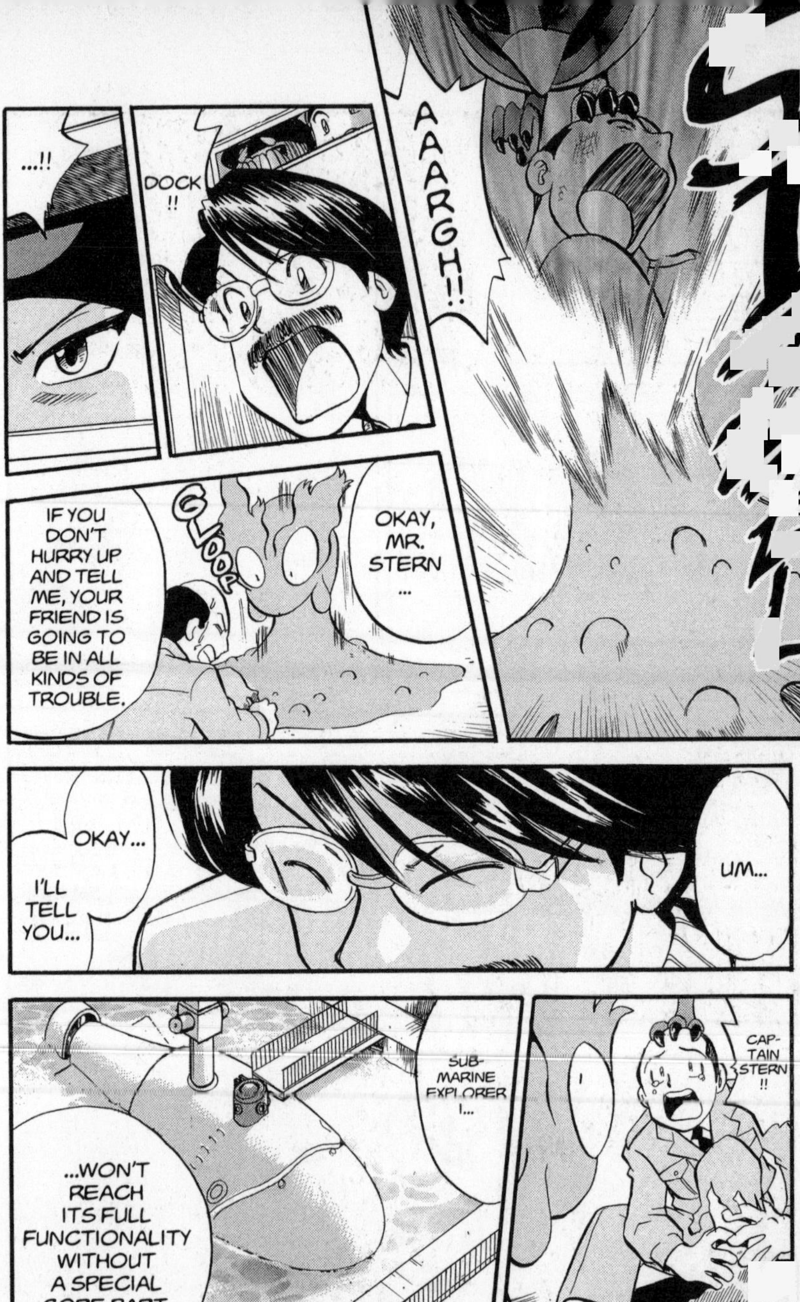
AAARGH!!
DOCK !!
...!!
OKAY, MR. STERN ...
IF YOU DON'T HURRY UP AND TELL ME, YOUR FRIEND IS GOING TO BE IN ALL KINDS OF TROUBLE.
GLOOP
UM...
OKAY...
I'LL TELL YOU...
CAPTAIN STERN !!
SUB-MARINE EXPLORER I...
...WON'T REACH ITS FULL FUNCTIONALITY WITHOUT A SPECIAL CORE PART.

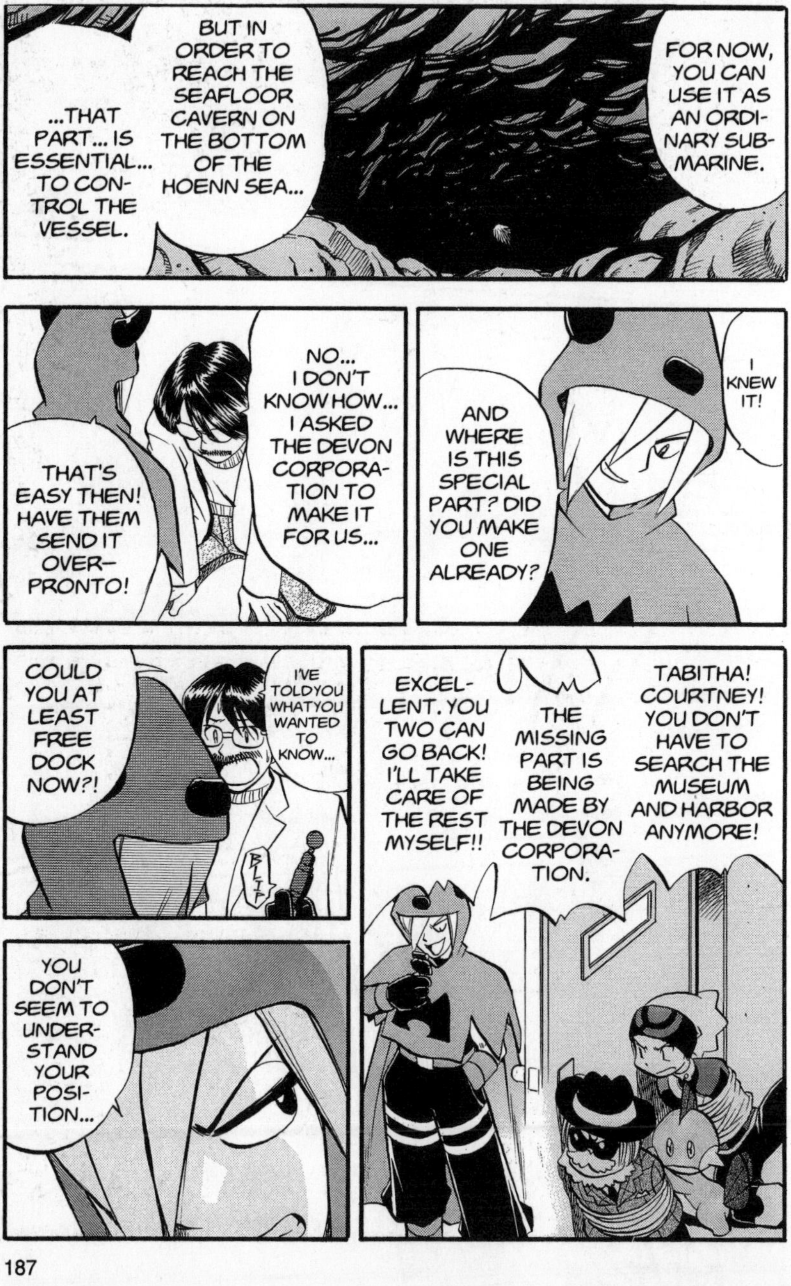
FOR NOW, YOU CAN USE IT AS AN ORDINARY SUBMARINE.
BUT IN ORDER TO REACH THE SEAFLOOR CAVERN ON THE BOTTOM OF THE HOENN SEA...
...THAT PART... IS ESSENTIAL... TO CONTROL THE VESSEL.
I KNEW IT!
AND WHERE IS THIS SPECIAL PART? DID YOU MAKE ONE ALREADY?
NO... I DON'T KNOW HOW... I ASKED THE DEVON CORPORATION TO MAKE IT FOR US...
THAT'S EASY THEN! HAVE THEM SEND IT OVER—PRONTO!
TABITHA! COURTNEY! YOU DON'T HAVE TO SEARCH THE MUSEUM AND HARBOR ANYMORE!
THE MISSING PART IS BEING MADE BY THE DEVON CORPORATION.
EXCELLENT. YOU TWO CAN GO BACK! I'LL TAKE CARE OF THE REST MYSELF!!
I'VE TOLD YOU WHAT YOU WANTED TO KNOW...
COULD YOU AT LEAST FREE DOCK NOW?!
BLIP
YOU DON'T SEEM TO UNDERSTAND YOUR POSITION...

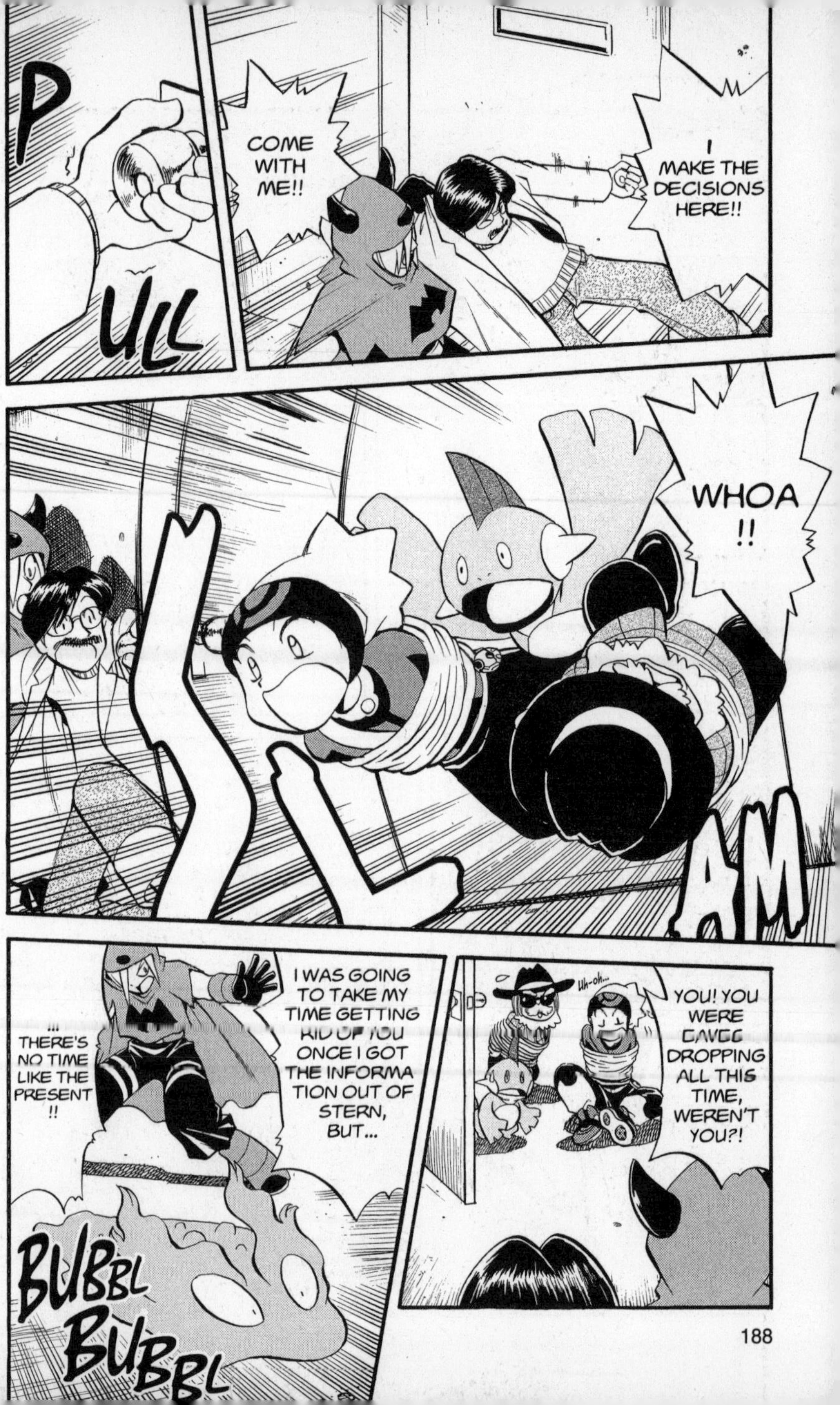
I MAKE THE DECISIONS HERE!!
COME WITH ME!!
P ULL
WHOA !!
AM
Uh-oh...
YOU! YOU WERE EAVES DROPPING ALL THIS TIME, WEREN'T YOU?!
I WAS GOING TO TAKE MY TIME GETTING RID OF YOU ONCE I GOT THE INFORMA TION OUT OF STERN, BUT...
...!! THERE'S NO TIME LIKE THE PRESENT !!
BUBBL BUBBL

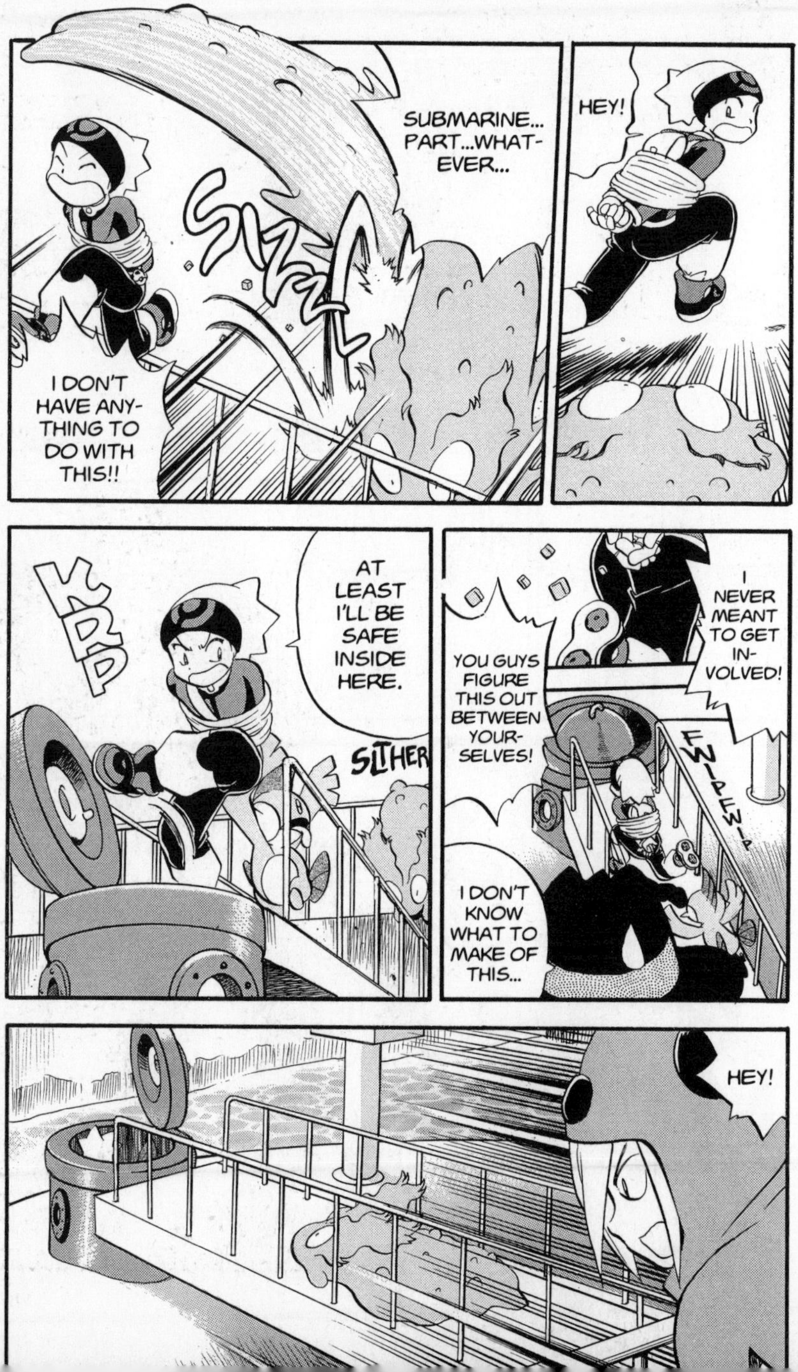
HEY!
SUBMARINE... PART...WHAT-EVER...
SIZZL
I DON'T HAVE ANY-THING TO DO WITH THIS!!
I NEVER MEANT TO GET IN-VOLVED!
FWIP FWIP
YOU GUYS FIGURE THIS OUT BETWEEN YOUR-SELVES!
I DON'T KNOW WHAT TO MAKE OF THIS...
AT LEAST I'LL BE SAFE INSIDE HERE.
SLITHER
KRP
HEY!

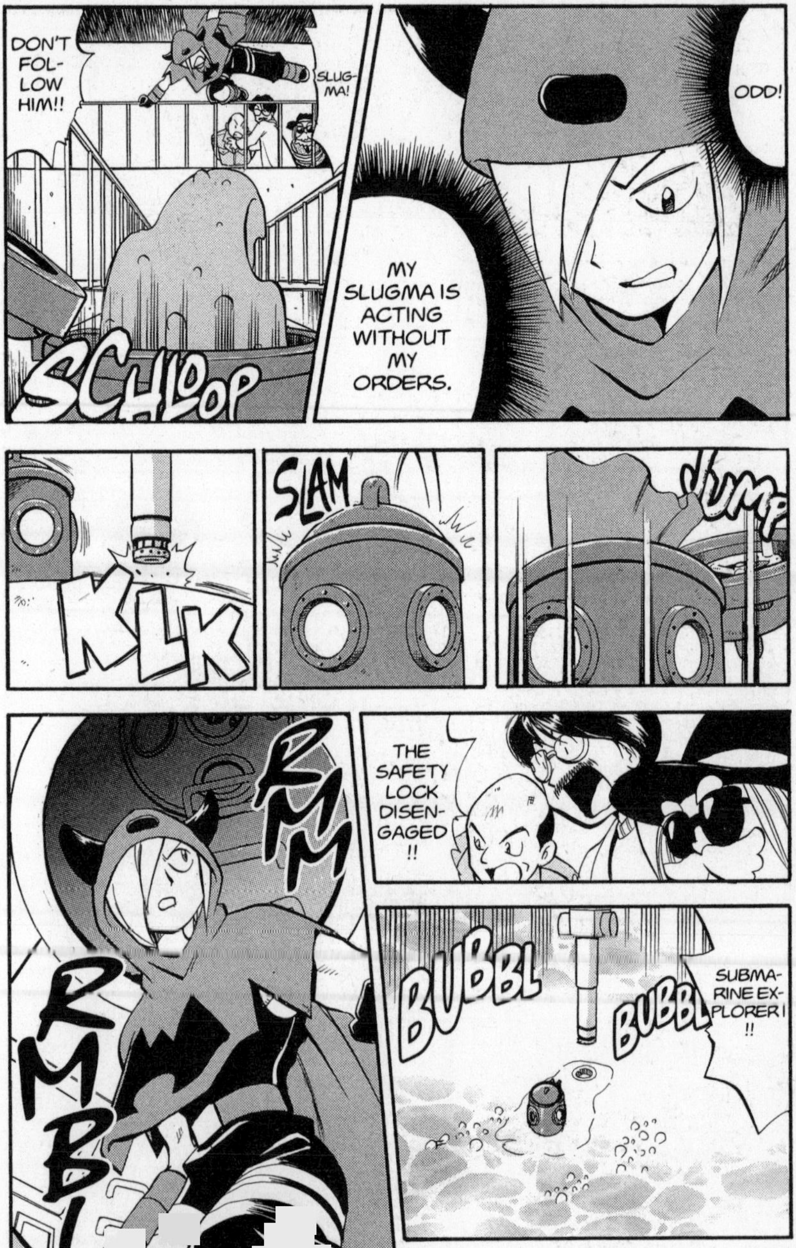
ODD!
MY SLUGMA IS ACTING WITHOUT MY ORDERS.
SLUG-MA!
DON'T FOL-LOW HIM!!
SCHLOOP
THUMP
SLAM
KLK
THE SAFETY LOCK DISEN-GAGED !!
SUBMA-RINE EX-PLORER I !!
BUBBL
BUBBL
RMM
RMBL

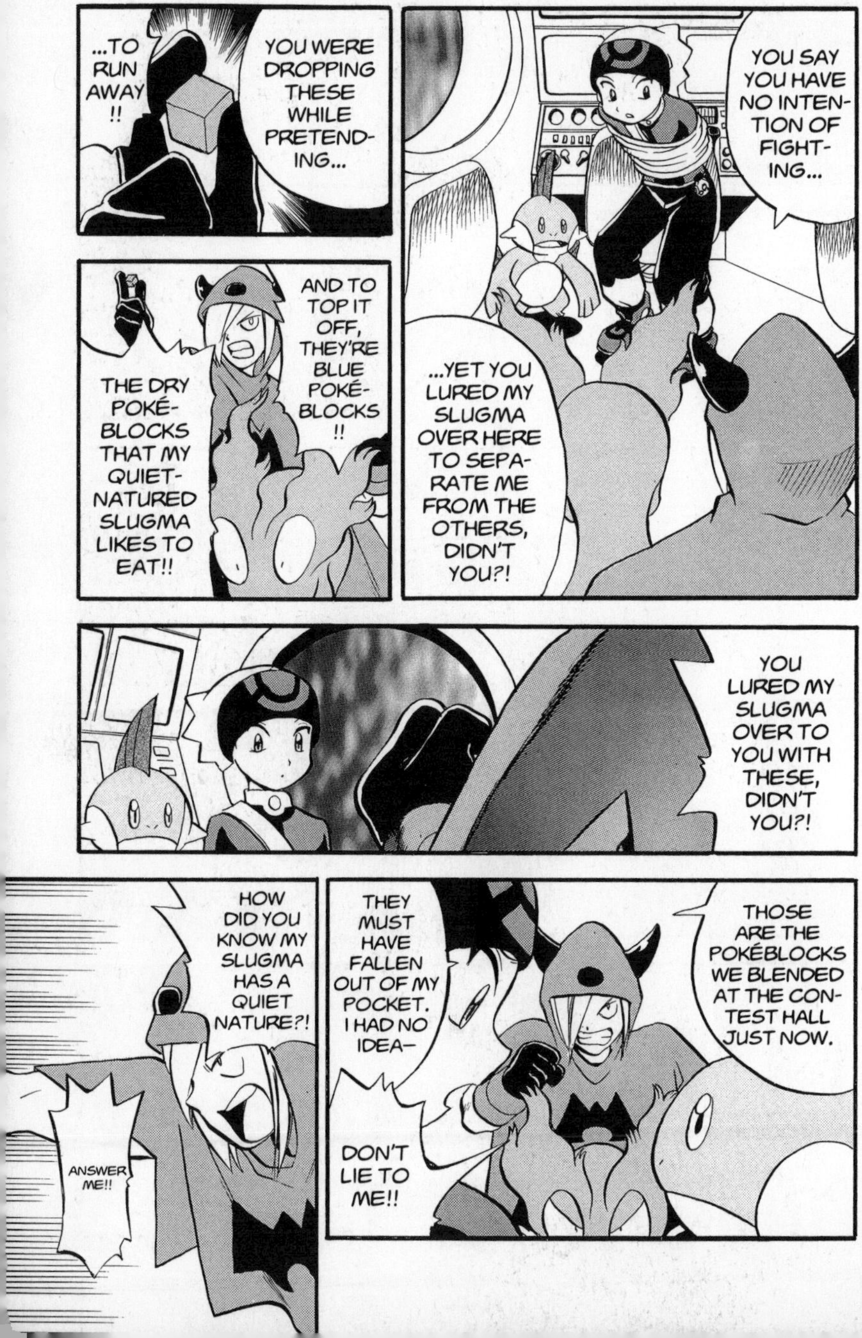
YOU SAY YOU HAVE NO INTENTION OF FIGHTING...
...YET YOU LURED MY SLUGMA OVER HERE TO SEPARATE ME FROM THE OTHERS, DIDN'T YOU?!
YOU WERE DROPPING THESE WHILE PRETENDING...
...TO RUN AWAY!!
AND TO TOP IT OFF, THEY'RE BLUE POKÉBLOCKS!!
THE DRY POKÉBLOCKS THAT MY QUIET-NATURED SLUGMA LIKES TO EAT!!
YOU LURED MY SLUGMA OVER TO YOU WITH THESE, DIDN'T YOU?!
THOSE ARE THE POKÉBLOCKS WE BLENDED AT THE CONTEST HALL JUST NOW.
THEY MUST HAVE FALLEN OUT OF MY POCKET. I HAD NO IDEA—
DON'T LIE TO ME!!
HOW DID YOU KNOW MY SLUGMA HAS A QUIET NATURE?!
ANSWER ME!!

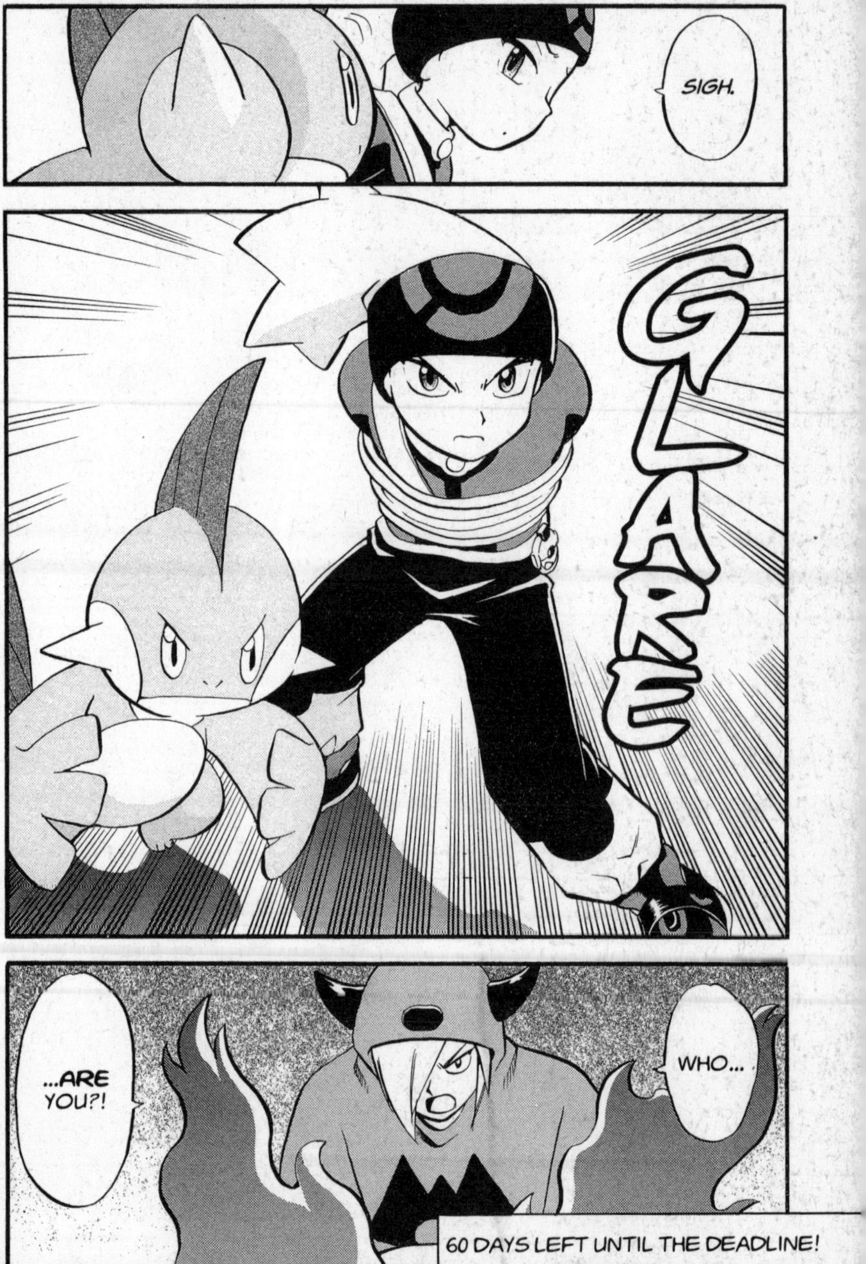
SIGH.
GLARE
WHO...
...ARE YOU?!
60 DAYS LEFT UNTIL THE DEADLINE!
TO BE CONTINUED...

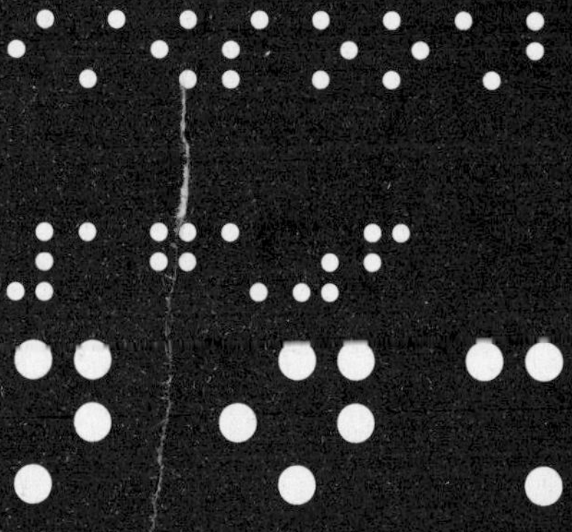

Special Feature: Team Aqua & Team Magma!!

TWO MYSTERIOUS ORGANIZATIONS SKULKING IN HOENN!!!

Myster ncidents have occurred all over the Hoenn region, and these two organizations seem to be behind them! Hence, we are gathering information on them.

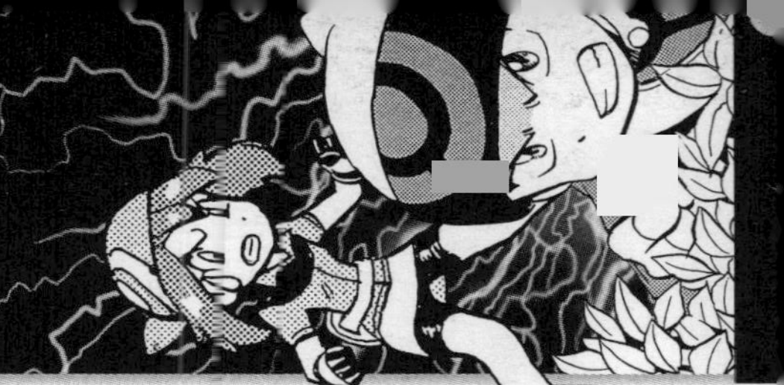

SECRETS REVEALED!!

TEAM AQUA

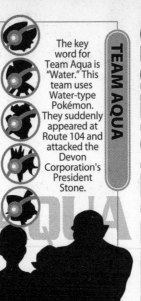

The key word for Team Aqua is "Water." This team uses Water-type Pokémon. They suddenly appeared at Route 104 and attacked the Devon Corporation's President Stone.

AQUA

TEAM MAGMA

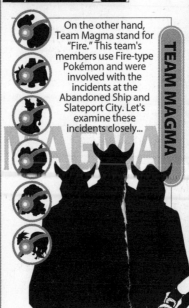

On the other hand, Team Magma stand for "Fire." This team's members use Fire-type Pokémon and were involved with the incidents at the Abandoned Ship and Slateport City. Let's examine these incidents closely...

MAGMA

INCIDENT 1

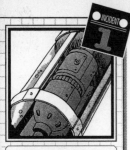

CORE COMPONENT

ROBBERY

— PETALBURG WOODS —

A DEVICE CREATED BY THE DEVON CORPORATION THAT WAS JUST ABOUT TO BE DELIVERED.

This special core component was stolen by Team Aqua during their attack in Petalburg Woods. What is their motive?

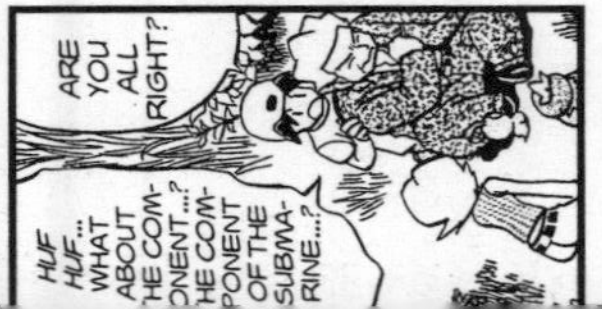

ARE YOU ALL RIGHT?
HUF HUF... WHAT ABOUT HE COM- ONENT...? HE COM- PONENT OF THE SUBMA- RINE...?

It seems to be a submarine part. Does this mean they're after something underwater?!

Cameraman Ty searched for the name of the organization that wears this symbol.

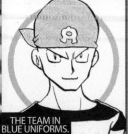

THE TEAM IN BLUE UNIFORMS.

TEAM AQUA

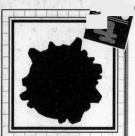

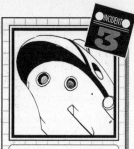

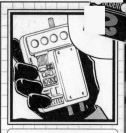

INCIDENT

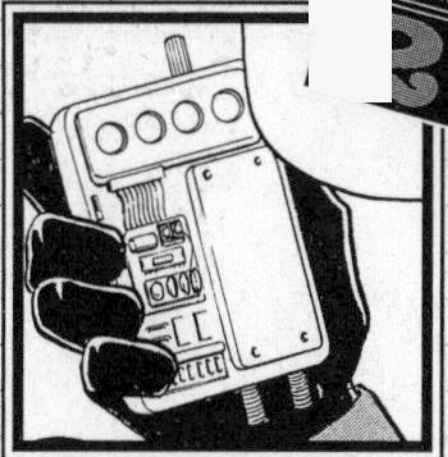

SCANNER

ROBBERY

—THE ABANDONED SHIP—

A DEVICE LEFT ON THE ABANDONED SHIP!!

Even though Ruby and Sapphire put up a good fight, Team Magma managed to steal the Scanner from the ship!

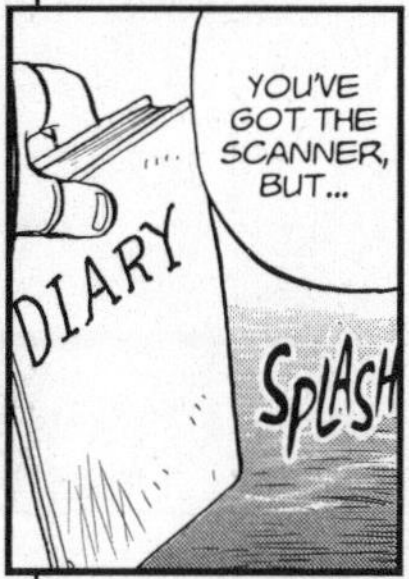
YOU'VE GOT THE SCANNER, BUT...
DIARY
SPLASH

◀ Did this diary belong to the creator of the scanner?

▼ The team in red capes. This organization's name is still unknown.

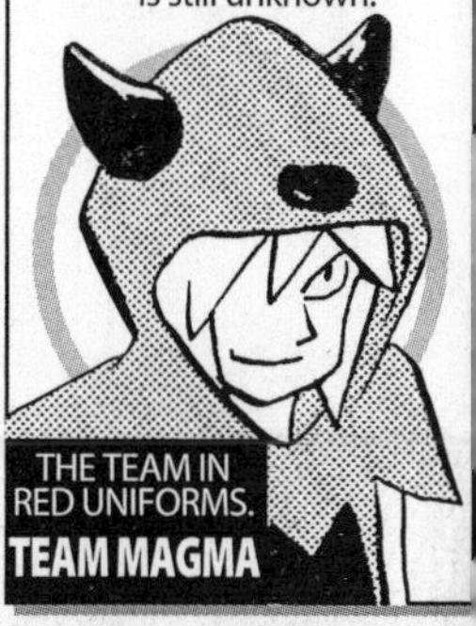

THE TEAM IN RED UNIFORMS.

TEAM MAGMA

INCIDENT 3

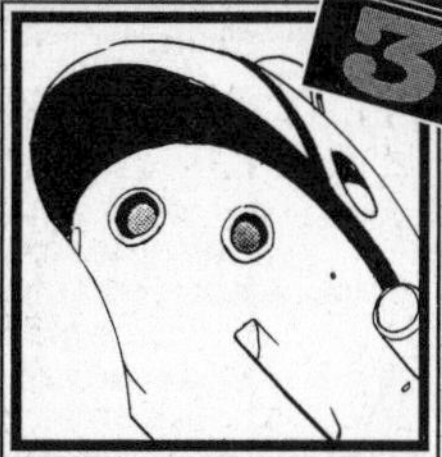

SUBMARINE EXPLORER 1

ROBBERY

—SLATEPORT CITY—

A DEEP SEA SUBMARINE!!

A deep sea submarine!! Team Magma also attacked the shipyard where the submarine was nearing completion—and stole it. This crime is still in progress. How will things turn out?!

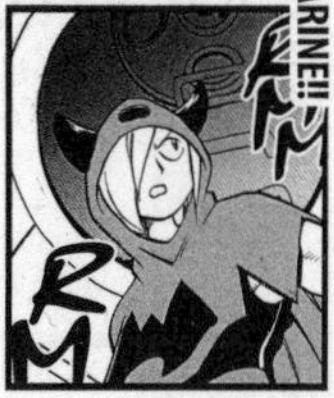
RM
RM

▶ The submarine sinks to the bottom of the sea...with Ruby and a member of Team Magma inside! (Chapter 201)

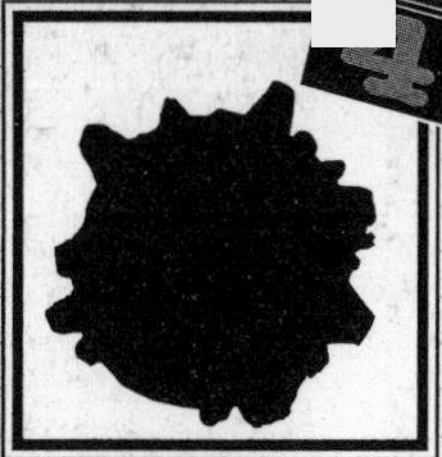

...?...

—METEOR FALLS—

WHAT WILL BE THEIR NEXT TARGET...?!

According to top-secret information, their next target is located at Meteor Falls. Is it some kind of energy source?!

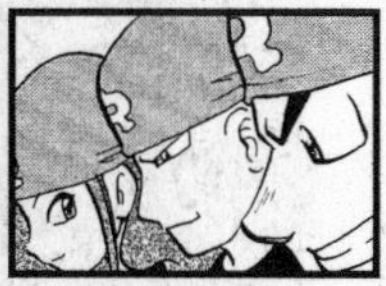

▲ Will Team Aqua get ahold of it...?

What did Steven mean by the following...?!

Steven, the young man who saved Ruby in Granite Cave near Dewford Town, spoke of "two great evils." Did he mean Team Aqua and Team Magma?! (Chapter 196)

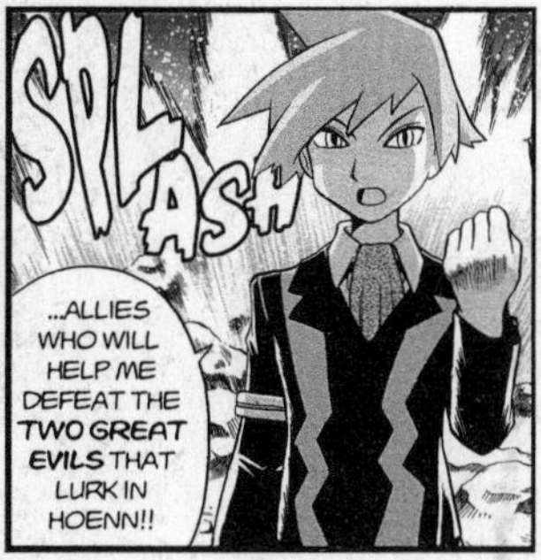
SPLASH
...ALLIES WHO WILL HELP ME DEFEAT THE TWO GREAT EVILS THAT LURK IN HOENN!!

▲ WHAT DO THESE REMARKS REVEAL ABOUT THE NATURE OF TEAM AQUA AND TEAM MAGMA AND THEIR LEADERS?!

Special Feature Team Aqua & Team Magma!!

THE TEAM IN BLUE UNIFORMS.

TEAM AQUA

A creepy group that coolly implements its schemes. How is their organization structured? Let's take a closer look at this cold water organization and their leader!

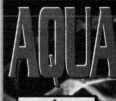

A CRIME SYNDICATE THAT WORKS IN THE SHADOWS...!

Team Aqua's schemes are all carried out in secrecy. Although we've learned the name of their organization, everything else remains veiled in darkness. And that's what makes them even more alarming!!

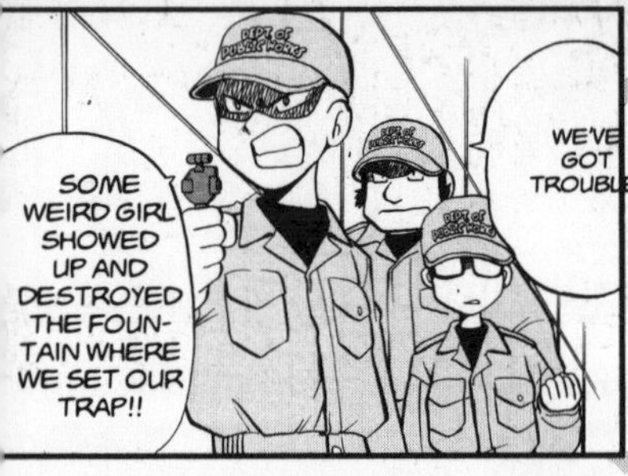

DEPT of PUBLIC WORKS
WE'VE GOT TROUBLE.
SOME WEIRD GIRL SHOWED UP AND DESTROYED THE FOUN-TAIN WHERE WE SET OUR TRAP!!

▲ Disguised as workers from the Waterworks Dept., they secretly cut the mesh over the intake hole. They're prepared for any eventuality!!

A WELL-DISCIPLINED SYNDICATE WITH A CLEAR HIERARCHY!!

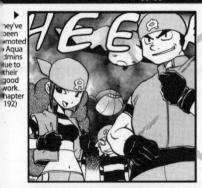

Team Aqua is a hierarchical organization. Superiors give the orders and are treated with respect. There are many ranks, and those who do a good job get promoted.

▶ ...hey've ...een ...moted ...Aqua ...dmins ...ue to their good ...work. ...hapter ...192)

DETAILED PLANS... WITH A RUTHLESS LEADER GIVING THE ORDERS!!

Archie is Team Aqua's leader. He doesn't seem threatening because he's soft spoken, but he's actually cold as ice. He'll use any means to achieve his goals, even to the point of treating his team members like dispensable tools! What are his sharp eyes observing now...?!

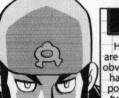

Aqua Leader Archie

His Pokémon are unknown. But obviously he must have extremely powerful Water-type Pokémon.

?

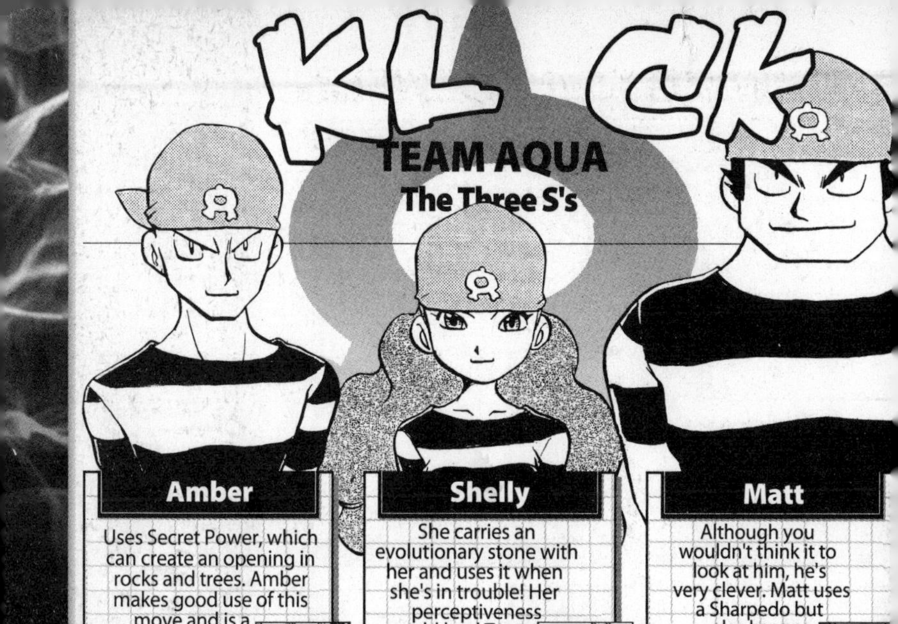
KL CK

TEAM AQUA
The Three S's

Amber

Uses Secret Power, which can create an opening in rocks and trees. Amber makes good use of this move and is a formidable foe!!

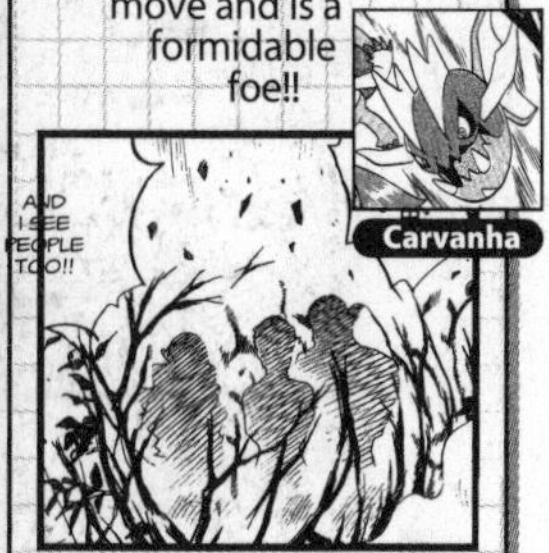
AND I SEE PEOPLE TOO!!
Carvanha

▲ Team Aqua might be lurking nearby...and about to use this move!!

Shelly

She carries an evolutionary stone with her and uses it when she's in trouble! Her perceptiveness could lead Team Aqua to victory!!

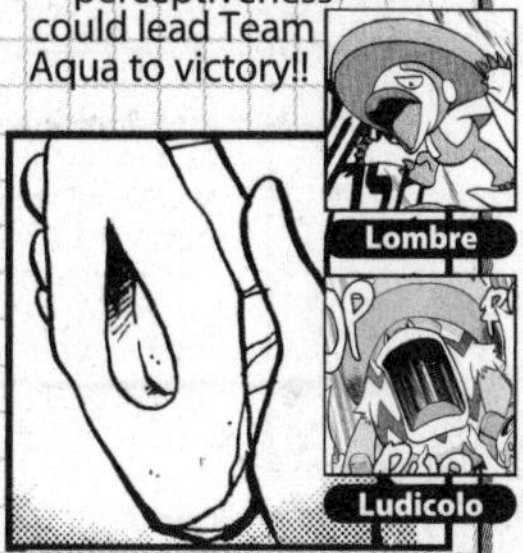
Lombre
Ludicolo

▲ Her deep knowledge of the energies inside the stones could determine the course of a battle!

Matt

Although you wouldn't think it to look at him, he's very clever. Matt uses a Sharpedo but also has an Azumarill. Fascinating...

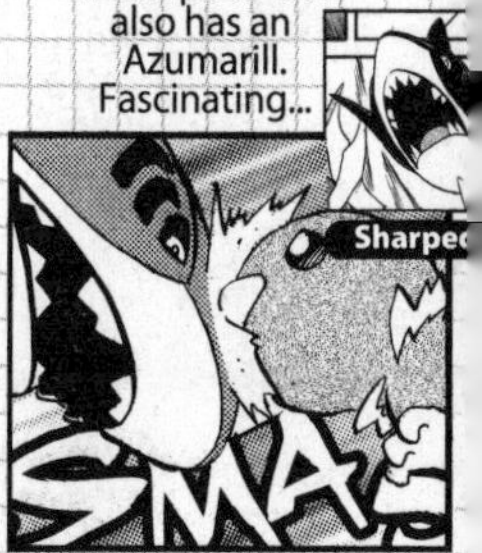
Sharpe
SMA

▲ Sharpedo's Ability Rough Skin damages its opponent just by touching them!

WHAT IS THEIR MOTIVE...?!

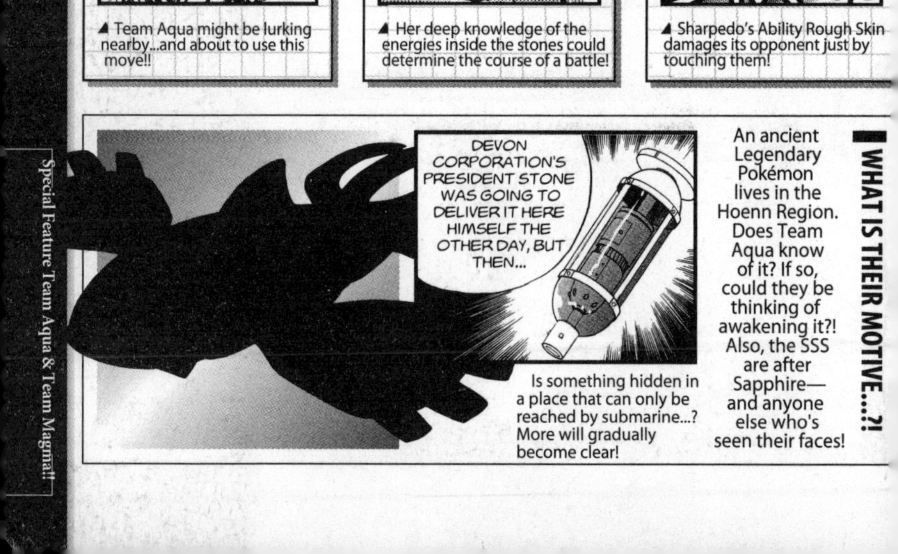
DEVON CORPORATION'S PRESIDENT STONE WAS GOING TO DELIVER IT HERE HIMSELF THE OTHER DAY, BUT THEN...

Is something hidden in a place that can only be reached by submarine...? More will gradually become clear!

An ancient Legendary Pokémon lives in the Hoenn Region. Does Team Aqua know of it? If so, could they be thinking of awakening it?! Also, the SSS are after Sapphire—and anyone else who's seen their faces!

Special Feature Team Aqua & Team Magma!!

THE TEAM IN RED UNIFORMS.

TEAM MAGMA

They create chaos without a thought to the consequences! What are the Leader and the Admins of fiery Team Magma like? What are their natures, schemes, and Pokémon like... Let's take a closer look!

MAGMA

THEY APPEAR OUT OF NOWHERE!! A MYSTERIOUS GROUP WITH NO PERCEPTIBLE ORGANIZATION!!

Team Magma uses Fire-type Pokémon. Their personalities are fiery too. They're hot-headed, violent and hard to catch. In fact, they are the complete opposite of Team Aqua, who are governed by clear rules and regulations.

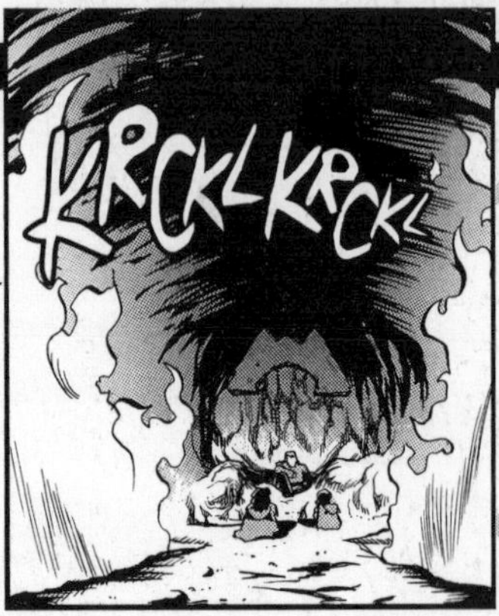
KRCKL KRCKL

▶ They have no head-quarters either! Wherever they meet becomes their head-quarters. (Chapter 200)

FREE WILL! EACH MEMBER IS FREE TO DO AS THEY WISH!!

This organization appears to be completely dis-organized. Each member attacks and steals with whatever strategy they dream up to achieve the team's goals. But that flexibility makes them strong!

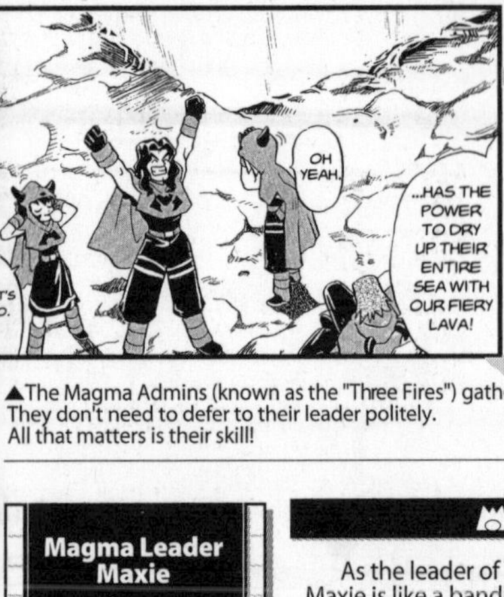
OH YEAH.
...HAS THE POWER TO DRY UP THEIR ENTIRE SEA WITH OUR FIERY LAVA!

▲The Magma Admins (known as the "Three Fires") gather together. They don't need to defer to their leader politely. All that matters is their skill!

AN OBSTINATE MAN! A FIERY BOSS WHO LEADS A FIERY ORGANIZATION!!

As the leader of Team Magma, Maxie is like a bandit king. He doesn't give detailed orders, instead, he lets the members choose their own course of action. That's what Team Magma is all about!

Magma Leader Maxie

His Pokémon is a Camerupt, a Pokémon who shoots magma out of the volcano on its back!

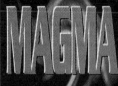

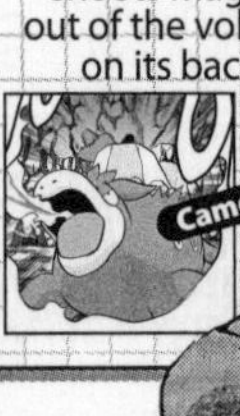
Camerupt

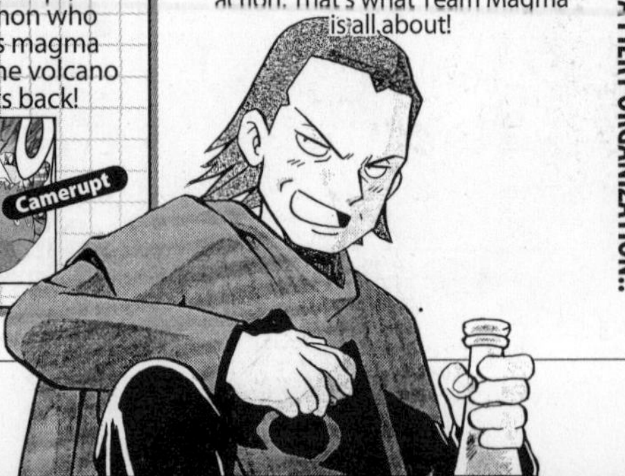

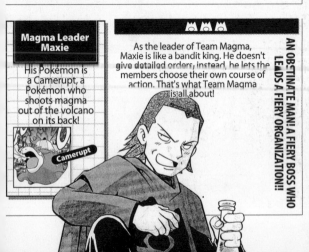

TEAM MAGMA
The Three Fires

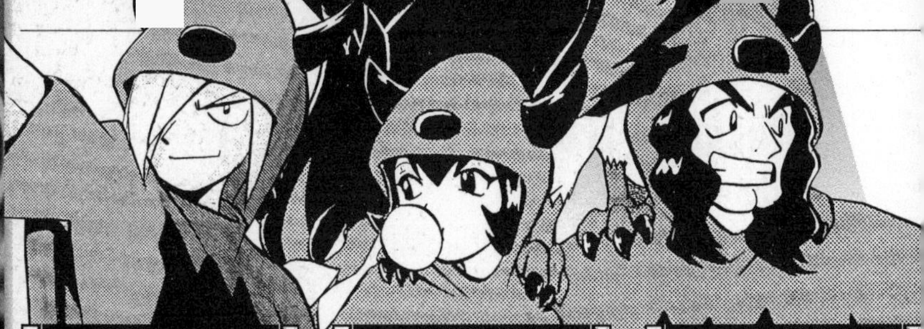

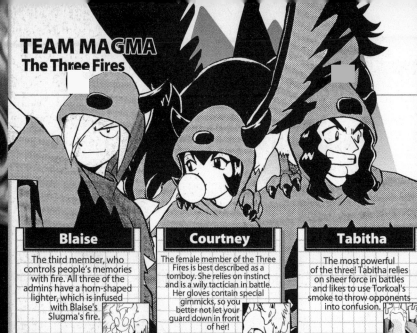

Blaise

The third member, who controls people's memories with fire. All three of the admins have a horn-shaped lighter, which is infused with Blaise's Slugma's fire.

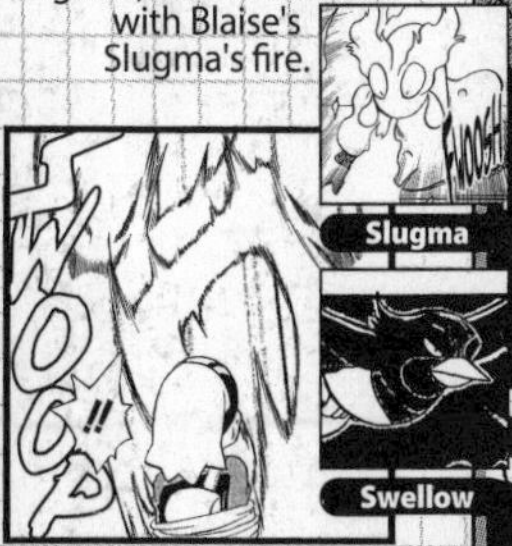
WHOOSH
FOOOO
!!
Slugma
Swellow

▲ Is this real or illusion?! We'll learn more about this battle tactic in the next chapter!!

Courtney

The female member of the Three Fires is best described as a tomboy. She relies on instinct and is a wily tactician in battle. Her gloves contain special gimmicks, so you better not let your guard down in front of her!

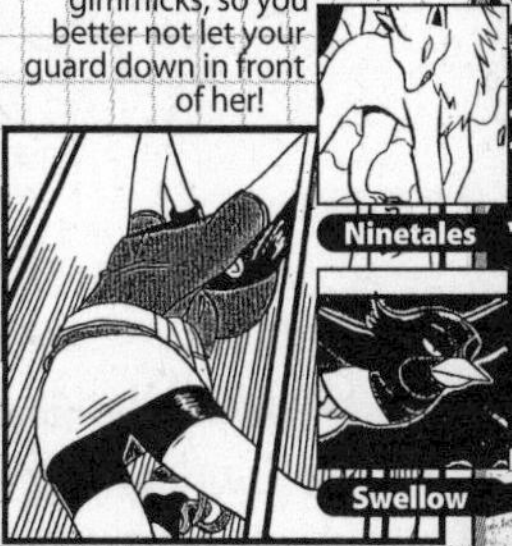
Ninetales
Swellow

▲ Tamato Berry juice squirts out of her glove to sting her opponent's eyes! (Chapter 199)

Tabitha

The most powerful of the three! Tabitha relies on sheer force in battles and likes to use Torkoal's smoke to throw opponents into confusion.

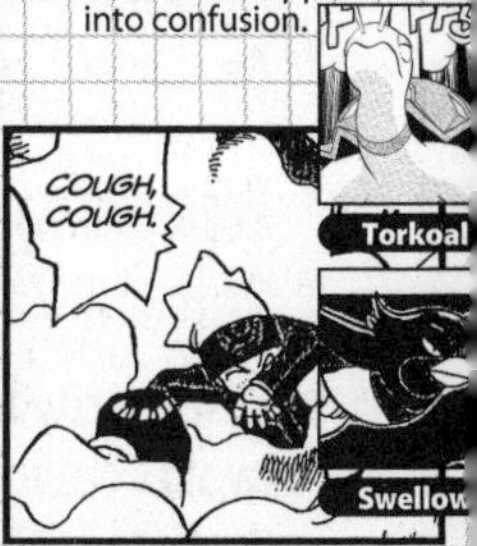
COUGH, COUGH.
Torkoal
Swellow

▲ The smoke emanating from Torkoal is powerful enough to knock out several people at once! (Chapter 200)

SO WHAT IS THEIR MOTIVE ANYWAY...?!

Why did they steal the submarine and the Scanner? What is their purpose? It's said that there's more than one ancient Legendary Pokémon in the Hoenn region... Team Aqua appears to be after one of them. Is Team Magma also after a Legendary Pokémon...?!

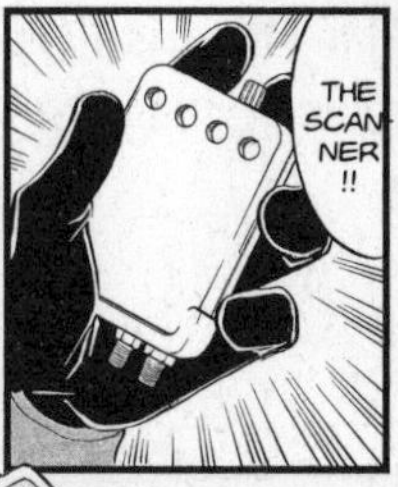
THE SCANNER!!

◀ We know it's a Scanner... the question is, what does it scan **for**? That would be a big clue as to what they're searching for!

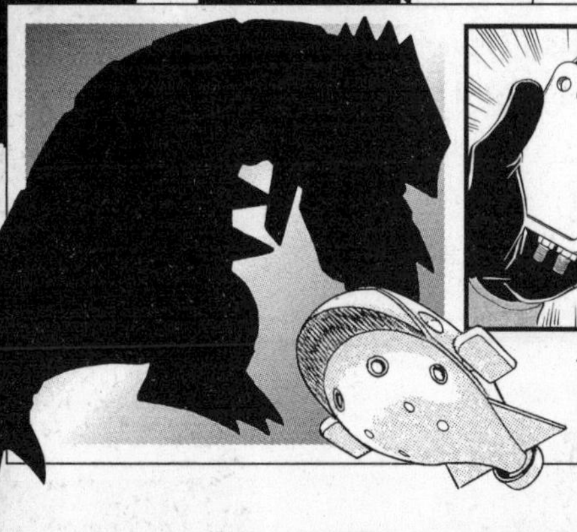

◀ Their goal is to reach the Seafloor Cavern, located in the deepest depths of Hoenn's sea! Stay tuned for more information!!

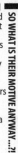

Message from
Hidenori Kusaka

The Ruby and Sapphire story arc is unfolding rapidly as our two heroes press on toward the deadline of their competition! The Gym battle against Roxanne at Rustboro and Brawly at Dewford... The battles at the Abandoned Ship and Slateport City... This volume is chock-full of my favorite episodes! I hope you enjoy Ruby and Sapphire's high-speed journey too!

Message from
Satoshi Yamamoto

Ruby, a city boy, loves beautiful things and prefers to avoid conflict and trouble. Sapphire, a wild girl from the woods, loves battles and action. These two main characters have very different personalities—but I love complex personalities. As I write, I enjoy starting each chapter wondering what the two of them will get up to next. To tell the truth, though, I think both of them would be really hard to get along with in real life.

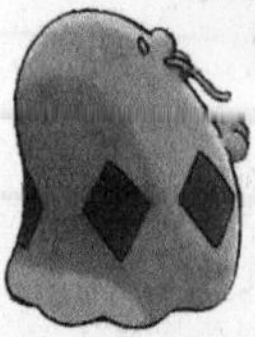

More Adventures Coming Soon...

On an accidental seafaring adventure in a submarine, Ruby discovers something mysterious deep beneath the waves. Then fishing nets him another Pokémon. But is his growing team bringing him closer to—or farther from—his dream? Next, Ruby must face his scariest opponent yet—his father!

Meanwhile, Sapphire is having trouble getting in her quota of Gym battles. One Gym Leader wants to just hand her a badge without a proper fight! And another has been...*kidnapped*?!

How are Team Magma and Team Aqua responsible for Ruby and Sapphire's difficulties?

AVAILABLE JULY 2013!

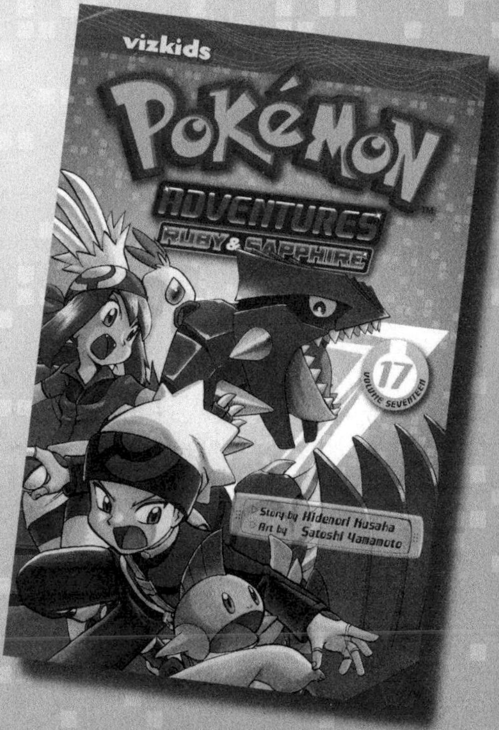
vizkids
Pokémon
Adventures
Ruby & Sapphire
17
Volume Seventeen
Story by Hidenori Kusaka
Art by Satoshi Yamamoto

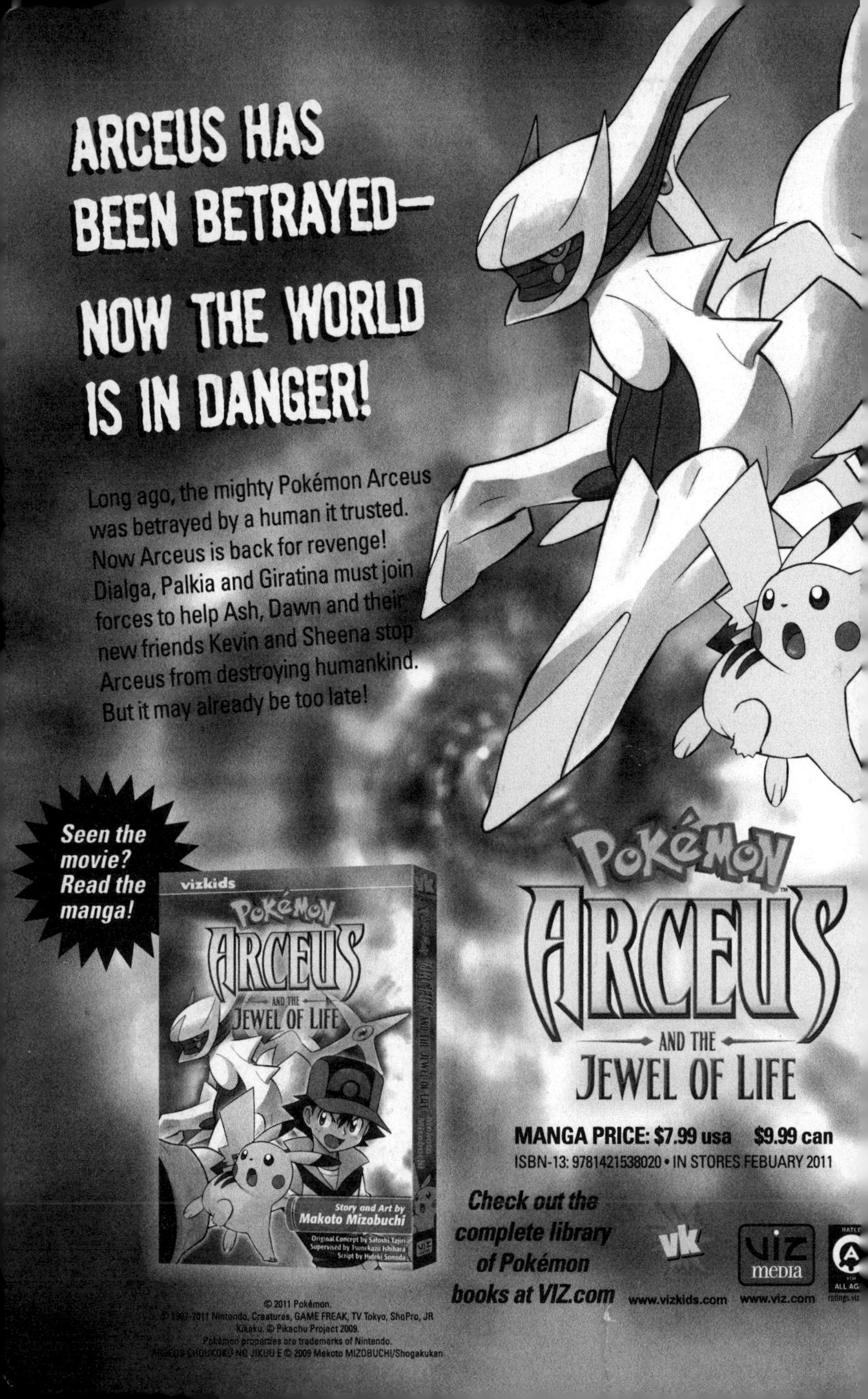

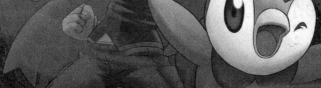

A BRAND NEW QUEST

Can a new trainer and his friends track down the legendary Pokémon Dialga before it's too late?

Find out in the *Pokémon Diamond and Pearl Adventure* manga—buy yours today!

On sale at store.viz.com
Also available at your local bookstore or comic store.

www.vizkids.com   www.viz.com

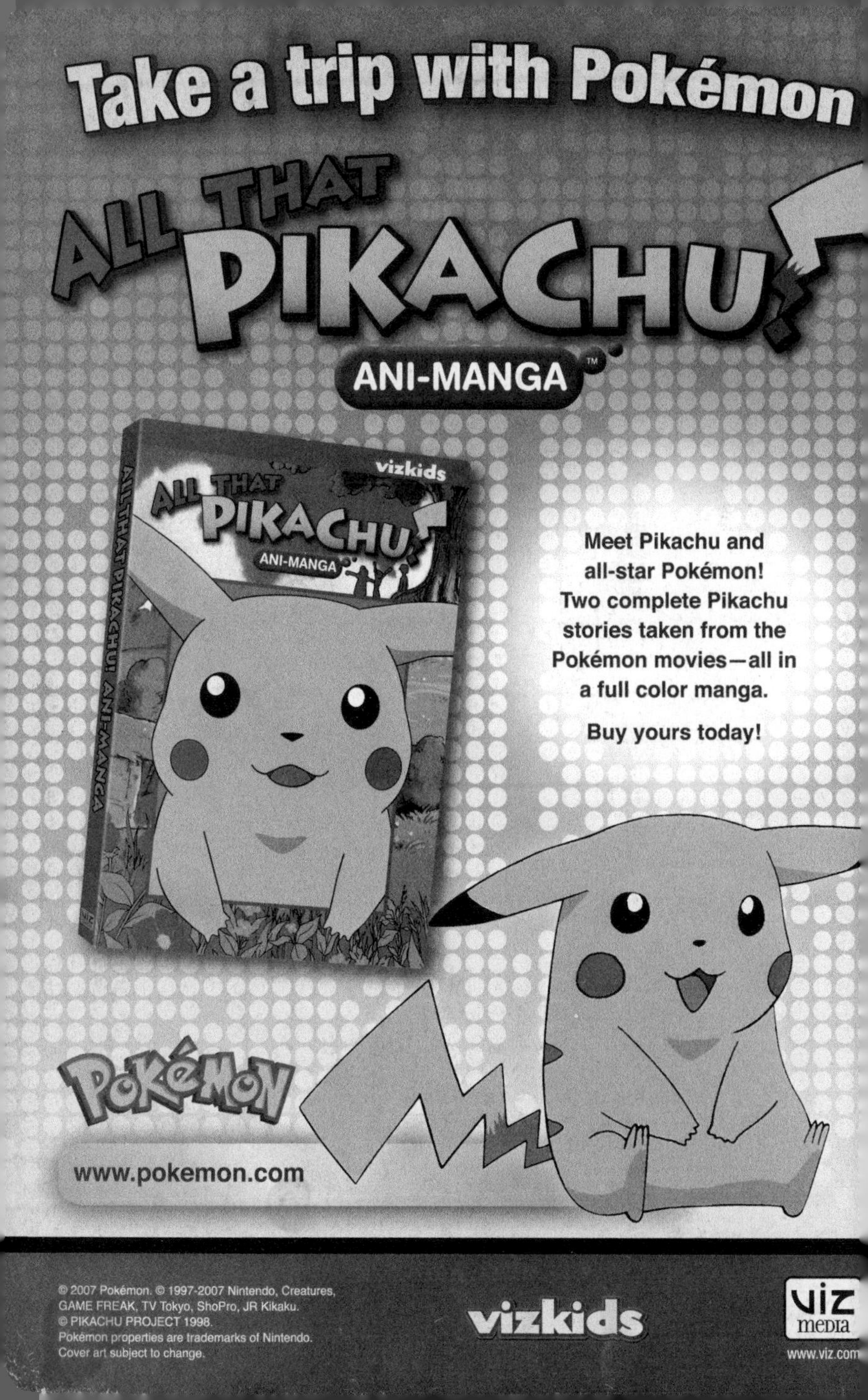
Take a trip with Pokémon
ALL THAT PIKACHU!
ANI-MANGA™
vizkids
ALL THAT PIKACHU!
ANI-MANGA
ALL THAT PIKACHU! ANI-MANGA
Meet Pikachu and all-star Pokémon! Two complete Pikachu stories taken from the Pokémon movies—all in a full color manga.
Buy yours today!
Pokémon
www.pokemon.com
© 2007 Pokémon. © 1997-2007 Nintendo, Creatures, GAME FREAK, TV Tokyo, ShoPro, JR Kikaku. © PIKACHU PROJECT 1998. Pokémon properties are trademarks of Nintendo. Cover art subject to change.
vizkids
VIZ media
www.viz.com

Pokémon
BLACK AND WHITE

MEET POKÉMON TRAINERS
BLACK AND WHITE

THE WAIT IS FINALLY OVER! Meet Pokémon Trainer Black! His entire life, Black has dreamed of winning the Pokémon League... Now Black embarks on a journey to explore the Unova region and fill a Pokédex for Professor Juniper. Time for Black's first Pokémon Trainer Battle ever!

Who will Black choose as his next Pokémon? Who would *you* choose?

Plus, meet Pokémon Snivy, Tepig, Oshawott and many more new Pokémon of the unexplored Unova region!

Story by
HIDENORI KUSAKA

Art by
SATOSHI YAMAMOTO

$4.99 USA | $6.99 CAN

Inspired by the hit video games
Pokémon Black Version and *Pokémon White Version!*

 Available Now
at your local bookstore or comic store

vizkids
www.vizkids.com

 HEROES OF MANGA

VIZ media
25 YEARS
www.viz.com/25years

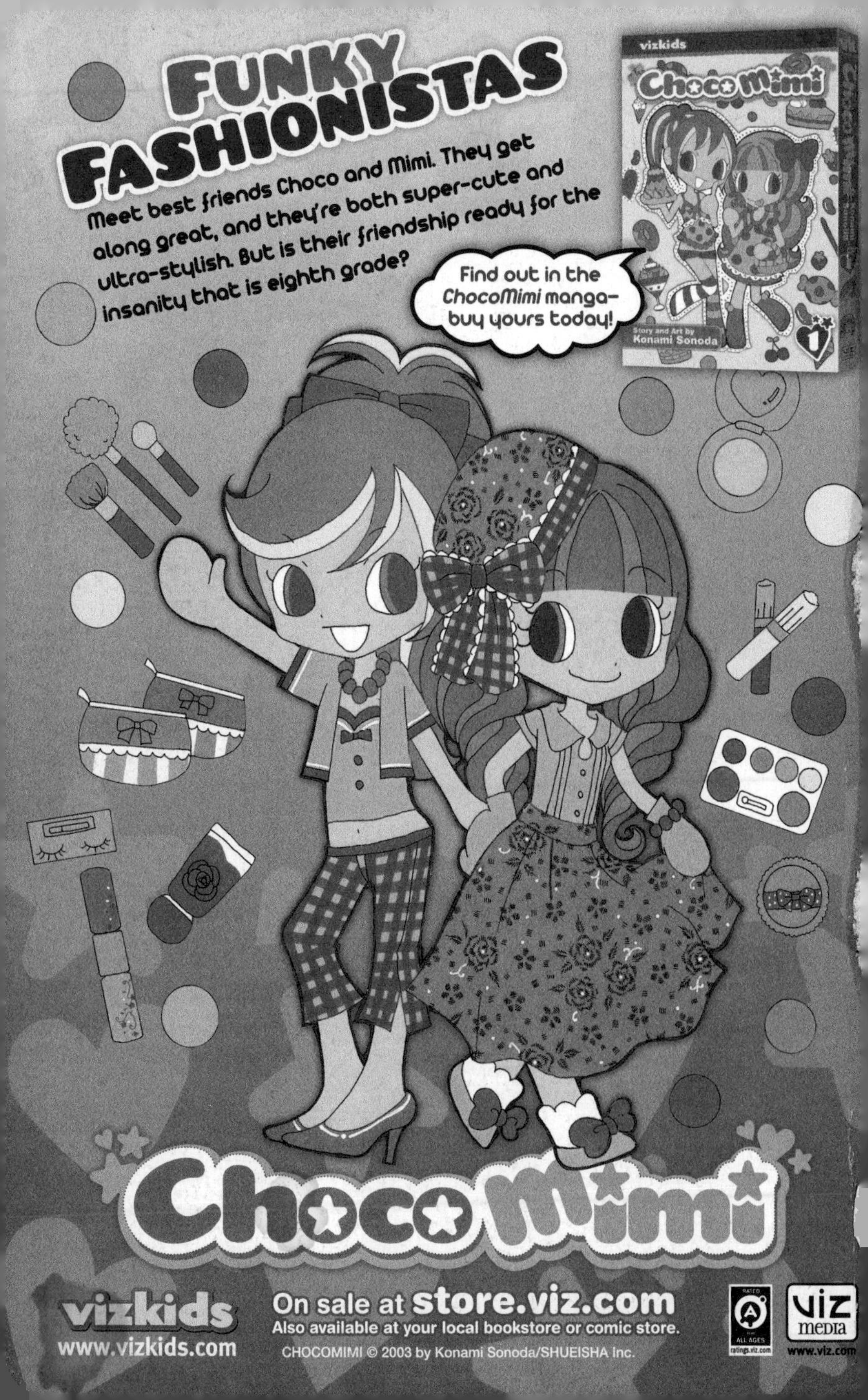
FUNKY FASHIONISTAS
Meet best friends Choco and Mimi. They get along great, and they're both super-cute and ultra-stylish. But is their friendship ready for the insanity that is eighth grade?
Find out in the ChocoMimi manga–buy yours today!
vizkids
Choco Mimi
Story and Art by Konami Sonoda
1
Choco Mimi
vizkids
www.vizkids.com
On sale at store.viz.com
Also available at your local bookstore or comic store.
CHOCOMIMI © 2003 by Konami Sonoda/SHUEISHA Inc.
RATED A ALL AGES
ratings.viz.com
VIZ media
www.viz.com

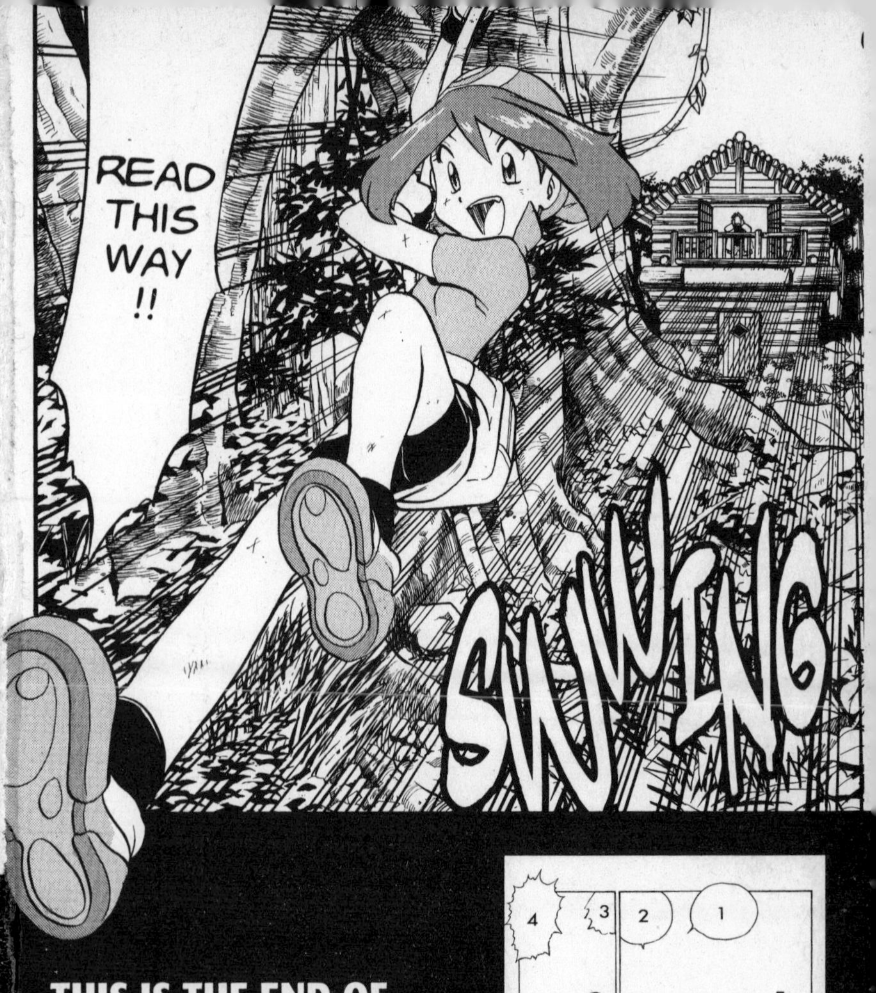
READ THIS WAY !!
SWWING

THIS IS THE END OF THIS GRAPHIC NOVEL!

properly enjoy this VIZ Media graphic ›vel, please turn it around and begin ›ading from right to left.

›is book has been printed in the original ›panese format in order to preserve the ›ientation of the original artwork. Have ›n with it!

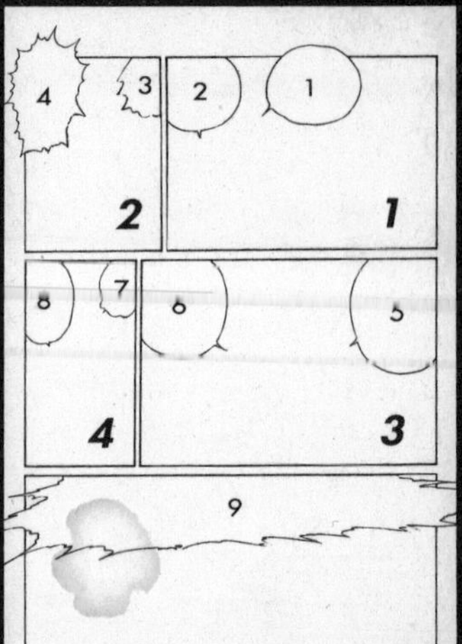
4
3
2
1
2
1
8
7
6
5
4
3
9
5
FOLLOW THE ACTION THIS WAY.
142